# VERSAILLES

British screenwriter David Wolstencroft is best known for his work on the TV series *Spooks*. He is the celebrated author of two spy novels. Simon Mirren has gained global acclaim for his work on the hit TV series *Criminal Minds*. Together, they sweep the reader away to the realm of the Sun King and the construction of the world's most beautiful palace. Elizabeth Massie has written several historical novels as well as the novelization of *The Tudors* TV series.

# VERSAILLES

BASED ON THE SCENARIO BY
SIMON MIRREN & DAVID WOLSTENCROFT

ELIZABETH MASSIE

CORVUS

Published in paperback in Great Britain in 2016 by Corvus,
an imprint of Atlantic Books Ltd.

Copyright © Michel Lafon Publishing, 2016

10 9 8 7 6 5 4 3 2 1

A CIP catalogue record for this book is available from the British Library.

Paperback ISBN: 978 1 78239 998 8
Open Market paperback ISBN: 978 1 78649 023 0
E-book ISBN: 978 1 78239 999 5

Printed and bound by CPI Group (UK) Ltd, Croydon, CR0 4YY.

Corvus
An imprint of Atlantic Books Ltd
Ormond House
26–27 Boswell Street
London
WC1N 3JZ

www.corvus-books.co.uk

*1*

*She was exquisitely* beautiful, young and small in stature yet fully a woman with bountiful curves visible through her sheer white chemise. She skipped ahead across the grass, glancing back over her shoulder, giggling, winking. Louis laughed and followed, trying his best to reach her but remaining several steps behind.

Into a labyrinth of hedge-lined pathways she hurried, out of view for a moment then back in again, patches of sunlight kissing her body. He ached with desire for her, every fiber of his body on edge, needing to have this woman. To hold her, to caress her, to take her and have her.

Through a shady grove of orange trees she danced, plucking ripe fruit from a tree as she passed beneath it. She turned and smiled. It was clear she wanted him, too.

Beyond the orange grove was a rise upon which sat a colossal, sun-bright palace, ornate and brilliant beyond imagination, looking as if the Mansion of God Himself had

1

come down to Earth. Louis' heart swelled. Though he had never seen this palace before, it was part of him. It was home.

The girl reached the palace and disappeared through an arched doorway. Louis followed and found himself in total, silent darkness.

He stopped.

He waited.

"Kings do not cry, no matter what they face," came a familiar voice. "No matter what they face."

He knew the voice. His mother. He turned slowly and she was there in a spear of light, a vision of pride and power, her body spattered with blood. Louis' younger brother knelt beside her, weeping and clutching her hand.

"Fear is a weakness," she said evenly. "It can crush a man, destroy him. Even you, my son."

Louis stood, frozen in dread.

His mother continued, her voice reaching out from the past. "You were anointed by God, blessed by the Sun. But you do not yet possess what really matters. The power. Without it, you will perish, and all of France with you. Of course you are scared. Your mother is dying. The world is on fire. Enemies wait around every corner. If history teaches us one thing it is this – terrible things happen to kings. Which is why you will need the strength of a hundred men. To do whatever it takes. To drag us from the darkness and into the light."

Louis and his mother locked gazes. He felt he could not breathe.

Then the beautiful girl appeared again, laughing, standing beside Louis' mother. Both women held out their hands, fingers beckoning. Louis hesitated then reached for the girl.

She pulled away and fled. Again he followed.

Out of the darkness and through bright, lavishly decorated rooms they raced, past marble statues, great portraits, and gilded moldings into a dazzling hallway where countless mirrors clung to the walls. Louis saw fragments of the girl's reflection repeated over and over – a bare breast, a porcelain-white shoulder, the small of her delicate back. She shrugged the chemise from her body and kicked it free. Naked, she ran into the room at the end of the hall.

"I can see Paradise," warned his mother from behind. "But you must build it for yourself. And let all the world know. Louis the Great has arrived."

Louis reached the room to find the girl lying on his four-poster bed, a teasing smile on her full lips. Slowly, she parted her shapely legs.

Louis tore his clothes off, flung himself onto the bed, and mounted the girl. With unstoppable and glorious urgency he forced himself into her. Again. Again.

Again.

He awoke as he came, his jaw tight, fists clutching the linen sheets, rising up into consciousness and the shadows of the bedchamber. His semen pooled on his bare belly, hot then cooling instantly. Sweat bathed his chest; his dark hair made a damp frame for his noble face. His eyes burned. He rubbed them, knowing he was awake yet not wanting to be.

A pre-dawn storm thundered outside the royal hunting lodge, the wind and rain battering the shuttered window. Louis' loyal valet, Bontemps, sat quietly at the foot of the royal four-poster bed. A man in his middle years, his face was patient and kind.

The dream was fading, but Louis held on to one particular image. "Tell the architect Le Vau that I want to talk to him," he said. "About mirrors."

Bontemps nodded.

Thunder rolled beyond the walls. Wind caught its breath then hurled another wave of rain at the window.

More awake now, Louis drew his nightshirt down over his abdomen. "How is my Queen, Bontemps? Everyone tells me it's going to be a boy –"

There was a sudden crashing of glass from outside. Over the noise of the storm Louis heard horses whinnying and men shouting. Then there were heavy footsteps and urgent, angry voices approaching the King's bedchamber. A moment later, a pounding on the door. Bontemps hurried to open it; Swiss guards poured into the chamber, followed by anxious courtiers. The guards flanked the royal bed, their faces hard. Louis shrunk back, his heartbeat quickening.

"Guard!" Bontemps demanded. "What business here?"

"An attempt on the King's life," said one guard.

"By whom? The Spanish? The Dutch?"

"We do not yet know. Fabien is moving to quell the threat."

"Bontemps," managed Louis. "Explain!"

"Sire," said the valet, his voice tight with concern. "Your bodyguards must escort you to the guard room immediately." He moved to the window and pulled the shutters back. The King's royal dressers reached out to remove the King's nightshirt, but Louis shoved them off. "On whose word?" he demanded. He clambered up and went to Bontemps.

"Away from the window!" shouted a guard.

"I do not know these men, Bontemps!" said Louis.

The guards surrounded the King and moved him forcefully from the window. Louis twisted in their grasp. "I'm going nowhere! And my second son will be born here, in Versailles. While I breathe I will show no fear. I will not leave!"

But the guards would not hear him, and the dressers did their duty. Then the guards hastened the King from the bedchamber and down the dark corridor. Wide-eyed courtiers bowed in pale candlelight as the King passed by. Louis managed to get free of the guards' hands but was unable to fight the human current that carried him along.

"Where is Philippe?" he shouted. "Where is he? Where is my brother?"

*The King's younger* brother Philippe, known also as Monsieur, drew his lips away and smiled up at the handsome, wavy-haired fellow in the velvet-upholstered chair. Chevalier, the handsome fellow, was dressed in a white shirt and nothing else. All the easier for Philippe to enjoy the delicious feast between the man's legs. Philippe's knack for obediently teasing and tasting had Chevalier gripping the chair's arms and tipping his head back in pleasure.

"God," said Chevalier through his teeth. "You are good at that."

Philippe smiled. Of course he was.

There was a sudden hammering on the door. Philippe glanced over dismissively then looked back at the rock hard, glistening organ before him. He leaned toward it, ready to take it again, but the pounding continued.

A footman shouted through the door, "The King summons you! Monsieur?"

Chevalier scowled. "We heard you the first time!"

Philippe brushed a strand of dark hair behind his ear and gave Chevalier an apologetic grimace. He pushed himself to his feet and shuffled to the door. Chevalier casually pulled at his shirttail and covered himself partway.

Philippe opened the door. "Is the baby born, then?"

"You are to come at once, Monsieur," said the footman.

Philippe rolled his eyes and yawned. He looked back at Chevalier.

With a wave of his heavily ringed hand, Chevalier said, "I'll send a for a snack."

"I couldn't eat another thing," replied Philippe. He stepped out into the corridor and pulled the door shut. Before he could complain about the interruption, the footman informed him of the planned attempt on Louis' life.

Erotic pleasures were instantly forgotten. "Have they caught the men?"

The footman shook his head. "They are still searching, Monsieur."

*The town square* of Versailles was dark, rain-drenched, and deserted, for the town folk had not yet awakened. Fabien, chief of the King's police force, stood in the center of the street, holding the reins of four skittish horses. His hazel eyes were narrowed with focus and determination. Another moment. And another. Then, yes! There they were. Four Spaniards, cloaked and furtive, came into view from an alley and turned in Fabien's direction.

The largest man stopped and looked at Fabien. He jerked his head in the direction of the empty hitching rail at street side. "Where are my horses?" he shouted over the sound of the rain.

"These horses?" called Fabien. He dropped the reins, slapped the horses' hindquarters, and the animals galloped off.

The man's face twisted in rage and he stomped through the mud toward Fabien. And at that moment, twenty guards appeared from side roads and surrounded the Spaniards.

"Have you lost your way, gentlemen?" said Fabien.

The large man snarled, clearly aware there was nothing left to do. He roared, grabbed a hatchet and carbine from beneath his cloak, and rushed at Fabien. He did not even have time to stumble on the puddle-rutted road, for at that moment the guards shot him to pieces. He fell into the mud. Fabien stepped on his head to hold him down as he thrashed and died. The remaining three spun about to run but guards blocked their way.

"Drop your weapons!" said Fabien.

The Spaniards tossed their carbines to the ground and stood still, backs to one another as lesser animals gather to protect themselves from predators. Fabien approached them, caught the gaze of the youngest – little more than a boy – and gave him a smile as cold as the rain.

✦ ✦ ✦

*Louis shrugged off* the hands of the guards who tried to keep up with him as he returned to his bedchamber. So many reaching for him, pressed in around him, cloying. *Get away!* his mind screamed. More faces, staring, true and perhaps feigned concern mingled into one distressing image.

*Get away from me!*

In his room at last, he stood at the window and leaned on the sill. His breaths were heavy and rapid, clouding the quarry glass and obscuring his reflection. Bontemps, guards, and a handful of courtiers stood at a distance, shuffling nervously. Louis felt their gazes on his back staring, waiting, silently demanding.

*Go away....!*

Then he heard a familiar child's voice, a boy's voice. Faint. Rising up from the past.

"Maman," the boy whimpered. "Where are we going?"

Louis turned his head and through a blur of distress saw a vision of his mother, Anne of Austria. She bustled anxiously about a lavish bedroom, packing boxes of jewelry into a large chest as a lady-in-waiting snatched gowns and slippers to pack a second chest.

*Mother...*

"We are leaving Paris," said Anne, her aristocratic face taut with purpose. "And we are never coming back. Hurry."

The little boy sniffed. "I'm scared!"

Anne looked at her son, sharply. "Kings do not cry."

*Kings do not cry…*

Louis closed his eyes, eased his breathing, and then opened his eyes again. The vision was gone, leaving only his silent subjects watching him. He looked away from them, out the window at the relentless torrents that seemed determined to drown the world.

The door opened and someone entered. Louis recognized the clearing of the throat. "Tell me, Philippe," he said without turning, "what is going on?"

"Another plot uncovered," said the King's brother. "They found four men in the village. Sent to kill you. We must all leave for Paris at once. This lodge is not safe."

"I decide where I go. I decide what to do." Louis hitched his head in the direction of the guards and courtiers. "Make them go away."

"Leave us," Philippe told the guards. Silently the crowd withdrew from the bedchamber, leaving only the King, his valet, and his brother.

Louis strode from the window to the central table. He leaned on it with his knuckles and studied the wood grain.

"You've had the dream again?" asked Philippe.

Louis snarled. His brother knew him too well. "You held her hand," he said at last.

"You could have done the same."

"They would not permit me that honor! My own mother…" Louis began to pace from the table and back to the window.

"Who permits the King but the King?" prodded Philippe.

"You will never understand! There is something bigger than you."

9

Philippe shook his head and made to leave, but Bontemps held up a hand. "The King has not given you leave."

"My dear Bontemps," Philippe scoffed. "I know that look well. And someone is about to get hurt. I rather it was not me."

Louis pointed a finger at his brother. "They mean to kill me. Let them come. Let them try!"

"The power lies with you," said Philippe. "Believe it."

Louis returned to the window. His gaze wandered out through the rain, seeking something beyond the storm, seeking the faint outline of the royal woods in the distance. Slowly the distress of his soul began to fade as he imagined the trees, the rivers, the tangled and beautiful wilderness. "The deer in our woods follow the same tracks as their ancestors," he said. "Going back hundreds of years. It's instinct. They simply follow. Once in a while one will turn. But those that challenge never win. For one reason. If you blindfolded me in that wood, turned me around a hundred times, I would find my way back. There's not a path I do not know, a tree I have not climbed. This is where I hunt." Louis looked around at Philippe. "You can leave now," he said brightly.

Philippe and Bontemps exchanged concerned glances as Louis looked back through the rain-drenched window glass.

*At last, as* if weary of itself, the rain eased, leaving the town of Versailles chilly and sodden. Flaming torches held aloft by Fabien's guards flickered and danced, reflecting on the road and the faces of the men.

The remaining prisoners had been beaten without mercy, and could barely stand as guards searched their clothing. There was not much to find, save some coins and a serrated hunting knife. But then a guard discovered a rolled paper in one prisoner's coat and handed it to Fabien.

Fabien held the paper up to the light of a torch and watched as a complex code became visible along the edge. It was a cipher, a collection of symbols and letters. It was what he'd been looking for.

Glancing up with smug satisfaction, he nodded at the guard with the hunting knife. "Hobble them." The guard leaned down and slashed the older prisoners' Achilles tendons with such force that their feet were nearly cut from their legs. The prisoners crashed to the earth, screaming in agony. The remaining boy closed his eyes and prayed.

*Jean-Baptiste Colbert,* the royal accountant, was a dutiful man. He sat in his office in the village of Versailles, collecting taxes and recording them in his ledger. Nearing old age, the man had no fondness for others, especially not those from whom he took money, yet his work was paramount. As he waved one smelly exciseman away from his desk and prepared to take the coffer from the next in line, Louvois, the King's War Minister, burst into the office, followed by Fabien and several guards. Louvois ordered the crowd of taxpayers out and shut the office door.

"You know," said Louvois, letting out a grunt, "I woke

yesterday in a goose-down bed with a view of my lands five miles to the river. Here, I sleep in a cupboard. We will finish the reckoning in Paris. Safe and sound." Then to the guards, "Secure the coffers and load the carriages. Four men to each."

Colbert rose behind his desk. "What is the meaning of this? I have work to do!"

Fabien rubbed at a bloody spot on his jacket. "Four Spanish mercenaries were found plotting an ambush in His Majesty's hunting grounds. They were prevented from doing so."

"Good," said Colbert. "They mean to end our new campaign with a single strike?"

"Madrid is not happy about our desires for the Spanish Netherlands. Neither are the Netherlands, for that matter."

Colbert swept a hand toward the coffers as the guards began to collect them from the desk. "They may be in luck. We cannot finance a war with this income. We could hardly finance a swordfight."

"The Queen must have her dowry," said Fabien. "They did not pay. This is their reward."

Louvois crossed his arms. "We really are out in the wilds here. Defenses are porous, nonexistent. The sooner we return to Paris, the better."

Fabien began, "The King is hunting this afternoon, I doubt very much we would leave –"

"I postponed the hunt," interrupted Louvois. "We can reconvene at Fontainebleau."

"Surely Monsieur Bontemps must –"

"I do not believe the King or his valet appreciate the full picture of this threat. In any case it's not up to him. The ministers, the council, we all must guide the ship. You think the country is governed by one man?"

With that, Louvois ushered the guards and coffers out to the street as Bontemps made his way in. His face was twisted with concern.

"Bontemps," said Colbert, "is the King informed of this? What does he say?"

"I...do not know."

Fabien angled his head. "Then where is he?"

Bontemps shook his head. "He told me he would be here."

Fabien clenched his fists and took a loud breath of air. "Then we must find him."

As Bontemps spun toward the door, Fabien grabbed his arm. "But," he warned, "calmly."

*The pounding of* the mare's hooves were like a heartbeat, rapid, powerful, driving down into the earth and up through Louis' body so that he felt he was one with the animal, one with the misty morning air, one with freedom. He leaned forward in the saddle, clutching the reins as they galloped along a woodland path of the royal hunting grounds. Yes, Philippe would be looking for him. Yes, Bontemps would be anxious. A search party would have already formed. But they were far behind him, and in this moment he felt the same joy and abandon as he had when a boy.

"Ah!" he shouted to the sky.

Around a bend in the path they went, Louis' cape lifting

and falling like a great wing. Warblers pecking the ground flew up in a mad spray to get out of the way.

Up ahead the trunks of ancient oaks bowed toward each other, their branches linking overhead, creating a dense, green canopy. Louis dug his heels into the mare's sides, spurring the animal onward into the lush tunnel. He glanced up at the spots of blue beyond the green then back down again in time to avoid being knocked from his saddle by a low branch. He ducked and laughed at the near calamity.

Onward they raced.

At last the path reached a narrow river and small grove. Louis urged his horse through the underbrush into the clearing and dismounted. He stood in silent awe, breathing in the simple beauty of pink wildflowers, waving grasses, and rippling water. He walked to the riverbank and knelt on the damp ground. For a moment he considered his reflection then cupped up some of the cold water and splashed it on his face.

Freedom. Clarity.

Suddenly his horse snorted, started, and galloped off.

Louis leapt to his feet and spun around.

A wolf was emerging from the undergrowth, lean, mangy, clearly hungry. The animal's lip lifted in a snarl. Louis tensed and moved his hand slowly to his short sword.

*Ah, king of the trees*, he thought. *You dare challenge the King of France?*

From the corner of his eyes he saw two other wolves, equally gaunt and hungry, moving out from the brush, heads low and eyes narrowed. Louis' fingers wrapped around the hilt of the sword. His own eyes narrowed. He was ready. Let them come.

"What are you doing?" came a furious cry. A horse was there then, skidding to a halt beside Louis, its rider's face red and angry.

The wolves shivered and ran off.

Philippe slid from his saddle. "You could have been killed, brother!"

Louis released his sword and shrugged. "Perhaps."

"Perhaps?" Philippe shook his head then chuckled in spite of himself. "Sometimes you surpass even yourself."

Louis glanced about to make sure the wolves were indeed gone, and then looked back at his brother. What a moment this was, just the two of them. Now he could speak freely.

"You and I have never been more alone than we are right now," he said. "We will never get this chance again. So I want you to listen. I am about to drag this country out of the darkness and into the light. A new France will be born and this palace will be her mother."

Philippe's brows drew together. "What palace?"

Louis pointed north through the trees. "That one."

"Our father's hunting lodge?"

"Versailles."

Horns and barking dogs could be heard back up the path. The search party was closing in.

"Neither one of us chose this," said Louis. "Fortune may have placed us here. We must build our own destiny. Right here."

The horns and barking grew louder.

"With great change," Louis continued, "enemies are quick to follow. We will soon know this for ourselves. I only need to know one thing. In this moment. No matter what. Are you with me, brother?"

Philippe let out a breath.

"Do you have my back?"

Philippe held Louis' gaze. "Where am I now?"

Louis considered his brother for a moment then nodded, satisfied. Taking the reins he swung up into the saddle then pulled Philippe up behind him. Louis spurred the horse back onto the path as the search party reached them.

"The King!" a guard shouted, but the royal brothers calmly rode past without a word. Fabien, Bontemps, and War Minister Louvois watched silently. Then the search party turned their heavily breathing mounts around to follow.

Back at Versailles, Louis sat down upon a bench in an anteroom to take off his boots as guards and nobles watched, clearly relieved that the King was safe.

"I'm hungry," Louis said simply as he dropped a boot onto the floor.

Louvois stepped closer, his hands clasped together. "Sire, thank God. The woods and the town are thick with conspiracy. We must get you to Paris at once."

The other boot dropped. "We are not going anywhere."

Louvois hesitated. "But – the councils of war – the generals are all waiting for you in the Louvre."

Louis stood with regal defiance, noticing among the myriad faces the sharp, aquiline countenance of the somber noble Montcourt, whom Louis could not tell was frowning or smiling. "Invite the generals to dinner," the King said, his attention back on Louvois. "Bring the war here."

*Fabien found little* pleasure in the daintier things of life, but he did savor power. Men who gained power were those who deserved it. Power had its responsibilities. And its privileges.

The youngest of the would-be assassins stood in the center of the poorly lit prison cell. And while youth had its bravado, it also had its emotional weaknesses.

The boy's bare feet were shackled. His body was streaked with mud, blood, and piss. His face was contorted in an attempt to hide the dread that his trembling arms belied.

On a wooden table lay one of the boy's co-conspirators, an older man, naked, breathing rapidly and shallowly. He was held in place with leather straps, drenched in sweat and filth, the end of one leg a raw, bloodied stump. On a second table lay the instruments that Fabien found most useful in torture – a hammer, blades, a pair of farrier pliers and other smaller instruments, one a kindly dentist might use in another setting, another circumstance.

Fabien eyed the boy indifferently.

"You will have been given a name," he said. "A friendly face. What was the name?"

The boy, unable to take his eyes from the mangled fellow on the table, shook his head. His eyes hitched in terror.

Fabien walked to the table with the instruments.

"Only…only Calderon knew!" the boy blurted out. "He said we'd receive word."

Fabien reached into his shirt and pulled out the map he'd retrieved at the arrest of the assassins. He pointed to the code at the top.

"This?" he asked.

The boy whispered, "I've never seen that before."

Fabien had guessed as much. The boy would talk but it would take a bit more encouragement.

Turning on his heel, Fabien selected the pliers and hammer, weighing them in his hands and then moving to the bound prisoner. He looked at the body to choose the best place to start. Then he slammed the hammer into the prisoner's lower leg, crushing the bone and flattening it against the wood of the table. The prisoner, who had been nearly unconscious, woke with a hellish shriek. The boy wailed.

The pliers were next. Fabien applied them skillfully to the bones of the man's forearms, squeezing until they cracked like tinder, and then snapping each finger slowly, methodically. The prisoner screamed the screams of the damned, thrashing against the restraints, pleading to God for mercy. Fabien grinned, feeling much like God, and in no way willing to give mercy to this scoundrel. The boy sobbed mightily, snot and tears flooding his cheeks and chin.

The prisoner died ten minutes later. There was nothing left to recognize him but a thatch of hair at the crown of his head.

Fabien tossed the pliers onto the table and walked up to the weeping boy. He wiped his blood-drenched hands on the young man's tunic.

"When I return?" Fabien asked in an almost fatherly tone. "The name."

*Henriette stepped up* from the pool, the water sliding in rivulets down the ivory skin of her voluptuous breasts to her flat belly and womanly hips. She ran her fingers through her drenched, sun-colored tresses; shook them out. Two of her ladies moved in then, enfolding her in a robe and following her to the door of the grand pool house.

The pool and pool house were situated on a well-manicured stretch below the royal hunting lodge. Flanked by pruned trees and hedges, they offered refreshment, beauty, and a bit of privacy when privacy was desired. Yet as Henriette glanced up toward the palace she noticed the ugly, one-armed gardener, Jacques, looking in her direction. He paused among the hedges with his trowel, staring long enough for her to know he was watching, and she quickly looked away.

Entering the pool house, she made her way down the hallway to the changing room, her ladies tapping along obediently behind her. As she stepped across the changing room's threshold, the door suddenly slammed behind her, leaving her baffled ladies in the corridor.

Henriette immediately noticed the white flower petals scattered across the floor. She picked one up and pressed it to her lips. She shivered, not from the damp but from anticipation. Her heart beat faster, and there was a delicious, undeniable current swelling between her legs.

"You look frozen," said he who had closed the door behind her.

"Quite warm, thank you," Henriette replied. Then she looked around to face her King, surprised once again how quickly his piercing gaze, dark hair, and raw manliness could make her feel at once weak, utterly alive, and in love.

She smelled the petal. "Narcissi."

"Spring has sprung," said Louis. He reached out and drew her tight against his body.

"Apparently so," she whispered. She shrugged from her robe and it joined the petals on the floor.

Louis gazed at her body as a painter would gaze at a masterpiece. "How is your husband?"

"Please, do not talk about him now."

"I like to hear your voice."

"You made me marry him."

"How else could I keep you here?" Louis pulled her even closer. Her nipples rose, sensitive, desirous, against the fabric of his shirt.

"What would you have me say?"

Louis nuzzled her neck. "I would have you tell me…" He kissed her mouth then cupped her breasts and licked each, slowly, in turn. "…everything he says and everything he does." Then Louis dropped to the floor, pulling Henriette with him. She rolled onto her back as he removed his breeches, flung them aside, and straddled her. She watched him, breathed him in – the sensuality, the power. There was nothing more she wanted in that moment than him above her, on her, in her. Louis forced her legs apart with his knees. *Ah*, she thought, *his royal member is more than ready to part my petals.*

And so it was.

*Chevalier's private chambers* were a flurry of activity. A young servant boy scurried back and forth under Chevalier's gruff direction, packing clothes in various trunks as his master sat at the table in a streak of dusty sunlight and dined on platters of oysters, wild duck, and smoked eel.

Philippe stood by the table, watching the boy packing, watching Chevalier eating.

Chevalier tossed an oyster shell onto the table and wiped his mouth on his sleeve. "I thought I might have lost you forever. I was worried about you."

Philippe scoffed. "No, you weren't." He nodded at one of the trunks. "And what are you doing there?"

"Tell me you're not seriously considering staying here another second? They just tried to kill the King. And if they get to him, who's next?" Before Philippe could answer, Chevalier raised a brow and pointed at him. "Now there's an idea."

Philippe drew back. "You would have *me* die?"

"You are so slow sometimes." Chevalier shook his head in mock dismay. "The prince, little Louis, he's always looked a bit…sickly, don't you think?"

"Stop it."

"My point exactly. How many children die around here? What chance does this latest one have of making it out of the royal merkin let alone walking to his own coronation? There's a reason your brother's desperate for another boy. That's why everyone around here appears to be willing another male child into existence."

Philippe glared. He did not want to hear this.

"But don't you see?" continued Chevalier. "When it all falls down it all comes to you. And what would you do? On that day? With all that power?" He grinned. "What would you be doing right now? Would you consign us to linger in the swamp? No. You would make Paris the capital of the world and we would dine and dance there every night."

Philippe shouted at the boy. "Put it back. All of it!" The boy flinched and dropped the bundle he was holding.

"No, keep packing!" ordered Chevalier. He draped an arm over the back of his chair and stared at Philippe. "What kind of king goes off hunting alone then gets lost? Your brother has lost all sense of himself. He also lost himself. What a prize idiot."

Aghast, Philippe slapped Chevalier soundly on the face. Chevalier jumped from his chair, knocking it backward, and drove his fist into Philippe's chest. As Philippe doubled over with pain, Chevalier grabbed his arm and shoved him onto the bed. The boy turned away and continued packing.

Towering over Philippe, Chevalier spoke through clenched teeth. "What's this now? You would try to rule me?"

Philippe stared up at his lover, cowed, furious, and greatly aroused by Chevalier's forcefulness. "You will not talk about my brother like that," he huffed.

Chevalier snorted and leaned in so his nose almost touched Philippe's. "You know me by now, mignonette. I talk in any way I choose." He grasped Philippe's trousers and yanked them down and off. Philippe was instantly hard. Chevalier unfastened his own belt and smiled darkly. "Judge not a man by his word but by his actions," he said. "Do not worry. I will be a merciful king."

*Without announcement, Louis* entered the private apartment of his Queen, Marie-Therese. Dark-haired and bright-eyed, the young Queen drew a breath and smiled when she saw him. Her lady-in-waiting curtseyed then stepped back.

The Queen's chamber was well furnished, yet there hung in the room a sense of joylessness, or loneliness. Louis realized he had not visited his queen a while, but such was the life of a King.

Yet seeing her husband seemed to bring great relief to Marie-Therese. She stepped forward and smoothed her green silk gown over the rise of her belly. She began to speak but then she spied another man, someone she did not know, standing with Bontemps near the door. Her smile fell away.

"This is Masson, your new doctor," Louis said, indicating the stranger, a balding older man with crooked teeth. "He will attend and deliver the boy when it is time."

Masson bowed to the Queen.

"Majesty," Masson said, "I consider this appointment the very apotheosis of honor, both to myself and to my family."

Marie-Therese looked helplessly at Louis. "Que?"

"She's from Barcelona," Louis explained to the doctor. Then, to his Queen, "Do not hide behind your language. It is most unbecoming."

Marie-Therese frowned, then nodded in apology. She

touched her belly again. "I think he waits for you. When do we go home to Paris?"

"The birthing bed is prepared," said Louis. "We're not going anywhere. Wouldn't you agree, doctor?"

Masson nodded. "Most certainly, Sire."

Louis dismissed the doctor, and Bontemps ushered him out.

Marie-Therese lowered her voice. Her brows furrowed. "I do not like being cooped up! I am jealous that you're going to Mass without me."

"It is for the welfare of the child. As well as your own."

"Then let us go back to Paris. Confine me there."

Louis led her to her bed and they sat. He stroked her hair as he would a child needing consolation. He would not, though, consent to her request and she knew it.

"At least," Marie-Therese said, "make them change the tapestries. You promised."

"I will."

"I wish you would keep more promises. My bed is very big without you in it."

Louis put his hand on her belly and felt a powerful kick.

"Strong!" he said, eyes widening.

"Like his father."

"Sire," said Bontemps from the door. "Father Bossuet is calling us to chapel."

Marie-Therese looked at the floor. She suddenly seemed more anxious than bored. "When the time comes," she said slowly, cautiously. " I do not want many people here."

"Why not?"

"I do not feel the same as I did the last time."

Louis kissed her cheek and the dry tears there. "All will be well. Fear not." He rose and left his Queen yet again.

*Abandoned once more*, Marie-Therese thought as the door closed and the King was gone. Any joy she'd felt bled away. She turned to her lady-in-waiting. "Tea," she commanded. "Bring it now."

Surrounding her were the silent walls again, the lonely bed, the charmless tapestries. Nothing to make her happy. Nothing, nothing…

Suddenly there was a tickling on the backs of her thighs, and she broke into giggles. She knew it to be…

"Nabo!"

A black African dwarf, dressed in bright and frilly clothing, poked his head out from the pleats of her skirt. "A baby is coming!" he said in his high-pitched voice.

"Nabo, you naughty thing!" the Queen said to her pet, happy for the diversion.

Nabo pushed himself all the way out, hopped to his feet, and bowed dramatically. Then he turned a summersault. The bells on his clothes jingled.

"Bed," ordered Marie-Therese with a snap of her fingers, and Nabo scrambled to a little bed on the floor and curled up like a puppy.

*Worshippers left the* chapel following the Mass, moving out through the ornate wooden doors and into the clouded sunlight. The King stood in the royal box above the lower pews, watching as the nobles passed by, bowing, curtseying, hoping to be seen by His Majesty, and hoping, in some cases, not to be heard.

Louvois moved along with Philippe and Colbert, speaking quietly. "So sad to be missing the lovely Seine at the time of year."

Philippe conceded. "We stay for a birth, it would seem."

"An expectant father," said Louvois, "and only a year since you lost your dear mother. That can be very hard on a young man. For the good of France we must return to Paris as soon as we can. Surely you agree, Monsieur?"

Philippe waved a fly from his face. "How do you imagine one would persuade my brother of this?"

Louvois shook his head. "I'm sure I do not know."

Farther back among the worshippers, Chevalier strolled with two stunning beauties, almost twins of one another – the Lady Beatrice, distant cousin to Chevalier, and her breath-takingly lovely daughter, sixteen-year-old Sophie. Beatrice chastised her daughter for her inability to move gracefully.

"Slow down," said Beatrice. "Eyes up, chin down. You're either looking or being looked at. Walking is a skill, like dancing."

Chevalier pursed his lips. "She needs help with that, too."

"Why does the King ignore her?" asked Beatrice. "She's the beauty of the court."

"The King cares more for character than beauty. No wonder he does not look on you."

Sophie, humiliated, and Beatrice, determined, moved on with the crowd as Chevalier shook his head.

The King watched them all, the gossiping of his subjects sounding much like the chatterings of well-dressed geese. With him were Fabien, Bontemps, and the chestnut-haired

Louise de la Vallière, who, though proper in a gown of pale blue and gold, was clearly nervous about being in God's House in her condition, and standing so boldly with the one who had put her in that condition.

"Bossuet spoke a beautiful Mass," Louise said, hoping to get the King's attention.

"Your piety becomes you, Madame Louise," said Louis. Without looking at her, he whispered, "I want you."

Louise nodded. "I serve Your Majesty as I serve God. With all my heart. Yet...yet, Sire, I feel a change in you. I know you. And I see it."

"You are very dear to me."

Louise touched her belly. "I...I hope with all my heart it will be a healthy child."

At last the King looked at Louise. His smile was what she'd hoped for. "No matter what, it will be a child of France. Of that you can be sure."

Louise stepped closer to the King. He did not put his arm around her but did not move away.

"Fabien," said Louis with a flick of his finger. "Was that the noble Montcourt I saw with Louvois a moment ago?"

Fabien nodded. "In blue, Sire. Yes. A word about this Spanish plot, if I may –"

But Louis shook his head. "Not now." He took Louise's arm and led her from the box.

Bontemps watched them go. "Answer his questions, Monsieur Fabien," he warned. "But where the King is concerned it is not your place to offer information."

Fabien scowled. "You would have me remain silent?"

"Yes. Deeply."

"*So we are* being robbed?" asked Louis. He slammed his pen down beside the paper on which he'd been drawing a design for a large, ornate building. He fixed an accusatory gaze on Colbert.

Colbert, seated at the large table with the other black-robed ministers of state, shifted uneasily. At the door, Fabien stood beside a tall, silent Swiss guard, watching, listening.

"Sire?" Colbert asked.

Louis spit air. "The tax revenues you outlined! You heard me. Nantes down seven per cent, Limousin down fourteen per cent, Anjou down twenty-one per cent, Bourbonnais twenty-eight per cent, Savoy and Auvergne both down thirty-one per cent, Epernon down thirty-five per cent. Robbery!"

The minsters glanced at one another. Louis shoved his drawing across the table to Bontemps and continued, "They do this because they don't fear the consequences. What's worse, they steal from the people of France. In *my* name. A common thief in a brocade shirt."

"Sire," said Colbert, "the expenses you asked for, the royal pension?" He handed the King a large ledger. Louis flipped through it, unimpressed and unmoved.

Louvois folded his hands on top of the table. "Sire, the taxation issue is a tedious mess. I would wish your royal attention be fixed on weightier matters. This is an administration issue and we intend to solve it once we return to Paris. The archives are there, after all. By the time our –"

The King slammed the ledger shut. "Who is our exciseman of Epernon?"

Louvois blinked, but before he could reply, the guard by the door pounded his halberd on the floor. A young, fair-haired messenger entered, bowed, and handed the note to Bontemps.

"Who disrupts our council?" demanded Louis.

"My lady of Ile Saint-Louis," said the messenger, his eyes trained on his shoes.

Louis turned to Bontemps, for Ile Saint-Louis was Bontemp's house. The valet cringed and moved to pocket the note.

"Read it," Louis ordered.

"I...I will, Sire," said Bontemps. "Once our business is —"

"Then I shall read it!" said the King.

Louis snatched the paper, studied it, and then slowly handed it back. Bontemps read the paper and his face went pale.

"Go at once," said Louis, his voice softer now. "Take a Swiss guard with you. There are bandits on the road."

Without a word, Bontemps bowed and left the room.

Louis sat for a moment, looking at the chair where his friend had sat. The council members waited to see if he might shed light on the urgent message that had called Bontemps away. But he did not. Instead, he stood, and pointed across the room at Fabien.

"Find the exciseman of Epernon! Educate him. And let me be clear. The state of these finances will not pass these doors. As far as the world is concerned, our cash flow is strong and the royal purse secure. Perception is all. Is this understood?"

Everyone bowed in affirmation.

"Louvois," said the King. "Do we know if this exciseman has transgressed before?"

"For that, Sire," replied Louvois, "we would need the archives. In Paris."

"Then bring the archives here!"

*The doctor Masson* maintained a practice and medical school in his house in the village of Versailles, in a large clinic filled with instruments and smelling of blood and iron, a place where those ailing came for aid and bright young men interested in medicine came to learn. This cloudy afternoon it was Masson's daughter, Claudine, in the clinic, examining the body of a woman who had recently died. The woman had not been old, but her corpse showed ravages of some undetermined malady. Claudine looked up when her father entered.

"Did you meet the Queen?" Claudine asked breathlessly. "Is she like you thought she would be?"

Masson nodded with a smile.

"And the King?"

"Yes, though taller than he looks in the paintings."

Masson moved to the table and pinched the corpse's sallow skin. "The cause of this should show itself under my knife." He noticed Claudine gazing at the lacerations on the dead woman's ankles. "And the letting of blood through vivisection purges the body of illness, of course." Claudine frowned. "Speak, if you must, Claudine. God knows I can't stop you."

Claudine was a small thing, but her fortitude and intelligence were sizeable. She leaned on the table and spoke directly. "It seems to me that doctors stand before corpses pronouncing reasons of death. Yet I wonder if they omit the most obvious cause of all. Their own incompetence."

Masson shook his head. "Strong as a mule, like your mother, and twice as obstinate."

"And like her I will keep asking. Why it is a peasant woman can birth six children and four of them grow on nothing but roots and straw, yet in that house on the hill children of noble birth suckle wet nurses and fatten on pheasants yet die and die again?"

"Peasants are hardy stock."

"Do you not think perhaps our medicine could be to blame? If the Lord himself ministered to these children would he drain them of blood?" She pulled dried sprigs from her pocket. "These herbs I carry, they relieve as much pain as letting –"

"Potions and poisons. A midwife's physic garden."

"Yes, I'm a midwife. And these are as strong a remedy as any."

Masson shook his head. "My dear girl. You are smart and kind. But few would see you that way. They see a woman of knowledge who speaks her mind, and the word they use is…"

"Witch. Say it."

"I will not see you burned!"

Claudine sighed, touched his hand gently, and left the room.

Alone in the hallway, Claudine studied the shelves on which her father had collected body parts in jars and buckets, the ripe and sometimes festering fruits of his surgeries. Tumors. Gout-swollen hands. Boil-infested feet. Hearts. Bowels. Eyes and tongues. She looked back to make sure her father had not followed then reached into a bucket and scooped out a bloody mass. She wrapped it in a cloth and stole away to her bedchamber. Closing the door, she sat at her table, and opened a journal in which she had made countless sketches of organs and limbs. She unwrapped the cloth, studied the bloody organs, then began sketching on a blank page with the heading, "Female Reproduction: Womb and Uterus."

*A large board* had been set up in the center of the royal lodge's War Cabinet room. The board was covered with models of castles, fortresses, and tiny soldiers and horses. As a child, Louis would have found these items just right for fun, fantasy play. *But to a king war is never a game. War is real. War means the difference between a kingdom and a country of slaves.*

Louis stood at the window as his generals worked out a plan, a plan that would carry France into its first war under this King, a war against the Spanish for their arrogant and daring refusal to pay the dowry for the Queen, the Infanta Marie-Therese.

"If we are to emerge victorious in the Spanish Netherlands," said Louvois, "we must claim our prize with both hands. The north and the east. Two fronts working together."

Louis frowned. "Two fronts? We discussed the single column."

"Your Majesty being so preoccupied with other affairs of state, we thought it best to –"

The door opened and Philippe sauntered in, dressed grandly in a red jacket with yellow bows. The generals bowed while Louis crossed his arms.

"Leave me, all of you," Louis said.

The generals bowed and exited.

Louis walked to the war board, keeping his eye on Philippe. He cocked his head accusingly. "You spent fifty thousand on shoes. I saw the report."

"Ah, but you haven't seen the shoes." He extended his foot, revealing exquisite mules with white heels.

*Damn him! Such frivolousness!* Yet Louis held his control. He reached out and moved several tiny soldiers closer to Bruges. Perhaps Louvois's plan had merit. He'd have to think it over. "When I asked you if you had my back, brother, I meant you would guard it, not remove it."

"You build your palace. I wear my clothes. As you've said, perception is everything. But I tell you this. If you let me go to war I would not only have your back, I would bring you glory."

"What do you know of war?"

Philippe pointed at the board. "Exposing your flanks. Dangerous. Given the terrain I'd think carefully about thinning out along the supply line. A well-timed thrust might just split you in two." He reached and picked up a piece to move it. Louis slapped his hand away.

"I just want to show you," said Philippe.

"Put the piece back."

"It's glaringly obvious –"

"Give it to me!"

Louis grabbed his brother's hand. The two fell into a tangle, wrestling for the piece.

"I have your back and what do I get?" shouted Philippe as he twisted in his brother's grasp. "Respect? Power? No!"

"You get money to throw away!" said Louis.

"The minute you have a chance, you belittle me!"

"Do not forget who addresses you! Give that back! We will not ask again."

Louis felt Philippe give in. The royal "we" let him know it was time to stop. He handed the piece to Louis. "You never were good at sharing."

"Go, play," said Louis. "Some of us men have work to do."

As Philippe turned away to leave, Louis put the piece back where it had been.

*Angry. God, so* angry! Philippe slammed into the private chamber of his wife, Henriette. She looked up from arranging a vase of flowers and it was clear she saw his mood.

"Do you think your brother will like these flowers?" she began. But Philippe did not answer. He grabbed her, tore off her skirt, and flung it aside. Then he reached up beneath her petticoat and ripped down her undergarment.

"I think I want a son," Philippe said through his teeth as he fingered the damp crevice between her legs.

"Then," Henriette said, her voice quavering, "then we should say a prayer."

Philippe pushed his wife back onto the bed and unbuttoned his trousers. "Say what you like," he snarled. "It's not going to help you."

*Louis invited the* skilled architect, Le Vau, and the well-respected landscaper, Le Notre, into his private apartment to see the plans he had sketched. The two men stood, considering the huge sheet of paper covered with the King's drawings.

"As I mentioned to you," Louis said, feeling ebullient at taking a final step toward his dream, "the envelope should be completed around the entirety of the lodge. Along the full length of the terrace, inside, a great hall of mirrors which should be reflected in the symmetry. We will need to buy in Venice for the glass. The gardens on this side will extend here to here."

"Very good, Sire," said Le Notre. "What is this large rectangle here?"

"A very big lake."

Le Notre touched his chin. His doubtful expression turned Louis' mood immediately. "Sire, to feed a lake of that size –"

Louis clenched his fists, anger blossoming in his throat. Deep in his ear, he heard his mother's voice. "You see the problem, of course," she whispered. "The moment you declare your hand, your enemies may move against you."

"Sire," Le Vau said, "there are not enough rivers in Versailles."

Louis stared at the landscaper. *They will obey me!* "Then bring the rivers here," he said sternly.

When Le Vau and Le Notre had been dismissed, Louis walked down to the gardens where dirt-coated men were digging and planting. He stopped before the gardener, Jacques. Jacques saw the King, dropped his trowel, and folded in a bow.

"How long have you worked for me?" Louis asked.

"Six months, Sire," Jacques said.

"And before this?"

Jacques looked up. "War, Sire."

"What happened to your arm?"

"Left it on a field in Malines."

"How forgetful of you." Louis chuckled. He looked up at the bright sun, savoring the warmth for a moment, and then turned his attention back to the gardener. "What qualifies a soldier for gardening?"

"Skills at digging. Trenches and graves. Those terraces are fortified. Your trees will march in formation. The planning of a garden such as this is not unlike that for a war. Centuries from now, people will walk these gardens and see enduring beauty. A war fought for beauty, against chaos."

"How much work would it be to dig a lake here? Half a league in length, to the trees?"

"Quite a while. I would need an army, Sire."

Louis glanced up at the horizon, considered this, then said, "Good day to you."

"Good day, Sire. May the Queen enjoy a healthy birth. May your dreams be full of wonder."

Louis looked back at the gardener. "Dreams?"

"My mother once told me, before a man becomes a father he will relive his own childhood."

*Ile Saint-Louis* was a grand mansion in Paris, a vast house filled with dutiful servants and, very often, joy and sunlight. Yet the rooms, as finely furnished as they were, were somber on this bright afternoon. Bontemps' young son was deathly ill.

The boy, pale and fragile, lay sweating on a cot. Bontemps, who had just arrived from Versailles, embraced his wife – held her for a long moment in a feeble attempt to reclaim a fraction of the time he'd been away – and then knelt beside his son to soothe the boy's brow with a damp cloth. His heart twisted and tears burned behind his eyes. Smallpox. *Oh, dear God.*

Two doctors from the King's court had traveled with Bontemps. They spoke quietly with each other before sitting at the foot of the cot, easing the boy's feet off the end, and placing a bowl on the floor. Bontemps' son shuddered when he saw the razor blade in one of the doctor's hands.

"I…I am feeling much better," the boy said hoarsely.

Bontemps continued to wipe the boy's brow. "They must continue their work. They are the King's men. The best doctors in the land."

"Father, please." The boy grabbed his father's hand and squeezed it as the blade moved to his ankle. "Please. Tell me a story." The blade sliced into the boy's ankle and the boy whimpered. Blood flowed into the bowl.

"Once upon a time," said Bontemps, keeping his voice as steady as he could, "there was a great and glorious King who lived in a beautiful palace in the middle of a forest. His first valet was an honest man who served the King with all his heart. The position came to him by his father, just as one day, he will pass it on...to you."

"I will work for the King? What will I do?"

Bontemps touched his son's fevered cheek. "You will be the first man the King sees in the morning and the last he sees at night. You will anticipate his every need so he might continue on his course of greatness with singular courage and purpose. You will meet no other man so wise, kind, and generous. You will be the luckiest man in the world, my son. You will be one of the few to truly know the King's most private mind. Then one day, you will tell your own son of your journey and pass these blessings on to him."

The boy licked his dry lips and in a voice only a father could hear, said, "But if I live with the King, when will I ever come home?"

*The whorehouse in* Epernon was no different from any whorehouse in any city. While they provided herbs, drugs, and other minor medical treatments, the main treatment was providing men with stinking, hairy cunts and wet, painted lips, both equally adept at sucking hot, angry desire from men with a few coins to spare.

With a bit of questioning, Fabien had learned that the

cheating exciseman was taking "treatment" at this whorehouse.

Fabien had traveled the forty-seven kilometers to Epernon with guards, a leather satchel, and a hatchet. Along the way he'd thought about the King and the threats on his life. Fabien was certain the Spanish had someone inside the court favorable to their cause. He thought about the cipher he'd confiscated from the would-be assassins and the fact that it had still not been translated. He thought about the bald, cheating exciseman and how he wanted the task of dealing with him over and done with.

With a flickering five-branched candelabra in hand, Fabien had searched the foul, narrow corridors and the sweltering whorehouse cells until he found his mark. The exciseman was on a sagging bed with two whores. One whore had her legs spread for another whore whose face was buried in her bush. The exciseman was taking the second whore from behind, slamming into her, sweating hard and grunting even harder.

Fabien cleared his throat. The exciseman looked around, lip twisted in confusion. The whore he was fucking rolled over and jumped to her feet with a screech.

"Hold this," Fabien said, passing the candelabra to the whore. She took it, her eyes wide.

The naked exciseman fumbled to regain his dignity. He stood and shook his fat fist, his emerald ring on his pinky catching the candlelight. "What is the meaning of this!"

"Arithmetic," said Fabien. "After what happened to Fouquet, I'd have thought you people would have learned something." He leapt forward, grabbed the bald man's hand, and shoved it back against the wall. He whipped the hatchet from his satchel and slammed it against the man's hand, cleaving off all five fingers. The exciseman squealed in pain and slid to the floor. Fabien put his knee on the man's chest and, with the candles from the candelabra, cauterized the finger stumps. As the man howled and clutched his butchered, charred hand, Fabien said, "Remind me now. As a tax collector, you can count, can't you?"

The exciseman nodded, barely.

"For future reference," said Fabien, "so can we."

*The time of* the Queen's delivery was near at hand. She tossed and turned on her bed as evening shadows cut intricate patterns across the floor, breathing hard as the contractions came, irregularly and increasingly painful. Masson and Claudine tended the Queen with steady yet anxious hands. Masson whispered to Claudine that should the baby be a girl, the two of them would need to be prepared to leave. To flee. For their lives might well be at stake.

As Marie-Therese clutched the counterpane and longed for her husband, Louis was in his apartment, preparing for a party and the reveal of something he'd been designing for months. How the court would thrill to his plan! A royal dresser played with the folds of the King's velvet cape and adjusted the frills of the sleeves. Then Louis considered himself in the mirror a second dresser held before him, turning this way and that.

Fabien stepped as close as was acceptable, determined to give the King his report, his warning.

"Sire," he said, his voice low. "There are members of court who are willing to sell details of our life to the highest bidder. Giving no thought to the implications for your safety. The Spaniards in your dungeon were confident that the money they spent would give them access to your court."

Louis looked away from the mirror. "These people you mention would report our business here to others?"

"Undoubtedly, Sire. Do you wish me to act?"

"No."

"But they came with a cipher that is currently unbreakable. They came knowing there would be a friendly face here. They came confident that –"

Louis held up his hand. "There will come a moment tonight when our Monsieur Montcourt will wish to leave. Let him. Have his horses ready."

Fabien stepped back and nodded.

"People think us weak," said the King. "Let them hear that we are strong. Say it once, and all shall hear." With that, he swept his arm, indicating that Fabien was to take his leave.

The party was underway in the Great Hall, and a lavish affair it was. Hundreds of candles glowed from tabletops and chandeliers. Flowers and feathers adorned the tables. Acrobats flipped and jumped, fire-eaters amazed onlookers by downing flaming torches, and a stringed quartet played in the mezzanine. When the music flowed into a cheerful allemande, partiers stepped to the center of the room to dance.

Fabien stood apart, watching the festivities, arms crossed. A pocket of commotion on the dance floor caught his attention. Chevalier was trying to teach the young Sophie how to dance. She was exquisitely lovely yet without grace, and the more Chevalier tried to set her feet and arms in the right positions, the clumsier she became. Fabien watched the awkward dance lesson then glanced over at Beatrice, who appeared quite mortified at Sophie's ineptness. At last Chevalier gave up and brushed Sophie aside in frustration. Philippe stepped in to take Chevalier's hand, and they danced together quite beautifully. At that moment, Beatrice looked over at Fabien. Their gazes met, held. Fabien felt a rush inside himself, a connection that was both stirring and frightening. She was so beautiful!

Heart pounding, he immediately left the party for the hallway. He was dazed by the look he'd shared with Beatrice. He stood silently, trying to gather his wits. He had work to do, things to get his mind off this. That would be good, that would—

The King appeared in the corridor, escorted by footmen and guards, and he entered the Great Hall with Fabien following.

To the north side of the room was an alcove closed off by a heavy curtain. At Louis' nod, the footmen drew back the curtain, revealing a large table covered by a richly embroidered cloth. Something large lay beneath the cloth. Chevalier ushered Sophie away from Beatrice to the front of the crowd.

Louis scanned the room then addressed his subjects. "Many of you have been asking why we are still here. The reason is I have a gift for you. A gift we will share. A wonder for the world." He nodded and the footmen removed the cloth.

Upon the table was the most amazing, enormous model of a palace Fabien had ever seen. It stretched as long and wide as the table itself, and was complete with countless arched windows and doorways, columns, tiny white statuary, and miniature gardens in stunning detail. The crowd, awed, went instantly quiet.

"Behold the mother of France's new destiny," said Louis with a sweep of his arm. "As a mother she will cherish us. As her children we will cherish her. A palace that once your eyes rest upon its beauty, your heart is hers forever."

Ladies touched their cheeks in amazement. Gentlemen nodded at one another. Fabien glanced at Beatrice saw, again, that she was watching him. His breath locked. And again he looked away.

"From the farthest reaches of the Earth," the King continued, "men will venture here just to look upon her. And those who do will never forget her. I give you… Versailles."

Chevalier was the first to make a sound. He laughed then applauded vigorously. The others joined in. The King smiled, buoyed by the admiration.

The crowd moved in even closer to study the model. Fabien turned his attention to Montcourt, who appeared to be fascinated with the model but then backed away and slipped quietly out of the room. Fabien looked at the King. Yes. Louis had seen Montcourt's exit, too.

Through a darkened delivery tunnel Montcourt strode alone, glancing over his shoulders, moving stealthily between the cold gray walls. His face was set, his thoughts focused and hard. He paused by the wall and removed one loose stone. He placed a small scrolled message into the void, replaced the stone, and stalked away.

*The morning sun* had not yet risen when Louis was awakened by Bontemps and told that the birth of the royal child was imminent. Dressed quickly in his burgundy robe, the King hurried along the corridors to the Queen's apartment, followed by Bontemps, Colbert, and his guards. Louvois, awakened by the tumult, appeared at his doorway as the entourage passed by.

"The Queen?" he asked. Bontemps nodded.

Louvois joined the procession, but as they reached the Queen's door, the King addressed him. "Your war plans have no merit, Louvois. We cannot expose our flank. Encircle them all, one city at a time. Make for the Rhine, and then north to the sea. Bring me all of it."

Louvois, taken aback, said, "I...I cannot plan a war this way. We cannot afford –"

"The money is there," said the King. "And more important, so is the glory."

Bontemps opened the door. All entered, but before Louvois could join them, the King slammed the door in his face.

*Marie-Therese screamed*, the sound piercing, agonized.

The King, Bontemps, Colbert, Masson, and Claudine flanked the birthing bed. The Queen's ladies-in-waiting, courtiers, several guards, and the Queen's pet Nabo, stood behind them, filling the room with tangible expectation.

44

Marie-Therese's eyes were red-rimmed and exhausted. "Too many people," she managed. "Too many."

Then she bore down again, wailed, and pushed. Louis smiled encouragingly. *My son. My son is here.*

"Here," said Masson. "The child comes." He peered into the folds of the blanket where, at last, a baby's wet head was visible between her legs. The Queen cried out and pushed again. The child was expelled, squawking with life.

Masson stood straight. He blinked.

Claudine, who had been watching closely, stared with terrified eyes.

Masson turned from the bed. "Everyone must leave," he said.

Louis frowned.

"At once!" said Masson.

Louis jerked his head and everyone cleared the room, leaving only the King, Bontemps, Masson, and Claudine.

"What is the meaning of this?" Louis demanded.

Masson looked at the Queen and baby still hidden by blanket. He swallowed hard. "I... Sire, I –"

"Speak! Where is your tongue?"

Claudine lifted the blanket to shield the sight of the child from the Queen, who lay panting on her pillows. Masson gently picked up the baby. It was a little girl, wailing with healthy lungs.

And the child was black.

# 2

*Impossible. This cannot* be true! Louis' mind raced, determined that this thing, this child, was a hoax. A nightmare! A horrific trick!

Yet it was quite real. The child the Queen had just delivered was not only female, but had skin as dark as an African.

Bontemps swept in and gathered the child from Masson's arms as Marie-Therese pushed herself up to see her baby. She gasped, whimpered, and dropped back to the pillows.

Bontemps folded the towel over the child and hastened it from the birthing chamber, through the outer room, and into the corridor. A young chambermaid nearly collided with the valet, and in that moment a flap of the blanket fell away and the maid saw the child clearly. She shuddered and looked away, but it was too late. Her eyes had witnessed what no one was supposed to witness. She quickly retreated down another corridor with her face downcast.

As Bontemps spirited the baby away, seeking a wet nurse

he was certain would be trustworthy, Masson stood in the Queen's bedchamber, trembling and glancing from Her Majesty to the floor to the King. Then he offered a stumbling explanation as to the child's condition.

"Sire, I…I believe that soon after the Queen became pregnant, her pet Nabo jumped out and…and he gave the queen a stare that corrupted her royal womb with darkness."

Louis resisted the delicious urge to slap the doctor. He merely replied, "That must have been quite a stare." Then he stalked from the Queen's quarters and into the corridor, where Colbert spied him and hurried to catch up.

"The child, Sire?" he called.

Louis stared straight ahead and did not slow. "Stillborn. The funeral is being planned. Now, are the tailors arrived for the pavilion?"

"They are en route, Sire. The pavilion is the talk of the court. Sire, I'm so sorry that —" But the King brushed him off and walked faster, his footfalls echoing like the pounding of an angry heart.

*Fabien found the* private room where his assistant, a plain-faced, humorless woman named Laurene, sat silently with the wet nurse. The nurse was an ugly blind woman with few teeth, but she hummed sweetly as the baby suckled her breast. She was clearly a healthy child, with bright eyes and lively limbs that kicked and peddled at the air.

At Fabien's nod, Laurene took the baby from the nurse and carried it to the door. Fabien caught her arm and whispered in her ear, "There was a chambermaid working outside the birthing room. Green eyes. A scar on her chin. I want her name."

*Chevalier stopped Beatrice* and Sophie in the corridor. He cocked his head and spoke to Beatrice.

"When you first came to court," he said, "do you remember what I told you?"

Beatrice nodded. "You said you would return any favor with interest. And yet I still wait after you had me spread those lies for you about your little blond friend, so very long ago."

Chevalier grinned slyly and handed her an envelope. "That is what I find so endearing about you, cousin. You are so patient."

As Chevalier walked off, Beatrice tore open the envelope. Sophie peered over her mother's shoulder and read the letter.

*The King invites you to a private showing of diverse suits of lace, velvet, and other fabrics from master tailors and mercers of Saint-Honoré. A grand carousel and banquet will follow in their honor.*

Beatrice smiled. His Majesty had noticed her daughter. An impressive step forward for herself and more importantly, for Sophie.

*Marie-Therese licked* her dry lips and struggled to sit up. Louis stood beside the bed, arms crossed, offering no help. "You've no color in your cheeks," he said. "Unlike your daughter."

"Where is she?" Marie-Therese asked. "Please?"

Louis scoffed. He walked across the room to the Queen's desk, picked up a sharp letter opener, and weighed it in his hands. Bontemps watched on silently.

Louis touched the tip of the blade, turned it around, studying it.

"Madre de dios!" Marie-Therese gasped.

"What we do here resonates throughout the world," said the King. "Do you imagine William of Orange in the north, if he knew what happened, would pause for a second at our borders? Would he see us, the King, and his country as anything other than a weak, debased, laughing stock? This was not the act of a wife or Queen. This was an act of sedition by a traitor."

"You...you are my King!"

"I know what your actions have cost me. But I do not yet know their *value*."

The Queen clasped trembling hands and began to pray. "Dios me ayuda. Dios me perdona!"

"French when it pleases you," sneered the King. "Spanish when you wish to hide. You long for uninvited visitors, perhaps. To remind you of home?"

"I am happy here."

"If you do not speak the language, no wonder you have no friends."

49

"If the court think me an idiot, at least they think me worthy of something, even if it is only pity!"

"You'll have no pity from me. Bontemps."

The valet bowed.

"Her Majesty looks unwell. Masson will tend her and she shall remain confined until she is fit to rejoin us." Louis drove the letter opener down, hard, into the wood of the desk and left, Bontemps following.

With the King gone, Nabo crawled onto the Queen's bed when the King was gone, and tried to snuggle with her. But she slapped him away. Nabo whimpered and returned to his bed by the fire.

*The afternoon air* was sweet and warm, laced with scents of colorful, blooming flowers of countless varieties. A new grove of orange trees was visible now, down from the higher gardens, planted by the clever soldier-turned-gardener, Jacques. Their leaves flipped and shimmered in a breeze.

Louis, his mind weighted down with many matters, took a sun-streaked pathway with Louvois and Colbert on either side, followed by Bontemps, Fabien, and Swiss guards.

"Sire," Colbert said, "we may have war or we may have splendor but I do not believe we can have both."

"Then," interjected Louvois, "it must be war."

Colbert countered, "Then the Dutch will secure the trade routes into West Africa and we shall have no part of it."

Louvois shook his head. "You cannot put a price on glory."

"The Dutch are mistaken," the King said. "And France has my wife to thank for that." Picking up his pace, the King left Colbert and Louvois behind. Bontemps tried to keep up but Louis waved him off.

The ministers and valet stood, frustrated, looking at each other without a word, until Fabien ordered the guards to follow the King and stay with him, keeping a reasonable distance.

Philippe, Chevalier, and several noble friends appeared from an intersecting, rose-lined pathway, laughing in the sun.

"Bontemps," Philippe asked, raising one finger in the air. "Are the rumors true?"

Bontemps replied, "Rumors?"

"Come now. My brother sent for the archives. Are we to stay here another *week*?"

Bontemps shrugged.

"Ha," said Chevalier with a hitch of his lip. "He cannot hear. His ears are old."

Bontemps spoke calmly, evenly. "I do not speak for the King. But the Queen is unwell. I imagine we shall be here until she recovers."

"Why should we even listen to you, Bontemps?" asked Philippe. "A servant who sleeps like a dog at the foot of another man's bed. What kind of man does that?"

Philippe and his friends laughed. Then Philippe noticed Chevalier winking at one of the more handsome members of the entourage and his smile faltered.

Bontemps paused then said, "A faithful one, Monsieur."

*Louis, followed by* his guards, entered the large grove where orange trees were set in large, silver pots. There was still much work to be done to make it as beautiful as Louis had envisioned, but the gardeners were busy, cutting diseased branches from the trees and tossing them onto a small bonfire. As soon as the gardeners saw the King, they fell to their knees. Louis gestured for them to rise and continue their work. Then he turned to Jacques, who was supervising the process by giving orders and referring to a paper in his hand.

"Tell me about our work here," Louis said.

Jacques pointed to one of the orange trees. "I make it my business to discern the provenance of every tree Your Majesty receives. This one..." he consulted the paper, "...came first from the botanic gardens at Montpelier. That one from the university at Strasbourg. Before that, Arabia, China." He looked squarely at the King. "To know the seed is to know the root. To know the root is to know the tree and the fruit that comes thereafter. So I burn the sick and preserve the purse. And the King shall have his orange blossom."

Louis nodded with satisfaction and some new ideas. And not far away, in the shade of an ivy-covered arbor, a noble from court had stopped to listen. He turned to his companion and said, "If we do not have proof of our title and provenance, then we have nothing."

*Fresh from wandering* among the flowers and hedges, Philippe and his dandy friends settled in Philippe's apartment to sample new perfumes. As a lone chambermaid swept along the walls, the men sat on chairs and divans, sniffing silk handkerchiefs and passing them about.

"And this," said Philippe, holding up a cloth embroidered with gold thread, "is the latest scent. Carmelite and lavender." He held the handkerchief to Chevalier, who put it to his nose and sniffed appreciatively. Another man suddenly leapt up, grabbed the handkerchief, and the men fell into a laughing, tangled game of tag, each one snatching for the cloth, tickling, shoving. The man with the cloth flapped it in the air, dropped it, and ran from the room, followed by the others, leaving Philippe standing alone, chuckling. He picked up the handkerchief.

Then he heard a soft sob from the corner.

Philippe turned.

"Forgive me, Monsieur," said the chambermaid. She was a plain girl with green eyes and a scar on her chin.

Philippe frowned and approached the girl. "What's the matter?"

The maid began to weep, her shoulders shaking. Philippe reluctantly handed the handkerchief to her and she dried her eyes.

"The royal baby," she said.

"We all have a heavy heart," said Philippe.

"I...I saw something."

"I do not understand."

The maid sniffed. "The child was alive. And...and the strangest color."

Philippe stepped closer. "What madness is this?"

"Sire, I beg you. I say this in the strictest confidence and the spirit of loyalty…my mother works for you at Saint-Cloud, thus I feel I must speak. Perhaps you might help me join her there in service?"

"There you are!" It was Chevalier in the doorway. He smiled a cool smile, walked over, and gave Philippe a passionate kiss. When Philippe turned back, the chambermaid was gone.

"Everyone is in a bad mood today," said Chevalier.

"The King has lost a child. And I, a niece."

Chevalier raised a brow then studied his fingertips. "Perhaps that's it."

"Do you take nothing seriously?"

"Not if I can help it."

*The royal orange* grove was splendid. Another affirmation of the glory of the Sun King, another step toward the future. Now, however, it was this moment that mattered. The ministers were gathered in the War Cabinet room, seated at the table with Louis at the head. Bontemps stood apart, always listening, always waiting and ready for what his King might need.

"Without the documents of law before us," said Louis, "my edict has no legitimacy. Where are the archives? Why are they not yet before us? Are they still on the road?"

All eyes turned to Louvois, who took a deep breath. "Sire," he began. "The decision was taken to turn the caravan around."

"What? Taken by whom?"

"The road from Paris is dangerous, especially as it approaches the royal lands around this lodge. We would not have court materials taken hostage."

Louis stood, pressed his hands against the table, and leaned forward. The council leaned away as if he was the wind and they were weeds. "But that is exactly what has happened, Monsieur Louvois! The masters of the tailors' guild arrived safely. One would think the King's guard might also stand a chance of survival."

"We think only of security," said Louvois. "We merely serve Your Majesty."

"For now," said the King.

Louis could see in Louvois' eyes that the man knew he had crossed a line. Louis stared at each of his ministers in turn and then dismissed them, leaving only himself and Bontemps in the room.

"If Monsieur Louvois does not soon hold his tongue," said Bontemps as he watched the door close, "I may volunteer to hold it for him."

Louis let out a breath. "I'd rather an honest critic than a false friend, Bontemps."

"Sire? He seems to talk only of his opposition to you. He takes contrary positions to your plans and declares it to anyone who will listen."

"And long may he continue."

Bontemps hesitated then stepped closer. His face looked oddly pale. "I'm…sure I do not understand, Sire."

Louis felt a rush of rage stirring within. It was not rage at Bontemps, but other things. Other deep things. The dark things…

Louis looked at the window, forcing himself to change the subject. "What news of your son?"

Bontemps did not reply.

Louis turned back. His valet was shaking and sweat had popped out on his forehead and cheeks.

"Bontemps?"

The valet's eyes rolled up in his head and he fell with a crash to the floor. Louis dropped down beside him, took his hand, and called his name over and over. *This can't happen!* Louis thought. *I can't lose you now!*

Then slowly the valet roused, panting and moaning. Louis helped him up and into a chair as maids cleaned the blood he'd spilled when his head hit the floor.

"The doctors made every effort to help my son," Bontemps said, looking at his hands, his throat ragged and raw, "but the pox was too strong. It took him. Dear God. He made a braver man than I will ever be."

Louis spoke gently. "I am with you in your loss. Go home."

"You are my home, Sire."

"Be with those you love."

"I am, Sire."

"Ah," said the King, looking at the ceiling. "God is punishing me by hurting those closest to my heart."

"He's testing you, Sire, offering a gift. Vengeance and mercy are His to choose. They are also yours."

Louis looked down; his expression altering, darkening.

"I believe," Bontemps continued, "God placed this child in your care for a reason."

Louis held up a hand. "No. I've heard enough."

"She is strong, let her live."

Louis leaned dangerously close to Bontemps. "And then what?" he screamed. "Answer me!"

"Sire…I do not presume any judgment…"

"Of course you don't! No one does!"

The silence held long, King and valet considering one another, friends yet separated by the vast sea of their positions. Then Louis' voice quieted but remained regally cold. "A secret such as this has the power of a tide. Once released it will go where it must, beyond our control. It will wash away everything in its path. And that will be the end of everything we know."

"Sire," whispered Bontemps. "I only meant —"

"Grieve your loss. But do not forget your place." Louis went to the door and the ushers opened it, revealing a crowd of courtiers waiting to see him. Always there, always waiting, always wanting. The King looked at them then motioned for the doors to be closed once more. He walked to the window, put his hands on the sill, breathed on the glass.

"Sire," began Bontemps. "Please forgive me."

Birds flew past the window, free and fleet of wing, heading across the gardens to the forested hunting grounds. Louis looked back at Bontemps. Bontemps could see the change of heart in the King's face. "Do as you must," he said.

And Bontemps, with new energy, concern, and resolve, raced from the room, the pain in his head forgotten.

*The chambermaid hurried* along the town square of Versailles, a basket of bread on her hip, going about her business but her mind on the baby. On having seen what she did not want to see, on knowing what she did not want to know. And certain her life was in danger.

"Hello!" came a voice from behind. She spun about, fearful to see a pistol at her head. But it was only Chevalier, Monsieur's friend. She relaxed a fraction.

Chevalier smiled. "Have you any money?"

The maid shook her head.

"I have lots of money. And I was thinking that perhaps I might give some to you. Then you could spend it getting to Saint-Cloud to join your mother. Would you like that?"

"Oh, yes, please!"

Chevalier's nose twitched. "Then tell me what you saw outside the birthing room, and you shall have it."

The maid glanced about and hesitated. *This*, she thought, *could be my only chance*. So she said, "Money first."

Chevalier shook his purse, peered inside, and then showed her it was empty. "Wait here," he said. He walked off, and in that moment the maid realized she had been betrayed.

*Marie-Therese continued* to suffer, her coloring splotchy, her breathing irregular. One of the ladies sat by the bed, reading *Aesop's Fables* in Spanish, though the Queen did not seem to hear it. In a corner of the room Masson and his daughter engaged in a whispered quarrel as to the Queen's care.

"She's not recovered," said Claudine.

"What's done is done. Are our bags packed? We must be ready to leave."

Claudine took her father's arm. "Stop this thinking, Father, or it will be the end."

"Of both you and me, child, unless we take measures."

Masson picked up a candle and gestured toward the door. "We saw what we saw, and we cannot un-see. And they will kill us for it."

But Claudine took the candle and slammed it back on the table, refusing to go.

*Behind the servants'* quarters, at the rear of the royal hunting lodge, was a storage barn filled with water barrels, grains, and supplies. Mice scurried in the walls and swallows fluttered in the rafters. In one dusty stall, Fabien and Laurene stood before a barrel filled with murky water. Laurene held the infant girl in her arms.

Fabien pointed at the water. "Baptize it. Thoroughly."

Laurene only then realized their reason for being there.

"Now."

Laurene held the baby over the water. The child began to cry pitifully. "I…can't," Laurene said.

"Gently," said Fabien. "You can." He put his hand on Laurene's and forced the baby down and under the water. The child's tiny legs thrashed but its determination was nothing compared to Fabien's resolve.

"See how life fights death? Cherish this God-given moment."

Laurene's eyes were averted.

"No, look," said Fabien. "We all remember our first time."

And then there was a roaring into the stall, someone with arms raised and eyes huge with anger.

"Fabien!" Bontemps cried. He knocked Fabien aside and pulled the baby from the water. The child coughed and kicked, then wailed.

Stunned, Fabien shouted, "Our work protects the King!"

Bontemps held the child close. "Your work here is finished!"

Fabien snarled. "What chance does that wretch have outside these walls?"

"That's not your concern. Tomorrow the *Gazette de France* will report the funeral preparations with all consideration of a royal passing. A grave is prepared." Then, cuddling the child, he walked out.

"A grave error, to be sure," Fabien said to the valet's retreating shadow.

"*Monsieur Colbert*," *said* the King as he swept into the palace anteroom where Colbert was hard at work over the ledgers, "add a monthly stipend to the royal household."

Colbert looked up, confused. "Whose name shall I place on the register?"

"Leave it blank. The pension must remain outside of the record." The King paused, then added, "Outside all record."

"Yes, Sire."

"Now then, is the pavilion prepared?"

"The tailors' guild and its masters await your word."

Louis touched his chin, nodded. "All nobles attending the banquet must wear French cloth. No Italian lace nor English wool. The night will reflect the glory of our French talents. Tell them all: bright colors and vibrant fabrics. For we shall all soon be tired of black."

*The chapel was* adorned in black for mourning – the bunting and altar cloths, the robes of the choir and priest. A tiny, intricately carved casket sat upon a black silk sheet at the front of the church. Noble mourners listened as Father Bossuet, in a voice deep and pious, spoke of life and death.

From behind a curtain, Louis watched the funeral. His fingers were tight, his heart even tighter. It was not customary for Kings to attend the funerals of children, yet he wanted to see. He needed to see.

Philippe slid up beside his brother. "What are you looking at?"

"My friends are here to mourn. The others to celebrate my misfortune and to gossip."

"The child's dead. What gossip could there be?"

Louis looked at his brother, sharply. What might he know? "I've no idea," he said evenly.

Philippe peeked through the curtain. "There is too much mirth in the chapel. If you will not attend at least they must pay you respect —"

"I will not. I cannot."

"If you say so."

"What is this insolence? Protocol demands it."

"Perhaps we should all be bowing to protocol, brother, and not to you."

Louis grabbed Philippe's collar. "You would usurp me?"

"Your child is dead. Her mother lies alone, sick, and scared."

"A lesson in morality. From a man dressed as a woman and who fucks the same way."

Philippe tossed his head. "Had your Queen the means, she would be here to grieve for her child. And you, without impediment, choose to hide. That's the only lesson."

"Oh," said Louis, letting go of the collar. "I do have an impediment. And I'm looking at him right now."

Flushed and furious, Philippe took the side corridor and entered the chapel from the rear. He crossed himself half-heartedly and joined Henriette on the pew behind Chevalier.

"How is the King?" Henriette whispered, wiping a tear from her cheek.

Philippe shook his head. "As you'd expect."

"He should be here."

"He does not mourn."

"In public, perhaps."

"Anywhere. The man does not weep."

"Not to you, perhaps. It takes a woman to see it. His heart will be full of sorrow."

"His heart," said Philippe, "if he has one, is a whole other matter entirely. Is it not?"

Chevalier turned in his seat and gave Philippe a teasing grin. "You look nice, Monsieur," he said. Then he winked at Henriette. She glared at him until, laughing silently, he turned around again. Then she lowered her head and cried openly.

*As Father Bossuet* lifted his eyes to Heaven and began to recite the Lord's Prayer, much was happening within the chapel:

Louise De La Vallière gazed at the tiny coffin, saddened, worried.

Chevalier stared at the coffin, wondering if this was a cover-up.

At the back of the chapel, Montcourt gave Louvois a smile in spite of the somber circumstance.

Even more was happening beyond the chapel's walls:

Bontemps, in a hooded cloak, rode his horse at a gallop along a rutted, muddy road away from the town of Versailles. For miles they traveled until they reached a small convent tucked up against a hillside. Two nuns stood outside the gate, waiting. Bontemps dismounted, went to the nuns, and opened his cape. There, tucked in safe, was Marie-Therese's infant daughter. He handed the child to one of the nuns. "Thank you, sisters," he said.

Laurene sneaked into a narrow hallway in the royal lodge

with a document in her hand. She plunged it into her coat just before a guard walked past her.

Fabien appeared in the servants' quarters and found the chambermaid he'd been searching for, alone and packing to leave. It took little effort to tie the sleeves of a robe around her neck, lift her onto a chair, lash the robe to the beams overhead, and kick the chair away. There. Suicide. Clean and simple. He spotted a flower-embroidered handkerchief on the bed and put it in his pocket.

*Henriette sat at* a small table in her inner chamber, her heart heavy, her hair loose and her face wet and puffy with weeping. "A dead child," she said as she touched her cheeks with a handkerchief. "What if the Dauphin follows him? And then His Majesty?"

Madame de Montespan, Henriette's witty and most graceful lady, reached across the table and took Henriette's hand. The Montespan was beautiful, tall, and slender, with golden-brown hair and bright eyes. Other ladies-in-waiting busied themselves nearby in the room, one tatting lace for sleeves, another reading, yet another mending a stocking.

"You already know the answer to that question," said the Montespan gently. "Your husband would be King, making you –"

"No!" said Henriette. She put the handkerchief down. "I would not wish to live in a world where my dearest, our dearest King is not! And Chevalier, God help us. He already divides the court. My marriage has three members, not two. If my husband were King, Chevalier would rule by the rod and my husband would be his rug!"

"Your husband is a good man and would make a good king. And you'd have power."

"I've seen what power can do to a man and how it can be taken away."

The Montespan nodded. "The fault of the English conspirators. And your brother has your father's throne."

"As long as he keeps his head."

"Calm yourself. Let's go look at the pretty things in the pavilion. All the tailors of Paris are here. I've never seen so much cloth."

"I'd rather you did my cards."

The Montespan nodded. She picked up a deck of Tarot cards and gave them to Henriette. With trembling hands, Henriette shuffled then dealt them face down.

The Montespan slowly turned the cards over. "The cards talk of past, present, and future. Your past is sadness. Yet there is a friend in your present willing to help you."

"If I could find this person," said Henriette, "I would ask only to protect my King."

The Montespan's hand hesitated over the last card and she studied the face of her young mistress. "You care for him greatly."

"There is nothing I would not do for him."

The Montespan smiled. She turned over the final card. It was Death.

65

*I remember . . . .*

His father, Louis XIII, dying…

Sick, in bed, a royal bed surrounded by grieving nobles and ladies. The old King's eyes were rheumy and faded, yet there was a rage and determination in them, yet.

Anne of Austria stood close to the bed, holding young Louis' hand. Louis was repulsed by the stench of death yet fascinated with the reality of it.

"Who's that?" the old King demanded.

"Your son," said Anne. "Louis the fourteenth."

The dying man's eyes fixed Louis with an icy stare. "Not yet he's not."

"Sire?"

Louis turned from the window, the memory dissolving. Fabien and Bontemps waited by a table with a sheet of vellum unrolled upon it. The vellum was covered with strange symbols.

"I've not seen this cipher before," said Fabien. "Even the brilliant cryptographer Rossignol cannot break it."

Louis looked at Bontemps. "This was in Montcourt's rooms? And yet he walks free?"

Bontemps nodded. "Free but not unwatched."

"I did not want to take action until I had heard from Rossignol, Sire," said Fabien.

Louis leaned over the vellum, eyed it closely. "So we do not know what it says."

"These symbols share a common thread with those we liberated from the prisoners."

"The Spaniards."

"I submit, Sire, we cannot be sure who they were. Whoever plotted this against you had no intention of their plan succeeding. This was a rehearsal to gain a measure of our defenses. Planning such an offense, one might plant a false flag of Span to divert attention elsewhere. And someone inside your court was helping them. Some inside was a friendly face."

Bontemps looked from the King to Fabien. "We shall summon Montcourt to us."

Fabien shook his head. "Better to lie fallow and collect information. This paper was placed freely upon Montcourt's bureau."

Bontemps considered this. "So he may not have known its true purpose."

"You are a friend of Montcourt?"

Bontemps said, "I am a friend of the truth."

Fabien turned back to the King. "One thing is clear, Sire. There is a plot against you."

The door to the apartment opened and a footman announced Colbert, who joined the men at the table.

"Only one plot, Fabien?" said Louis. "To my left my excise-men rob me, to my right the Spanish want my neck, and now a chambermaid has hanged herself. Was she plotting, too? Or did she not pay her taxes?"

Bontemps looked hard at Fabien at the mention of the chambermaid. "A minor contribution at that."

"A larger sum than any noble," said the King.

Colbert nodded. "The nobles pay no tax whatsoever."

Louis walked around the table, thinking. Then, "How many noble families attend our fashion pavilion for the tailors' guild of Paris?"

"Every family within a day's ride have been summoned, Sire," said Colbert.

Louis stopped. "Make sure they are all there. Montcourt, too. After all, the true measure of a mousetrap is not the weight of the block."

"It's the smell of the cheese," said Fabien.

Bontemps glared at Fabien.

"Touché," replied the King.

*Behind the closed* door of the tack room in the royal stable, Louvois spoke in a low voice to the Swiss Guard members who had been responsible for turning back the caravan carrying the archives. There were two knocks on the door, then two more, then one. The recognized code.

A guard opened the door to admit Montcourt. Beneath his heavy brows his eyes flashed with fear.

"Meeting here is too much risk," he said.

Louvois crossed his arms. "We cannot leave while the Queen is sick. The King will not have it."

"Perhaps that is his intention."

"Many nobles ride in for the carousel of fashion," said Louvois. "They will ride out again afterwards. This is our moment to make our case and let the message fan out to all four corners of the country. To the ears of many more who will join in our opposition. The building of the Versailles palace *must* be stopped. Not even a king can stop a tide."

$\mathcal{C}hevalier\ lunged\ with$ his sword, laughing, as Philippe grinned and parried with his own weapon. A platter of fruits and meats sat on Philippe's table, a snack brought in by order of the King's brother but as of yet untouched.

"Touché!" cried Chevalier as his sword came up and knocked Philippe's away. Chevalier stepped close, put the point of his sword against Philippe's throat then slowly drew it down his chest.

"A maid comes crying to you and tells you she has information on the royal baby," Chevalier said teasingly as the sword tip paused just above Philippe's crotch. "And now she's dead. Now we're told we cannot move from Versailles because the Queen is unwell. I wonder. What is your brother hiding?"

The fun of play instantly gone, Philippe stepped back and stared. "You be careful about what you say and how loudly you say it."

"Perhaps the baby was alive after all."

"We saw the child buried."

"We saw a box. Your brother thinks you weak. A bitch! You have more power than you realize. Use it."

Philippe went to the table and picked up a pastry. "We're still cut from the same cloth. Raised under the same roof." Then he dropped the pastry and turned to look at Chevalier. His face suddenly lightened. He grabbed Chevalier and kissed him. "Of course!"

"What's so funny?"

"Come!" said the King's brother. "If I'm going to be a bitch I may as well look like one."

*Henriette's ladies dressed* her in a new gown, a sun-yellow dress of silk with gems sewn along the neckline. She would wear it to the Carousel of Fabrics. Philippe, of course, would care little for her appearance except, perhaps, to chide her. On the other hand, the King…

The door to her apartment opened. Louis entered, head high, adorned in a plum coat with an ermine collar, an embroidered vest, and a gold chain around his neck. His dark hair was swept back and his gaze was bright with passion.

Henriette looked down but Louis said, "Do not avert your eyes from a king. Especially when you look as you do right now." He waved his hand at the ladies-in-waiting. "Leave us." The ladies scurried off into adjoining rooms.

Louis walked toward Henriette. "You were never more beautiful than at this moment. Now, take it off."

Love swelled in Henriette's heart. Passion flooded her body. She undressed before the King, her flesh cooling to the touch of the air, then stood naked and ready.

"There is talk of war," she said.

"Always." The King's fingers moved along the rise of her breasts. Her nipples hardened joyously.

"My husband would love to fight."

Louis unbuttoned his shirt. "Is that what he wants?"

"He talks of nothing else. Almost."

The King removed his shirt and trousers. Then he pulled her to himself. "If I send him to the Spanish Netherlands, he may not return."

"A glorious death would not displease him. Or me." His breath was on her neck, his lips an inch from her throat.

"That is my brother you are talking about," he whispered.

"I speak it, Sire, but you think it."

Louis stroked her hair and stared into her eyes. His gaze was strong, certain, and loving. He turned her chin up and kissed her deeply, completely, and she felt into his arms, in that moment truly and wholly his. And in that moment death was forgotten.

As Louis and Henriette clung to one another in the privacy of her apartment, the Carousel of Fabrics opened to the nobles at court. It was grand, a bright, bustling, and colorful bazaar where countless tailors displayed exquisite fabrics as well as superbly finished gowns, cloaks, capes, and trousers. Every room and corridor of the pavilion was filled with life-sized dolls modeling clothing as well as tables displaying masks, shoes, perfumes, gloves, and jewelry set with all manner of rare gems. Noble men and ladies, from the court and from a day's ride away, were awed by the offerings. They strolled through the displays, touching, holding, and purchasing. Montcourt gathered beautiful fabrics and piled them high to carry away. Fabien wandered around, pretending to be interested in fabrics but watching the crowd, instead.

Beatrice and her daughter Sophie moved among the throng, Sophie admiring plumed hats and lace gloves, Beatrice primping her daughter to make sure she was a fine display all her own. She was greatly pleased with the admiring stares Sophie drew from the noble men.

"Men are at war," Beatrice whispered to Sophie as Sophie held up a gold silk gown. "They use swords, but we use our beauty. But the end is the same. Conquest."

"I want this dress," said Sophie.

"You'll need more than a dress. A filigree bracelet and necklace of diamonds."

"How will we pay?"

"Let me worry about that. Your job is to bring me a king."

There was a sudden commotion at the pavilion entrance. All heads turned to see Chevalier stride in beside Philippe, who was dressed in an exquisite ladies' gown of scarlet and silver with rouge upon his cheeks. Noblemen and their wives went silent, uncertain of what to say. Some applauded, others glanced at each other nervously.

Fabien sidled up to Philippe and handed him the flower-embroidered handkerchief. Chevalier saw it and quickly pulled Philippe away. They continued to promenade through the crowd. Philippe took elegant steps, his head high.

Then several teenaged boys tittered behind their hands. This caused a ripple; adults began to whisper carefully to one another, confused and off-put. Neither Philippe nor Chevalier seemed to notice.

But then came a loud, throaty chuckle that quickly grew into roaring laughter. Philippe turned to face the man, a battle-worn, middle-aged warrior with steely eyes.

"You mock me," asked Philippe, pursing his lips.

The warrior smirked. "How can I not? You are an embarrassment to the King."

Nobles gasped. Swiss guards stepped closer, watching, ready.

"Mock me," said Philippe, "you mock my brother. Which makes you a traitor."

"I defeated the Turks at Saint Gotthard in the name of the King. That sound like a traitor to you?"

"You sounded like one when you opened your mouth."

"If I smite you, you will fall. Which makes me a dead man."

"You have my word, you are free to strike. If you dare. Coward." Philippe pointed at the guards to make sure they knew to let the men fight. The nobles stepped back. Tailors scrambled anxiously to protect their wares.

The warrior bowed mockingly then charged Philippe, grabbed him with both hands, and slammed him against the wall. Philippe coughed, struggled, pulled free. He drove his fist into the warrior's jaw. The warrior stumbled but regained his footing. He took hold of Philippe's arm, ripping the sleeve of the dress then hurling the King's brother backward again. Philippe twisted about and landed a solid blow to the warrior's face. The warrior clasped his fists together into a club and brought them down on Philippe's head. Grunting and spitting blood, Philippe crashed to the floor. His face struck, hard, tearing a long gash into the flesh of his cheek. The warrior stood over him, panting, his yellow teeth bared.

Guards stepped closer but Philippe managed to lift his hand. "Stand down," he coughed. "He has my word."

The guards withdrew. Philippe wiped blood from his face, kicked off his shoes, and staggered to his feet. The warrior snarled, snatched an iron from a dressing table, and swung the thick metal block. Philippe ducked out of the way. He grabbed a long hatpin from the model behind him, jumped forward, and drove the pin deep into the warrior's eye.

The warrior dropped the iron and bellowed. He flailed, unable to grasp the pin with his sweaty fingers, and collapsed to his knees. Philippe grabbed a halberd from a guard and approached the wounded warrior. With an expression of satisfaction and exoneration, he raised the heavy staff, ready to bring it down.

"Stop!" shouted Chevalier. "I think you've made your point." Philippe reluctantly lowered his weapon, brushed himself off, and stared at the crowd hard enough to send them back to the business they'd been about in the first place.

*Alone in the* King's apartment, Louis and Philippe circled each other. Fury flashed in the King's eyes and it was matched by the rage in his brother's.

"You can choose who I marry and where I live and how much money I spend," said Philippe, "but you do not get to choose what I wear and who I fuck."

Louis angled his head; a wolf challenged in his forest. "Everything you do reflects on me."

"I've been dressed like this since I was three months old," said Philippe. "It's been my duty to be less than you. You think it's hard to be King? Try being a king's brother for a day. You could never trick me. I know what you are planning here. And what you are hiding."

"I've given you nothing but my love and respect, brother."

"Is that what you tell yourself when you're fucking my wife?"

Louis snorted. "Someone has to."

"Everything I have I share with you. But you will not share the truth. How can I have your back if you won't tell me the truth?"

Louis stopped circling and studied his brother. "Some things only a king can know."

"What happened to the baby?"

"It did not survive."

"Don't you understand how rumors start? Your silence fuels the fire. Let me help you. I've never uttered an ill word against you, my brother."

Louis' smile was sour. "It's not your words that worry me."

*The King gathered* his generals and ministers in the War Cabinet room. The model battlefield sat upon the table. Men upon ladders held up large maps of the Spanish Netherlands with the enemies' positions highlighted in red.

Louvois marched about, vigorously pointing out Spanish positions. "The Spanish have fortified the towns of Charleroi, Tournai, Douai, and Lille. General d'Aumont has troops in the north. Turenne's battalions lie east of Cambrai."

Philippe was announced and he entered, no longer dressed in feminine garb but as a man with fresh wounds who would be a warrior. He bowed and asked the King for permission to speak, which surprised the ministers in the room. Permission was granted.

"Cut off all of Flanders, from the large Spanish bases to the east," said Philippe, stepping up to the table. "Bruges. Ghent. Brussels and Namur."

Louvois shook his head. "To achieve your goal we would have to cut the Spanish off from Tournai and Douay. Who could lead our men? Every man is accounted for."

"There is one, perhaps," said the King.

Philippe looked hopefully at his brother.

"But in truth, he may not be ready."

*The Montespan strolled* arm in arm with Henriette, down the corridor on their return from a walk in the gardens. So much had been accomplished by the gardeners – new, expansive sections with hedges and pathways, flowers and trees, statuaries, fountains, and marble benches set back in the shade. A perfect place for an afternoon of womanly chatter and gossip.

As they reached the door to Henriette's apartment, the King, Bontemps, and guards rounded the corner. The Montespan and Henriette curtseyed.

"Sire," said the Montespan, touching her full lips with one hand and her heart with the other, hoping the King took note. "I am full of sorrow at your recent loss."

Louis nodded but then turned to Henriette.

"I received word from my brother in London." Henriette

spoke quietly to the King. "The Dutch fear our presence in the Spanish Netherlands encroaches on their borders. They are arming against us. My brother fears without help, we will not be successful against the Spanish."

Louis frowned. "Your brother the King forgets your husband the soldier, who amongst his other appetites has an extraordinary appetite for war."

"I wonder," offered the Montespan, "if it's because both activities require men."

Louis looked at her and she blushed. "Oh, Sire. Please forgive me. My tongue sometimes runs so far ahead of my brain it bumps into it from behind."

The King hesitated then burst out laughing. He smiled and winked at the Montespan. *Yes*, she thought. *You see me, Sire!* But the King took Henriette's arm and ushered her away into her apartment. The door was shut in the Montespan's face.

*No matter. It is not my time. Yet.*

The Montespan turned to Bontemps and gave him her most beguiling smile. "A little bird tells me you have one of the finest libraries in France. You wouldn't happen to have a copy of the fine atlas of the seas by Pierre Goos?"

Clearly flattered, Bontemps said, "Indeed I do."

"I should love to see it one day," said the Montespan. "I simply adore maps."

*Refreshed and restored* by his visit with Henriette, Louis sat in his apartment, studying the detailed map of the Spanish Netherlands brought him by Louvois. The two had begun discussing military intricacies when Philippe stormed in. His cheeks were red and his face was tight.

"You took it!" he cried. "You took my tactic and gave it to him! All my life I have longed for war. And you deny me again and again. Now this false hope is killing me beyond all pain."

Louis said nothing for a moment then stood slowly. "Ask me who will lead the charge."

Philippe let out a huff. "Who, brother, will lead the charge?"

"You will."

Philippe's eyes widened. Astonished, Louvois blustered, "Sire. You…you had mentioned that you thought the man not ready."

The King gazed at Louvois. "I was talking about you." Then to Philippe, "Congratulations, brother. You are going to war."

As Louvois stared and the royal brothers clasped hands, a footman rushed in.

"Sire! Quickly! The Queen!"

Followed by several guards, Louis rushed to Marie-Therese's apartment to find the Queen writhing on her bed, sweating heavily into the sheets. The room smelled of blood and agony.

Masson had ordered his daughter to prepare a poultice, but Claudine had refused. She knew the Queen's illness was because of the birth and knew only one thing that could save her life. She opened her journal to the drawing she'd made of a uterus, and placed it on the bed. Then, shoving her father aside, parted the Queen's legs and inserted her arm deep into Her Majesty's raw vagina.

"God in Heaven!" cried Masson.

As her heart pounded mightily, Claudine moved her fingers until they located a slick mass. Then carefully, slowly, with a firm grip, she pulled it from the Queen's body. It was a portion of placenta, left behind following the birth.

Masson, still horrified, checked the Queen's pulse. "Stronger," he muttered. "And it appears the bleeding is easing."

Claudine let out a breath. "I knew it would work, Father."

"But we shall never speak of this!"

"Speak of what?" It was the King in the doorway, flanked by Bontemps, Fabien, and guards. He instantly noticed Claudine's blood-soaked arm and looked sharply at Masson. "You may leave," he ordered. Masson, devastated, exited the room.

"What is in your hand?" Louis demanded.

Claudine lifted her chin. "Afterbirth, Sire."

"Is this how you stopped the bleeding? Lie to me, you lie to God."

"I removed it from her uterus."

The King stepped closer. His face was dark, challenging. "How did you know it would stop the blood?"

"I am a midwife. Trained by my father. But I'm also a student of anatomy and medicine."

"I do not recall signing a law allowing women doctors. A justice would assume the worst and have you burned at the stake."

"If that is your command, Sire."

Louis glanced at his wife then again at Claudine. "My command is that you stay close to me on medical matters. You father will remain our physician in the eyes of the court, but the advice I will heed will come from you. Bontemps, let in some air. Unless," he said to Claudine, "you advise against it?"

Stunned, but refusing to let it show, Claudine answered, "As long as we cover her, fresh air will offer much benefit." Claudine gently pulled the Queen's blanket up over her, and Louis reached out to help.

"Don't look so surprised," he said with a small smile. "I've put many women to bed."

*Alone in her* apartment, Louise de la Vallière removed her chemise and stood naked before a gold crucifix on the wall. On her back were rough, brutal scars from earlier self-flagellations. She picked up the leather whip from her dresser, whispered a prayer to God for the life of the Queen and for her own forgiveness, and then proceeded to slap the whip across her shoulders into the flesh of her back. Blood cut zigzagging rivulets to the floor.

*"As best he* could, the proprietor of the Epernon whorehouse has written down every noble purchasing services there for the past twelve months," said Fabien. "I have good authority his records are accurate."

"Let us hope so," said the King, leaning on his desk, candlelight dancing on his face as rain drummed the windows.

Fabien handed a leather journal to Bontemps, who then passed it over to the King. Louis opened it and read several entries, his face remaining stoic.

Fabien addressed Bontemps, "If I may continue, Monsieur?" Bontemps was surprised that Fabien would ask permission of him rather than the King, but such behavior was right and proper. Bontemps nodded.

Fabien unrolled a parchment onto the King's desk. There was a large "L" for Louis written in the center. Fabien began to draw concentric circles around the L. "You, Sire, are the sun. Around you circulates not only our celestial court but those who would harm you. You have ministers who openly defy you. Nobles who pay no taxes and believe France is theirs, not yours. Beyond our borders are Spain, the Dutch, English, and the Holy Roman Empire. They will smile and deal but would all see you destroyed. A strong France scares them."

Bontemps frowned. "You would wish a weak France?"

"I wish for the power to protect His Majesty."

"You have sufficient resources, Fabien."

But the King said, "Bontemps, get him what he needs. At your discretion, of course."

Bontemps felt Fabien's power-grab. Yet he would obey the King. He would always obey his King.

*Had God Himself* planned an expanse of gardens, His handiwork would have been no more glorious than the new royal gardens of Versailles. The King ordered a banquet and party in the garden while the nobles who had attended the fabric carousel were still at court. As the sun lowered itself below the distant woods, countless candles were lit upon tables and posts, giving the appearance that the sun was going nowhere at all. Servants scurried in and out, bearing great platters of foods. Nobles wore pieces inspired by those at the fashion parade, and they strutted about, showing them off.

Montcourt walked with Louvois along a path toward the banquet, speaking softly. "Opinion is ours," he said. "We have the room."

Louvois looked to make sure no one was near enough to hear. "We shall have to have more than a room if we are to persuade him."

"The noble Beauvais shares our intent," said Montcourt. "We have exchanged letters on the subject."

"Be that as it may, Beauvais does what he will. He has nearly as much money as the King. Should we persuade Beauvais, we have half the nobles in France."

"At the banquet, then."

"You're a braver man than I, Montcourt."

Montcourt huffed. "We've our tinder. But now one of us must strike the flint. If it is to be me, so be it."

They entered the arena of the banquet and stood among the crowd, watching and waiting for the King, at his table, to speak.

At last Louis rose. His gaze swept the gathering. "I believe," he announced, "that very soon we shall have a revolution in our country. The world knows France to be masters of the battlefield. But one glimpse around this glorious banquet will tell you. Soon, it is our textile mercers and master tailors who shall transform the world. Our fashions will be revered just as much for beauty, elegance, refinement, and grace." The crowd murmured their approval. "Many of you," Louis continued, "mentioned at the carousel your desire to acquire one of the fine emerald rings on display. This was never possible because I had bought every single one – I wished you all to have one as a gift at this very special evening."

As the crowd applauded, footmen handed emerald rings to everyone in attendance. Sophie put her ring on her finger and, giggling, compared it to those of her young friends. Beatrice slipped her ring onto her own finger, unaware that Fabien was watching her intently.

The King swept his arm in the direction of the orange grove. "I hope you are enjoying the orange blossoms. I can trace the root stock back to the ancient citrus plantations of Arabia. Which reminds me. Montcourt. How is your mother?"

Everyone fell silent and stared at Montcourt.

Montcourt caught his breath. He steeled himself. "Dead, Sire. Gone six weeks."

"I see you didn't have time to change clothes after the funeral."

Muffled laughter erupted around the audience.

"These are not my mourning clothes," said Montcourt.

"Neither are they evening clothes. Nor even French clothes. One look at your cuffs would tell you that.

Now, your father, the Baron, inherited his title from his grandfather, no?"

"Yes, Sire."

"Yet this was a title originally bequeathed to his grandmother, the Baroness of Saint-Maur. She married no higher than seigneur."

"Seigneur Charles de Saint-Maur no less, Sire."

"A farmer's son might call himself Charles de Saint-Maur if that is indeed where he was born. You father was a common man with a fiefdom, a vassal to his overlord, the true noble, the Grand Seigneur."

Dread crawled up Montcourt's throat. He glanced at Louvois who was watching the King.

"You might be labeled a vassal, perhaps," said Louis. "Or a peasant. Yet you raise yourself above these men whom would gladly sweat and toil to feed their families, pay their taxes and honor their duties to the King. But you would pay nothing and do nothing. So I must ask. What is a nothing doing at my table?"

"I can find the papers, Sire. I beg you allow me to prove my worth."

"The papers are all here, Montcourt. After an inexcusable delay."

Louvois spoke up. "As to the delay, Sire, as I mentioned we did not wish to bother you with such trivial affairs of state –"

"I am the state!" Louis shouted. He strode angrily from behind his table. Courtiers backed away to give him room. "And we shall all soon discover where we come from. It has come to my attention that many of you are uncomfortable here on our visits to Versailles. Many of you prefer Paris, or your estates that you miss. Some only a short ride away. To all of you I say this; You will soon get used to it." He stepped close to Montcourt and stared at the man. "Your noble birth freed you from our taxes. Your falsehood has condemned you to pay."

"Sire, I have no money but my estate."

"Take his keys," the King directed two guards. They moved in, tore Montcourt's estate keys from his jacket, and then stripped the man to his undergarments. The King handed the keys to the trembling, elderly noble next to Montcourt. "Your name?" asked the King.

"Pierre de la Croix, Sire," said the noble.

"God smiles on you, la Croix."

Then, as Montcourt stood mortified and disgraced beside the pile of his clothes, the King announced, "I do not know that man. He does not belong here. And the time has come to prove to me who you are. All of you. You can rest assured I will do the same."

Nobles glanced at each other uneasily as the King returned to his table, picked up a roasted leg of stag, and took a bite.

*The party continued* as the King retired to his apartment and watched the festivities through a window. Full night had arrived, and with it a spray of silver stars across the black sky. A bonfire blazed brightly in a wide area between sculpted evergreen hedges as bats darted back and forth on the periphery of light.

At Louis' encouragement, Bontemps pulled a chair up beside the King and the two sat like old friends. Candles flickered on the nearby desk, catching their faces at curious angles, reflecting in their eyes.

"I'd like very much to hear stories about your son," Louis said.

Bontemps rested his arms on the chair. He sighed silently. "In his last hours he asked me to speak about my life with you."

"What did you tell him?"

"The truth. That it is God's gift to me that I am by your side. That life is only beautiful when I am here. That the gardens are so glorious, they themselves gave birth to beauty. I also told him he would one day work and live in my place. That he might find himself part of the noblest family in the world, all of whom dream they might one day live like a king. Or queen."

Louis nodded, soothed by Bontemps' words.

"I told him that one day, when we are all gone, they will write stories about this place of wonder. Those who hear it may not believe it for it seems like a fairytale."

"Did your son approve of your story?"

"He asked if that was where he was going. I told him yes."

"I happen to believe," said Louis, turning to Bontemps, "that true paradise lies in his father's arms. To be here, with you, in this moment." Bontemps' eyes welled with tears. Louis placed a hand gently on his shoulder. "But that is not our choice. God has made His plans. We cannot question His design. Just as my people should not question mine. But they will." Louis' gaze moved to the dancing candle flame. "They mean to kill me, friend. They would kill us all to preserve the past. They may even succeed. But change will come no matter what. And if we are to endure, there is only one course. We must lay our own foundation. Here."

"Why here, Sire?"

"Because I will not be the King of Paris. I am Louis XIV. I am the King of France."

Louis peered out the window again, leaning from his chair. What he could not see was that out in the darkness, Sophie and her friends, overly warmed with wine, dredged about in a marble fountain to recover an emerald ring one had dropped there. They discovered, stuffed in a water pipe, a small, dark, bloated body. Nabo. What the King could see were the nobles beginning to abandon the party. Having spent enough time to appear loyal, they clambered into carriages with baggage and bundles, glancing over shoulders and up at the lodge. Anxious.

"See, Bontemps," said Louis. "See how they run."

# 3

*The King's barber* was a precise little man with a pointed nose and steady hands. He snipped and combed Louis' mustache with the utmost care and brushed stray hairs from the King's silk shirt. Bontemps stood by, holding the King's new crewelwork coat. The morning was bright, and light from the windows danced delicate patterns on the walls and across the tapestries and paintings.

"Sire," said Bontemps, "the dignitaries from Issiny have been waiting a month for an audience. They've come a long way. Monsieur Colbert is deeply anxious they will leave. That we may lose any hope of an agreement."

Louis sniffed. The barber snipped. Then the King asked, "What kind of man do you think I am, Bontemps? Merciful?"

"If you desire it."

"Vengeful?"

"If conditions merit."

"All things to all people?"

88

"Equally and without condition."

Louis nodded thoughtfully. The barber waited until his head was still again. "As a King, yes. I ask as a man."

"You are both," said Bontemps. "We cannot separate one from the other."

"When I send my brother to war, I do so as a king. Should he die there, I would mourn him as a man. It is as a man I could gain favor in the eyes of another. As a king, I cannot."

"You are forever in our favor, Sire."

"You think Montcourt feels the same?"

The barber stepped back, finished, and bowed deeply. Louis rose and Bontemps helped him with his coat. The King considered himself in the bronze-framed mirror on the dresser.

"A king will be resented as much for good deeds as for bad," said Louis. "This much I know."

There was a moment of silence then Bontemps said, "The jacket fits well, Sire."

Louis looked at himself again, staring into his own eyes, seeking what was there. And what looked back at him was determined, regal, powerful, and prepared.

*Louvois was glad* to get outside for a while. Though an important man of the court, he savored the sounds and scents of the outdoors. He strolled through a wooded area of the royal gardens, breathing deeply, trying to calm his tumbling thoughts when he heard rustling behind a tree. He stopped to look. A deer, perhaps, or a badger. But no, the face that appeared around the trunk was a bedraggled, frightened human.

*Fates be damned!* Louvois looked to see that no one was nearby then hurried to the tree. "Montcourt! What are you doing here?"

Montcourt's eyes were red with desperation and lack of sleep. His clothes were filthy and smelled like a barn. "I've nowhere else to go," he pleaded. "My wife's family will not take me in. She married for the title! Now that I have none, they've no need for me."

"You have my sympathy, but I cannot help you."

"You are my only friend at court."

"And a loyal friend will tell you the truth. Your days here are finished. I must go."

Montcourt's lip hitched. He snarled, "My commendations to His Majesty's health."

Louvois considered responding but went on, instead, and for a moment thought he heard his former friend begin to cry.

*Louis squinted across* a vast stretch of lawn from his seat in the open day carriage. He ordered the driver to rein the horses in. *Well, well!* Louis thought as he opened the carriage door and got out.

A young man, rakishly handsome with wavy brown hair, strode toward them across the grass with his arms outstretched. "Majesty!" said the young man.

"Dear Rohan!" said Louis. "You've returned!" Seeing his childhood friend brought a surge of joy, an almost tangible remembrance of earlier, easier days.

"You see?" said Rohan cheerfully. "I always do what you say!" He reached out to embrace the King but then remembered himself and pulled his arms back. "I've missed you."

"And I you," said Louis, clapping his friend on the shoulder.

"There are more pretty women here than I recall."

"Your memory is failing you," laughed Louis. "You're getting old."

"But," Rohan bowed dramatically, "I've learned my lesson, and return to you atoned, anew, and at your service, Sire. I hope I am worthy to be part of court with all this time passed? I so enjoyed my former position as master of the hunt."

Louis smiled, feeling buoyant and carefree with his companion. He and Rohan fell in together and strolled down to the orange grove. Butterflies drifted on spears of sunlight. Dragonflies buzzed in for a closer look.

"I saw plans for the stable," said Rohan.

"Your thoughts?"

"Either we are doing a very large amount of hunting, or you are building something quite different here."

"A palace," said the King.

"A city!" laughed Rohan. "A most glorious city, Sire!"

*I am a warrior. I have always been a warrior at heart,* thought Philippe. He turned back and forth before the mirror, admiring his trim jacket, new trousers, stockings, and black polished boots.

"How do I look?"

Chevalier crossed his arms. "I dressed you myself, how do you think I think you look?"

Philippe grinned.

"Speaking of which," Chevalier continued, "who puts a dwarf in a drainpipe? If the little man was sad he might have done it himself. Or perhaps the Queen tired of him. Perhaps he was trying to mend the King's fountains and restore himself to favor but accidentally shoved himself in there like a cork?"

Philippe rolled his eyes. "You've too much time on your hands. Come with me to the front."

"You're inviting me to a war? Are you mad?"

"Not any war."

"Your brother says one thing and does another. Do not hold your breath. But if you do make it I will remain here, naturally, ensuring your place at court remains assured."

"Is that so?" asked Philippe with a rueful chuckle. "'My place.'"

Chevalier followed Philippe into the anteroom where Henriette waited, elegant in a laced-trimmed gown.

"You look handsome," she said to her husband.

"I already told him," said Chevalier.

Philippe blew air through his lips. "You did not, in fact."

"Husband," said Henriette. "Is there news?"

Philippe stalked from the room, calling over his shoulder, "Not yet," leaving Chevalier and Henriette to stare at one another.

Then Henriette broke the silence. "Perhaps he will send you instead."

Chevalier shrugged. "I would be honored to serve, of course."

"Do you really think he does not see you exactly as you are?"

"He sees me, my dear. And he is happy. And that is what divides us."

"The only thing that unites us is division."

"At least when your husband is gone, I'll know where to find you."

"If you come to my rooms I will not answer."

"I would not think to seek you there. Just as I would not seek the King at the chambers of Her Majesty."

Henriette, though shorter than Chevalier, lifted her chin definitely in an attempt to look down at him. "You imply much but say little."

Chevalier stepped close, his voice like that of a snake. "I know how much you enjoy swimming. I might find you at the pool house, for example. I hear that is popular for young lovers of nature." He reached out to fondle her curls and she slapped him away.

"You are warned, sir!"

Chevalier smiled a dark smile. "Constantly, my dear."

*The Queen stood* at her window in her mourning gown, clutching her handkerchief and weeping. She had wept so long it amazed her there were still tears. But they were there, and they were plentiful. Her ladies sat nearby, silently sewing, embroidering, and reading.

The door swung open and the King entered, followed by Bontemps. Marie-Therese looked over with blood-shot eyes and managed a curtsey.

"How is my Queen?"

"Much better, thank you." Her throat was sore, her words raspy.

"Change your clothes. The season for mourning is passed. It is time to resume your official duties."

"Yes, Sire."

Louis stepped to the window and looked out across the gardens to the road. "We are to receive a guest at court. You are to host them personally. Shower your attentions on them with your customary warmth and grace."

Marie-Therese blinked. "Who is this person, so I might prepare myself? Are they Spanish, perhaps?" Louis gave her a sharp look. "You have my word," she muttered.

"I will depend on it."

Before she could say more or plead for a fragment of his time and tenderness, he was gone.

*Montcourt wiped snot* and rain from his face, gathered his resolve, and pounded on the door of the great and ominous Chateau Cassel. Rain had made night of day, and everything from grasses to trees appeared as gray as cold ash in a fire pit. He knocked again, desperately, harder, as the rain pounded him. At last the door was opened.

He begged to be let in.

An hour later, Montcourt was seated on a low stool before a crackling fire, dressed in a clean shirt and trousers, the stubble on his face being shaved away by a footman with a sharp razor. In the darkness beyond the reach of the firelight, two brawny thugs named Mike and Tomas stood watching. There was no sound but the fire popping, the scraping razor, and the heavy rains outside.

The noble Cassel, a middle-aged man of cunning and strength, stepped forward into the light. He considered his visitor with hooded, unreadable eyes.

"What do you wish from me, Montcourt?" he asked at last.

Montcourt looked up as the footman made the last stroke with the razor. "In a downpour one seeks shelter under the largest tree. Here, in the north, there is no one stronger, no one more powerful or resolute than the mighty oak, Cassel. I am a refugee from this royal deluge and seek protection, my lord. I am your servant."

"Servant," said Cassel. He snapped his fingers and Montcourt stood.

Several nobles appeared from shadows and stood by Cassel. They considered Montcourt with pity, fear, and loathing.

"Here is your King's new law," Cassel said to the nobles. "Stripping a true noble of all dignity. Defiling the reputation of a man whose family forms the bedrock of our country. Not long ago, we all knew where we stood but now…now we must prove ourselves. Sing for our suppers!"

The nobles grumbled agreement.

"This causes me great pain. As you know, the King has always had my respect. But now he says, 'I am France.' But I say, 'It is we who are France.' Our friend Montcourt's condition is a message. And soon he shall have his reply."

A footman brought cologne and sprayed Montcourt's body to mask the ripe smell. A second footman combed his hair.

"This playground in the woods," said Cassel. "The King obsesses over it. He sees Versailles and nothing else. Were we to remove this new distraction perhaps the King will forget himself. Then Versailles can return to the weeds, the King to Paris, and we to our lands and our lives."

Mike placed a pistol on the table by the fire.

Montcourt looked at the weapon then at Cassel. "You would persuade the King by force?"

"He's lost his mind. No other appeal to reason will work. You wish my protection, Montcourt?"

"I serve your lordship with my life."

Cassel nodded slowly. "Indeed you will."

*A line of commoners* stood before a table on a terrace in Versailles' ever-expanding gardens. Jacques sat at the table, giving serious consideration to those who wanted employment as gardeners. Behind them, the royal hunting lodge was being transformed into the King's palace, with countless sections of scaffolding clinging to the exterior walls and pallets loaded with massive marble bricks on the ground being hoisted up to the bricklayers.

An elderly man in rags stepped forward, nodding hopefully, his old eyes squinting. Jacques inspected the man's hands.

"I need men who can dig, not men I should plant!" scoffed Jacques. He held up his remaining hand. "This hand killed ten men at the Battle of Saint Gotthard." He smacked the skinny man hard across the face and the man scurried off.

The next to step up to the table was tall and young, with toned muscles, light hair, and a confident expression.

"I've also done my share of killing," the young man said. "Rigged a thousand sails in storms higher than mountains. Must be worth something?"

"Not to me," said Jacques.

The man shrugged and turned to leave.

"Wait. Bricklaying," Jacques called after him. "Easy work for a navy man. They need bricklayers, with several fallen or crushed last week. I know the foreman. I'll vouch for you." He got up and marched off toward the scaffolding.

"I'm Benoit," said the man as he followed. "Tell me, friend. Have you ever seen him? The King?"

"Many will claim they have," snorted the gardener. "All I can say is this. I am a friend to no man. This way."

*The carriage was* resplendent, edged in gold and adorned with painted images of angels, flowers, and exotic animals. It pulled up to the entrance of Louis' palace and footmen scurried out to hold the horses and place steps at the door. A brightly colored macaw flew from a carriage window and settled on the shoulder of a guard by the door. The guard, in proper fashion, did not move even as the bird pecked at his hair.

A stately man of black skin and flashing eyes stepped out and down. This was Prince Annaba of Issiny, the Ivory Coast of Africa. His flowing cape was scarlet and sea-green, the scarf at his neck was blue, and his hat was trimmed with rainbow plumage that might well have come from his pet bird's twin. Annaba was followed by his younger brother, Kobina, who was dressed as elegantly as Annaba. A second carriage stopped behind the first and several men and women climbed out, all adorned in clothes of brilliant colors.

Bontemps raised his hand in greeting. "Prince of Issiny," he said. "Welcome to Versailles."

Annaba glanced around. "Nice house," he said mildly.

Bontemps ushered Prince Annaba and Kobina into the palace and along the corridors to the receiving room of the King's apartment. Annaba's entourage followed silently, their heads high. Courtiers stared at the newcomers to court, and Annaba, his macaw sitting upon his shoulder, returned their smiles with a smirk of his own.

"That's right," he said, loudly enough for the courtiers to hear, "I'm a stupid black man. I come from the trees. Hello, how are you? You think it's going to be easy to fuck me? Wonderful. Keep thinking that."

"Brother," said Kobina. "Keep your voice down."

Annaba waved his hand. "The French need money, so they need us."

"Then why did they keep us waiting in Paris for a month?"

"How many times do I need to tell you, brother? Power is a game played with mirrors." They reached a corner, turned into another long hallway. More courtiers and nobles gawked.

"We're not safe here," whispered Kobina.

"Come now," said Annaba. "Wipe that look off your face. We've arrived at the center of the world."

"The center of the world is very white."

"We are pioneers, making history. They want what we have. So do the Dutch. We let them fight over us. Either way, we are victorious."

They reached a set of closed, arched doors where guards stood on duty and Fabien and his assistant Laurene waited. Annaba leaned into his brother. "They will speak of this moment long after we're gone."

"It's the gone part that worries me," said Kobina.

"Honored guests of the King," Bontemps said with a respectful nod. "Annaba, Prince of Issiny."

"Son to the King of Eguafo," added Annaba, "inheritor of the Coast of Ivory and Teeth, Lord of the Sky. And this is my brother, Kobina."

"Prince Annaba," said Bontemps, "you will accompany me, please." But as Annaba beckoned the others to join him, Bontemps stopped him. "Alone. Your brother will accompany Monsieur Fabien."

"And my friends?" asked Annaba as his macaw flapped its rainbow wings and hopped over to Kobina's shoulder.

"Shall bask in the full warmth of the King's hospitality." At that, Laurene stepped forward. Then the three parties departed in different directions, to differ encounters throughout the palace.

Bontemps ushered Prince Annaba to a small, sparsely furnished chamber. There was but one window, a second, closed door on a far wall, and a heavy green curtain to one side of the room. Annaba peered behind the curtain to find an alcove with a bed. Something was up, and it did not feel right. He glanced out the window and asked as casually as he could, "Bontemps, how far is it to the trees?"

He heard the door shut and turned to find Bontemps gone, leaving only two guards. Annaba moved toward the door but the guards leaned in to block his way.

*What is going on? What does –*

The door opened again. Surely this was the King, coming to greet him.

But it was the Queen. Marie-Therese stood there in all her noble beauty. The two gazed at each other for a long moment.

Then, "Good day, Prince Annaba."

Annaba bowed. "Good day to you, Highness. Such a pleasure to see you again."

*A covered cargo* wagon rumbled along the road to Versailles, carrying a load of wine barrels. A rosy-cheeked monk sat on a bench inside with the barrels, the rocking wagon and squeaking wheels nearly putting him to sleep. It was a fine day, a sunny summer's day. God was in His Heaven and all was right with the world.

And then he heard an angry shout outside. "Halt! Your cargo or your life!"

The monk's mouth went dry. He dropped to the floor and tried to make himself small.

"Wine!" shouted a second voice. "For the King!"

The driver shouted something unintelligible and with a violent jerk the wagon took off. The monk was tossed back against the barrels. Hoof beats followed the wagon, and then *boom!* The wagon shuddered and fell to its side. The monk rolled over and struck the corner of the bench. Blood poured down through his hair.

A man appeared at the window and looked down at the monk. A man with aquiline features, dark brows, and an impassive face.

Montcourt stared at the helpless monk, raised his musket to the window, and blew the monk's face away.

*Bontemps caught up* with the King and Colbert as they stood admiring the fountain of Bacchus, a striking, enormous figure now situated in a pool around which new trees had been planted.

"Majesty?" Bontemps said, wiping his brow. "As requested, it is done."

Louis smiled. "I've received word that my good friends, the Parthenays, are riding to Versailles from their estates in the south."

Bontemps brightened. "Little Francoise is coming?"

"With her husband and family."

"How time has flown," said Bontemps.

The King nodded and began walking. "The Parthenays are well-regarded in the south. A strong influence. As a favor to me they are coming here to submit their noble credentials as an example to the rest. We'll ensure the *Gazette* reports on this. Perhaps also strike a medal, Colbert? The political arithmetic must augur great things to come."

"'The great nobles of the south submit their credentials to the King,'" said Colbert. "That should do it."

"Or better this," said Louis. "'The King receives the credentials from nobles of the south.'"

Ahead was a cart filled with manure at the edge of a newly dug section of the gardens, and Jacques was overseeing the unloading of the smelly mass.

"That's a lot of shit," called the King.

"The finest shit from His Majesty's horses at the Louvre," said Jacques.

"Sire," he continued, but then he looked away and went silent.

"Speak," said the King, moving closer. "What is on your mind?"

"On my way through the woods I found an old man cooking a rat by a stream. I thought he was a tramp."

"But you recognized him?"

"From your father's court. He fought for Constantin of Auvergne."

Louis' smile faded as he remembered. "During the Fronde," he said. "Oh, had they been successful..."

"You'd be dead."

"One day," said Louis, "I would like very much to know more about my father." Then, with a wave of his hand, he took a meandering, tree-lined path alone. Down he went to the pool. Down to the pool house where he knew Henriette was waiting.

And she was there, waiting in the changing room with her ladies in the outer hall again. She came to him and placed her head against his chest. He ran a finger through her wet hair and turned her face up to his. *So beautiful*, he thought. *My dearest*.

"You are shaking," he said tenderly. "Is it the chill from your swim?"

"Other reasons," she replied. Her blue eyes were troubled. "You. Us. Him. Chevalier."

"Chevalier makes you tremble?"

"Yes. He scares me. The way he looks at me. The way he talks about you. The way he uses my husband's better nature to demean himself. Please. Make them disappear for a while. They can have each other and so can we."

"What kind of King sends his brother to war?"

"I would have you send both of them."

Louis kissed Henriette's forehead, her neck. "Do you remember when you were sixteen? You stepped on a rose and your foot was bleeding."

Henriette smiled slightly. "You kissed my toes."

"I took the pain away?"

"In an instant."

"I want you to know," said Louis as he drew his hands down the small of her back and cupped her soft buttocks. "I will always take away your pain. You will never have anything to worry about when it comes to Chevalier. I am your safe harbor."

Henriette gasped and arced her body, pressing hard against the King as he slid one hand around to her belly, then lowered it to caress between her legs. She gasped and whispered, "You...you will protect me from the waves."

"Even as they roll over us, my love," he said. He scooped up his love, carried her to the settee, and guided her hand to his trousers to show he was more than ready. "Even as the tide takes me."

*Prince Annaba and* the Queen faced each other, alone but for the guards in the little room. They spoke of many things, pleasantries mostly, passing the time.

Then Annaba said, "On my last visit, I left you a gift."

The Queen nodded.

"Has it given you pleasure?"

Marie Therese paused then said, "A great deal, thank you."

"I am pleased to hear it. It was very precious to me."

At long last there were footsteps outside the door. The guards stepped back to let Bontemps enter. "He is ready for you now," he said to the prince.

Bontemps opened the chamber's second door, revealing a bright room filled with nobles and courtiers. The King sat in a large ebony chair upon a dais, dressed regally. Behind him on the wall hung a large gold emblem – a radiating sun with the face of a man in its center. The countenance of the face was the image of Louis XIV. The Sun King.

Marie-Therese took her place beside her husband.

"Prince Annaba of Issiny," said Louis. "You are welcome at my court."

Annaba bowed. "Sire. Versailles is more beautiful than I can imagine."

Louis presented Philippe, Henriette, Colbert, and Louvois. Each nodded, acknowledging one another. Then the King stared steadily at Annaba and said, "And you have already met my wife."

When the formal meeting had concluded, Louis and Bontemps led Annaba and his people on a tour about the gardens, explaining what had been done and what was yet to be completed, to not only the gardens but the palace as well. The Africans nodded, appearing to be impressed with the scale of it all.

"When I hosted a party here several years ago," said Louis, "we did not have enough room for my friends. Now we shall have enough – four hundred apartments, all told."

"Ah," said Annaba.

"Tell us about the countries of Africa," said Bontemps.

Annaba stopped and frowned. He looked from Bontemps to the King. "When do we negotiate?" he asked.

"In France we have a different way of doing things," said Louis.

Annaba tipped his head. "Perhaps I've made a mistake. Perhaps I should talk to the Spanish, the Dutch, the English. All are keen to discuss the future."

The King faced his guest. "Are you not enjoying our hospitality?"

Annaba nodded. "There…there is a great deal of it."

Louis laughed. "And more to come, as you will see tonight."

"What happens then?"

"Then," said Louis, "I shall sit down with you."

"*Our visitor from* Issiny has inspired me," Philippe said as he stood before the mirror, adding colorful bows and scarves to his military garb. "I think I require more color. Oh, how does one dress for a war?"

Henriette sat at her sewing, watching her husband, her heart torn and heavy. "If you go," she said, "please come back."

"If I were to die your life would be simple."

Henriette added several stitches to the skirt in her lap. "You know my problems will never be solved. And I would rather you did not die."

"You say the sweetest things, poppet." Philippe looked at her. "Since we were small, my dream has been war. Yours has been my brother. Look how lucky we are. Perhaps one day, very soon, we will both live our dreams." He turned back to his reflection and did not see his wife cry into the skirt.

"*Construction is on* hold?" Louis paced the private outer chamber of his apartment as Bontemps, Fabien, and Colbert stood by, tense, waiting to speak. "Appearance is everything! The prince is a guest in my house and so far has shown more grandeur in his clothing than I can show him in my palace!"

"A shipment of marble went missing on the road, Sire," said Colbert. "Men cannot work without materials."

"There are thieves on the road, Sire," added Bontemps. "There have always been thieves on the road."

Louis paused in his pacing, his face red. "This is organized sabotage!"

Bontemps worked to keep his voice even. "The more we build, the more we need. The more we need, the greater number of goods we transport to Versailles and the more likely these moments are."

"These moments can build to movements!" Louis shouted. "Before we know it, our land is on fire! The King's road is sacrosanct! Whoever did this is declaring war!"

"My men and I will set up patrols on the road," said Fabien.

"At once," said Louis. With that, he left for his bedchamber, beckoning Bontemps to follow.

Bontemps leaned into Fabien and spoke quickly. "With war upon us we don't have enough men. I'll handle the roads. We have visitors at court. We are striving to live up to His Majesty's standards and build his dreams. The King is better served by you here. What do we know of the Issiny party? Are you sure they do not spy on us? That they are here on behalf the Dutch?"

Fabien's eye twitched. He knew Bontemps could be right.

"Much more depends on this visit than you realize. Our foremost duty is to safeguard the King."

"Bontemps!" shouted Louis through the door.

"Even if it is from himself."

Fabien nodded. "Make sure your men are of quality. I need them as my eyes and ears."

Bontemps hurried after his King. Fabien went to the window and saw Annaba's obnoxious macaw sitting upon a stone railing, looking back with unblinking eyes.

Inside his bedchamber, Louis gripped the back of a chair,

his heart pounding with rage, his breath hot and rapid. The room around him began to shimmer, undulate, and fade into the past....

The King's royal bedchamber was gone. He now stood in the room where he'd slept as a youth. His mother entered the room and he watched himself turn from the window and the raging fires outside. At thirteen he was tall for his age but his face still bore the round innocence of boyhood.

Seeing his mother unnerved him. He loved her, but could not understand her.

"There is someone I want you to meet," she said.

A second woman entered the room, a lady nearly his mother's age, with eyes as piercing as those of an eagle and a beautiful, full body. She smiled confidently.

"This is Madame de Beauvais," said Anne. "She is here to tutor you."

"But Maman," Louis began, glancing toward the window. "The men outside –"

His mother raised a finger. "Don't let them distract you. Pay attention to your studies."

His mother left the room. Madame de Beauvais began to unbutton her blouse.

"What are you to teach me, Madame?" Louis asked.

The lady opened her blouse, pulled her chemise down, revealing her breasts. "Call me Catherine," she said.

"Sire? Do you agree?" Bontemps' voice came from somewhere else, from beyond. "Sire?"

The memory vanished. The King's room was back. Louis turned to Bontemps who had asked some sort of question.

"I do not know," Louis said. "Yes. Or no."

Bontemps looked confused. "Sire?"

Louis straightened his shoulders. "Where is my brother?"

*Beatrice and Sophie* wandered the lower gardens following a gentle rain, talking jewelry and fabrics, when Fabien rounded a hedge and nearly collided with them. Beatrice locked eyes with Fabien, took a sharp, silent breath, and smiled coyly.

"Madame…de Clermont?" Fabien said. "Did I get that right? We have seen each other but have never spoken."

"Indeed. Monsieur Marchal."

"Fabien."

"Beatrice."

"And," said Fabien nodding at Sophie. "Your sister?"

"Daughter. I'm Sophie."

Fabien's eyes widened. "Daughter? Is that so."

Beatrice shot Sophie a withering glance and then spied Chevalier on a distant path. She needed to talk to him. Yet she wanted to spend time with Fabien. *Curse the fates!*

"A fine day for a walk –" Fabien began.

"Yes," said Beatrice, glancing at Chevalier then back at Fabien, trying not to let her nervousness show. "And it was nice to have met you."

Fabien appeared disappointed at the abrupt dismissal. "Yes, ah, well, good day," he fumbled. He bowed and walked off. Beatrice grabbed Sophie's arm and hurried her toward Chevalier.

"Mother," said Sophie as she stumbled along. "I think Fabien likes you."

"Be quiet now, sister."

"You're angry with me."

Beatrice shook Sophie's arm. "And one day you'll know how much!"

They intercepted Chevalier at a marble fountain. He swept his arm dramatically. "Greetings, cousin!"

The trio strolled into a maze-like path bordered by low-trimmed boxwoods. Birds, startled from the hedges, flew out and away.

"Sophie, my dear," said Chevalier. "Some help if you please. A moral quandary. If someone I adore fucks someone without my consent, is it not right for parity to be restored that I fuck someone else of my own choosing?

"Enough teasing," said Beatrice. "We should count our lucky stars. So many families are being thrown out of court."

Chevalier shrugged. "None had papers in place."

"I suppose none had anyone to vouch for them."

"These are the laws we must now comply with."

Beatrice took Chevalier's arm. "At least we have you."

Chevalier gave Beatrice a cautiously curious look. "Why are you being so nice to me?"

"My folly," she smiled. "I know in my heart you will use us up and cast us out like all the others."

"Naturally. But I will watch out for you in this madness, have no fear of that. Especially you, my pretty." He pursed his lips at Sophie. "Even though you walk like a milkmaid."

They continued on in silence for a bit. The maze brought them closer to the palace where men on wooden scaffolding worked at precarious heights laying brick and fashioning new sections of sloped roofing.

Sophie glanced up to see one muscular man with light hair gazing down at her. She stopped. Smiled.

"Sophie!" Beatrice called from up ahead. Reluctantly, her daughter followed.

From his vantage point on the scaffolding, Benoit watched the beautiful young girl walk away then scooted along the plank to Jacques who was dining on cheese and bread. "I heard her name!" he said. "It is Sophie!"

"That's a death wish," said Jacques.

"Better to die for something you believe in, right?"

Jacques took a bite of bread. "What's your name again?"

"Benoit, sir."

Jacques handed some bread to the stone layer. "I'm Jacques."

"What is a gardener doing up here?"

"The view helps me measure the lines of the garden."

Benoit grinned. "And the girls who walk in it."

"Be careful with that business. You think about your future."

"I am," Benoit said dreamily. "And I see Sophie in it."

*Philippe knelt upon* a pillow in the War Cabinet room as the priest stood beside him and uttered an incantation for the protection of a warrior. Philippe's clothing bore no fancy ribbons or bows. They were tossed away, leaving only the clothing of a soldier of serious and focused intent.

Louis entered and watched him without speaking, yet his brother immediately sensed he was there.

"I thought if I began my departure," Philippe said, his head bowed, "you might sanction it."

"I do not understand," said Louis.

The priest finished the blessing and left the room. Philippe rose and faced the King. "I await your word, brother. And when I can wait no more, I ask deliverance from my God."

The brothers stared at each other, tension between them hanging like dust in the air, and then they turned to gaze at the models on the center table. There was more detail to it now; the projected positions for battle had been expanded with additional soldiers, horses, and written plans. Louis nodded at the display. "Which one are you?"

"A horse," said Philippe with a small smile.

Louis sighed. "Philippe."

"You want me to be serious."

Louis continued studying the model. Then he said, "Stay close to your bodyguard at all times. Protect your flank."

"I will bring you glory. I vow it."

"May God watch over you and bring you home safely. You leave today."

"Go then," said Philippe. "Run to Henriette. You have my blessing. God knows you don't need a priest for that." He waited for a reply, but none came. He left without another word.

The sun fell silently behind the trees to the west. The day with its suspicions, sadness, jealousies, and hopes turned its back on the world, and on Versailles, once more. Creatures of the forest bedded down in dens and burrows as candles were set ablaze in the palace.

"If your friends the Parthenays prove as meaningful as I believe," Colbert said as Louis sat before a meal of swan pie, pears, and pork, "once they have visited and shown their loyalty we could persuade much of the south to comply. Leaving the north and east."

Louis stabbed the pie with his knife. "Who defies me there?"

"The Duc of Cassel, Sire. Half the nobility in the north and east are in his debt."

"He's our keystone, then. If we extract him from the wall, the entire structure is demolished. If not, the collapse will be ours."

"But he does not heed our letters, Sire."

Louis left the table and walked over to the portrait of himself above the fireplace, an elegant likeness by the painter Hyacinthe Rigaud. Louis looked up into his own dark eyes, into the determined, royal face that ruled France. *All* of France. "Then I must send him a gift alongside an order to comply with our laws. He will supply proof of his nobility or suffer the consequence." Louis turned back to Colbert. "To which all of France shall bear witness."

*The great and* imposing Chateau du Cassel stood on its tree-covered hill, clothed in the gray dusk of early evening. Cassel, Montcourt, and other nobles lounged in the dank-smelling Great Hall in front of the hearth, downing goblets of red wine. Wine too good for monks. Wine good enough for a king.

"The road to Versailles is the only thing that keeps the King's new love alive," said Cassel as he wiped his lips. "Choke it and the project dies on the vine. They will thank us all later, I'm sure."

Tomas appeared from the shadows. "A messenger has arrived bearing gifts. From the King."

Cassel's lip twitched with a sarcastic smile. The messenger appeared, carrying a flat package of significant size, wrapped in paper. He put the package on the table and carefully removed the paper. It was a portrait of the King.

"Ah, how kind," said Cassel.

The messenger straightened. "Louis the Great commands your presence to court as required by the rule of law and the Grand Inquiry into Nobel Legitimacy. You are required to present proof of your nobility."

Cassel looked at Montcourt then took another sip. "Really," he said into his cup.

*The party was* in full swing by the time Annaba, Kobina, and the Issiny entourage were called from their chambers and led through the palace by Bontemps. At last, Annaba was certain, he and the King would negotiate. It was well past time.

But what lay behind the large double doors was not what he expected and his confidence slipped a little.

The salon was brightly lit and filled with noisy, drunken nobles. A quartet on flute, violin, lute, and chalémie played lively music, causing some nobles to sing, others to attempt to dance. Yet it took only a moment to see that this was a gambling den, for in the center of the room was a large roulette table. People placed bets and cheered as the wheel spun round and round.

But when the nobles noticed the black men at the door they fell silent. The Africans moved into the room, several walking to the roulette table, causing the nobles there to back away.

Kobina whispered, "I think we are not wanted here."

"I think," replied Annaba, nodding in the direction of a second, adjoining room, "that the negotiations have indeed begun."

In the adjoining room the King sat, elegant and regal, at a table set with flowers and food. Beside him was his Queen, Marie-Therese, and around the table were a handful of nobles. There was an empty stool across the table from the King, and Annaba moved forward to join the royal gathering. Two guards stepped in and blocked his way.

Seeing the guards' action, Marie-Therese put her hand on Louis' arm and whispered, "Please, husband, don't toy with Annaba this way."

Louis looked up and casually waved his hand, and the guards let Annaba proceed. The prince stopped before the table, and after an uncomfortable moment Louis nodded, allowing him to sit.

Slowly, conversation swelled again, filling the rooms. The music resumed and the roulette wheel spun round as bets were laid. Kobina waited by the wall, glancing back and forth, arms crossed. Annaba turned his attention from the King to the game. He watched several minutes and then shouted above the din, "I believe I have a good measure of this game!" He motioned to one of his entourage, who placed a large bag of gold on the roulette table.

The Montespan, who was seated with the nobles at the King's table, smiled, tossed her head teasingly, and leaned toward Annaba. "You are a man after my own heart, sir." She stood, laughed, and threw a few coins next to Annaba's bet.

As the drunken hubbub grew even louder, a footman slipped to the King's table and handed him a black envelope. Marie-Therese rose to add her coins to the game, but Louis stopped her. Then he announced to the room, "Alas, fortune at this table does not favor us tonight." He rose and escorted Marie-Therese from the room.

Annaba watched after them, then got up to join his brother by the wall. The game-playing resumed yet again.

"Brother," said Kobina, his voice low, "when you came to the French last year, you told me you had an audience with the Queen."

"What of it?"

"What did you talk about?"

Annaba looked at the door through which the King and Queen had gone. He smiled with a fond memory. "Everything," he said.

"*What are you* doing?" Marie-Therese asked as Louis escorted her from the game room and into the hallway, followed by guards.

"I'm winning," he replied, the expression on his face one of pure satisfaction. The Queen's heart leapt with hope.

"There is a spring in your step," she said as they turned into another corridor.

"And a mud-spattered man in my path," said the King.

Before them stood Fabien, Bontemps, and the messenger who had been sent to visit Cassel in the north. The messenger was disheveled and covered in filth.

"Your Majesty," said Bontemps. "Urgent business that requires your immediate attention."

The King looked at Marie-Therese, who inclined her head and was escorted away by guards.

"Now what is it?" asked Louis.

"Cassel replied to your message, Sire," said Bontemps. He handed Louis a small note to which a single gold coin was affixed by wax.

"'Here is your proof,'" Louis read slowly. "'A contribution to your noble project.'"

"Such insolence!" said Fabien. "May I reply to him in person?"

Bontemps shook his head. "If I may, Sire? To arrest him will end your plan as quickly as it starts. If you put Cassel in prison you might as well put all the nobles in jail, because that would be the end point of it all."

"At least let me bruise his face, Sire?" said Fabien, his face twisted in anger.

But Louis held up his hand. "Cut off one head and another will take its place. To strike him down is to beg for civil war. And we saw how well that went for the English."

Before Fabien could plead his case further, Louis turned and followed in the direction his Queen had gone.

In her bedchamber, Marie-Therese's ladies helped her from her gown, placing it carefully in the tall armoire and then guiding the Queen to the table where she sat before the mirror as her favorite lady unpinned and brushed her hair. *A strange evening*, Marie-Therese thought, *but so much improved. Louis seemed pleased with me, thank our Heavenly Father. Now if only he would…*

And then she heard him. He was there, behind her, his eyes watching her face in the looking glass.

"Husband," she said, turning, her hair falling in long, dark curls. "I am not ready yet."

"I'm not here in duty," said the King. He sent the ladies away with a flick of his hand then led his wife to her bed. He eased her back upon her pillows and traced his fingers along the fullness of her breasts and the curve of her hips. She felt passion, long since repressed, rise in her heart, her body.

*I care nothing for ugly tapestries if my King cares for me again!*

"I'm here in gratitude," Louis said as he removed his trousers, revealing his readied manhood. He climbed onto the bed with her and straddled her. "For keeping your word to me and showing such hospitality to our guest. You availed yourself very well." Her nipples hardened against the cool caress of air. "I wish to bestow upon you a gift."

"I…accept," she whispered. *I am ready!*

"The gift is a secret," said Louis. He reached down to finger her and found her damp and ready. He stroked her, probed her, and she panted. Then he whispered in her ear, "Your daughter is alive."

Marie-Therese's eyes opened wide with joy and disbelief. "Oh, my God!" she cried as her King drove himself into her.

*Annaba had been* startled into wakefulness by the King in the middle of the night. Leaving a frightened Kobina behind in the bedchamber, Annaba was now seated in a coach with His Majesty, rumbling at a mad speed along a road through a dark, imposing forest. Outriders galloped close by on either side. At first Annaba was certain that finally, after so many delays, he was going to spend time with the King to negotiate.

But now he wasn't so sure.

The King sat silently in the rattling carriage, watching Annaba and then watching the night beyond the window.

"What would you offer me?" asked Annaba, breaking the silence. "The Dutch do not have your hospitality, but they do have money."

Louis said nothing. *What is going on?* Annaba wondered. And the coach continued onward.

At long last the coach slowed and came to a stop. The faintest morning light was beginning to stream through the trees, yet Annaba could see no town, no chateau, no structure whatsoever.

"Where are we?"

"A brief stop," said the King.

Through the window, Annaba watched as Fabien, who had driven the coach, jumped down and walked out into the woods. In the dim light Annaba could determine a small, poorly constructed hut amid the trees. Fabien disappeared inside the hut then dragged out a frail, old, balding man. As they got closer, Annaba noticed that the old man was so terrified, he had shit his trousers. His mouth worked as if he wanted to plead his case but dread had stolen his voice.

"My gardener chanced upon this man on his ride," Louis told Annaba, his voice cool, even. "His name is Constantine. He fought with my father's brother against my family in the Fronde. He thought himself safe here in the woods. But I never forget a face."

As the old man folded his wrinkled hands for mercy, Fabien pulled a rope from his pocket, stood upon a log, and tied the rope around a tree branch. Then Fabien forced the little man onto the log and looped the rope around his neck. It was then the man finally spoke. "God help me!" he screamed. He clawed at the loop, trying to loosen it, but Fabien shoved the log from under the old man's feet and he swung there, gurgling, his eyes popping.

Fabien returned to the coach, climbed into the driver's seat, and urged the horses forward. Annaba watched as long as he could until the old man, still thrashing and twisting, was swallowed up in the trees and shadows.

"Onward," said the King.

A hard ride and nearly an hour later, Louis, Annaba, Fabien, and the King's guard were inside an ancient, isolated convent, being ushered quietly up a narrow set of stairs by an ancient, pock-faced nun. Candles flickered on the wall along the stairs, and small statues of Virgin Mary and Jesus stared sightlessly from tiny alcoves in the bricks. At the top of the stairs was a hallway with several doors, the nun led the men to the last one. She rapped gently on the door and eased it open.

Inside the small cell sat a nun holding a baby. A black child who gurgled and babbled, kicking her arms and waving her arms.

Annaba stared, his mouth suddenly dry. He hesitated then walked toward the child, watching her intently. Louis moved closer, keeping his eyes on the prince.

"The Dutch do have money but no power," said the King, his voice steady, certain. "We have both."

"Why did you bring me here?" asked Annaba.

"To finish our negotiations."

"We've not even started."

"Annaba, we have been negotiating since the moment you stepped off our coach."

Annaba looked at the King. "You offer me little choice."

"I offer you security and a fair stake in revenue. I also offer a gunboat to secure your port. You've been away from home a long time and your enemies are moving on your capital."

"My father will deal with them."

Louis tipped his head toward the baby. "Do you see this loud little life before you? A friend once told me God had brought this life to me for a reason. Only now do I understand. Her existence begs the question, because in any other country she would be long dead. And her mother, too. Yet here she is. And here you are. You can be sure of one thing. You can make a deal with the Dutch, or English, or Spanish. Rest assured they will smile and agree then bring their armies, burn your lands, kill your families, and take everything you hold dear."

Annaba swallowed hard. Cold traveled his arms but he looked Louis in the eye. "You would do the same."

"Not I. And I suggest you decide quickly. A country without a king will eat itself in war."

"King?"

Louis removed a black envelope from his coat. "We received word that your father is dead. My condolences, Your Majesty."

Annaba stared at the baby, the nun, and then the King. "Power is a game played with mirrors," he said to himself.

Louis nodded. "The world is not what *is*. It is only what appears to be. You are a king now. You must understand that."

"I am beginning to, Sire."

*The Parthenay family* was tucked comfortably in their coach, heading north toward Versailles in the early morning, happily anticipating their visit with the King. Sebastian, the patriarch, was an aging yet handsome warrior; his wife Francoise a demure beauty with flaxen hair. Their sixteen-year-old son and twelve-year-old daughter were bright and inquisitive, full of energy that both exhausted and charmed their parents.

Charlotte, the daughter, caught her mother's hand and smiled. "Are we nearly there, Maman?"

Francoise looked out the window and peered at the winding road ahead. "I cannot tell, dear, but –"

*BANG!*

The carriage shuddered, rattled, and drew up short.

Exasperated, Sebastian put his hand on the door handle. "A wheel has come off, I fear," he said. Climbing from the coach, he joined the driver and the guard. They examined the coach but none of the wheels were gone or damaged.

"I don't know what that was," said Sebastian as his guard took a step toward the trees to have a look.

Then two deafening cracks exploded from the trees, one immediately after the other, slamming into the guard and the driver, blowing holes in their chests. The men fell like axed trees.

"Get down!" Sebastian cried to his family in the carriage. They crouched low, terrified. And in the next second a third shot tore into him and he dropped to the road.

The men who had fired the shots rode up on horseback. One ordered, "Take their money and their clothes."

Inside the coach, Francoise gasped. "I know that voice!" *Montcourt!* The moment she spoke, she knew she had sealed her family's fate. Montcourt peered through carriage window, beckoned Mike to join him, and they shot the terrified mother and son at close range.

But then he looked closer into the carriage.

*Where is Charlotte?*

Montcourt glanced about anxiously for the Parthenays' young daughter. She was not in the carriage, not under nor behind it. *Damn it to hell!* Then he heard faint panting, rustling, and turned to see the girl racing into an open field past the woods. Montcourt raised his pistol, leveled it, and aimed. But then he hesitated, watching her run, seeing her youth, innocence…

*Boom!*

Charlotte fell in the tall grass. Mike lowered his smoking musket and looked at Montcourt with a satisfied sneer. Done.

"With speed, then," said Montcourt. "Begin."

Mike and Tomas began snatching up clothing and valuables from the coach as Montcourt tucked his pistol into his coat and strolled out to the field. Needing to see the child, to rob her corpse, yet feeling a twinge of regret. *So young.* He reached the place where she'd fallen.

And she was gone.

*Alive? Oh, God. Is she alive still?*

Mike whistled and waved anxiously. "Hurry!" And Montcourt raced back to his horse.

*At the palace* of Versailles, Annaba hugged his brother warmly. "We're going now," said the new King.

In the private chapel in her apartment, Queen Marie-Therese knelt before the priest and whispered, "Bless me, Father, for I have sinned."

In his bedchamber, Louis admired the new, gold-framed, full-length mirror being installed in a corner. "The Venetians have been working hard on the new glass, Sire," said Bontemps. "They hope this one will be to your liking." Louis nodded, and heard the voice of his mother reply, "Better."

And at Cassel Chateau, Cassel gazed at the portrait of the King that had been gifted him, took a sip of wine, and then tossed the painting into the roaring flames of the fireplace.

# 4

*Hot blood coursed* down the King's cheek and caught in the collar of his hunting jacket. Oblivious to his wound, he slammed into his private chambers, stalked to the table, and slammed his fist into the wood. "The Parthenays came at my personal invitation!" he shouted. "They drove on that road secure in the knowledge they were guests of the King!" He stared at Bontemps. "If a child of France is not safe on royal lands what chance is there for anyone else? Until their killers are brought before me I shall not sleep again! Where are the Parthenays? I will pay my respects."

"Sire," said Bontemps. "You're injured."

"More than you can know! Any news from the front? At least tell me the siege is ended?"

"Not yet. But Sire – you are bleeding."

Louis looked at Bontemps, confused. Then he held out his hand as blood dripped into his palm. He let out a breath, remembering. "Low branch," he muttered.

Masson was called in to tend the wound. Louis sat on a cushioned settee as the doctor nervously cut the skin from around the wound. Louis stared ahead without wincing, gazing at the portrait of himself and Philippe as children. Louis in boys' clothing. Philippe dressed as a girl.

"Debriding the dead flesh will allow full healing," Masson explained. "Egg yolk and turpentine will permit drainage."

"Why not simply close the wound?" Louis asked.

"Permissible for battlefield injuries, Sire, but modern doctors use modern methods."

Done with the cutting, Masson packed small bits of cloth into the wound. Bontemps picked up the *Gazette*, and as the King's attention turned to his valet, Masson took a quick swig from a small blue bottle from the medicine box.

"'We report with joy the success of the King's infantry against the troops of the Spanish,'" read Bontemps. "'Siege is now laid to the town of Cambray, in the north of France.'"

"At last," said Louis. "Some good news."

"'Most remarkable of all heroes present in the King's name is His Majesty's brother, Prince Philippe, the Duke of Orleans, who has shown bravery on the battlefield...'"

"That's enough for now."

"...beyond all measure, a true and everlasting hero –"

Louis jerked his head toward Bontemps, causing blood to seep. "I said enough!"

*Thick, acrid smoke* lay across the battleground in the Spanish Netherlands. Hundreds of troops littered the scorched field like butchered cattle, the mortally wounded writhing pitifully, weeping for lovers, for home and the dead. Most were the green-uniformed Spanish. Fewer by far the French in blue.

Philippe, in his armor, walked proudly across the field, surveying the carnage. Here was glory! Here was victory!

As he paused to study the strangely peaceful expression on the face of a dead trooper, a young French soldier shuffled past with a heavy, bloodstained sack on his back.

"The siege is broken," Philippe called. The soldier continued walking. "Where are you going? Our camp lies the other way."

The solider turned slowly, mechanically, his eyes dulled in shock. "I promised our mother I'd bring him home," he said. It was then that Philippe noticed that in the sack were an arm, a leg, a ragged torso, and the raggedly severed head of a young man with eyes still open to the world.

*Upon tables in* the medical room of Masson's house, the bodies of the Parthenays lay wrapped in muslin. Claudine waited in the corner, her head bowed respectfully.

Louis and Bontemps stared at the wrapped bodies. Neither spoke for many seconds, and then the King ordered, "Let me see her."

Masson unwrapped the first body. The foul smell of decay was strong on the air. Louis' cheeks hitched but he said nothing. These were his friends, had been his friends. He nodded for Masson to unwrap the second. The stench was the same, the proud and putrid odor of death.

"She bled," said the King, brows furrowing. "Yet he did not?"

"I believe she was shot from a very short distance, Sire," said Masson. "And...and he was shot from afar. Those shot with muskets do not bleed very much."

"Why?"

"Ah, well, that is the way the wounds behave, Sire. They are very large."

"Which would produce more blood, not less."

Masson licked his lips. "Ah, indeed, Sire, um..."

Claudine spoke up. "What I believe my father is saying is that the musket shot tends to fragment. It makes channels twice as large but also crushes the flesh around the entry wound. It seals the blood where it sits so it cannot flow."

Masson looked at Louis, clearly mortified that his daughter has shown more knowledge than he.

"I see," said the King. "Thank you...Masson. Now, the boy."

Masson lifted the sheet, keeping his eyes averted.

"And where is Charlotte?" asked Louis. "The Parthenays had two children."

"I do not know, Sire."

Louis turned to Bontemps. "Find Fabien!"

*Fabien stood on* the road where the Parthenays had been slaughtered. There were large patches of dried blood on the dirt and crusted on the nearest trees. He studied the ground carefully, searching for clues as to the ambush. Then he spied a small set of footprints leading from the road into the field by the woods. He traced the prints to the meadow's edge and discovered a flattened path through the grasses. Someone had run through here. Waving gnats from his face, he followed the path to a spot where that same someone had lain down. No, had fallen. There were clots of browned blood on the crushed weeds.

He walked toward a far copse of trees, following another trail of trampled grasses.

And she was there. Curled up at the base of an almond willow tree.

Charlotte.

Fabien knelt beside her and drew her gently into his lap. The amount of blood that had soaked her gown told him her wound was fatal.

Charlotte's lashes fluttered but her eyes remained closed. "Will I die?" she managed.

Fabien sighed. "Yes."

She tried to lick her lips. "Can you help me?"

"No. But you will not be alone."

There was a brooch upon her collar, and her feeble fingers fumbled for it as if it were a rosary. Fabien listened, waited. It would not be long. Any moment.

Suddenly Charlotte's eyes opened and she looked straight at Fabien, her gaze filled with a terrified ecstasy."

I saw angels!" she cried.

And then she folded into herself and her life flew away.

*Cassel awakened the* snoring, drooling Montcourt by pissing on his face.

"Filthy dog!" sputtered Montcourt into the cold floor as he struggled into consciousness. "I will end you!" Then his eyes focused enough to see it was Cassel pissing and he went quiet.

"You deserve it!" said Cassel. "You arrived here so drunk that you donated the contents of your bladder to the corner of my kitchen and now lie like a pig in the fireplace. Consider this merely the repayment of the loan."

Montcourt sat up. He ran his hands along his face, streaking black soot like war paint. "Where…where is our share?"

"Here," said Cassel. He leaned over and slapped Montcourt soundly. "Is that enough or would you like more? You murder a noble family on the road, then come to *my* house?"

"She heard my voice." Montcourt struggled to his feet. "She knew me."

"How is that possible?"

"Unlikely, but I could not take the risk."

Cassel glared. "You murdered a noble family where they stood. Every single one."

"Not quite. A young girl escaped into the field. But she's wounded and won't live long."

"You did not follow her?"

"I did not think it safe to linger."

Cassel leaned in to the piss-smelling, soot-covered man. "Return! Finish what was begun! She still has her tongue, I presume?"

"Why? You have the chaos you wanted. Think a moment, my lord. Noble blood is spilled on the road to Versailles. Who would follow the Parthenays now? The King will soon tire of his project and move back to Paris. Then we shall own our country again."

"But until that day," said Cassel, "I own only my lands. And I shall own you too, murderer. You've made your mess. Now clean it!" With that he took a small bag of coins from his coat and hurled them at Montcourt.

*Charlotte's body lay* on the floor in Fabien's office, bound in cloth. Fabien sat at his desk, writing in his ledger as Laurene looked on, her hands folded and fingers fidgeting.

"But," Laurene said, "if the court were to know she is dead then they could mourn."

"No. They think she died with them. The family was murdered in the road. Everyone is talking about it."

"But her body was not found."

Fabien looked at his assistant. "Three people know this. Me. Laurene. And the man who meant to kill her. He'll know his shot missed its mark. And he might use that knowledge to make a mistake."

✦ ✦ ✦

*In the privacy* of the room of the War Cabinet, as Bontemps and the other ministers looked on, Colbert unrolled a map on the table to show some progress regarding the nobles, but how those in the north continued to follow Cassel's lead.

"Who else delays?" demanded Louis.

"Fourteen families in all," said Colbert. "All wait for assurance for their safety before venturing on the road."

Louis looked at the map, then at Colbert. His face was tight. "Is there any good news? How are the stables?"

Colbert let out a nervous breath. "Work has ceased, Sire."

"What now?"

"Traders are reluctant to send supplies. If their goods do not arrive, the traders are not paid."

"So," said the King, leaning on the table, "the nobles of the south stay quiet, the east remains cowards, and the north…"

"Without Cassel," said Colbert, "there will be no more cooperation from the north. He's a man of great influence in the region."

"Perception of influence, nothing more."

"Which is just as dangerous."

The King lifted his fist. "Secure the road! Why is it we are laying siege to Chambray yet it is we who feel surrounded?"

A guard at the door spoke quietly to Bontemps, who then said, "Fabien is here, Sire."

Fabien entered the room and Louis stared at him. "You

have failed me, Monsieur Fabien. Just as you failed my friends, the Parthenays. Had your patrols been on the road they would have arrived safely. Instead their deaths will send a message to the world that traveling to Versailles is not safe."

Fabien held the King's gaze. Bontemps tried to catch Colbert's eye.

"Your continued presence in this court demands nothing less than absolution,"Louis continued."You will bring me the men responsible."

"May I speak, Sire?" asked Fabien."I believe a noble may be accountable for this act."

Colbert frowned."How would you know such a thing?"

"The musket shot that killed Parthenay was fired from horseback. The angle of the wound tells me the horse was many hands high, almost impossible for an untrained rider, only a nobleman or cavalry man might be capable of such a feat. But since most of our men are at the front, this leaves suspicion where I say it lies. With a noble."

Retired to an anteroom near the War Cabinet, Bontemps poured himself a glass of wine and took a deep drink. Fabien entered and stared at the valet with furious eyes.

"Say it,"Bontemps said.

"Your plan was ill conceived and badly executed! A force of two hundred would have secured the road."

Bontemps put the goblet down."Drawn from where? Our soldiers are at the front."

"There is your problem."

"It's a problem we all face. And a threat to the King."

Fabien paused, eyeing the wine."Or indeed, it may be a solution."

"A solution?"

"I do not know yet." He snatched up the goblet and drank down the rest of the wine. "The only thing we can be sure of is these men will never strike again." He left the anteroom, carrying the goblet.

*Henriette put down* her hand of cards and shook her head. "You win. I lose."

Madame de Montespan collected the cards from the table, touched the deck to her chin thoughtfully, and gave her mistress a teasing smile. "You aren't trying. Can't we play for matchsticks? After all, if there are no stakes to play for, why play at all?"

"Perhaps later."

The Montespan nodded, placed the deck into its little wooden box, and opened the copy of the *Gazette* that lay on a chair beside the table. "Your husband is the talk of France. Astonishing."

"Not really," said Henriette. "Since we were children, Louis was protected and Philippe was exposed. For the sake of the crown."

"Is that why the King loves to hunt?"

"Perhaps."

"Men never feel more alive than when they are cheating death," said the Montespan. "It turns some into children, others into warriors. Many do not know which one they are."

"Or have the chance to find out."

"I talk of the King."

At that moment a guard announced at the door, "His Majesty!"

The women stood and curtseyed as Louis entered. The Montespan immediately noticed that the King was smiling – a good sign. A good moment, this. Louis took the *Gazette* from the Montespan's fingers. She shifted her hands slightly, hoping his would touch hers, but they did not.

Louis spoke to Henriette. "Your husband's a fine warrior. But it is also true that a soldier's best friend is Fortune. And he has no idea how lucky he is."

The King smiled.

And the Montespan planned.

*Cassel, seated by* the fireplace with the *Gazette* in hand, looked up as Montcourt entered the hall. He spit out the seeds from the grapes he'd been chewing. "Is the problem solved?"

"There are plenty of men on the road with questions. I'd rather not provide them with an answer."

Cassel waved the paper. "Meanwhile, the King gains territory. Claims the land of the Spanish in kind for unpaid dowry. A pretext, naturally. But victory for him is more than land. It's confidence and power. He must be stopped."

Montcourt nodded. "They will not find the girl and if they do, she will be dead. A few days and the roads will be ours again."

"So you are ready to work."

"At your service."

Cassel dropped the *Gazette* onto the floor and crossed his arms. "Protocol doesn't permit us to own or run a business. So I administer my affairs by proxy. Thirty companies under my control. My most trusted man has a brother in a royal warehouse in Paris. He told me about a shipment soon to make its way to Versailles. It will be heavily guarded. They will fight to the end to protect it."

Montcourt bowed. "You raised me from the dead. I would be pleased to lay down my life for you."

"Good," said Cassel. "Because from what I hear, this is a cargo worth dying for."

*My timing is perfect*, thought the Montespan as she swept down the corridor in her loveliest aqua gown. The King was coming her way, with Bontemps and several guards to his sides. As Louis passed she smiled demurely then she stumbled and nearly fell.

Louis turned, his face showing genuine concern. "Madame?"

"Forgive me," said the Montespan, bowing her head daintily. "It is no matter."

"You are ill, perhaps?"

"If…" She looked at the King. "If I feel anything, I am nervous about this war."

"The glory will soon be ours."

The Montespan brought her hands to her heart. "You are already glorious, Sire. If I may be so bold."

"You may, Madame. Be well." And the King took her hand and kissed it. The Montespan made as if to swoon, but then curtseyed deeply. Louis walked away, smiling.

And from a distant doorway, Beatrice watched and glared.

*What did it* matter if Chevalier watched as his lover's wife was undressed by her ladies and helped into her nightgown? He had no interest in the feminine other than to use them to his own ends. This was something Henriette knew all too well and so when he entered her bedchamber, sat on a chair, and threw one leg over the arm, she merely turned her face away. He gazed at her, his lips twitching with sarcasm.

"Misery suits you," he said with a sniff. "You wear it well."

Henriette let out a breath. "What do you want?"

"Did you read the *Gazette*? Your husband is glorious."

"It's the King's glory."

"Not from what I read."

Henriette spoke to the young, curly-haired girl, the newest of her ladies. "Angelique, could you find some blue ribbons?"

Angelique curtseyed graciously and moved past Chevalier. He called to her, "Angelique, I've been meaning to return this to you."

Angelique stopped and looked back to see Chevalier dangling a sparkling diamond necklace from his finger. Her eyes grew wide and her face went pale.

"A chambermaid found it in your drawer and removed

it by mistake," Chevalier continued. "I will make sure she is disciplined."

"My necklace!" said Henriette.

Chevalier cocked his head. "*Your* necklace?"

"Yes, it is very dear to me. I thought it lost." Henriette looked at her young lady, shocked at this turn. "Angelique?"

Angelique shook her head, terrified. "It was not in my room."

"Of course it was," said Chevalier. "And well hidden."

"Madame!" pleaded Angelique. "I did not take your necklace. I absolutely did not!"

"Be quiet," said Chevalier.

"My lady, please!"

Chevalier handed the necklace to Henriette. "Your lady's a thief, Madame. That is clear. And I doubt you are in the habit of employing pickpockets in your household. You may be sure you've not heard the last of it."

Tears spilled down Angelique's cheeks as Chevalier smiled and walked out.

*Noble ladies gathered* in their salon in mid-morning, visiting and sharing gossip as sunlight flooded through the windows. Clusters stood about, talking of husbands, children, and clothing.

The Montespan had gathered a small group around her, and a middle-aged courtier with silvered hair and rubies around her neck spoke to the Montespan in an urgent, dramatic tone. "Lissette begged her husband not to come! After what happened to the Parthenays can you blame her? But she said with the King's new edict he told her they had to, that they must find a sponsor or be doomed."

Beatrice and Sophie entered the salon and sidled up to the group. But rather than let them join, the ladies drew together more closely.

"I heard the real reason," said the Montespan, "is that they cannot find their papers. There was a flood a few years back. What if the papers were washed away? Poor lambs."

"There will be remedy, I'm sure," Beatrice interjected from outside the circle.

The ladies glanced at her. The Montespan eyed her coolly. "That remains to be seen, does it not? Not everyone can have such credit with the Chevalier."

Beatrice smiled, holding her own. "As much credit as he is inclined to give is as much as I have."

"Should your coffers empty I'm sure your daughter will offer some security. Beauty unlocks many doors."

"You of all people should know that first-hand, Madame. And beauty without wit is merely vanity."

The Montespan returned the smile, and Beatrice led her daughter away.

When out of earshot, Sophie said, "Mother, that was unkind."

"Daughter, when you pass through a door in court you aren't walking into a room. You are entering a marketplace. The center sells to the inner circle, the inner circle sells to the outer circles. And the outer circles sell to the rest. Transactions mean contacts and contacts mean credit. Credit means power.

Power means everything. Do you think the attention Madame de Montespan receives happens by chance?"

"I thought you didn't like her."

"Speak softly! I saw the King look at her today. A lingering gaze. Think what that might be worth."

"What does it matter to us? We've our papers and our lineage."

"Not yet."

"What can happen to a piece of paper on the road from Pau?"

"Ask the Parthenays," replied Beatrice, "and say no more." With that she steered her daughter away from the salon and out into the gardens.

They made their way along a stone pathway next to the west side of the palace, each deep in her own thoughts, when something bumped Sophie's shoulder. She spun around to find a bucket had been lowered by rope from the scaffolding above. She peered inside to find a single pink flower, and glancing up, saw a handsome man grinning at her. The same man with light brown hair who had caught her eye before. He nodded at the flower, indicating it was for her. She reached into the bucket to take it out.

"Sophie!" Beatrice had turned back and was glaring at her daughter and the man above her.

Sophie left the flower and hurried to her mother. Beatrice grabbed her arm and shook it fiercely.

"Listen to me!"

Sophie scowled. "What have I done?"

"Do not make eyes at boys like that! You only have eyes for the King. Even if I succeed in marrying you to a noble, men in court are stepping stones. Nothing more, nothing less. And men like the one on that scaffold are pond scum over which you walk. Do you understand?"

Sophie pouted. "You're clear on what you want for my life. But you've been silent on what life I wish for myself. You would have me marry some noble corpse to advance our station."

"Without money there is no life!"

"If lying with a noble is so important, why don't you take your own advice?"

"I am doing this for you! This is a hard, cold world for women!"

"I do not think you are telling me everything."

Beatrice let go of Sophie and stood tall. "You are still young. You can be sure of it."

At that moment, at a distance across a circular pool filled with swans, Sophie spied Fabien walking with Laurene. Across the hedges and shrubs, Fabien nodded and smiled in Beatrice's direction.

"What about him, Mother?" asked Sophie, wrinkling her nose. "Stepping stone or pond scum?"

*Louis and Rohan* sat upon pillows in the King's private chambers, facing each other, sipping wine, and laughing. It was as the old days had been; comfortable, light-hearted, two friends reveling in memories, sharing the best of times.

"She wore her hair in bows," said Louis, running his finger along the top of his goblet.

"Yes, at the picnic," replied Rohan. He took a drink. "Midsummer."

"I was angry at you."

"Because Françoise chose me!"

"To make me jealous."

"She was successful. For she truly had eyes only for you."

Louis held up his goblet to his friend then drained the rest of the wine. He pushed himself up from his pillow and went to the window. Rohan joined him. The reflections of the two, side by side in the window glass, revealed nothing of status, of position, of power. They looked to be, in that moment, equals.

"Thank you, my friend," said Louis. "I needed this."

Rohan nodded. Then he held up a finger. "We should celebrate her tonight. And every night after that. I shall tie a bow on the next beautiful woman I see and call her Francoise!"

Louis smiled. "Yes!"

Out on a garden pathway, Rohan spied the Montespan with several other ladies. He pointed. "What about her?"

Louis shook his head. "Her you do not touch."

"Shame."

The men returned to their seats and poured more wine. "I have a position in mind for you," said Louis. "I hope you might take it."

Rohan's brows lifted. "The answer is yes, of course. What is it?"

"As you know, the stable is done. The hunt needs a new master."

Rohan nodded. This was what he had hoped for. Master of the hunt was the position of his dreams. "I know just the man," he began.

"I was hoping you did."

"It would be my pleasure!"

"Send me his name, then. I will need to put him in place while you go to war."

Rohan swallowed hard. "War?"

Louis placed the goblet on the table. "As our war continues I find that my brother is foremost in my mind."

"I…I understand."

Louis leaned forward in his chair, his face morphing from close friend to monarch. "I wish you to go to the front. Be my brother's shadow. See that no harm comes to him."

*War! I do not want to go to war!* But Rohan forced a smile. "I will do as you ask."

Louis patted his friend on the shoulder. "That's the Rohan I remember," he said.

"Yes, Sire," said Rohan, keeping the smile he could not feel in place.

*Louis stood in* Fabien's office, sensing the tall dark shelves and countless books closing in on him, the mid-day meal a painful knot in his belly, furious that he, in that moment, felt helpless with grief. He stared at the brooch in his palm, the brooch that was encrusted with flakes of Charlotte's blood. "Where did you find her?"

"In the woods near Marly," answered Fabien.

"Where is she now?"

"Buried with her family."

"Without a sermon?" asked Bontemps. "Beneath dignity."

Fabien shook his head. "A full sermon might attract attention."

The King closed his eyes for a moment then looked back at the brooch. Anger raged behind his eyes, but he spoke evenly, slowly. "What would be wrong with that? You let me live in hope then break my heart again? Why did you hide *her* from me?"

"Because you have armed me, Sire," said Fabien, "not just with weapons but with choices. My choice was to protect the truth, which is that Charlotte Parthenay did not die with her family. This knowledge gives us something her killers do not possess. Certainty. This means they will make a mistake."

Louis nodded, and crushed his fist around the brooch. There was so much to say, so much to scream, but Fabien's point was valid. The anger in his soul melted into grief, and he clenched his jaw to keep tears at bay. "Did she suffer?"

"A great deal."

"I hope it did not last long."

"She was in considerable pain for an extended period."

Louis pinned the brooch on his own jacket. "Monsieur Fabien, you do not seek my approval in any way, do you?"

Fabien's brows furrowed in confusion, uncertain as to the right answer. And so he said, "No, Sire."

Bontemps gasped quietly, but Louis smiled slightly. "Your honesty is also a weapon."

"If you say so, Sire."

Louis removed the brooch, pocketed it, and left the office with guards falling in behind. Fabien moved to follow but Bontemps stopped him.

"When the King addressed your failings, I did not speak up in your defense," Bontemps said.

"Yes."

"I hope you can understand why."

Fabien stared without passion at the valet. Then, "Will that be all?"

Bontemps nodded curtly. Fabien walked toward the door but then turned back. "There is a man at court. His face is unfamiliar to me. No one told me of his arrival and yet he's given protection and access to the King. Who is he? What is his name?"

Bontemps waved him off. "You have work. I suggest you apply yourself to it."

*Select courtiers gathered* that evening in a private palace salon at the invitation of Beatrice and her daughter. The room was gaily adorned with late-season fruits and flowers and candles in silver floor stands. A handsome, blond cello player had been appointed to play cheerful tunes to set the mood.

As Beatrice and Sophie greeted each guest, Chevalier strode in, dressed for the party in a burgundy cape, and scanned the room. He immediately took note of the handsome cello player and grinned lasciviously.

"Cousin?" called Beatrice, waving her hand. "You seem to be in a good mood."

Chevalier sauntered over. "How can I not, with such beauty around me?" He winked at Sophie. "Speaking of which, Henriette's entourage is looking rather tired. I've made an opportunity for my darling girl here."

Beatrice frowned. "With Henriette? Should Sophie consign herself to her, when Madame de Montespan grows in stature day by day?"

"My decision is made. I am head of this family, or have you forgotten?"

Beatrice stared at Chevalier. There was a long, silent moment. At last she spoke, angling her head as she regained her composure. "When will this position become available?"

"Soon. One of her ladies is fond of pilfering."

Chevalier took Sophie by the hand and took her onto the floor to dance. As Sophie stumbled along, trying to keep up, Chevalier watched the cello player. "Dance is formalized conversation, my dear Sophie," he said. "Full of rules and restrictions, much like the dress you are wearing."

"Do you like it?"

Chevalier drew her against himself, watching the musician, imagining what it was like to have the man in his bed, to touch him, fondle him, consume and command him.

"I never asked you," said Chevalier into Sophie's ear. "Are you still intact?"

"Intact?"

"Have your fingers ever been…curious?"

"I don't know what you mean."

"Oh, you will," he whispered as he pulled her even closer,

146

so much so that she could feel the hardness in his trousers. She struggled but he held tight, pressing into her, against her, thinking of the delicious, tantalizing cello player.

The party was over. Chevalier hurried along a forest pathway in the faint light of the sickle moon, the ground damp beneath his feet. But oh, the warm, damp treasure that awaited him in the darkness.

And there he was, the cello player, leaning against a tulip tree by the path, his arms crossed.

"I'm a little early for my lesson," said Chevalier. He took the cello player's hand and nibbled it. The musician cupped Chevalier's face and kissed him fully, pressing his body against him and groaning with expectation and pleasure.

"Ah," purred Chevalier. He pulled his mouth from the musician's, tore the man's shirt open, and then drew his tongue down the man's well-muscled chest to his waist. He quickly unfastened the musician's trousers. The musician tensed and arched his back, forcing his groin into Chevalier's face. Chevalier chuckled at the man's enthusiasm and kissed the warm hair just above his cock. But then he tasted something hot, slick, and salty. He drew back to see.

Blood.

"What in God's name!"

Chevalier leapt to his feet to find the musician grasping his neck – which had been sliced open. Blood poured through his fingers. His eyes rolled up in his head and he slumped to the ground.

Then a man stepped from the shadows, a man whose face was hooded, and he put the point of a knife against Chevalier's throat.

"Oh, my God!" cried Chevalier. "Please!"

"Shh," said the hooded man. "You're an easy person to find. Since your infidelity is so constant." Then the man spun Chevalier around and caught him in a chokehold. His words were hot on Chevalier's neck. "Here's what happens from this moment on. We will tell you what to do, and you will do it. Many already crave what we seek. We will do anything to see it won. Deny us and you die. Apply yourself and all shall rejoice. Your lover will be the King. But you will have the power and the future is yours. As long as you do exactly what we tell you. We will talk again."

The man squeezed Chevalier's throat, harder, then dashed off into the woods. Chevalier tried to scream but he could only cough. And then see that he had pissed himself.

*The night beyond* the open window of Louis' bedchamber was noisy with autumn insects chirring to one another in the trees. The silver moon hung in the black sky like a sharp, curved weapon waiting a Divine command. Eagle-owls with golden eyes flew silently, seeking out their helpless prey.

Inside the bedchamber, Louise de la Valliere paced before the King, her hands clasped over the swell of her belly, her voice trembling. "I wish to make peace with God," she said.

Louis caught her arm, brought her to himself, and caressed her cheek. "I used to be your God," he said.

Louise crossed herself. "I cannot stay in this house of sin. A convent has given their consent to take me in. Sire, please, release me to God's care!"

"Have I not given you everything?"

Louise looked at the floor. "I used to think I was a person of quality. But now I do not know myself or my place. I only wish to serve God."

"I love your piety, Madame Louise." Louis leaned in to kiss and nuzzle her gently. Louise drew back.

"I will soon be gone in your eyes. I see who will come after me."

"God wishes us to be together."

"Sire, let me atone for my life!"

Louis' patience and tenderness was gone. "Enough!"

"What if I am to burn for eternity?" Louise pleaded. "What if it's too late for me?"

But the King only pointed toward the door. "Go to your room!" And she scurried away, her cries muffled in her sleeve.

Louis stared after her and then left his apartment, ordering Bontemps to stay behind, and with two guards following quietly and discreetly, he made his way down the palace's widest corridor to the dining room. He found Madame de Montespan alone in the empty grand dining room where the serving tables were still spread with delectable pastries the courtiers had been too over-filled to consume. The Montespan gave him a coy smile as she lifted a macaroon from a platter. She held it seductively to her lips then took a bite. Louis moved close and picked up a macaroon, as well.

"I commend you on your excellent appetite," said Louis.

"Why, Sire? You hardly know me or my needs."

"I know you are still hungry."

The Montespan wiped a crumb from the corner of her mouth. "Perhaps. How many have you had?"

He stepped even closer. *We are not talking food,* he thought. "I do not recall."

"In which case, why would another make any difference?"

Louis smiled and held her gaze. "Hard to tell without partaking."

"I wonder why that is?" she asked. "After a certain time, it's just a number. Isn't it?"

"That depends on the number," he said. Louis finished his macaroon, wiped his hands on a cloth napkin, and gave the Montespan a bow.

*Henriette lay naked* on her bed, clutching a pillow and smiling at the King as the earliest birds of morning stirred outside her window and began their noisy, pleasant calls to one another. Louis, seated on the bed's edge, was dressed but for his boots.

"You're bold," Henriette teased, running her fingers through her tangled hair. "Coming to a lady's chamber like you did."

Louis lay back across Henriette's legs and stroked her calf. He wanted to feel satisfied. As King, he should feel satisfied. Yet he was torn; his soul struggling. "I believe I was invited."

Henriette reached down to stroke his cheek. "You're tired."

"I won't sleep until I catch the men who murdered the Parthenays."

"I hope you will sleep soon, then," she said as he stared at the canopy overhead. "I want to do this every night. So I know you will keep me safe."

Louis sat up and tugged on a boot. "Do I not already protect you, Madame?"

"Sadly, where Chevalier is concerned, I cannot see how anyone can. He caused my lady Angelique great pain."

Louis turned to Henriette, his jaw tight. "Is it not enough that I protect you? Must I now protect your ladies?"

"He made up a terrible story and put a problem in my lap."

Louis pulled on the second boot.

"And now you're sad."

Henriette got on her knees and put her chin on Louis' shoulder. "Françoise Parthenay was very dear to you. I was even jealous of her for a silly moment."

Louis stood and pulled his coat from a chair. "I'm going to war. Where it is safe."

Henriette blinked. "I do not understand."

"And you are coming with me."

Henriette frowned and pushed her hair back from her face. "Why?"

"Would you wish to be somewhere else?"

"Of course not."

"A new day is coming." Louis buttoned his coat and walked to the door.

151

$\mathcal{A}$ *private meeting* was held in the King's apartment, with only the King and the Emissary from the Holy Roman Empire in attendance. Bontemps and Fabien waited obediently outside the closed door with a pair of guards.

Louis, dressed in his most royal garb and wig, sat in his chair while the Emissary sat upon a lower stool, presenting his case. "The Spanish grow weary with our silence, Sire," the Emissary said. "They wish us to intervene."

"You have claim by inheritance," Louis replied. "We have claim by the law. We need not fight each other for the prize. Though many in your council would benefit from war, I am sure."

The Emissary folded his hands on his knees and took a deep breath. "The circles are divided. But if our present discussions were to establish a policy between us –"

"Your Prince Auersperg, of the noble Austrian family, might get his cardinal's hat."

The Emissary smiled, impressed. "Indeed, Majesty."

Louis leaned forward, fingers linking. "Let us move, then, to a treaty." A small trickle of blood began to run down his face from under his wig. "A treaty in secret between the Kingdoms of France and the House of Habsburg to divide the territory on the death of the Spanish king." The blood continued to run, a wider rivulet now, covering his cheek and his chin. "The health of the ruler is paramount to the security of state."

"Your Majesty." The Emissary's cheek tightened with concern and a bit of embarrassment. "Your face."

"My face?" Louis touched his face then studied his hand, now coated with bright red.

The Emissary hurried to the door and pulled it open. Fabien saw the Emissary's face – it was the man Fabien did not know, the man he had worried about, had asked about. He drew back in surprise and distrust.

"Quickly!" shouted the Emissary. "A doctor!"

Fabien hesitated.

"Did you not hear me, man?"

Louis appeared at the door, blood still streaming, holding on to the sill, his vest now soaked.

"I will fetch Masson, Sire!" said Bontemps.

"Not that doctor," said Louis. "The other one." He closed the door.

Bontemps raised a warning finger to Fabien. "No one must enter," he said, and then he took off down the hallway.

Hardly a half-hour passed before Claudine entered the King's bedchamber through the private rear door, ushered there by Bontemps, and approached the King with a quick and silent curtsey. She removed the heavy hooded cape she had worn so that no one would know she was female and draped it over a chair.

Seated at the bed's edge in only his trousers, Louis pulled his hand away from his forehead. "Your father's work," he said, "I'd like you to inspect it."

Claudine checked the wound and the leaky dressings. She grimaced but did not criticize what her father had done. "It will need to be stitched."

Louis nodded.

"It will hurt."

Louis looked across at the portrait of himself and his brother; children, then, not yet knowing their fates. "Good," he said.

*Louise de la* Valliere entered the Queen's outer apartment hesitantly. She curtseyed before Marie-Therese and drew her shawl more closely around her shoulders.

"You received my message," said the Queen.

"Yes, Majesty. I've been praying for your lost child every day."

"You are kind to say such a thing."

Louise rubbed her back and winced, her pregnancy making her uncomfortable.

"Be seated," Marie-Therese said.

Louise lowered her head and sat.

"It is warm," said the Queen. "Take off your shawl."

Louise hesitated then handed her shawl to the Queen's lady.

"My words to you were not kind," said the Queen. "I said them in a moment clouded by my own failings. I'd like us to be friends. Not because I do not still resent every moment you've stolen from my husband and me, but because I sense something in your soul. The fabric is torn."

The Queen walked around Louise and noticed the savage red marks on her back, the barely healed wounds of self-flagellation.

"My concern is not as such for you, but the innocent life

inside you can feel this pain."

Louise looked over her shoulder at the Queen. "I will join a community of prayer, Majesty, when the time permits."

"Do you love the King?"

"I love God."

"That is not an answer."

"I…also love the King. But the price is too great."

Marie-Therese came around again to look Louise in the eye. "Your back. What have you done to yourself?"

"Nothing I do will ever be enough. It hurts so much."

"It's supposed to," said the Queen as she looked away.

*The door to* Masson's house opened and Claudine entered from the street, the mist of night following her into the warm firelight of the kitchen. Masson glanced up as he stirred a pot that boiled on the stove.

"I'm making potage for supper," he said. His voice was ragged, suspicious. "Potatoes, carrots, celery. I thought since you are now the man of the house I would take on a more wifely role."

"Father," Claudine interrupted as she removed her cape. "Let me do it."

"Sit. Rest. You've had a full day of it at work."

"You're not saying what you mean and I do not like it."

Masson's eyes narrowed. "You would make mockery of your father?"

"What are you talking about?"

"Where have you been?"

"I am not at liberty to say."

"So your silence speaks for you. My work on the King's head was rushed, yes? Simplistic too, perhaps. But my own daughter? He would seek to destroy my reputation."

"Your reputation remains intact, Father. You're jealous."

"I'm scared, child!" Masson hurled the spoon and it clattered on the floor. "Scared for you. This is not a place of warmth and trust. It's a cold, brutal circle of lies, and while they might use and discard me, as long as there is breath in my lungs I will not permit them to do the same to you. The King has his favorites. Then, one day, he becomes tired of them and no one sees them anymore."

Claudine let out an exasperated breath then looked around for Masson's small blue bottle. She found it on a low shelf, opened it, and without taking her eyes off her father, poured out the contents.

$\mathcal{T}$he old priest listened silently in the darkness of the King's bedchamber. It was well past midnight, yet the priest was always available should the King need him. He was perched on a stool with the King beside him, kneeling on a cushion with his head bowed. There were no sounds but the clock ticking on the mantle, a wind rattling outside, and the King's anxious breathing.

"Bless me, Father, for I have sinned," Louis said.

"What is your reconciliation?"

"The mortal sins of envy and wrath."

"Remember, Sire," the priest began. "Some transgressions by the State are necessary, whereas if committed by Man —"

"Do not address me so," Louis challenged. "In this moment I am a man, alone, burdened by sin, doing my penance under God."

The priest nodded.

"How shall I repent?"

The priest folded his wrinkled hands and thought before speaking again. "Acts of contrition take many forms, Sire. One may atone in kind by practicing the sin's corresponding virtues in their stead. The sin of envy, for example, is mirrored by kindness. The sin of wrath is mirrored by the virtue of patience."

Louis stared into the shadows. "We are at war, where wrath has its station. And war is no place for kindness."

*Rohan and Philippe* stood side by side at the edge of a forest, staring out across a wide stretch of uneven pastureland toward the distant enemy camp where soldiers in green uniforms moved back and forth on patrol. French guards watched from nearby in the trees, silent, keeping eyes on the adversaries. A cold autumn wind passed by, stirring downed leaves and dust into the air and causing dead grasses to undulate like waves upon a sea. A callous sea that waited to embrace those who might fight and die there.

"We are far inside the line," warned Rohan. "We're in great danger here."

Philippe said nothing.

"Sire, I promised your brother."

Philippe gave Rohan a sharp look. "Promised him what?"

Rohan clearly did not want to answer. Still, he said, "That I would ensure your safety." Philippe glared at Rohan then stalked away into the trees. He should have known Louis had sent Rohan for that very reason, but he'd chosen not to believe it. He could hear Rohan following and raised his arm to wave him back. *Leave me be!*

After a good many paces through briar and brush, he stopped by a tall, broad oak to relieve himself, and as he did he heard a scratching sound nearby. He peered around the oak to spy a bare-chested man in a gully, digging a shallow hole in which he first placed his sword and then his shirt. A green shirt, the uniform of the enemy. *Here we have a deserter*, Philippe thought. *Fascinating.*

"It's not that easy, you know."

The man looked up, shocked. His eyes widened and he looked about to see if others were with Philippe. Then he sighed. "I did not choose this war," he said.

Philippe stepped from behind the tree. "Nor I. But it is what we do. I stand on one side, you on the other."

"Your army's cannons have killed many of my friends."

"We are making history."

The man scraped soil into the hole. "You stay and make history. I'm going home to my wife and child."

"They live in a world forged by war," said Philippe. "We are part of this creation. You cannot clean war out of your body because it is our body."

"A father needs to see his child and tell him he is loved more than life."

"How can you teach your son to face the future with courage if you cannot face your own? Your words will mean nothing."

The deserter scowled. "Who are you?"

"Philippe, Duc d'Orleans."

The man laughed. Then realized Philippe was telling the truth. He stood on shaky legs and bowed dramatically. "Perhaps we will meet on the field tomorrow."

"Perhaps."

As Philippe turned he heard the deserter digging back into the hole to retrieve his sword and shirt.

*Henriette tossed her* wet hair back from her shoulders, shivered, and walked quickly from the pool to the pool house with several of her ladies. Soon it would be too cold to bathe outside, but she would still want her precious time in the pool house. She watched her slippered feet as she walked, thinking of war and warriors, of Philippe and Chevalier. And Louis. Always Louis.

She looked up to see the Montespan standing at the pool house door.

"What a surprise to find you here," Henriette said.

"I wanted to talk to you, away from the usual ears," said the Montespan.

The two ladies moved away to sit on a stone bench. A chittering chaffinch watched from a branch overhead.

"What Chevalier did to your poor Angelique," the Montespan said.

Henriette nodded, frowned. "He was being himself, unfortunately. And now I have a new lady."

"Mademoiselle Clermont."

"Yes, Sophie. I've found her pleasant enough. And she is talented with hair."

The Montespan leaned closer. "I've a scheme that would bring a delicious revenge on Chevalier. Would you consider it?"

"No, thank you, Athenais."

The Montespan's eyes widened slightly in confusion. "Might I have a reason?"

"I already know what it is you want, and I cannot help you get it."

The Montespan blinked. "I am sure I don't know what you mean."

"Think awhile. You will get there in the end." Henriette stood, smiled, and walked off, leaving the Montespan alone on the bench.

"I suppose I will," she said to herself.

*Louis scanned the* faces of ministers he'd ordered into the War Cabinet room. His eyes were shadowed by anger, determination, and defiance. "We are surrounded by conspirators," he said as he leaned on the table, his head lowered like that of a wolf. "By criticism. By wilderness and danger. Defense is no longer our option. We must break the siege. We must attack. Bontemps, arrange a force to guard the roads."

"They are assembled, Sire," replied Bontemps, though the valet could see by the twitch of Fabien's eye that he was not convinced that was true.

"Make their clothing uniform. Make their presence felt. To deter and reassure as we do in Paris. Purse the roads. Police them. Contact every noble who defies me. I wish to understand their concerns. And they shall be informed of our intent. Their King is going to war." Louis rose and the men followed suit.

Fabien sought out Bontemps at the door, but Bontemps spoke first. "Four squads of one hundred on the roads. Five men per shipment. All on the road shall have a guard."

"But these men are untrained," said Fabien.

"Most are at the front."

Fabien sneered. "Leaving only children!"

Three busy days passed, with preparations for the King's journey to the war front. When the morning came for him to leave, nobles, courtiers, guards, and servants gathered in the courtyard in front of the palace, a cloudless sky overhead, cheering and waving handkerchiefs as the King and his mistress Henriette climbed into the royal carriage. Three of Henriette's ladies, including Sophie, boarded a second coach that was waiting behind the King's.

The Montespan had not been invited along. She pushed her way through the crowd to stand beside Louise, and stood on tiptoe to see the King and to make sure he saw her. She wanted to make one last connection with him before he left for the war. *Look at me*, she thought. *See me. Here I am.* As the driver slapped the reins on the horses' backs, Louis looked out the window and nodded at the Montespan. *Yes!*

"Bravo, Madame," the Montespan said, leaning in to Louise. "The look is yours."

"Oh, no," sighed Louise. "I believe you are mistaken."

"You are upset?"

Louise shook her head sadly. "I cannot reach him."

"Nonsense. You are his mistress."

"He's chosen her. He's taking her with him. To war."

"No. He's delivering her to her husband."

Louise looked at the Montespan, her eyes filled with hope. "Can you help me? I need to make him like me but I am boring. Perhaps when he returns you can put him in a good mood for me? Talk to him, make him laugh. If he's in a good humor I might have a chance."

The Montespan watched as the carriage disappeared down the winding road. She brushed a stray strand of hair from her face. "I suppose I could try."

*They rode in* silence for a while, watching barns and cottages and hedgerows passing outside the carriage windows. *The fruits of the peasants' lives*, Louis thought. *Simple lives, lives with no true understanding of the burdens shouldered by royalty. Are they free, then? Or are they slaves to their menial lots in life?* Henriette reached over and touched Louis' hand.

He did not reciprocate and she pulled her hand back.

"Do you miss England?" he asked at last.

"I miss you," said Henriette.

"Have you heard from your brother recently?"

"You would know if I have."

Louis adjusted the frill of his collar then stared out at a pasture filled with grazing cattle. "The summer of our lives has been full of blossoms. But autumn is here and nights are drawing in. In the growing darkness we must remind ourselves that life is more than love. And marriage more than duty."

Henriette turned her feathered hat so that he could not see her face and her need to cry. "My life is yours," she said softly.

*The sputtering candle* offered only the faintest of illumination to the palace corridor. The hour was late and Fabien was deep in thought as he carried the candle on his way to his chamber; so deep that he was startled when a shadow appeared at the light's edge.

"Monsieur Fabien?" The voice was soft, sweet, and feminine.

Beatrice stepped into the pool of light. Fabien's heart skipped a beat.

"You are lost, Madame?" he managed.

"In truth, I am scared," said the lady, her brows furrowed. "The war. The night. The palace is not the same when the King is away. Two nights gone and every room is empty and dark. Would you walk me to my apartment?"

Fabien felt himself nod.

Beatrice stepped full into the candlelight. *So beautiful!* he thought. *What do I say to her? How do I behave?*

They began walking, and Fabien tried his best not to let the candle tremble in his hand. "Despite the news of your friends, you seem in good spirits," he said.

Beatrice stared. "What about my friends?"

"The Parthenays. They lived close to your family in Pau, yes?"

Anxiety flashed across Beatrice's face. "Known to me, yes. A tragedy I cannot bear to ponder."

They reached the door to Beatrice's apartment. She turned to him and smiled. "Perhaps we can walk again for a while. In the garden during the day? And talk of happier things."

Fabien nodded. *How do I conclude this? Do I dare touch her? Dear God, I want this lady.*

But then Beatrice kissed the tips of her two fingers, and placed the fingers on his shoulder. With that, she entered her apartment, leaving Fabien alone.

*The young man* stood beside a road to Versailles and sobbed as he dug a grave with a small shovel. His friend knelt beside him, his arms bound, his mouth slack with shock. Scattered beyond the two of them, across the road, were ten other men, their heads blown apart. Their broken carriage lay on its side, one wheel spinning in the wind.

Three men with black masks stood over it all with weapons on their arms, watching. Silent. Then one stepped forward, put the muzzle of his musket on the forehead of the bound man, and fired. The man fell backward into the half-dug grave. The young man with the shovel screamed.

One of the armed men pulled off his mask. He aimed his musket at the young man. The young man gasped. "I…I know you!" he said.

"You used to know me," sneered Montcourt. He pulled the trigger. The man's head shattered and flopped over, blood pouring into the dirt.

Montcourt snatched up the shovel and handed it to one of Cassel's two thugs. "Tomas," he said, "nobles do not work." Tomas began but then Montcourt took the shovel back. "I have a better idea," he said.

With ropes they found in the carriage, Montcourt, Tomas, and Mike hung the twelve police officers from roadside trees by their ankles. They swayed and creaked in the wind like foul fruits among the branches. Then Montcourt nailed a sign to one of the trees from which a body dangled.

"ROAD CLOSED."

*French military tents* covered a huge swath of ground, standing amid trees along an icy river and across a portion of pastureland, creating a city of its own. Thousands of soldiers relaxed before fires, walked with one another, talking of battles and loved ones left behind.

Inside the largest tent sat a table on which papers bearing the most recent war plans were unrolled. Philippe stood with his feet planted apart slightly, his face flushed and his soul empowered by war and all it had asked of him.

"Here." Philippe spoke to War Minister Louvois as Rohan looked on. "If we pulled our line back into this valley —"

Louvois, dressed in an elegant velvet jacket with decorations indicating his superior rank, held up his hand. "They would follow our retreat," he said.

"Allowing our cavalry to ride in from the east, closing the circle. They'd have nowhere to run."

Louvois considered this then nodded in agreement.

There was a shout outside. "The King!"

Philippe turned from the table, his chest swelling with pride. *Now my brother will see all I've done and plan to do for France.*

The tent flap opened and Louis walked in, followed by several guards, Henriette, and Sophie. He strode to the table as Louvois bowed and Philippe smiled.

"Wonderful news, brother—" Philippe began.

"Indeed," Louis interrupted. "The war is over. Negotiations for a ceasefire are to begin this day at Tournai."

Philippe's mouth opened then closed. Shocked, he glanced at Louvois, at Rohan, and then back at his brother. "But we've battled hard for this moment! Many men have died to attain it!"

"We will maintain our line," said the King. "But no more. In a day, perhaps two. But this war is over."

Anger stirred in Philippe's arms. His fists drew together and his jaw clenched. "For what? We can win the war. Here. Today."

"The odds are not with us."

"We've lost too much to stop now!"

Louis maintained a countenance of calm. "I would speak to my brother alone," he ordered. He nodded at a guard who pulled back the tent flap and all within exited, leaving the brothers alone.

"I'm here to bring you home," said Louis.

"And I am here to fight. And fuck. This ceasefire, I am wondering, will it just so happen to be announced on your return with 'All hail King Louis, who went to war and won the peace'?"

Louis stepped closer to his brother. Philippe did not step back. Eye to eye, King and Warrior.

"Our spies report there is a price on your head," said Louis. "The Spanish have engaged mercenaries to seek you out of the field. They wish to make an example of you, to use you against me. I will not countenance the risk. You are to come with me."

"Without me beside them, those men may die."

"This will be the last battle. I will not have it be your last act."

"On the field there are no Kings. No nobles or peasants. Every man is equal. Fighting to survive the day. Tomorrow, on that field, I will have more in common with my enemy than with my own brother." He spun toward the tent's door. "Henriette! Where is my wife?"

"I envy your brotherhood," said Louis. "For me there is only solitude, the likes of which you have never known."

"Tomorrow," said Philippe, "I will be with my brothers."

"They mean to seek you out and kill you," said Louis.

Philippe stepped out of the tent, finding the King's entourage standing nearby. He walked to Henriette, snatched the feather from her hat, and tucked it into his jacket like a jaunty flag. "Then I had better wear something bright or they will not know who I am."Then he pulled Henriette to himself and kissed her with the raw and angry passion of a man at war. A man ready to conquer.

And the following morning, in the light of early dawn, two thousand French troops marched out across a field toward the enemy. Cannon and musket fire boomed around them, but forward they marched. Some were struck, screamed, and died. But the others marched forward, unfazed, determined.

In the midst of them, leading them, with them, rode Philippe upon his horse, with Rohan riding close beside him. Philippe sat tall, possessed with bloodthirsty fury, and a sense of brilliant, terrifying destiny. He checked his face in the mirror from his pocket, lifted his face to Heaven, then drew his sword, spurred his horse, and charged down the hill into the mist.

# 5

*"Noble steed, quiet* now." Philippe sat cross-legged on a hillside, deep in a tangle of charred weeds, surrounded by dead enemy soldiers, holding his horse's head in his lap. The animal lay trembling with a mortal wound to his chest. He snorted and strained, his eyes flashing white, each movement causing the wound to bleed all the more. After many long minutes the struggling eased, slowed, as the horse seemed to accept what was to come. The gray muzzle twitched. The great eyes dimmed. His sides bellowed one last time, and his breath was warm on Philippe's arm.

"Be at peace," said Philippe. "Well done."

*A broken carriage* lay on a tree-shadowed stretch of the road to Versailles, downed like a horse in battle. The coachman and two police outriders stood trembling with their muskets drawn, facing three masked men whose weapons were also drawn.

Montcourt smirked behind the cloth over his mouth."How much are they paying you, gentlemen? I can assure you, it is not enough."

There was a rustling in a tree and a policeman glanced over to see a crow flying away. And in that second, the outlaws fired.

*Emissaries, diplomats, and* generals flanked the table in Philippe's tent, eyeing one another as King Louis XIV lifted a white quill pen and held it above the Treaty of Aix-la-Chapelle. Marie-Therese had been brought in from Versailles for the occasion and she stood behind her husband, her hands folded, dressed in purple, her dark hair piled high and threaded with pearls. Philippe waited by the tent's door, watching it all, his gaze tight, his arms crossed.

Louis dipped the pen into the inkwell and with dramatic flair, signed the paper, and dated it May 2nd, 1668. The war was over. The attendees applauded politely. Philippe pushed his way out of the tent where countless soldiers waited for him. They burst into applause, much louder than that inside the tent.

The following morning, the King's carriages traveled back toward Versailles along the rutted road. Louis and Marie-Therese rode together without speaking. The velvet curtains were drawn over the windows and the interior of the carriage was stuffy.

At last Marie-Therese spoke."You are troubled, husband. Tell me."

"It does not concern you."

"Concern me? This war was fought for me. You killed my countrymen to defend my honor. At least, that was your excuse."

"Your father made a promise to me he did not keep. I lost five thousand men to make him honor it."

"But the treaty is signed. What war remains?"

Louis ran his hand along the fringe of the curtain."When I was ten years old, I learned what fear was. I saw my mother scared to death. The nobles were coming for us and she thought she was about to die. Ever since then I have had a plan to ensure that will not happen again."

"But you have guards, a palace, and an army who march at your command."

"They obey me but do not fear me."

"What power does any man have over you?"

Suddenly something heavy slammed into the side of the carriage. Marie-Therese gasped. Louis flinched, rose, and yanked the curtain back. *It cannot be thieves! It will not be assassins! I have my guards!*

There at the window, clinging to the side of the carriage like a monkey, was Philippe.

"Are we there yet?"he shouted gleefully as his hair batted in the wind.

Louis scowled.

"I am bored!"said Philippe. He pulled open the door and

swung inside, wavering, laughing then plopping onto the seat, quite drunk.

"We've no wine if that's what you're looking for," said Louis.

"Ah! I seek conversation! When you've killed as many Spaniards as I have, it's hard to talk about the weather." Philippe looked at Marie-Therese. "No offense. Some of them were very nice."

The carriage continued as Philippe rambled on with disjointed stories of soldiers, army food, his horse, and the smell of victory as Louis stared at him silently. But then the carriage shuddered, slowed, and stopped.

"What is this, now?" asked Philippe.

"Rains, perhaps," said Louis. "The storm took out parts of the road near Chaville."

Then there were angry shouts outside. Philippe's drunken expression changed immediately, as if snatched back to soberness by the voices. He pushed the door open. "Stay here!"

A smaller coach had been knocked over and the coachman and two outriders lay face down beside it, dead, their flesh torn apart by musket fire. The body of a fourth man was sprawled in the mud, apart from the others, a large thug with a black, bloodied cloth around his neck. One of his eyes was gone and his leg was badly shredded.

Louis climbed from his coach and Rohan dismounted his horse. They joined Fabien and Philippe beside the bodies.

"It was a shipment from Paris, Sire," Fabien said. "Stripped of its valuables."

Louis noticed Fabien staring at the one-eyed thug. "Do you know these men?"

"No, Sire, it pains me to say."

Philippe bent over the thug to have a closer look. "This one's alive! There is breath in him still!"

"Deliver him to a doctor!" ordered Fabien. "If he speaks again, it will be to me."

As the thug was hoisted onto a horse, Fabien turned to the King. "My congratulations."

"For what?"

"The treaty. Our war is ended."

Louis surveyed the massacre on the road. "Has it?"

*Jacques and Benoit* sat upon the scaffolding beside the palace, breaking with a meal, gazing out at the gardens and the intricate and endless patterns created by trees, hedges, pools, and statues.

"If I were King we would not have gone to war," said Benoit. "We would have stayed here because it is so beautiful. Because it is becoming something even more beautiful."

Jacques scowled. "And it would have remained so for a week at least. Until the Spanish or Dutch or English ran over us roughshod."

"Every man needs to build something in his life, whether it abides or not."

"We're all dust, Benoit. Nothing last forever."

"This will. I know it."

*The Montespan hummed* as she gazed in her mirror, adding ribbons and feathers to her hair. She would be perfect when the King arrived back at the palace. He would not be able to look away; he would see and want her.

A snide voice spoke from the doorway. "So beautiful and pure."

The Montespan turned to face Chevalier. "Are you in the habit of loitering around ladies' dressing rooms?"

"Every chance I get. I live for it."

The Montespan crossed her arms. "Is that so?"

"No." He stepped closer. "I'm lying. I can think of five things more appealing right now. A warm fire. New stockings. A down pillow. A breeze on a summer's day." He stroked his chin, thinking. "Oh, and cabbages. They're fun. Speaking of which, I love your hair."

"So you're a kind and gentle soul."

"I am, aren't I?" He pointed at the ribbons and feathers on the dressing table. "I hope he's worth it."

The Montespan slammed her hands on the table, stood, and strode defiantly toward Chevalier. So unlike most of ladies at court. "He? Who would that be?"

"Your husband, of course."

"He's in the south, I'm happy to say."

Chevalier wrinkled his nose tauntingly. "Then what other gentleman could possibly inspire you so?"

"The mind boggles. Or rattles, in your case. Like a dead mouse in a box."

"I do so enjoy your tongue, Madame."

"So do I."

"I am an admirer of its edge. So keen. A lacerating organ if ever I saw one."

"No doubt you've seen a few."

"You remind me of a swan on the river, graceful on top but underneath, two fat flippers, thrashing away."

"And a beak that can break your arm."

Chevalier laughed, and there was little gaiety in the sound. "I'd rather you didn't."

"The campaign was long but now they're coming home. I hope you were patient?"

"Oh, I adore waiting. Just think of what it does to wine."

The Montespan glanced at Chevalier's crotch. "Personally, I think it all comes down to the grapes."

*Louis and Marie-Therese* stepped out of the carriage at the palace door to face a vast, welcoming crowd of courtiers. The nobles were dampened from a late afternoon rain, yet all smiled and applauded for the King, including the Montespan, who had worked her way to the front of the throng in her new gown and ribboned hair. Yet the King's mind was elsewhere. Bontemps joined him and the two walked past the throng, noting no one in particular, as the Queen joined her ladies.

"We've won the peace, Bontemps," said Louis. "Now we shall use it. We shall unite the country in celebration, right here. We shall host a Grand Entertainment to be seen by the world. Every noble family shall be represented. Our victory is their victory. Has Cassel replied to our invitation?"

Bontemps shook his head. "Not yet, Sire."

"Send another. And have Louvois tell my armies. There is work for them here as builders. For any able men who want it." They took the steps and entered the palace, the King pausing to stare at Fabien before disappearing into the shadows.

Colbert caught up to Fabien at the base of the steps. "The King grows impatient," he said. "The nobles. The building. The road. Your failure in this regard begins to reflect on us all, Monsieur."

Fabien's voice was cold as iron. "The King shall have justice."

"For all our sakes," said Colbert, as he climbed the steps, "I hope you are right."

Philippe waited in the carriage until his brother had entered the palace, then he got out and swept through the crowd with great flourish. Once inside, he strolled down the wide palace hallway, feeling much the conquering hero with his head high. Guards along the corridor began pounding their halberds upon the floor rhythmically as the King's brother passed, the sound growing louder until it became thunderous praise for their returning champion.

Footmen at the door to Philippe's apartment bowed then opened it on his approach. He walked in, still smiling, with Henriette not far behind.

Chevalier was lounging in a chair, one foot tapping the floor. "Welcome home," he said.

Philippe reached for a leather satchel a servant had placed on the table. He opened it, withdrew a book, and handed it to

Chevalier. "I brought you a present, rescued from a burning monastery. A volume of sacred anthems written by men of chastity." Philippe poured himself a goblet of wine. He sniffed it then drank deeply. "Of course, I thought of you."

"You know me so well," said Chevalier, opening the book. At the top of the page was a symbol that looked like a lower case "h." There were small markings at the top of every page, as well. "Someone's scribbled in it," he scoffed.

Philippe put the goblet down and snatched the book. "Then you shall have no present," he said. He flung the book at Henriette. It barely missed her and fell to the floor. "Here, have a psalm."

Chevalier grabbed Philippe's arm and took him into the bedroom, closing the door behind them. *I know what he wants,* Philippe thought. *I know what he needs, but this time will be different, oh, this time…*

Chevalier shoved Philippe onto the bed. "I've been waiting for this moment for months!" he snarled. He straddled Philippe then reached down to remove his trousers. But in an instant Philippe grabbed Chevalier's shoulders and flipped him over forcefully. Philippe was now on top, savoring Chevalier's stunned expression. "Lies," he shouted. "You wait for no one!"

"Amusing," said Chevalier. "Now let me up."

"Perhaps. When I am finished."

"What on Earth has gotten into you?"

Philippe leaned in close. "That's the fascinating thing about war. You learn so much about yourself. Do you know what I discovered on the line, my sweet Chevalier? When the enemy attacked, when the fighting was close and urgent and the blood flowed bright and red, in the glorious moments nearest to my death, my heart would thunder. My breeches would grow tight because the sword inside them was full and hard. Can you imagine to be in the middle of a battle and your prick is set to burst?"

Chevalier began to struggle, his face growing red with the effort.

"I never knew a Scotsman," said Philippe. "But now I know what a sporran's really for."

Chevalier bucked against Philippe's weight. He could see the enraged passion in the warrior's eyes as well as the bulge of his trousers. "Let me be!"

Philippe stayed atop Chevalier, shaking his head. Then he got up and waved Chevalier away. Chevalier scrambled from the bed and threw the door open, startling Henriette and the young chambermaid fluffing cushions on a chair. Philippe followed, breathing hard, his eyes narrowed, his passion unsated. He looked at Henriette then at the chambermaid.

"Have you ever tasted champagne?" he asked her.

The maid looked desperately at Henriette then at Philippe. She slowly shook her head.

"You may be about to," said Philippe. He took the maid's arm, forced her into the bedroom, and slammed the door. Henriette stared after them, her hands to her mouth.

Chevalier picked up Philippe's wine goblet then put it down. "Honesty," he said, "I don't know what you see in him."

*"You're home,"* *said* Marie-Therese, "but you have not arrived." She stood in the King's outer chamber watching her husband as he gazed from the window at a visible portion of the palace under construction.

"The body travels on wheels, the soul on foot," he replied.

"You're not a faithful man. You can deny it but I see it in your eyes. As only a wife can." Louis glanced at her then back out the window. There was brief sorrow in his eyes, a sad understanding, that he did not want her to witness. "I had never seen you in love until you came to Versailles," she continued. "I'd never seen it shine inside you. And now you would persuade the world to share in it. Even those who wish you ill."

"Not all of them may come."

"You're reaching for the stick when you should offer the carrot. After all, what is it that men truly want?"

Louis looked at her again.

"The answer is simple," she said. "If you're a woman."

*Henriette sat by* herself in one of the ladies' sunny salons, a book in her lap, gazing forlornly at the pages but not seeming to read. Louise and the Montespan nibbled from a dish of dates and watched her from the far side of the room.

"She looks so sad," said Louise.

The Montespan tossed her head and made a face. "I wonder why."

"It's not for us to judge."

"What else are we going to do all day?" She picked another date.

"Athenais, do you recall the favor I asked of you?"

The Montespan took a bite. "Of course."

"Bontemps has told me the King has asked for time alone in the chapel this afternoon. Perhaps… perhaps today is a good day to thank God for our victory."

"Lucky me."

Louise smiled. "To have a friend like you to help me, the luck is all mine."

The Montespan raised a brow, looked at the date, and tossed it back into the dish.

*The war was* over, the treaty signed. It was time for new battles, ones that did not require weapons of the hand but rather weapons of the mind and were as important in their own way.

Louis arose from a restless night, dressed, and went to the War Cabinet room where his ministers were waiting. He walked around the table considering the plans that had been laid out for his consideration. Plans for a party. A party that was to have purpose much more serious than that of mere gaiety.

"Cassel will sit next to me…" said Louis. He glanced at Bontemps, "…and he will come, I assure you."

"If he does not, Sire?" began Louvois.

Louis gave the War Minister a stern stare. "What then, Monsieur?"

"Then you can be assured that neither will de Havilland, de Menthon, Gagnac, all of the northern nobles who are clients of Cassel. You would be sitting alone, Sire."

Louis stared. "How kind of you to remind me." Then he picked up a paper to study it.

Colbert motioned Louvois to the door to speak privately. "Good God, man. Watch your tongue! Unless you are twice the idiot I already take you for."

"Correct me if I'm wrong, but I thought we won the war."

"We could have," said Philippe, strolling into the room, "if you only had let us. Sire."

Louis looked up. "Official business, brother. Let the men do their work."

"I think everyone knows full well the reason the war is over. You are standing in it. Right here."

"Sire," said Colbert. "Your brother has returned to court without remembering where he is."

"Unlike you, Louvois," said Louis, "my brother knows exactly where he is standing. Of that I'm sure."

Philippe hoisted himself up on to the table and sat there, swinging his legs. "Three cheers, then! Let's dance on the broken backs of your bravest men."

Louis frowned. "Cease. Now."

"Oh, you mean, halt! Now *there's* a command!"

"Sire," said Bontemps, "it's clear your brother is not himself."

Louis spoke slowly, evenly. "If not himself, then who is he?"

Philippe laughed sourly, "I am the sound of distant thunder!"

"Clear the room," Louis ordered his ministers. "Leave us."

The men hastened from the room, leaving Louis and Philippe alone. Apart. Staring at one another.

"Your first act on return is to shame me, brother?" Louis asked.

Philippe looked at the papers on the table. "You took my victory. So I take from you your pride."

"Your victory?"

"Your pride."

"*Your* victory?"

"And all you hold dear."

Louis studied his brother, taking in the presence before him, balancing good and distant memories with these words of disloyalty and resentment. "You're not well, brother."

"I wish you could see yourself! Deaf to advice, blinded by sin. Indifferent to everyone but your own dreams. No matter how great, you will have your new palace!"

"What did I tell you in the woods?"

"Good men died in the lie you spun!"

"You said you could be trusted."

"You were sure of the outcome before the first cannons fired. A game to you!"

Louis paused, then, "You told me you had my back."

Philippe jumped off the table and stood behind the King. His smile was cold. "Where am I now?"

*Cassel's men rolled* barrel after barrel of wine and other goods into the chateau's Great Hall as Cassel silently counted the barrels. In his hand was an invitation he'd received from the King. Montcourt stood beside Cassel, rubbing at a gash in his arm, received during the latest skirmish.

"These barrels look familiar," said Cassel. "Oh, yes, of course. They belong to me."

"Thieves, my lord," said Montcourt. "On the road."

"Is that so?" said Cassel. "Terrible business." He smiled at Montcourt then slapped him soundly. "You would attack the cargo in the shadow of the King's convoy? And kill my drivers?"

Montcourt's face stung but he did not acknowledge it. "We did not have accurate information."

"Does your whoring separate you from your brain? Six thousand soldiers home from war, new uniforms on the roads! A force to police it all. Why did you not attack earlier? I gave you as much information as you needed!"

The thuggish Mike came into the hall, stood at the hearth, and spit into the fire. Cassel's eyes narrowed. "I appear to be missing a man."

"Tomas is dead," said Mike.

"A fine and loyal servant was Tomas! And now the King may trace him to me."

Montcourt shook his head. "No witnesses were left alive."

Cassel walked to the fire, studied the dancing flames. "You'd better be right. Because the only person who hangs for this will be you, Montcourt. But cheer up. You shall have his share. Try to stay alive long enough to spend it." Then Cassel threw the King's invitation to the flame.

"*Where are you* hiding it?" Claudine demanded as she searched the cabinets throughout the kitchen. Masson followed on unsteady legs, breathing heavily, reaching for his daughter. "Claudine, I beg of you…stop."

Claudine turned on him. "Don't try to deny it, father! I smell it on your breath! You mask the bitterness with honey and sherry, do not pretend otherwise."

She pulled a large box from the cupboard. On the side was written, *XIV*. Claudine opened the box and studied the bottles containing medical potions meant for the King. There was a small blue bottle among them.

"And you should never take any from here," she said. "You know better!"

There was a sudden pounding on the door. "Open in the name of His Majesty!"

Claudine sat her father down onto a chair, smoothed her apron and hair, and answered the door. Fabien and two Swiss guards pushed their way into the room, carrying a large, bloody, nearly lifeless man who had but one eye and a mangled leg. He was dropped onto the kitchen table, knocking bowls to the floor where they shattered.

"The King commands you save this man," said Fabien.

"I fear he might be too far gone," said Claudine.

"His heart is still beating. I'm not medically minded but I would consider that a good omen."

Claudine bit her lip, looked at Fabien and then at the dying man. Her life depended on this act, she knew. She also knew she needed to act immediately. She snatched a cleaver from beside the stove on which a pot of water was boiling for dinner. "Bring me the kettle and the blue bottle from the box!"

Fabien nodded. One of the men lifted the pot from the fire and the other snatched up the bottle. Claudine found a rag in her pocket, emptied the contents of the blue bottle onto the rag, and stuffed it into the thug's mouth. The thug struggled weakly, a stench of fear and pain rising from his body. Then Claudine tipped the kettle and the boiling water poured over his crushed leg. The thug's cry was muffled against the cloth.

"I said cure him, not cook him," sad Fabien.

"He can lose his life or his leg," said Claudine. She raised the cleaver, grit her teeth, and with all her might drove it down into and through the thug's leg. Blood sprayed.

"Finally," said Fabien. "Some real medicine."

*Louis'* and *Bontemps'* footsteps echoed through the chapel as they walked up the aisle toward the altar. Then Louis spied the back of a head in a pew, a head with golden-brown hair adorned with ribbons. Bontemps stopped in the aisle as the King approached her. The Montespan turned, stood, and curtseyed.

"I only come here when I need to think," she said, cocking her head in a most charming way.

Louis smiled. "I do the same."

"I confess, Sire, the thoughts I am here to think about concern you."

Louis smiled. "And mine. I believe you know a man of interest to me. The Duc de Cassel."

The Montespan's smile faltered then returned. "Why, yes, Sire. I'm quite well acquainted with that…person."

"You've known him a long time, I'm told."

"When I was a young girl I knew him very well. Our families were on terms in those days. Cassel had many clients, as you know. I do not care to remember it."

"I want you to pay him a visit. He refuses to attend our celebration. Since you know him well he may receive you and listen to you. You must persuade him of the error of his ways." He looked at her, and she held his gaze. "And deliver him to me."

The Montespan hesitated, intentionally, seductively. "You knew I would be here, Sire, did you not?"

Louis nodded.

"Then you will also know my answer."

Louis looked back at Bontemps then again at the lady. He smiled. "Take whoever and whatever you need."

The Montespan touched her lip. "There is one person, Sire, who I would ask to join me."

"And you shall have them. And when you return, you shall also have your reward."

The Montespan curtseyed again, and her smile was now brilliant.

"*Hurry up, my* dear, or Henriette will be waiting for you," Sophie's mother called from the other side of the dressing screen. "It's supposed to be the other way around."

Sophie stood behind the screen, dressed and ready, gazing at the note that had been lowered in a bucket from a scaffold, a note from the handsome builder. It read, *Top of stairs behind the chapel. Tomorrow noon. – Benoit.* The clock on the mantle beside her read ten minutes to the hour. *Ten minutes!*

"You go ahead, Mother," Sophie said, running her finger gently over the note, thinking of his eyes, his hair, wondering what his touch might be like.

On the far side of the screen Beatrice sighed, then said, "Very well."

Sophie listened as her mother walked to the door, as the door opened, as it was shut. She smiled, let out a deep breath, and came around the screen.

There stood Beatrice in the center of the room. Her face was flushed with rage and fear. She saw the note, gasped, and ripped it away from Sophie.

"Give that back!"

"Shut up!"

Beatrice read the paper then crushed it in her hand. She stood, breathing hard, shaking the fist with the note. "You will not associate with this creature!"

Sophie tossed her hair. "You cannot tell me who to speak to."

"Oh, I can, my little one. You have not a clue. Not a single, dust mote of an inkling what you are dealing with. And what you are doing to me!" Sophie tried to push past her mother but Beatrice shoved her back. "You must promise me you will never see this boy! If you do, you will destroy everything I have worked for! Do you understand? Everything!"

Sophie stared. Her mother had been upset with her before, but this was different. This was so much more. "What is wrong, Mother?"

"The King wants proof! Surely you know that. He demands we all provide our proof!"

"It is coming from Pau, Mother, you said so." Then she saw furious tears in her mother's eyes, tears that lingered then fell to her cheeks. "It isn't coming?"

"We are not who we claim to be."

"I…I do not understand."

"No, you don't. But that doesn't change the truth. You were born a Huguenot. A Protestant, just like your mother."

Sophie put her hands over her ears. "Please! Don't. No more!"

"I found a way to make us noble and keep us noble. But to do so requires your help. If you work against me, all is lost."

"But how can I be noble if I'm not?"

"Do you feel noble? In your heart?"

Sophie nodded.

"Then you are. And you will never think otherwise again."

"What happens if the King finds out?"

"Then we hang. Like all the rest."

Sophie buried her face in her hands and began to cry.

"Oh, dear," said Beatrice, her lips pouting. "Is your mother scaring you? Let it out. There's a good girl." Sophie looked up for some motherly compassion, and Beatrice slapped her soundly. "Now never do it again!"

Sophie drew her arm across her face, wetting her sleeve with tears. "Why are you telling me this? I don't believe anything you say anymore!"

"You had better," said Beatrice, stony resolve returning to her eyes. "Because your life now depends on doing exactly as I tell you."

*Sophie's mind reeled* with her mother's revelations as she hurried on her way to the Henriette's apartment, not wanting to be seen by any other nobles, who might see through her and know her terrible truth. And what of Henriette? Would she read the deceit in her face? And if she did, what then?

"There you are." Sophie turned slowly to see the Montespan coming up to join her.

"Madame," said Sophie with an awkward curtsey.

"Sophie, dear," said the Montespan. "I need to borrow you for an errand."

"But my lady will not permit it."

The Montespan smiled an odd smile and touched Sophie's cheek. "At the King's request," she said.

It was only a matter of an hour before the two were in a coach heading north. The Montespan sat on a bench across from Sophie, gazing alternately out the window at the passing French countryside and at the girl she'd brought with her.

Sophie's expression was hard to read, though it was not a happy one.

"You do not speak much,"said the Montespan."I like that."

Sophie turned her gaze toward the lady."I'm here to serve you. And my King, of course. I'm in your debt."

"Oh, believe me. It's my pleasure entirely. After all, the King asked for you himself."

"Is that so?"

"Yes. That's what I said."

Sophie took this in. Then,"How is your husband?"

The Montespan stared at the girl. She shook her head."Oh, dear. And you were doing so well."

"I…My lady, please accept my apology. I had no idea."

"None, clearly. But to answer your questions, I do not know. But luckily he is far, far away."

"Don't you miss him?"

"When I was a child I had dysentery, typhus, and rickets. I miss them all more than I miss my husband." She brushed hair from her eyes."Marry for power and rut for love, my dear. If you get a good one, do both. If you retain anything from this journey, let that be it."

*Henriette was startled* from her reading when Louis entered her outer chamber. She put down the book of psalms.

"A diverting volume?"he asked as he approached her.

Henriette sighed."Not in the least, I'm afraid."

Louis looked around the room, then back at Henriette. "I've stolen your lady. Madame de Montespan had need of a young girl."

Henriette tried to hide her disappointment. "Well, of course. Anything for Athenais."

Louis picked up the book and flipped casually through the pages. "Where did you get this?"

"My husband brought it back from the front. It was a present for Chevalier, but he did not want it, so —"

"A hand-me-down."

"I'm used to it."

Louis stared more closely at the pages, then thumbed through them slowly, noting the symbols scrawled on each one. One looked to be a lower case "h." His eyes widened.

"The pages are all defaced," said Henriette. "Such a shame."

Louis looked up at Henriette. "Where did you say my brother found this?"

*Chevalier leaned against* the windowpane in Beatrice's apartment and linked his fingers atop his head. "How is Sophie settling in?" he asked.

Beatrice put down the sleeve she was embroidering and gave him the most confident smile she could muster. "She's shown great promise."

"Indeed? Then perhaps you can explain why she was seen leaving in a coach with Madame de Montespan."

Beatrice's needle went still. "I…I had no idea."

"When she returns, I want a full daily report on how Henriette spends her time. Who she meets, what she writes, all of it."

Beatrice made another stitch. It was crooked. "Ah," she said. "Of course."

Chevalier raised a brow. "What is it?"

"Why you were so keen to place her there."

"You surprise me, my darling cousin. I would have thought you were always two steps ahead of me. If I were you, I'd make sure of it." He looked out the window. In the distant blue above the forest a flock of starlings created intricate, delicate murmurations. "And for Heaven's sake, Beatrice, put your papers in order. Your lack of compliance is starting to reflect badly on me."

"Our papers are to come by road."

"Then I would suggest praying hard for their swift arrival."

*Fabien unrolled the* map cipher and placed it on the table in the War Cabinet room. Then he opened the book of psalms and placed it beside the cipher. Louis, Bontemps, Colbert, and Louvois stepped closer. The air in the room was heavy with anticipation.

"What is it?" asked Louis.

"It's been identified as a Cistercian codex," said Fabien. "Hailing from the low countries. Very rare and almost forgotten. Used, it appears, as an alternative to Roman numerals."

"So these are merely numbers," said Louvois.

"Which correspond to letters." Fabien looked at the King. "The book hails from Cambray, Sire, in the Spanish Netherlands. Which suggests the plot to kill you started there. The Dutch were nervous of our war. And they meant to stop it by any means in their power."

Louis let out a low breath. "You suppose William of Orange would send a man to kill me? Posing as a Spaniard?"

"I do not just suppose, Sire, I believe it. And what is more, they were sent to find a friendly face. Which means their supporters are amongst us. And they will certainly try again."

Louis' nod was slow, measured.

"The first message is very simple," said Fabien, picking up a paper on which translations had been written. "It says, 'Kill the men who bring this map.' The second is more intriguing. A riddle, in fact." He handed the paper to the King.

"'The end is near,'" Louis read. "'Make your peace with God.'"

*Louise dreamed she* was alone in a large room without windows, without doors, yet one lit by a blindingly bright sun. She moaned but could not cry out. She struggled but could not move. Then someone came up behind her and kissed her neck. She felt a rush of hope at the touch; she knew this man. She leaned back into him, coming up out of the darkness of her dream…

Into the darkness of her bedchamber.

"I was not expecting you tonight," she whispered through sleep-sluggish lips, trying her best to see the King's face in the candlelight. His kisses continued on her neck. Then he pulled up her nightgown and kissed her belly and the sensitive flesh down to the space between her legs. "But I would recognize your caress anywhere."

He kissed the moist crevice, licked it. She sighed.

Then he looked up at Louise. This time the light fell fully upon his face. "It runs in the family, my dear."

Louise screamed and rolled from the bed. "Christ have mercy!"

Philippe sat back on his heels on the bed, his eyes narrowed ominously. "I will say this for my brother. He has great taste."

"Get out!" cried Louise. "I will tell the King!"

"Tell him what, exactly? Dear heart, I am his *brother*. I will always be his brother. You are merely passing through, so if I were you I'd enjoy it while you can. It feels warm when the sun shines but believe me, as soon as he's done with you…" Philippe grabbed Louise's arm, twisted it, and forced her back onto the bed, "…all the lights will go out."

*A guard helped* the Montespan and Sophie step out of the carriage in front of the towering, ominous Cassel Chateau. Dead leaves rattled across the broad steps leading to the front entrance. The evening air was bitter.

"I do the talking," the Montespan said, gripping Sophie's arm and speaking sternly. "And if he does succeed in cornering you, pretend to enjoy it. Take it from me, he loses interest if there's no one to fight."

Sophie shivered. Her insides tumbled like the dead leaves. "Yes, my lady," she whispered.

"Good girl."

They took the steps as bravely as either was able.

Inside, a servant directed them to sit on a bench in the foyer. They waited in the light of a single candle on a sideboard, listening to the sounds deep within the other rooms. There was a portrait of Cassel upon the far wall, but the Montespan did her best not to look at it.

There were footsteps heading their way. It was Cassel, his head high, his gait confident. "Ah! My little fig. What an unexpected pleasure."

The Montespan and Sophie rose and curtseyed.

"My lord," said the Montespan. "Delightful to see you again."

"Little Athenais, all grown up." Then he looked at Sophie. "So much beauty in one afternoon. I was born under a lucky star."

"I'm here, sir, on the King's business," said the Montespan. "He's not heard from you since inviting you to his party."

"Did I not reply? How remiss. Pass on my apologies to His Majesty. I trust he will understand why I cannot attend his celebrations, as joyful as I am at our glorious ceasefire."

With that he turned to leave.

"The gathering at Versailles is of course a celebration," said the Montespan. "But it is also a memorial to pay homage to those noble men who have given their lives for this peace."

Cassel turned back. "You will thank His Majesty but I prefer to pay any homage I have quite alone."

The Montespan and Cassel's eyes met, locked. There was a long silence. Then Cassel continued, "I appreciate your traveling so far to act as royal postman. I'd be honored if you and your lady would be my guests for super. But be advised, my mind will not change."

"I hope to persuade you otherwise."

Cassel tapped his lips. "You've done well for yourself. I knew you had potential. I flatter myself you've come so far. Admit. I taught you well, yes?"

Sophie glanced anxiously between the two.

Then the Montespan said, "Is it not said that Christ teaches us that only by going through Hell can we reach Heaven? So yes, I suppose I have you to thank for that."

"Ah, sweet Athenais," replied Cassel without smiling. "Always fighting back."

A clock chimed low within the bowels of the chateau. Cassel extended his arm to usher the ladies down the hall. Sophie could see the cold, hard iron in the Montespan's eyes, and it terrified her.

The dining room reminded Sophie of that in Louis' ever-growing palace, with vaulted ceilings, countless portraits of stern-faced men, and a table long enough to accommodate forty or more guests. Yet in spite of the roaring fire in the fireplace and the silver dishes on which the food was served, there was a sense of age and decay in the place.

The Montespan took a bite of boiled duck then looked at

Cassel, who sat beside her at the head of the table. "My lord," she said, "the King believes that without you his celebration would be incomplete."

"His Majesty flatters me," said Cassel.

"But he's aware of your mind, of your love of your lands. And so he has an alternative proposition."

Cassel's eyebrow lifted. "Yes?"

"If you cannot come to the party, the party will come to you."

"What do you mean?"

"You will host the party. The King will move the court here. He will send his army of builders to transform and rebuild your chateau and outbuildings to be ready to receive the many thousands of guests who will come to celebrate."

Cassel laughed a strange, nervous laugh. Sophie anxiously clutched her hands together beneath the table.

"His Majesty jokes at my expense," said Cassel.

"No, my lord," said the Montespan. "It is the party that will be at your expense."

Cassel waved one hand. "It would not be a problem, of course, but –"

The Montespan tipped her head. "Come now. I've seen your house. Cushions are frayed. The walls grow mold. Your chateau is just like you, a decent exterior but underneath the façade it is rotten to the core."

"I'm wealthy even beyond your reckoning!"

"You used to be. You would brag of your assets and your proxies in Paris. But they are not working anymore, are they? I expect your staff have not be paid in a long while."

Cassel picked up a piece of bread then put it back on his plate. He rubbed his chin, trying to maintain calm but his rage was visible in the reddening of his face. "It would be too inconvenient for His Majesty to attend."

"Not as inconvenient as you being absent from Versailles. At his invitation."

There was nothing more to say. The trap laid and the prey snared. Cassel squirmed slightly in his chair, then looked past the Montespan at Sophie, seated beside her.

"Beautiful, isn't she?" asked the Montespan.

Cassel patted his knee. "Come here, child. How old are you?"

Sophie leaned back in an attempt to hide behind the Montespan.

"I love it when they play hard to get," said Cassel.

"Now, now," said the Montespan. "The sweetmeats come at the end of the meal, sir, not during. And I assure you, the King is planning a most extraordinary banquet."

Sophie stifled a cry, and felt she would lose everything she had just eaten.

*Midnight approached. Louis* and two guards entered Henriette's bedchamber where the lady and her husband lay sleeping. Henriette was startled awake at the creak of a floorboard, but Philippe continued to snore loudly and drunkenly, his face against a pillow. Henriette slid her feet off the bed to receive the King but he waved his hand, indicating she needn't get up.

Louis stood at the bed and nodded at Philippe. "I'm told he drank nine bumpers of the Turin Rosa Solis after supper."

"Yes," said Henriette. "And three more after arriving here. Then he fell asleep."

There was affection in Louis' eyes as he leaned closer, over his brother. "When he sleeps, he could be a child again."

"We all could," said Henriette.

Suddenly Philippe's eyes flashed open. He roared and grabbed Louis by the throat and then he screamed as if in the midst of battle. Louis gasped in the chokehold as the guards hastened forward. Then Philippe saw whose throat he was clutching and let go. Louis jumped back, coughing and massaging his neck.

"Oh. It's you," said Philippe, his voice thick with drink and fatigue. "My brother. The magician."

Louis frowned. "Magician?"

Philippe pointed at Henriette. "Her brother in England allied with two others against you. The prospect of a winter campaign and the supply lines of grain running thin. Only you could sign a ceasefire and call it a victory."

Louis shook his head sadly. "My brother, we'll talk in the morning."

"Better now," said Philippe. "I do not think I'll be awake tomorrow."

"You have not officially replied to our invitation. I'm assuming you intend to come."

Philippe pulled himself up to sit on the bed's edge. He lifted a glass half-filled with wine from the bed-stand. "Oh, yes, sir. I do as commanded by my superiors."

"Drink your fill tonight," said Louis. "I wish no repeat of this at our entertainment."

"I will entertain myself, then. As you always said, brother, there is no greater glory than dying for one's King and country. But I have to disagree based on personal experience. I have to say the greatest glory lies in living."He held the wine glass up as if toasting the King, then downed it in a gulp.

*Tomas, Cassel's thug,* lay unconscious on the table in Masson's kitchen, the stub of his amputated leg charred black so he wouldn't bleed to death. Claudine watched him closely as her father sat in his chair, nervously picking at the skin on his knuckles. Fabien stared at Claudine and then Tomas. Claudine knew the peril she faced should the man on the table die.

But then Tomas' eyelid fluttered. He coughed, moaned, and blinked. Claudine saw in his eyes the realization of what had happened and the mortal danger he now faced. With his broken hand he beckoned Claudine closer and then he whispered,"Help me, please."

Fabien stepped closer to the table and stared at his captive. "Impressive," he said. "I shall call him Lazarus. And you, woman. I do not yet know what I shall call you."Then he went to the box on the counter and took out a scalpel.

"Who is this man?" asked Claudine. "What did he do to you?"

Fabien brought the scalpel back to the table and held it up so that it reflected the light of the kitchen. Tomas struggled to get up but Fabien put his hand on the man's chest and held him down.

"He's done nothing. Said nothing," said Fabien.

"Do not undo the work —" began Claudine.

"Quiet," said Fabien. Then he leaned in to Tomas and put the scalpel close to his face. "Charlotte Parthenay died in my arms. Your musket, was it?"

"I didn't kill her," said Tomas.

"But you were there. Who did?"

"I did not see!"

"Well, then. If you were not looking, you won't need this, will you?" With that, Fabien drove the scalpel into the socket of Tomas' remaining eye. Tomas screamed and thrashed. Fabien worked the scalpel around and cut the eye out. He handed it to Claudine, who stared at it, horrified. "For your collection."

"Please!" said Claudine. "Let him live."

"I promise I will. I just need him to answer a simple question."

"Give me your word!"

"I give you my word. I will let him live." Then Fabien leaned over Tomas again. The man's eyelids flapped uselessly over the raw, bleeding sockets in his face. He drooled and whimpered. "Whom do you serve?"

Tomas caught his breath. "The King."

"Yes, yes. But who is your Lord? To whom have you sworn your oath?" He pressed the tip of the scalpel on Tomas' throbbing jugular.

"Cassel!" said Tomas. "Duc de Cassel."

"Thank you," said Fabien. Then he slashed Tomas' neck, opening the artery. Tomas wailed again and bled out on the table.

Claudine raised her hands in horror. "You promised me! You said you would let him live!"

"And I did. I let him live an extra three seconds. I'm a man of my word."

*Jacques was on* his knees with his trowel, filling soil around one of the newest orange trees, his shirt unbuttoned against the warming afternoon. He was so engrossed in his work he saw the royal boots before he realized the King had approached him. He scrambled to his feet and bowed. "Sire, I'm honored."

Louis looked at Jacques and then out across the vast gardens that had been planned and created, and at those on the peripheries that were still being created. Then he said, "What does war do to a man?"

Jacques brushed dirt from his knees. "You are no stranger to it, Sire."

"When he returns home, for example," said Louis.

"No man leaves a battlefield the same way they entered. Many see ghosts. The smell of meat roasting on a fire can spark a memory as fresh as when it happened. Some go mad. Some take to drink. Some take their own lives." One side of his lip hitched in a half smile. "Some grow orange trees for the King."

"You returned as another?"

"I only felt aggrieved when I was not paid."

"What happened then?"

"I took whatever measures were needed."

"What did your family make of your choice?"

"I lost my family in war. Three sons, all dead, killed in your service."

"My prayers are with them."

"No need, Sire. There's no place for us in the house of God."

"There is if you are reconciled."

"I've nothing to confess, Sire. I know I committed no sin."

It was then he saw Louis gazing at the large, raised scar on the gardener's chest. Louis nodded slightly. "If you say so," he said.

As Louis walked away, Jacques called, "May the celebration be glorious, Sire."

"I will make sure of it," said the King.

*The celebration was* held in the palace's amphitheater, a large, beautiful open-air auditorium in the gardens. The night was dark but the celebration bright, with fire throwers entertaining as musicians played. Garlands of ivy were hung in nearby trees, and centerpieces crafted from fruits and feathers adorned the tables. Large golden planters, as tall as a man and bearing the face of the Sun King, were filled with evergreens shaped into animals. Louis sat on a dais in the center of the amphitheater as a long line of nobles waited to take their turns paying their respects to the royal family. Marie-Therese sat to the King's left and Louise was to his right. There was an empty chair beside the Queen, meant for Philippe, who had yet to show himself. Henriette sat beside the empty chair and Chevalier and Beatrice stood behind the King, all watching the procession.

Amid the procession of nobles were the Montespan and Cassel, with Sophie on Cassel's arm. Beatrice, who stood behind the King with Chevalier, smiled with pride. Nobles noted the presence of Cassel, and spoke to each quietly, astounded to see the powerful, headstrong northern noble right here at Versailles, here at the King's beckoning. Sophie's friends likewise nudged each other, surprised to see the beautiful yet clumsy girl with such an esteemed noble.

Louis nodded at the Montespan, then looked at Cassel and Sophie. "A handsome couple, don't you think?" he asked Louise.

"No, Sire, I do not," replied Louise. She and Marie-Therese exchanged uneasy, disapproving looks.

"Cassel," called a noble in the crowd as Cassel, the Montespan, and Sophie passed by him on their way to the dais. "You surprise me, that you are here."

Cassel smiled elegantly, determined to play the part, determined to retain his power and dignity in spite of the place where he now found himself. "How could I stay away?"

Then it was his turn to be presented before the King. Louis motioned with his hand. Cassel took Sophie's arm to lead her forward. But the Montespan took Sophie's other arm and drew her back. "Sorry," she said. "I must return her. She isn't mine to give away. She's on loan."

Cassel spoke angrily through his teeth, his smile never fading. "You cunt."

The Montespan grinned. "Men think to shame us by calling

us the name of our sex. Of course I'm a cunt, and proud of it. You, on the other hand, are a prick. A tiny, shriveled, pointless prick." Then she turned to Sophie. "Go, be free."

Sophie vanished into the crowd.

"You will pay for this," said Cassel.

"I already have," said the Montespan. "And it was worth every penny."

Cassel stepped up to the dais as Louis extended his hand. At that moment, Fabien whispered in the King's ear. Louis whispered something back, and Fabien retreated.

The last thing Cassel wanted to do was kiss the royal hand. He hated losing. But even more, he hated losing face. He leaned forward to kiss the hand. And in that moment, Louis lowered his hand so far down that Cassel was forced into almost a kneeling position.

"Bow to your King," said Louis with great satisfaction as Cassel kissed the royal hand. And the nobles spoke quietly to one another, muttering in amazement that the mighty Cassel had bowed to His Majesty.

Near the edge of the party, Sophie waited and watched until her mother was otherwise occupied with several noble ladies, and then she wandered away from the celebration, away from the complexities and intrigues of those in power, seeking solitude and peace that might lie in the darkness of the outer gardens.

"Pssst!"

She spun around to find Benoit beckoning to her from beside a boxwood. She looked to see that no one else was nearby, and went to him.

"You ignored my invitation," said Benoit.

Sophie looked at him, at his handsome face in the moonlight, at his hopeful yet sad eyes. "I could not come. My duty called me elsewhere."

"I want to believe you."

"Please try."

Benoit stepped close to Sophie, so close their bodies almost touched. "Follow me," he said.

"No."

"You want to. I can tell."

"It can never be, between us."

"I know. But come with me." Then he reached out for her hand and she did not resist. She ran with him into a grove of roses, losing a shoe as she went.

*Louis commanded Cassel* to sit beside him on the dais, and silently, together, they watched the fire performers juggle, toss, and catch flaming batons and hoops.

At last Louis spoke, leaning casually on his elbow. "As children we're told not to play with fire, but they seem to enjoy it."

"I see no merit in it," said Cassel. "No true skill."

"A little burning is good for the soul, don't you think?"

"Joan of Arc, France's courageous heroine, might disagree with you," said Cassel. "Or Lucifer."

The King looked straight on at Cassel. "I fancy that in another life we might have been friends, Cassel."

"I do not give myself to fancy. I have no time for it."

"That gives me surprise."

"I don't care for those, either."

"How unfortunate for you."

There was a sudden *BOOM!* The partiers spun about, some gasping, others screaming, to find the source of the noise. And then overhead a huge, flaming flower exploded, sending out a sparkling shower against the black sky; the fireworks had begun and the guests applauded. Cassel made a face and rose from his seat.

"So soon?" asked Louis.

"I've seen burning paper before." Cassel stepped from the dais and called to his servants, who waited at the periphery of the party. "Bring my carriage!" Then he stormed off.

As Cassel departed, Philippe wandered onto the dais, carrying two glasses of wine, and plopped down on the empty seat. "I thought he'd never leave. Here, drink with me." He handed a glass to Louis and smiled.

"I am grateful you are here, brother," said the King. "Truly I am."

"And," Philippe said, lifting his glass in an informal toast, "for once I am inclined to believe you." Louis raised his own glass in answer to the gesture, and they drank together.

*As fireworks exploded* overhead, Benoit and Sophie watched from a bench at the edge of the orangery, protected by the night. She leaned into him and he into her.

She lifted her face to his and he kissed her, deeply. And her soul burst with joy as bright as any firework.

*Philippe put down* his empty wine glass and looked up at the fireworks. His body was loose and his head light; it felt as if the chair below him were spinning. *Another drink*, he managed to think. *I need more wine.*

Then three fireworks rocketed upward and exploded simultaneously. The sound was deafening, much like musket and cannon fire on the battlefield. Philippe blinked, stared, and instead of flaming sprays of stars he suddenly saw flaming bodies flying outward, wounded and dead soldiers in the air, severed arms and legs plummeting earthward, blown apart in battle.

He stood from his chair, his face blank, his eyes glazed. He wobbled a moment then staggered away.

"Brother?" called Louis.

Philippe disappeared into the crowd. Louis hurried from his chair to follow, waving back guards and guests. Philippe stumbled from the amphitheater, along a stretch of rose bushes, and down toward the pool house where there was no one to see or hear but the moon, the stars, and a polecat sniffing about the vegetation for mice. There, he fell to the ground, covered his head with his hands, and wailed.

*My brother!* Louis knelt beside him and drew him into his arms. He felt the heat and the angst that raged there. Then Philippe pushed away, holding up his hand as if it was a shield.

"On the field, I saw a young man," he said. "He carried his brother in a sack over his shoulder. He told me he'd made a promise to their mother, to take him home." He paused, then, "Would you do that for me? I wondered. I would, I know. But you? I do not know."

Louis nodded compassionately. "Philippe, you think because I am King I am not also a brother. That I may have all I want and yearn for nothing. Even a King can't have all the life he would want to live. It's you who live those parts of my life for me. It's you who truly lives the life yearned for by a King."

Philippe drove a fist to his forehead as if wanting to bash the terror from his mind.

"The war still rages in you," said Louis.

"And it will never cease."

"Stop."

"You cannot resist the last word, can you?"

"Brother."

Philippe snarled. "Why do I do this to myself?"

Louis reached for Philippe again, gathered him, and held him for the barest moment until Philippe wrestled free. "Go!" he shouted. "Leave me! I command you!"

Louis stood. And this once, he obeyed his brother's command.

*As the fireworks* continued to fire upward and explode in dazzling showers, a figure in dark clothing entered the empty chapel, stepped silently into the penitent's side of the confessional, and pulled the door shut. With gloved hands the figure placed a small roll of parchment into a gap in the slats, a gap that would be overlooked unless someone knew it was there. Then the figure quietly slipped away.

*Beatrice approached Fabien* as he gazed at the loud, brilliant display overhead. "I believe I was promised a walk in the garden," she said.

Fabien glanced around. "We are in a garden now."

"So we are."

Fabien studied her, his face unreadable in the night. "Follow me," he said at last.

They walked in silence for several minutes, away from the celebration and into the obscurity of a dark garden maze, and then Fabien said, "I need to know more about you."

Beatrice cocked her head. She would not let the conversation go as she feared he wanted it to. "Are you someone who enjoys music?"

"Where were you born?" asked Fabien.

"Do you enjoy theatre, perhaps?"

"Where would you like to die?"

"How do you spend your time away from your work?"

Beatrice stopped. Fabien did, as well, and gazed at her with a mixture of longing and hesitation. "I would like to ask you all of these things," he said, "but my problem is I cannot stop looking at you."

Beatrice smiled, her lips pouting ever so slightly. "Well, that is most kind of you to say."

"I find you distracting. For when I look upon you –"

"All thoughts stop."

Fabien stepped closer. Beatrice felt his desire enveloping her, almost burning her. "Then we are in agreement," he whispered.

"I suppose we are."

His hand touched hers, briefly, a spark ready to ignite a blaze. She moaned in expectation. Then he threw his arm around her waist, pulled her into himself, and kissed her. She kissed him back and then drew him down with her to the grassy pathway. Where their fireworks exploded.

*The party was* over. The Montespan entered her apartment, shut the door, and moved to the hearth, where she leaned on the mantle and wept openly. *I am strong! I must be strong! Nothing matters but cunning and strength and beauty!* Yet now, alone, she felt as vulnerable as a newborn foal.

There was movement behind her. She turned to see the King standing by her bed. Quickly she blinked away the tears and lifted her chin.

"I'm grateful to you, Madame," said Louis. "You understand more than all of them."

"Understand what, Sire?"

"In order to rule, the first thing you must learn is sacrifice."

The Montespan watched, waited, as the King came to

her, and ran his hands along her face, her shoulders. *Yes*, she thought. *At last!*

He kissed her cheeks, tasted her lips, and pulled her gown off her shoulders, releasing her breasts to the cool of the room. She closed her eyes and cupped them, lifting them so he could touch and suck the nipples. He did so fervently, drawing on them so hard that a most delicious pain coursed through her body. Then he lifted her, carried her to her bed, and she gave herself to him completely.

*Morning dawned gray* and dreary. Cassel climbed from his carriage and stared in horror and disbelief. His ancestral home, his chateau, which had sat so long upon the hill amid the trees, was burned to the ground, leaving only a hulking, smoking shell. And hanging from the gatepost was the body of Tomas, a swarm of flies around his head, his red, empty eye sockets gazing accusingly at Cassel. A few servants and peasants had gathered near the gate, watching in stunned silence.

Ruins. All was ruins.

There was the sound of hoof beats. Cassel spun about to see a messenger on horseback coming his way. The messenger reined in his horse and pointed an accusing finger at Cassel.

"The King requires your papers! Your noble papers, sir. Your lineage."

Cassel shook his head. "They are ashes."

"Then you are without proof?" The messenger pulled a scroll from his sack and handed it to Cassel. It was closed with the royal seal. "Only true nobles are exempt from tax. Arrears are to be repaid in full."

"I have nothing. It is…all gone."

"Then," said the messenger, standing in his stirrups and waving his arm, "you are in the King's debt!" A small cadre of uniformed police rode up and circled Cassel. "Place this man under arrest!"

As two police dismounted to take hold of him, Cassel looked once more in despair and fury at the smoke and the devastation. And from a nearby hill, Montcourt watched it all.

*The new line* of young police recruits stood at attention along the royal road, listening intently, ready to swear their allegiance to their King and their new positions. Among the recruits stood a tall, thuggish man who had once made his home at Chateau Cassel.

Mike.

With Bontemps at his side, Fabien lifted the paper with the oath and began to read, "I hereby swear to protect this road and the lands that surround it with my life. To police it, in the King's name…."

*Philippe lay on* his bed, his hair disheveled, his head on the pillow, asleep at last. Louis sat on one side of him and Henriette sat on the other, each holding one of his hands and watching his face. So peaceful now, lifted in slumber from the hellish torments of war. Then Henriette looked at Louis and he looked at her. Both felt the desire for one another, the longing and the despair at the impossibility of their love. When Henriette reached out for Louis he did not take her hand. Tears filled her eyes and she let her hand drop.

# 6

*Louis walked briskly* along the wide stone walkway beside the palace of Versailles with the Montespan, Bontemps, and guards beside him and Philippe and the newly arrived guests smiling and doing their best to keep up. He strode as the Sun King he was, powerful, passionate, and confident, basking in the glory of all that had been accomplished in the past many months and the opportunity to show it off.

One of the guests, the dashing Pascal de Saint Martin, gazed in awe at the splendor of the sun-kissed palace, a structure so majestic no one could take in the entirety of its grandeur at once. Only birds of the air would have the proper perspective, and even they could not comprehend the majesty of it all.

"Later," Louis called back, "we shall tour the gardens. But first, the east wing, extended beyond the original lodge built by my father. It is here that you and your families will be accommodated. It is my wish that you see Versailles not as the royal palace but as your home. A place of leisure and conversation, of light and joy!"

They rounded a corner to find a large crowd of builders seated on the ground and on the scaffolding, their arms crossed, tools down.

Louis slowed his step and his smile faded. "The workers are idle," he said to Bontemps.

At the top of the scaffolding stood a dark-haired, one-eyed builder, a former soldier. He shook his fist and glared down at the nobles. The nobles looked at him then at the King, confused.

"Our shared glory!" the veteran shouted. "Look, Sire!" He wavered at the scaffolding's edge, his arms out as if he wanted to fly. Bontemps motioned urgently to the guards to get the man down.

"What victories I've seen! I fought for you at Douai, Sire! I lost an eye for you at Besançon."

"For which you shall be compensated," called Louis.

"And how much for my brother, Sire? Crushed by a stone as he built your walls? Or my nephew, half dead of gangrene?"

The guards grabbed for the scaffolding but a young builder scrambled up ahead of them.

"What do you want?" shouted the King.

"You promised France would honor its heroes." The veteran teetered precariously.

"I did."

"Lies! We live and die like slaves! You say you are France, but if you truly were you would know our suffering! You would take the pain away."

The builder reached the top of the scaffolding and crept toward the veteran. "Don't be a fool," he said.

The veteran laughed hopelessly. "The King makes fools of us all."

Bontemps shouted, "Come down at once!"

The veteran held up a rope noose and slipped it around his neck. "You wish me to descend? Very well." He directed his gaze at Philippe. "As your brother commands."

The builder grabbed for the veteran, but it was too late. The veteran leapt as the crowd gasped and covered their faces. When he reached the end of the rope, there was a sickening snap. His body jerked and his mouth spewed blood. His dangling body came to rest directly in front of the King, and Louis turned to stare accusingly at his brother.

*A summit meeting* was held in the War Cabinet room. Louis paced back and forth as his men stood around the table, glancing at one another.

"The man believed he and his fellow soldiers have not been given the honor and respect they earned on the battlefield," Colbert offered.

Louis continued walking. "They were soldiers! Do they not now take their orders?"

"Their grievances are many, Sire," said Louvois. "And many suffer from injuries sustained in their work that are still untreated."

"How many have joined this stoppage?"

"Two thousand, Sire," said Colbert. "Unless they return to work, construction cannot continue. Winter is fast approaching. With no completed lodgings, I fear our new arrivals might soon depart."

"We must speak to these men," said Louis. "In the meantime, the rest of the builders shall continue."

Colbert shook his head. "They refuse to work, too. They claim working conditions are too harsh and little attention is paid to their safety. We lose half a dozen men per week. Many more injured. We have a reckoning of compensation."

"What will that man's family receive?"

"Nothing, since his injuries were self-inflicted."

"Pay him, anyway."

"That may assuage the grief, but not the anger of the men."

Louis moved to the large globe by the window and touched the surface where Europe lay. "By the age of thirty, Alexander the Great had created an empire stretching from Greece to India. But without his men, King Darius would have driven him into the sea. We retook the Spanish Netherlands. Soon, we shall turn our eyes to Holland. We profit from our trade with the lands of King Annaba even as the Duc de Cassel bows his head. I will not be pushed into the sea by a builder on a scaffold." He looked at each of his ministers in turn. "Order them back to work."

*Bontemps led Cassel* along a palace corridor. "The king will be delighted to see you here,"Bontemps said. "He has extended to all nobles a financial inducement. Those who wish to build a house at the periphery of the grounds will be forgiven all outstanding debts."

"Then I shall begin my planning at once,"replied Cassel, head high with satisfaction, taking in the elegance of his new surroundings, the tall arched ceilings, the elegant artwork and gilded frames, sparkling chandeliers, and luxurious furnishing.

"In the meanwhile,"Bontemps continued, "we'll do our best to make you comfortable within the palace."

They reached a door at the end of the corridor. Bontemps unlocked it to reveal a tiny room with a wooden bench, a plain desk, and a single small window. Cassel's face fell."It's hardly bigger than a broom cupboard!"

Bontemps nodded."I believe it was a broom cupboard. Welcome to Versailles."

Cassel walked inside and Bontemps closed the door. Cassel stood in disbelief as several drops of water leaked from the ceiling onto his head. This was to be his new home? He clenched his fists, sat on the bench, and then stood up again.

There was a soft whooshing sound. Cassel looked down to see a letter with a seal and a lower case"h"sliding into the room beneath the door. He picked it up.

And at the same moment Cassel was opening his letter in his tiny palace room, other letters of the same content were being clandestinely folded, sealed with wax, and marked with an "h," then being delivered hand to hand beneath a card table, slipped in saddle bags, and pressed between the pages of a Bible, shared most carefully and cautiously with just the right persons.

*As Louis' personal* dresser adjusted the folds on the King's jacket, Bontemps ushered Marie-Therese and Louise de la Valliere into his chamber. Marie-Therese gave Louise an encouraging look but Louise remained silent, her eyes downcast.

"Your horses are being fed extra grain, Madame de la Valliere," said Louis. "Are you planning a journey?"

"She yearns for release, Sire," said Marie-Therese.

Louis waved the dresser away. "From what?"

Louise slowly lowered her shawl and turned, exposing the wounds on her back. "From torture, Sire," she said.

"You only torture yourself, it seems."

"She desires a cloistered life in a convent," said the Queen. "She's suffered enough."

"It appears no one's content with what they have been given." Louis crossed the room to a table on which a gold candelabra was placed and stared at the flames.

"I loved you, Sire," whispered Louise.

"And I you," said Louis, "once upon a time. But all stories must end." He pinched out one of the candle flames.

"May I go?" asked Louise.

Louis turned back. "This is your home, Madame. It is everyone's home. I will not permit it."

"But Sire," begged Louise. "My son. Our son. Louis de Bourbon."

"He is cared for?"

"In Paris."

"My promise to you remains the same. A child of France. No matter what." With that, he left the room. Louise stared forlornly at the candelabra, and the extinguished flame suddenly reignited. Louise put her hand to her mouth. *Is God watching? Will He help me?*

*Chevalier lounged in* a chair in Philippe's outer chamber, reading the *Gazette de France*. "Oh, dear," he said. "The Duke and Duchess of Vierzon have announced the impending marriage of their daughter Delphine to the Marquis of Agen. Poor thing."

Philippe, lying on the divan, cocked his head. "Why poor?"

"Delphine's a charming creature of fifteen, whereas the Marquis is past seventy and suffers from every venereal disease known to man. And he's a beast, if the rumors are to be believed."

There was a soft rapping on the door. Philippe picked up a wine glass.

Chevalier dropped the paper onto his chair and went to the door. When he opened it, he found a pair of elegant shoes. He picked them up and spotted a note inside, a note sealed with wax and marked with an "h." He carefully read then pocketed the note, his hands trembling.

"Who is it?" called Philippe.

"The valet bringing back shoes. They'd better be polished this time." He brought the shoes into the room and placed them beside his chair.

"Did you hear about the builders?" asked Philippe.

"I try not to hear anything about builders."

"One man dead. Right in front of us. The rest downing their tools. Now my good friend Pascal de Saint-Martin has no rooms."

"If I were him I'd go back to Paris."

"And if you were him you'd be taller and twice as handsome."

Chevalier ignored this. "I fancy taking the air. Join me?"

"I thought you hated the outdoors."

"I do. But not today." He pulled Philippe to his feet. "I know I vex you from time to time. I'm vain, lazy, and excessively fond of frivolity. But a quick turn around the gardens before dinner is good for the soul."

Chevalier pulled on the gayest expression he could muster and grabbed his coat. Philippe put down his wine glass and followed.

Daylight sparkled off a sheen of frost. Chevalier made a point of admiring the late season flowers and new pathways. "We should do this more often," he said. "We spend too much time indoors." He realized his voice was wavering.

"Honestly," said Philippe, stopping in his tracks. "What is the matter with you? Why are you so nervous?"

Then a voice spoke from behind. "We need your help, Your Highness."

Philippe turned as Chevalier hurried on. Philippe frowned

and stepped forward. "I recognize you. Who are you?"

"A sergeant in His Majesty's army."

"You're the builder who tried to save the man from hanging himself. Are you also one who refuses to work?"

The sergeant nodded.

"What could you want from me?"

"We may not be on the battlefield, but we are all in loyal service and demand fair treatment. We ask you to speak to His Majesty about our demands. Respect. Our wounds tended. Decent lodge, fair pay, compensation. As benefits of soldiers of the King."

"Why would I plea on your behalf?"

"You could count on our support in the event of a change in circumstances."

"What change?"

"If your brother were no longer King."

Philippe stared. "I could have you hanged for talk like that."

"I know. Yet you shall not. And why is that?" The sergeant looked at the pale blue sky. "The sun is setting." He turned and vanished into a line of trees.

Chevalier wandered back to Philippe, looking innocent. "What did he want?"

"You knew he would be there, didn't you?" Philippe's jaw tightened. "You delivered me to him. What are you playing at?"

"I'm doing what you do so poorly."

"Which is what?"

"Looking after your best interests."

223

*While courtiers waited* in line outside the palace dining room for the King to arrive, Colbert sought out Beatrice and Sophie, who were both dressed impeccably for the meal in gowns of coral and pale green, their coifs laced through with glimmering beads.

"Madame de Clermont," he said, "you informed me some time ago that your papers would soon arrive from your estate. Many months past, in fact."

Beatrice flashed a smile. "They will arrive presently."

"Good. Though I must say His Majesty has declared that all those unable to produce proof of their noble blood within the month must leave. We would not wish that fate to befall you of all people."

"That is most considerate of you."

Above the civil murmurs of the crowd came Louvois' voice, loud and angry. "If we were back in Paris," he said, addressing two aging nobles, "and rid of this place, we would not need any builders at all! The worst kinds of headaches are unnecessary ones, isn't that so?"

Colbert left Beatrice, hurrying his way through the crowd to reach Louvois. "Watch your tongue in public," he said, grabbing the other's arm. "We all know your feelings about the King's project."

Louvois scowled. "Is that so?"

"In fact, it is often difficult not to hear your criticisms whilst in public. You should know I plan to air my concerns to the King."

Louvois pulled away from Colbert. "Do as you see fit."

At that moment a guard cried out, "The King!"

Dinner was an elegant affair as was always the case, yet a bit more so with the new guests at court, who were to be impressed beyond measure according to royal command. Select courtiers had been assigned the task of bringing food and tending the others, offering their smiles and most courteous attentions as well as fine wine and elegant dishes. Louis sat at the high table, flanked by Marie-Therese, the Montespan, Henriette, Philippe, and Chevalier, chatting about the palace, the food, the charm of the evening.

"I notice your friend Pascal de Saint-Martin has come to Versailles," Louis said, turning to his brother. "You persuaded him?'

Philippe picked up a chunk of Roquefort cheese and licked it. "He came of his own accord. But now he has nowhere to sleep."

"He shall be accommodated in due course."

Philippe put the cheese down. "Your builders are unhappy. Let me talk to them."

"I won't discuss politics at dinner, and certainly not with you."

"Many of them followed me into battle. Perhaps they might follow me back to work?"

Louis lifted his wine glass and took a sip. "We shall go hunting in the forest tomorrow."

"You're ignoring my offer?"

"Yes. I'm glad you noticed."

Philippe drew several sharp breaths. "My own house is ten miles away! If I've no function for you, no position of which you deem me worthy but that of your brother, why must I stay here? I can be your brother in the comfort of my own bed. If you wish to see me, send up a firework."

"I want you here. That's reason enough." He resumed eating, stabbing a slab of venison with his knife.

Several seats down from the King, the Montespan watched Henriette for a moment then touched her lady's arm. "You've not eaten a bite. If I didn't eat I'd have no energy for the other pleasures in life."

Henriette's smile was tired. "I'm quite all right, thank you, Athenais."

"But I know you, Henriette. If no one pushes you to eat, you'll shrivel up and disappear."

Henriette continued to gaze at her food.

Dinner continued into the evening, with nobles chatting and flirting with one another with winks and laughter. Cassel, in his best clothing, tried to join in but was ignored and ended up in the corner where he kept his head high and his disgust under control.

At a table in the center of the great room Beatrice preened her beautiful daughter subtly between bites of lamb and junket. Sophie picked at her meal and gazed around at the display of glamor and wealth. Her eye caught Rohan's and he smiled and nodded. Sophie blushed and turned away. "Mother," she whispered, "when I was small, you told me stories about noble life. You said these stories were true. I believed you. Why should I believe you now, Mother?"

Beatrice kept her smile but her voice was terse. "Now is not the time nor place, my poppet."

"Who am I? Who are we really?"

Beatrice pinched Sophie's thigh under the table. "Hush! Would you give all this up?"

"I would know a thread of who I am."

"A thread of truth is enough to hang you, my dear."

Sophie looked up at the King's table. "And our cousin, Chevalier. Is our family a lie as well?"

"Chevalier believes only what is in front of his nose. As long as he feels he might profit, he will be our friend and maintain our place in court. At least, that was the case until the King demanded proof."

"If we cannot convince him, then what?"

"We do whatever it takes to survive."

Sophie glanced down at the sliced pear on her plate then around to find Cassel staring at her. She looked back at the pear, her stomach clenching, her appetite waning.

A moment later Fabien stopped by the table and smiled at Beatrice. "You looking very comely this evening," he said with a bow.

Beatrice touched her hair. "Why Monsieur Marchal," she replied, her voice now light and airy. "You are most kind."

*The whorehouse sat* at the edge of the village of Versailles, a rustic, small establishment never wanting for patrons. The house's drug lounge, a dark, low-ceilinged room, smelled of liquor, smoke, sweat, and sex.

Montcourt lay with his head in the lap of a fleshy whore, smoking an opium pipe as she pleasured him with her hand. He drew on the pipe as she drew on him, the sensation building until, with a groan and arc of his back, he came hard and hot.

There were other men in the room, each with a favorite whore. Two sat nearby with their own red-lipped trollops taking care of business.

"I'm an exciseman," one grumbled to the other. "If the King is losing revenue to road bandits, I cannot be held responsible. Even with a force to protect them, there's not a carriage from here to Paris that isn't vulnerable. If the King's police cannot control the roads, the King cannot expect his taxmen to ride them."

Montcourt rolled away from his whore, fastened his trousers, and walked over. "It sounds like you gentlemen need some help," he said.

The taxman sneered. "We've no need of help."

"What you have need of," Montcourt tapped the man's shoulder, "is protection."

$\mathcal{T}$*he gambling room* was filled with cheerful nobles, spinning the great roulette wheel, placing bets, and drinking great amounts of wine. Rohan, well into his drink, stood before a small gathering, regaling them with a story as Louis and the Montespan, seated nearby, listened in.

"We were lost in the forest," said Rohan, "and happened to pass a small hut where we stopped to seek food and directions. Two sisters lived there, peasant women who didn't even know who we were. When His Majesty relieved them of that burden, they stared as if he'd come from the moon!"

The crowd chuckled.

"They agreed to give us food, drink, and show us our way on one condition. That we…how can I put it…*serviced* them! The problem was," said Rohan with a thrust of his hips and a wink at the ladies,"who would service which? One had warts and no teeth, the other had bandy legs."

Everyone laughed aloud except for Cassel. As soon as he saw Louis staring at him, he forced a laugh, too.

The Montespan leaned into the King."Are you pleased with the pet I bought you?"

"Cassel? Yes, delighted," said Louis.

"I see you're still training him."

Louis smiled, and he gazed out at the room, taking in the faces, the voices, the bright candlelight and cheer. *This moment is good and right*, he thought. *Here, in the palace with my subjects. If only our clock would stand still a while, if only the moon would hold the night in place until I gave it leave.*

Done with his tale and quite drunk, Rohan wandered over to the King's chair."Someone must speak to your builders," he said, his words slurring."They're tired and hungry. I do not think harsh measures will work against them."

Louis' smile faded."I will address them. And I would be grateful if you would keep your voice down."

"If I may be so bold, Sire," continued Rohan, wobbling on his feet, "it will only diminish their respect for you. Soldiers understand orders. Perhaps if a military man were to approach them, reason with them." He bowed, clearly offering himself.

"You are right. I will send Louvois."

Rohan's mouth opened then snapped shut. It seemed he wanted to say more, to demand the position, but had suddenly remembered his place. He bowed half-heartedly and wandered off.

As Rohan vanished into the crowd, Henriette approached the King. Her face was pale and her forehead furrowed. "Forgive me, Your Majesty. I'm feeling faint and will retire."

Louis leaned forward. "What is the matter with you? You used to be the brightest light in the room. Now you seem… absent."

"My apologies, Sire." Henriette curtseyed, beckoned Sophie, and the two left the room with Philippe and Louis watching after them. Then the Montespan took the King's hand and he led her to her bedchamber.

Their lovemaking was frantic. The Montespan bucked beneath the King, growling with desire, her breath hot and insistent on his neck. He held her down, her arms pinned against the bed, and she twisted and thrashed as if trying to roll away though clearly savoring his power and dominance. He thrust himself into her, taking her with a formidable need that would not be denied.

And yet his thoughts went to Henriette.

He forced himself into the Montespan again, his fists clenched and his teeth bared, but then the sense of urgency began to wane. She screamed with orgasm, and threw her legs around the King to pull him into her more deeply.

And yet again, he thought of Henriette.

Abruptly he pushed himself up and rolled away, unfulfilled.

The Montespan brushed damp hair from her face and touched his shoulder. "Did I not satisfy my King? Let me try again." But Louis stood and began to dress.

"I'll return," he said.

Collecting a candle, Louis took a secret back corridor to Henriette's chamber. There he found the lady asleep in bed, her hair tussled, her hands folded together beneath her chin like a child in prayer. His footsteps awoke her, and she roused herself, pulling the sheets up to her breasts.

"Your Majesty," she said, her voice deep with interrupted slumber.

Louis put the candle on a table and sat on the bed. "I was concerned about you."

"I'm tired, Sire. That is all."

"Your eyes tell me a different story."

The door was suddenly thrown open and Philippe strolled in. "He does this, doesn't he?" he shouted. "Waits until you're tired to have that big talk. He's always done it to me, but it's reassuring he does it to you, too."

"Some privacy, brother," Louis ordered.

"I think you forget where you are."

Louis shot his brother a challenging glance. "You forget who addresses you."

Philippe struggled, choosing his words, and then, "Louvois will not help you. You know that."

"Not *now*!"

"They've no respect for the hilltop general. A warrior only trusts the man who stands beside him."

Louis rose from the bed and walked toward his brother, who held his ground. "Take care with your words."

"You defend yourself always. But from what? How can you be blind to those who want to help you? Not everyone is trying to knock you down. If you stopped attacking for a moment you might see it. Let others aid your decisions."

Henriette moaned and pulled herself up from the bed, dragging the sheets with her.

Philippe's voice rose. "Brother! You think I oppose you. You think the world opposes you. But you are mistaken."

"Husband," muttered Henriette. She clutched the bedpost, panting. "Please stop it."

Philippe turned to his wife. "For heaven's sake, *eat* something!"

"Yes, sit," said Louis. "Eat. What on earth is the matter?"

Henriette looked at both men, at the table on which a bowl of fruit sat. She shook her head and then dropped the sheet, revealing the roundness of her belly. "I am expecting a child."

Louis and Philippe looked at her, then at one another, momentarily struck dumb.

*Cassel grit his* teeth as he stepped into the whorehouse's drug lounge. He was there to meet Montcourt, but this was a place most foul, an establishment he'd not enter for any other reason. He moved past the wasted men and the writhing, giggling, naked women and rubbed his nose in disgust.

Montcourt waved him over to a bench. "I've a proposition for you," he said as Cassel sat and sniffed.

"I'd rather you paid your share."

"It's here, my lord. I have not forgotten." He dropped a coin into Cassel's hand.

"And the rest of it?"

Montcourt grinned and leaned back. "Every day more nobles attend court in Versailles. On the road the forces of police grow every day. Bandits still roam and the fear is still there. But the risk to us is greater than it's ever been. So I've decided on a new plan for us. To offer protection to the excisemen."

"Here is gratitude for you! I found you discarded and gave you life."

"As a father to a child you saved me. But look now, Papa." He wiggled his fingers, showing several expensive rings. "See how I've grown."

"You've grown into a bigger idiot than I took you for."

Montcourt shrugged. "I won't go back on the roads with a musket. There are too many police."

"We have friends in the police."

"Not enough."

A whore lowered herself to sit on Cassel's lap but he waved her away. "You bring me money, Montcourt. How you come by it I no longer care. The King's builders have downed tools. They share our frustrations with the King's plans."

"The King will simply find more."

"The builders fought for him, you fool. Many are soldiers. His army has dissent in its ranks." Cassel stood and leaned over Montcourt. "Let us see what we might do to encourage it."

Montcourt picked an opium pipe, considered it, and then put it down. "The King will stop any insurrection with his armies."

"Puh. If he has any left by then."

Dawn had not yet broken over the village of Versailles, but Masson was up, searching through the bottles of medicine in the cabinets of his kitchen. The thumping and clinking aroused Claudine, who drew her shawl around her shoulders and tiptoed from bed to find the source of the noise.

Masson, blue bottle in hand, saw his daughter in the doorway. The piteous yet critical expression in her eyes drove a shard of anger into his chest.

"Father," she said, "you know what laudanum can do, yet you persist."

Masson rubbed sweat from his forehead. "I need it to keep the ship afloat."

"It will embrace you and sink you! The King needs his doctor well. Come now. Let's dress and be ready for the day. We cannot spend our lives waiting for His Majesty to catch cold. Many of his builders are injured. We should tend them while we can."

Masson sat and put his elbows on the table. "I shall stay here."

"But, Father –"

Masson's face twisted. "Get out!"

Claudine stared at Masson but he looked away. She nodded then, more to herself than to him, and went back to her room.

*Louis' mid-day meal* of cheeses, eggs, and pastries had been well prepared as always, and presented upon fine blue and white Nevers porcelain, yet Louis had been so preoccupied with Henriette's news and the issue of the striking builders, he had not enjoyed a single bite.

He put down his knife and addressed Fabien, who stood near the table. "Find accommodations for the new arrivals on the ground floor of the east wing. The rooms and view contingent on wealth and title."

"Yes, Your Majesty," said Fabien. He hesitated then continued. "But, Sire, our spies report unrest in the village of Aubenas –"

"I know Aubenas. They grow some of the finest olives in France."

"One of your tax collectors there was stoned to death, in protest at the increase in taxes proposed by Your Majesty."

Louis pushed away from the table. "Why is this of concern to me?"

"Such sentiments seem to have a habit of spreading. This is not the first village to voice such protest."

"Then have the men rounded up."

"But they are women, Sire."

"Where are the men?"

"Working for you, Sire. Here."

Louis drew back, shocked.

"*Hello.*"

The soft voice brought Benoit out of his gloomy reverie among the other striking builders on the scaffolding. He looked down to find Sophie smiling up at him.

"I've sent you a dozen notes," he called. "Did you not receive them?"

Sophie glanced about to make sure no one had seen her stop. Her mother was with several other ladies out by one of the garden's fountains and her own friends were in the palace, trying on new dresses. Benoit swung down a rope to join her.

"You're not working," she said as he landed.

"I want to but how can I? The builders must be paid."

Sophie's lovely face was clouded. She tapped a pebble with her toe. "Who cares about the palace? What's the point?"

"You cannot mean that. What is the point of a mountain? Or a perfect morning? They all make the world more beautiful."

Sophie's lip quivered.

"What's wrong?" asked Benoit.

"I must renounce our love. There are things about my past I've hidden from you."

Benoit's heart kicked painfully. "What can that matter? The past is gone. We are here. Now. Building the future."

"We build nothing. Not here."

"Of course we build."

Sophie looked at Benoit, her face pinched in grief.

"Why try? One day the rain will come and wash everything away."

"The point is not that it lasts forever," said Benoit. "Only that it *is*. Because then, it always *was*."

"You must forget you ever saw me." Sophie turned to leave but Benoit grabbed her arm.

"Please," he said. "We've two paths. This, the one you've decided on. Or another. More treacherous, more difficult, more impossible."

"And where does that path lead?"

Benoit bent and kissed her tenderly. "I don't know. But at least we will walk it together."

*Henriette rolled over* on the bed to face her husband, who stood in the center of her room, staring at her accusingly. She knew his thoughts. "I cannot say if the child is yours," she said.

"Cannot," asked Philippe, "or will not?"

"Abandon me, if you wish. Confine me to a cloister."

"I can do neither, as you know, even as I feel betrayed. By you. By him. By myself."

Henriette sighed, exhausted and heartsick. "Do you hate me?"

"How much more straightforward if I did." Philippe walked to the window and tapped his reflection on the glass with his fist. "He will use this, you will see."

"How?"

"To get what he wants. It will be his child on a Monday, and mine on a Tuesday, depending on his needs, his mood, his whim, his health, or which way the wind is blowing. You are not giving him a child." He turned back and pointed a finger at his wife. "You are giving us a club for him to beat us with."

*Louvois, in the* long blue jacket and tall black boots of his high military rank, sat astride his horse by the east wing of the palace, a cold wind stirring dust around him. Four guards stood with him at the ready. Nearly one hundred builders had gathered yet again to protest their conditions: Some stood on the ground; others clung to the scaffolding at various heights. Their faces were set and their eyes cold.

"His Majesty understands that you feel you have not been shown the respect you merit," Louvois called out. "You are mistaken. Without you, France would not exist. There will be more wars to fight and battles to be won. But as you stood side by side on the fields of Flanders, the King asks you now to stand side by side again, here at Versailles."

The builders did not reply. The tension in the air was as thick as the rain-threatening clouds overhead.

"Who is your leader?" said Louvois.

The young builder who had tried to prevent the builder from jumping stepped forward. Louvois thought he recognized the man as having been one of many sergeants in the King's army. "We have no leader. We speak with one voice."

"If you do not return to work, I shall have you hanged."

"Kill me," said the sergeant, "and two more shall take my place."

Louvois' horse shifted his feet; Louvois shifted his approach. "I understand your complaints. I was at Cambrai and Compiegne –"

"Yes," said the sergeant. "I saw you. In a tent on the far horizon two leagues behind the rear guard."

Louvois' jaw tightened at this, but he let the sergeant finish.

"Tell the King that we will fight for him again. Build for him again. And show trust and loyalty again. But first the King must show us that he is a man who will honor his promises." The striking men nodded, and the motion, in unison, looked almost to be a silent declaration of war.

*Freezing rain drenched* the forests of Versailles and the main road to the palace. In the middle of the icy mud a carriage had been stopped. A masked man stood with his musket aimed at the driver. Another masked man, bearing his own firearm, yanked open the carriage door and climbed inside where an exciseman sat, eyes wide with expectation.

The masked man pulled the cloth down from his face. It was Montcourt. "Your money!" he shouted.

The exciseman, the same one Montcourt had approached in the whorehouse with his plan, sat mute.

Montcourt made a face and whispered, "Now you say –"

"Oh, yes," said the exciseman, his eyes widening. He shouted, "Never!"

"You would rather die?" cried Montcourt.

The exciseman shook his head. Montcourt rolled his eyes and mouthed, *Say never!*

"Never!" shouted the exciseman. He lowered his voice. "What happens now? I forgot. Do I give you –"

"You give me half, you keep half."

"Then I hit you?"

"Then I hit *you*."

"Oh yes, of course." The exciseman handed Montcourt two bags of coins. Montcourt then struck the man hard in the face, and handed one bag back.

The exciseman rubbed his bleeding lips. "Next time," he said quietly, "we might save us both some time and do this in the warm?"

"That would be my pleasure," said Montcourt, striking the man once more. He pulled his mask back up, pocketed the bag, and climbed from the carriage into the rain. He and the other masked man disappeared into the dark cover of trees.

*Guards waited, attentive* and nearby, as Louis approached Jacques in the garden. The gardener was pruning a row of young beech trees, his coat unbuttoned, his face focused.

"You, at least, do not withhold your labor," said the King.

Jacques looked up and blinked against the sun. "I'm not a builder, Sire."

"When you fought for me, did you ever encounter rebellion in the ranks?"

Jacques scratched his cheek with his trowel. "Occasionally."

"Tell me, how did you come by your scar?"

"Rebellion."

*Ah, yes.* "How did the generals react?"

"That depended on the kind of men they were. But I can tell you this. The King that brings soldiers to face down soldiers is rarely king for very long. All men lash out when in pain."

Louis was silent for a moment. Then, "I see no resolution. I've sent emissaries to them. They do not pay attention."

"There is one man, Sire. One man to whom they might listen. He has their respect. He fought alongside them."

*He means Philippe.*

"Brothers can disagree with each other without opposing each other," said Jacques.

Louis turned away, shaking his head. "You were clearly an only child," he called back.

Inside the palace, the King called for Rohan to join him in his apartment. There, he instructed his friend to find the disgruntled soldiers and speak to them one on one. Rohan was to offer nothing specific but give a listening ear and encouragement.

"The winter will soon bring frost and the ground will harden," Louis explained. "If we are to build we must have foundations, if we are to have foundations they must be dug now, and if they are to be dug I must have builders."

After Rohan was on his way, Louis ordered Bontemps to send for Bruand, the architect, and Leclerc, the director of bullion at the Royal Mint. Then the King left his apartment, followed by his guards.

*I must speak with her*, he thought as their footsteps echoed up the corridor. *I must make my position more than clear.*

He found Henriette seated at her dressing table as Sophie combed her hair into long twisted tendrils that hung down around her shoulders. A guard announced Louis' arrival and Henriette immediately stood and Sophie retreated to an adjoining room. The King approached Henriette and put his hand on her stomach. As she moved to put her hand over his, he pulled his away. The corners of her eyes tightened with disappointment.

"We cannot continue as we have done," he said.

Henriette nodded sadly. "I understand. We are yours to own and discard as you see fit."

"I've never done either so far as you are concerned."

"His Majesty hides behind words but his sense is clear," she said gently.

"The child you carry is a symbol of doubt," he said. "A doubt I do not myself wish to bear. Would you want me to own you to the exclusion of all others? To the exclusion of my brother?"

Tears welled in Henriette's eyes. "I cannot answer that. Forgive me."

He walked away, feeling the task done and yet feeling no better for it.

*A house in* the village of Versailles had been converted into a makeshift hospital. Rohan was directed there by an old pig farmer guiding his cart filled with squealing piglets through the town square. Rohan approached the house, his cloak wrapped around him, his breath fogging the air. The door creaked when he opened it, and he stepped inside.

The front room was filled with wounded soldiers, some on the dirt floor, others on benches, waiting their turns to be treated, massaging bad legs, holding broken arms, touching gashed heads that had healed poorly. Claudine, the doctor's daughter, was probing a bloated abscess on one warrior's shoulder.

"You tend these men?" Rohan asked, stopping just inside the door. Claudine looked over and nodded. "What do they suffer from?"

"Gastric fever. Gangrene. Crushed limbs that cannot heal."

Rohan took several steps closer to the line of soldiers along the wall.

Claudine shook her head. "I wouldn't advise you approach them, my lord."

Rohan stopped. "Why not?"

"There may be a miasma. A pollution in the air."

"These are brothers-in-arms," said Rohan. "I shall take the risk." He walked up to a young soldier who sweated with fever.

"Drummer Brebant, unless I'm mistaken," Rohan said. "We took the town of Rochefort together."

The soldier ran his forearm across his eyes, and then smiled. "Lord Rohan!"

Rohan leaned down. "You are in pain?"

The soldier nodded.

"All of France feels your suffering."

The soldier's smile faded. "And the King?"

"The King, too."

Before the soldier could say more, Rohan moved on to the next wounded man and then the next, sharing sympathy and words declaring the King's compassion.

*The new architectural* designs were rolled out upon the table in the War Cabinet room, and Louis studied them carefully. They were first drafts, but well imagined, and the King was pleased. Liberal Bruand, the young architect, stood back as the King considered each detail.

The door opened and without announcement, Rohan strolled in, smiling widely. "Good day, Sire," he said. "I've good news."

Louis looked up. "Say."

"I visited some of the soldiers. For all their ailments and woes, their affection for Your Majesty is undimmed. They will soon tire of this petty show of rebellion. Stand firm, make no compromises and the field will be yours."

"I am pleased to hear it."

Rohan saw the papers on the table. "Another day, another edifice?"

But Louis stepped over to block Rohan's view. *This is not for your eyes yet, friend.* "A matter of government," he said. A brief look of disappointment crossed Rohan's face but then it was gone. He bowed and left the room.

Louis turned his full attention back to the drawings.

"Sire," said Bruand, "I would put the courtyard here and the chapel here."

"With respect," replied the King, "the other way around."

Bruand tilted his head and thought, then nodded. "A fine idea, Sire."

As the two studied the architectural plans, the guard at the door announced, "Monsieur Marchal." Fabien entered with a placard beneath his arm and a scowl on his face.

"Sire," he said, "this sign was found in the town."

Louis took the sign and held it up. Bruand's eyes darted nervously from the sign to the King. It read: FIGHT FOR JUSTICE AGAINST THE TYRANT LOUIS.

Without a word, Louis tossed the placard onto the floor and turned his attention back to the drawings on the table.

Fabien fumbled for a moment, shocked at the King's lack of rage. "Sire? Word of the builders' grievance has spread. A man called le Roure has taken up their cause, traveling town to town gathering support and spreading sedition and revolt. Do you wish me to act?"

"Not yet." Louis waved his hand to end the discussion, leaving the chief of his police force confused, troubled, yet silent.

*Sophie sat at* the table in her mother's chamber, her face in her arms, weeping piteously. Beatrice stood over her, exasperated and desperate.

"What do you expect me to do?" Beatrice demanded. "Tell you this all ends happily?"

"I have no idea who I am!" Sophie cried into her arms.

"Twenty-one years ago you were born. I loved you, cared for you, and kept you safe in any way I could."

"Where was I born? Pau?"

Beatrice hesitated. "La Rochelle."

"And my father? A noble?"

"A kind man. An artist. Crushed by the strictures of the King."

Sophie looked up. Her eyes were red, her face creased. "Why would the King crush my father?"

"Because of who he was."

"A criminal? A traitor?"

"Worse. A Protestant."

Silence hung in the air, an agonizing silence that had no balm. Then Beatrice noticed a new vase of flowers on the sideboard. "Flowers," she said without emotion. "How lovely."

Sophie wiped her eyes. "I thought they were for you."

Beatrice walked over and spied a note nestled in the leaves. She slipped it out and saw a lower case "h" on the outer fold.

"Who are they from?" asked Sophie.

Beatrice grabbed her cloak and went to the door. "I have a toothache. I need to visit the apothecary." She looked at her daughter. "I shall be a while."

On foot and with her cloak to hide her face, Beatrice ventured from the palace into the town of Versailles with several coins in her pocket. Returning to the palace in the fading sunlight, she did not go to her apartment but directly to Fabien's office. She did not knock, but pushed the door open to find him alone at his desk, hunched over, holding a magnifying glass and studying a paper with strange writings. The room was dark; the single candle burning so low it would soon be in need of replacement.

"You are fond of your books, aren't you?" said Beatrice.

Startled, Fabien looked up. "Ah…yes," he replied. "I'm at present reading a treatise on espionage in imperial Rome." He put down the magnifying glass.

"I like a man who reads." Beatrice stepped from the shadows into the faint candlelight, glancing at the paper on the desk. Her lips had been reddened and her hair was loose and seductive. She walked past Fabien, running her hand along his shoulders as she passed, and opened the door on the far side of the office. Fabien got up to follow.

The room behind the door was Fabien's torture room. Shelves held ropes, iron pinchers and shackles, drills and hammers and pokers. Tables were stained with dried blood. Beatrice picked up a pair of manacles. "Do you enjoy your work?"

"I would not say enjoyment but rather satisfaction."

"Does it pain you to see people suffer?"

"I do not consider such matters." Fabien came up behind Beatrice, brushed her hair away, and touched the nape of her neck. The softness of it caused his heart to pound hard against his ribs.

"Do you look them in the eye when you punish them?" asked Beatrice.

"Always," said Fabien. He grabbed her shoulders and turned her around to kiss her. She slapped him in the face, splitting his lip and drawing blood. Then she traced her finger along the blood and licked it off.

Fabien watched her, his mouth stinging, at once shocked and thrilled. So this was how it would be. "The line between pain and pleasure is fine," he said.

"There's a line?" she said. "I hadn't noticed." With that she shoved him down into a chair and mounted him, her skirt hiked up around her waist. His hands instinctively grabbed her flushed, naked buttocks. *Oh, God!* She bit his neck as if ready to consume him. He bared his teeth, and with a single buck threw her off onto the floor, where he straddled her and ripped the bodice of her gown down, revealing her bounteous breasts. She lay, heaving and grinning with pleasure.

Then he stopped, his hands hovering over her.

"What's wrong?" she asked.

"I…I've never been with a woman before."

Beatrice laughed. "My stars! You have so much to learn!" She yanked his trousers down and off and threw them aside. He stood, snatched her up, and slammed her against the wall, chains and manacles rattling. Beatrice threw open her legs so he could enter her and he did, over and over again as she writhed and wailed against the wall.

Neither noticed Laurene open the door, stare in horror, and pull the door shut again.

*They sat in* the quiet darkness of Henriette's bedroom, Henriette on her pillows, Louis beside her.

Candlelight caressed the bed and their faces.

"When we last spoke,"Louis said,"I was not as gracious as I could have been. Do you remember when, as children, we used to go down by the stream in summer?"

"I remember."

"The path led over a ditch, past the farm with the dog that barked, then through the spinney which we thought was haunted."

"Yes."

Louis went silent. Henriette waited, uncertain of his mood, his thoughts. He seemed to be confronting fears before her eyes.

"Why do you remember this, Sire?"she asked.

Louis smiled at her, and she felt again that he was her lover, her friend."I've always thought I was running toward the stream. Now, I think perhaps I was not running towards it at all. I was running away." He looked away, then back."When I'm with you, I run away. To be with you, I run to our past, and ignore what is right in front of me."He gently placed his hand on her belly and kissed her forehead."I will not run away any more."

Then he stood and left her. She watched, heartbroken and astonished that he would leave her yet again.

*As Masson sat,* passed out in a chair in his kitchen, a cloaked figure climbed in through the window, opened the box marked "XIV", and placed a blue bottle in with the other bottles. Then the figure went back out the window into the night even as Masson shuddered and snored in his sleep.

*Fabien leaned over* his desk with his magnifying glass, daylight replacing candlelight, studying the cipher. Laurene stood beside him with her arms crossed.

"I saw Beatrice enter the whorehouse in town," she said accusingly. "She spoke to the apothecary there and ordered two bottles of arsenic."

Fabien moved the glass along the paper. "So? A fine cure for toothache. I use it myself from time to time."

"And one bottle of Eros. Claimed to aid the vigor of amorous coupling." Fabien put down the glass and stared at his assistant. She continued, "Which gives me cause to believe you and she have become...intimate."

Fabien's voice took on the chill of winter. "I pay you to spy on others, not me." He hitched his head toward the door, ordering her out, then turned his attention back to the paper.

*Bontemps led the* striking soldiers along the wide, sparkling corridors of the palace and into the War Cabinet room where Louis waited with his guards, smiling. The soldiers, filthy and unkempt, stared at the opulence around and above them, their faces registering wonder, suspicion, and resolve. Some bowed grudgingly to the King. Others removed their hats.

"Good morning, gentlemen," said Louis. "It is an honor to welcome you. I live here but this is not my home. It is a home for France and her aspirations."

The men shifted on their feet and said nothing.

"I want to thank you for showing me the error in my thinking. You were right to put down your tools and refuse to work."

Philippe appeared at the door and Louis looked straight at him. *What I have to say is for you, brother,* he thought, *even more so than these soldiers.*

"I've brought you here today to ask your forgiveness and to try to renew your faith in me," Louis continued. "You are, all of you, an army in the service of your King, whether on the field or scaffolding. You've risked your lives for France. It's time for France to give you something in return." With that, Louis pulled the cover from off the central table to reveal the designs for a grand structure, a large and intricate building with countless rooms and gardens and courtyards. "This shall be known as Les Invalides. It will boast the finest medical facilities, refectory, dormitories, and church. It will be located in Paris near the river. Every soldier wounded fighting for France will be treated there, and every solider unable to return to his village will be able to spend the rest of his life there in comfort, free of charge."

Louis nodded at Bontemps, who stepped up with an ornate box.

"I've also struck a medal in honor of our recent victories,"

Louis said. "I wish to give one to each of you. But the first to receive it is the man to whom I owe the most. A brave brother soldier, known to you all. Philippe, Duke of Orleans, who I am also honored to call my brother."

Louis took a medallion from the box, went to Philippe, and hung it around his brother's neck as the soldiers watched in awe. Then Bontemps distributed the other medals, placing them around the soldiers' necks with great solemnness and respect. The soldiers looked at one another as if to assure themselves that this was, indeed, happening.

"Hurrah for the King!" shouted one soldier, raising his arm in the air. The others joined him in shouting, "Hurrah for the King!"

""I feared you would not come," Louis said to Philippe as the soldiers gathered around the table to discuss the drawings.

"You really believed what you said, didn't you?"

Louis smiled but did not answer.

One by one the soldiers left the table and approached the King, their faces full of humble gratitude. One by one they knelt and Louis extended his hand in a blessing. Philippe watched the spectacle, his anger growing. He lifted the medal around his neck to take a closer look. On it was the image of the King and the inscription, *Ludovicus Rex Victori Perpetuo*, "The perpetual victories of Louis the Great." Turning on his heel, he left the room.

A feverish, red-faced soldier with cracking lips pushed through the others to reach the King. "Your Majesty?" he said.

Louis took the soldier's hand. "France thanks you," he said.

The soldier leaned in close and whispered in the King's ear. "The enemy is closer than you think."

Louis frowned. "What enemy?"

Then the soldier spit in Louis' face. Louis gasped and shoved the man away.

Two guards quickly dragged the feverish soldier away.

"The poor fellow is sick!" said the King, stunned by the assault but maintaining his dignity. He turned to Bontemps and the look he gave his valet was full of a dark yet certain meaning. "Let him be tended to."

Moments later, on the other side of the palace, Philippe stormed into Henriette's bedchamber, demanding they leave immediately for their home in Saint Cloud.

"Philippe!" she cried as she stood from her table. "Please, wait. Explain yourself!"

"I just realized we have a choice. We don't have to do everything he tells us. We've been cowards! We merely need the courage to resist him."

"I don't understand!"

Philippe grabbed Henriette and pulled her close. "What do you really want?" he snarled. "To come with me or remain here waiting day and night for his knock on the door?"

Henriette hesitated.

"Let us leave him!" said Philippe. "I don't care if the child is mine or his. It will be ours."

Henriette stepped back, fear and indecision in her eyes. "But our lives are here! You are brother to the King. You cannot leave. This place is who you are, who we are."

Philippe snarled. "If that is true then we are already rotten inside."

*In the dark*, ruined interior of an isolated Huguenot church, an hour's ride from Versailles, a man standing in the shadows spoke to the one who had come to meet with him.

"The cipher has been broken?" he asked. "Are you sure?"

"Yes."

"Then we must form a new codex. This will take some time. Until then we will need to meet in person. I do not like the risk."

The other stepped closer. Beatrice. "They demand my papers," she said.

"You were sent forgeries."

"Next to useless. When do I have a replacement?"

"I will inquire."

Beatrice shook her head. "I'll deal with my papers myself. Our first priority must be the cipher. If they can read it, they can read our thoughts. However, they do not know we know it, which also means we now have an opportunity."

*Louis woke to* the silence of his bedchamber. He rubbed his eyes and peered into the darkness. There! Movement, shadowy figures he could not quite see.

"Is that you, brother?" he asked.

The figures came closer and a faint, yellowed light revealed the faces of Philippe, Rohan, Colbert, Louvois, and Fabien. Their eyes were closed, but when they opened them they were devilish and ghastly bright. Louis struggled to sit up, but discovered his arms were lashed to the bedposts. Philippe stepped to the bed's side, brandishing a dagger.

"What are you doing?" Louis screamed.

"I'm so sorry it had to turn out this way," said his brother calmly. "But you would not listen."

Henriette appeared to Philippe's right, smiling sadly. Louise appeared at Philippe's left. She lifted her hands and began to chant the last rites.

"*Per istam sanctam unctionem et suam piissimam misericordiam…*"

Philippe raised the dagger. It glistened viciously.

*No! Dear God, no!*

"You forgot to make your peace with God, didn't you, Louis?" asked Henriette.

With that Philippe plunged the dagger into Louis' chest as Louis thrashed and screamed.

He awoke to Bontemps hurrying to his bedside, his eyes wide with worry. "Sire!"

Louis grabbed Bontemps' shirt, panting, sweating, panicked. "Where is my brother? And Henriette?"

"Both left for Saint Cloud, Sire."

Louis clutched his head and moaned.

"Your Majesty!" said Bontemps. "You are sick!"

# 7

*The King sat* upon a lush green hillside, a landscape he knew but could not name. Scattered across the hill were the ruins of once grand, ancient buildings. A white-haired man in a golden robe reclined in the grasses nearby, writing upon a tablet. A godly halo encircled his head, and an eagle stood, alert, behind him in the grass.

Then Louis realized where he was. He was inside Poussin's painting, *Saint John's Meditation at Patmos*, part of the scene yet not belonging.

*I don't want to be here,* he thought. *I need to be in Versailles!*

Saint John lifted his face and stared directly at Louis, and his face was not that of the holy, wizened apostle but that of the young and fevered soldier who had spit on the King. "And the fourth angel poured out his vial upon the sun," the soldier said, raising his finger threateningly, "and power was given unto him to scorch men with fire. And the fifth angel poured out his vial upon the seat of the beast, and his kingdom was full of darkness."

Suddenly clouds began to roll and churn in the sky, bleeding together and blocking out the sun. Lightning flashed and thunder growled. Louis struggled, trying to get up, to run away, but was unable to move.

Saint John's eyes blinked, changing from blue to fiery red. "The enemy is closer than you think!" he shouted. The eagle leapt into the air and flew at Louis, its beak snapping, its talons flashing like daggers. Louis screamed.

"Sire!"

Louis heard Bontemps' muffled shout from outside his dream.

"The King's doctor!" cried the valet. "At once!"

*Philippe had brought* Henriette back to Versailles from Saint-Cloud in mid-October, missing the extravagance and excitement of court. And missing Chevalier. Life had settled down much as it had been, Henriette in her apartment and Philippe in his.

Philippe and Chevalier, in their nightshirts, were enjoying a late night party in Philippe's bed. They drank wine and listened as a palm reader told them their fortunes. The palm reader, a fine-featured young man, lay across Philippe's lap, holding Chevalier's hand and running his finger along his heart line. Chevalier was already bored.

"There is love in your future," crooned the palm reader with a wink. "Twice as much as you might think."

Chevalier wrinkled his nose dismissively and rolled off the bed. "I'm off to water the garden."

"I think that's a no," Philippe called after him. He stroked the palm reader's hair. "You know, when I was home in Saint-Cloud, Versailles seems like a stone's throw away. But when I'm here, it feels like a distant land across the sea. Chevalier, are you listening?"

Chevalier grunted an affirmative and padded across the room to the door of the antechamber. He stepped inside, pulled the door closed, and stood over a chamber pot. Raising his nightshirt, he began to piss into the pot.

Suddenly there was a large hand over his mouth and a cold, sharp razor at his groin. The stream of urine stopped instantly, and Chevalier drew a terrified breath. The man behind him spoke softly, menacingly, into his ear.

"You did not respond to my last message."

"In all honesty," replied Chevalier, trying to keep calm, "it didn't seem all that pressing."

The edge of the razor pushed harder against the flesh of Chevalier's penis, nicking the flesh. "And now?"

"You have my full attention."

"Read. Follow." A letter was stuffed into Chevalier's hand and his nightshirt was yanked up over his head. When he pulled it back down, he was alone.

"Chevalier?" called Philippe from outside the door.

Chevalier stuffed the letter into his nightshirt and stepped out of the anteroom, hoping on one hand to catch a glimpse of the man who had assaulted him and praying on the other that he would not.

A King's messenger hurried into the apartment, unannounced, and rushed to Philippe on the bed.

"Were you raised in a cattle shed?" demanded Chevalier.

"You must come at once!" said the messenger. "The King's Circle!"

Philippe shoved the palm reader away. "Wake my wife! Do it now!" he shouted as he grabbed for his trousers and shirt.

Chevalier stumbled into his own clothes and followed Philippe into the corridor.

"I must talk to you," he said, walking quickly to keep up.

"You're still drunk," Philippe replied with a shake of his head. "It can wait."

"You don't understand the gravity of my need!"

"Every need of yours weighs exactly the same."

"But a great tide is stirring! It pertains to your future in the court. Your place at its center."

"Go to bed. Please!"

Side by side they turned a corner and encountered guards in front of the War Cabinet room. The guards stepped back to let Philippe enter then drew together again, blocking Chevalier's way.

A nervous group gathered inside, waiting as Colbert and Bontemps closed the door. The only sound was the clock on the mantle between mounted shields and swords, ticking away the time.

Colbert looked at each person in turn – Philippe, Louvois, Fabien, Marie-Therese, Henriette, and Rohan. "In the King's book of names you will find a circle of trust, those he believes are the most loyal, faithful, and true. You are the names on that list. This circle of trust will not be broken. We all know what is at stake."

Henriette's eyes brimmed. "How is the King?"

"The fever is consuming him," said Bontemps.

Colbert nodded solemnly. "Protocol now demands we begin work on the issue of succession."

"I will not hear it," said Philippe.

"He is stronger than a malady," said Rohan. "Stronger than a hundred fevers!"

Colbert held up his hand. "As we hope for the best we must plan for the worst, as –"

Rohan interrupted. "Where did this distemper come from? Are we sure it's not poison?"

Bontemps stared at Fabien, who immediately spoke up. "Whatever the cause, I promise I will root it out."

"I hope you will be more successful," said Bontemps.

"More?"

"When a sick man gains close access to the King I do not call it a victory."

"The Dauphin is the direct successor but would require a Regent," said Louvois.

"The protocol is clear," said Colbert. "If the King –"

"Don't say it!" snarled Rohan.

"If the King dies, or if he is incapable of exercising his duties, a regent shall be appointed."

"But who?" asked the Queen.

"That," said Colbert, "is the choice before us."

The King's Circle glanced at one another and the clock ticked.

*Masson and Claudine* entered the King's bedchamber through the rear, secret door, to find the King in bed, sweat-soaked and raving. Bontemps and Marie-Therese stood by, their faces tight with fear.

Masson examined the King and then took a bottle from his medical box. He lifted Louis' head from the pillow. "Majesty, drink this. It is an herbal cordial to allay your pain and aid your rest: laudanum, saffron, and bruised cloves."

Louis turned his face from the bottle and looked at Claudine with pained eyes. She shook her head ever so slightly.

"Sire, I beg you to listen to your trusted medical advisor," said Masson, pressing the bottle to Louis' lips.

Louis addressed Claudine through fever-dried lips. "What…do you say?"

Claudine looked at her father then back at the King. "In… in the beginning a malady is easy to cure but difficult to detect. But in time, if allowed to grow, the ailment will be easy to detect but difficult to cure."

"When you last had a fever, what measures did you take?"

"To permit my body to cure itself, it was necessary to purge. There is an herb, sagewort. It grows wild on the edges of the forest."

Louis nodded with effort.

"Fetch your remedy," Bontemps ordered Claudine. "And quickly, but with a calm air. No one must know of his condition."

As Claudine hurried out, Louis turned his head away from Masson. "Leave me."

"But Sire," said Masson, "a physician must attend you."

"All of you, leave. And bring me Madame de la Vallière." The

King sank back into his pillows, exhausted, the illness pulling him back into troubled sleep.

*The Montespan found* Henriette and Marie-Therese in the corridor leading to the Queen's apartment, and she took hold of Henriette's arm.

"What is the news?" she asked, her brows knit and her lip quivering. "The King was not at Mass and you know how people gossip."

The Queen looked away.

"Majesty, please! Rumors are flowing. To know the truth might stop them."

"His Majesty is unwell," said the Queen. "That is all."

"Why such secrecy?"

"So that rumors do not start," said Henriette.

"Did someone tell Madame de La Vallière?"

The Queen nodded. "They will."

"Then…it is serious."

Marie-Therese looked at Henriette, then she nodded.

"What…what would happen if –" the Montespan began.

"There is no if," answered Henriette sternly. "He will be well." She and the Queen walked off, leaving the Montespan alone.

"Yes, of course he will be!" she called after them, but wasn't sure they heard her.

*Hunched over his* desk in his tiny room, Cassel dipped his ink into the well and prepared to write. At that very moment several large drips of water leaked through the roof and onto his paper. He looked up in frustration, and another drip caught him in the eye. *Curses! Can a noble not even have a closet that does not leak?*

As he slammed back in his chair in frustration, he saw a note sliding beneath his door. He jumped up, grabbed the note, and opened the door.

But no one was there.

He looked at the note. It bore the same wax seal as before.

*At the edge* of the forest as a light rain fell, Montcourt was hunting with his spaniel. The dog ran out into the trees for a pheasant but returned with a note tied to her collar. It bore the familiar wax seal.

*There was nothing* out the window that he wanted to see, but Chevalier stared anyway, his eyes following the clouds, a flock of birds, and a late season fly crawling on the other side of the glass. When he heard Philippe enter the chamber, he didn't turn around. "If the King's hair hurts," he said, "perhaps it was the wine last night? They say, 'Eat the fur of the beast that bit you,' but who wants a mouthful of fluff for breakfast?" He felt Philippe's angry gaze. "Did I speak out of turn? Come now. How is our King?"

Philippe's fists clenched and unclenched. He looked as if he had something to say but feared the speaking.

"Talk to me," said Chevalier, looking around at last. "What is all this secrecy?"

Philippe went to the table, picked up a half-filled wine glass but then let it fall to the table. The wine ran across the table's surface like blood. "You must vow to me."

"On my father's life."

"Your father's dead."

"My mother's, then."

"Forget it."

Chevalier walked over and took Philippe's arm. "Your distress pains me."

"Make your vow, then. That what I tell you will go no further."

Chevalier put his hand over his heart. "On my life. I vow my oath."

Philippe drew his finger through the spilled wine. "My brother is very sick."

"I always said you'd make a marvelous King."

Philippe glared. "Stop it."

"You were serious? Goodness."

"He's gravely ill. Should he die it is possible I will be regent."

"I had no idea."

Philippe grabbed Chevalier's collar. "Not a word to anyone. This is a testing time but I know with you by my side,

I can overcome anything."

"Of course. Now, I must have air. Come, join me."

"I cannot." Philippe hesitated. "I have…to think."

Chevalier called for a footman, standing at the door, to bring his coat. "As you wish," he said to Philippe, caressing his cheek. "He is in my prayers. As are you."

As Chevalier strode to the door, Philippe called, "What did you mean when you said 'a great tide is stirring'?"

Chevalier looked back. Their eyes met. "Did I say that? I must have been drunk."

*The stench was* ripe and foul, an odor of sickness so heavy that Philippe covered his nose as he walked into the King's bedchamber. Others stood back, watching helplessly as the King tossed about in restless sleep. Philippe stared, uneasy at the sight of the King so frail, so helpless.

Moments later, Rohan entered and looked to the others for permission to go to the King, but Bontemps shook his head. "Only his physician may approach."

Rohan nodded.

More painful minutes passed. At last Philippe demanded, "Where is the King's doctor?"

"He's fetching a remedy," said Bontemps.

"Good God, where does the doctor live? In Marseille?" Philippe growled, and walked toward the bed. Rohan grabbed Philippe's shoulder to stop him but Philippe gave him a withering gaze. "He is not a leper!"

"It's not safe," said Rohan.

Philippe stared coldly at the King's childhood friend. "Do you forget who addresses you?" He went to the bedside, gently took Louis' hand, and offered a short prayer. Louis shuddered and his eyes slowly opened. He pulled Philippe close and whispered in his ear. "Thrust in thy sickle, and reap; for the harvest of the Earth is ripe."

A chill ran down Philippe's back. He was familiar with the Bible and knew the passage that followed spoke of the blood, death, and the Apocalypse. He could only pat Louis' shoulder in an attempt to comfort himself and his brother.

In the King's outer chamber, Henriette, Marie-Therese, Louvois, Fabien, and Colbert waited for an audience with the King. Colbert sniffed when he noticed Henriette's pregnancy. "Madame, you should not have come in your condition."

Henriette lifted her chin. "I will not be away from my King."

"We're beside ourselves with worry," said the Queen. "Of course she is here."

"There are reports of typhus in the rank and file," said Louvois.

"We'll leave the medicine to the doctors," replied Colbert. "The Council must meet to move the business of government forward. And Your Majesty." He turned to the Queen. "Your presence would also be welcomed at our discussion."

"When do we convene?" asked Marie-Therese.

Before he could answer, the priest Bossuet walked past them and into the King's bedchamber. The Queen crossed herself. Colbert said, "We convene as soon as possible."

And the Montespan, standing unseen in an alcove, heard everything.

*Claudine was collecting* her jars of samples from the cabinet in her kitchen, placing them into a large satchel, when her father stumbled in, growled, and drew his arm along the cabinet shelf, sending the other jars to smash on the floor.

"Jezebel!" he shouted. "Delilah!"

Claudine grabbed for his arm. "Control yourself! Stop this!"

"You may have shaved my seven locks and sold me to the Philistines, but I am not yet on my knees!" With that he spun about and slapped Claudine soundly. She fell back, striking her head on the edge of the door. Masson stared at her, at her motionless body. With a satisfied nod, he reached into her satchel, found a bottle of laudanum, and took a swig. Then another.

His stomach cramped violently and he clutched the table, heaving. Through the fog of pain he looked over at his daughter on the floor. A single clear thought stung his brain. *Dear Jesus, I've killed her!*

He crawled over, put his hand on her arm, and sobbed, "Forgive me." Then a more violent wave caught his stomach, twisted it inside out, and he collapsed.

At last Claudine roused, her head throbbing mightily, her mind unclear. With great effort she opened her eyes and there, lying unconscious on the floor beside her with blood streaming from his mouth and an empty bottle of laudanum in his hand, she saw her father.

She forced herself to her knees and cupped his face in her hands. "Father!" she cried.

He did not answer.

"Father!" she cried again. *"Father!"*

The door banged behind her. She looked back to find Bontemps standing there.

"Help me!" she pleaded. "He's dying!"

There was sympathy in Bontemps' eyes but urgency in his voice. "You must come. The King."

Claudine looked back at her father, her heart pounding.

"We both know who his doctor is," said Bontemps.

"But my father will perish!"

"As will your King."

Claudine folded her hands and held them up before the valet. "Don't make me choose. He's all the family I have."

"Save your father, or save France," said Bontemps. "The choice is yours."

*The soldier who* had spit upon the King awoke to find himself lashed to a table in the shadowy torture room, with Fabien, the King's chief of police, staring at him with contempt.

"Are you dead?" asked Fabien.

The soldier licked his cracked lips. "By your hand or by my sickness, it doesn't matter. I will be soon."

"Your destination is not in doubt. The issue before us is merely the amount of pain you will endure on the journey."

Laurene entered, her face flushed with excitement. "I was just in the laundry," she said. "And I found this in one of the pockets."

Fabien put out his hand. Laurene removed a letter from her skirt, unfolded it, and held it up. It was a cipher. "The same shapes," she said. "I may not be able to read but I saw they were like those in your book!"

Fabien took the letter and studied it. Then he turned to the soldier. "Don't go anywhere." He and Laurene left the torture room for the office, locking the door behind them.

Using the book codex, Fabien sat at his desk and labored over the cipher. Laurene stood by, thrilled at having accomplished something so important, even as the work took the time of one and a half candles burned down. At last Fabien stood and put on his jacket. "A meeting is planned today. Is my horse ready?"

"Fed and watered this morning."

Fabien waved the letter at her as he strode out the door. "You have done well!"

*Bontemps and Claudine* entered the King's chamber through the secret door to find him gone and the guard staring at the wall.

"Guard!" demanded Bontemps. "Where is the King?"

"His Majesty ordered my eyes to the wall but he has not yet ordered them back."

Leaving Claudine in the bedchamber, Bontemps hurried

out of the King's apartment and into the corridor. There, he stopped in his tracks and stared at his master with pity and horror.

The King was dancing. In the center of the corridor, in his sweat-stained nightshirt, he was pivoting and circling, his head wobbling back and forth to unheard music. He spotted Bontemps and motioned him closer. "There you are! I cannot decide whether this will be a courante, a pavane, a passacaille, or a gavotte."

Bontemps spoke as softy as his fear would allow. "Sire, you must return to bed. Your doctors −"

"Bontemps! I've created a new dance! And I wish my court to perform it."

"Very well, Sire, but first −"

Louis stopped for a moment. "Everyone must learn it immediately. Bring me pen and paper. And a gardener."

Bontemps glanced over at the guards who stood nearby, then back at the King. "Gardener?"

"Jacques! My gardener. Bring him here. I see this dance unfolding in a garden, an orangery full of blossoms." Then Louis began dancing again. He tipped his head toward his valet. "Bontemps, dance for me. Now. Follow me. First, a pied largi, then sissonne, pirouette, then pas de bourree, contretemps…"

Bontemps, mortified yet always obedient, tried to follow the King's steps but stumbled awkwardly.

"The dancers will orbit the sun in the order of rank," said the King as he twirled. "The King, an Emperor, a Pope, a laborer, a child, on down the line of precedence. You can be Pope if you like, Bontemps."

Bontemps bowed uncertainly. "If these are your steps, Sire, then your dance is a passacaille." *How pale he is! How weak! I must get him back to his bed lest he die!*

Louis stopped dancing. His eyes narrowed and his head lowered like that of an animal ready to strike. "I do not trust you. I do not trust you at all. Guards! I do not know that man!"

Bontemps stepped back. "Sire, please!"

"I need my gardener! My enemies are coming!"

Bontemps turned to the guards. "Avert your eyes!"

"Guards! They mean to kill me! Bring me Jacques!" Then Louis' eyes rolled back and he fainted. Bontemps leapt forward and caught him in his arms. He dragged the King back toward his apartment as Louis muttered, "My gardener will know what to do."

*A late afternoon* wind rattled the broken walls of the Huguenot church and caused its deteriorating shingles to flap upon the roof. At the door, Montcourt glanced about then hastened inside and pulled the door shut. He found Cassel in one of the remaining pews and sat down with him.

"We're risking our lives being here," said Montcourt. "I had to conceal my horse half a mile away."

"You're the one to talk," scoffed Cassel. "Why the urgency?"

Montcourt sat back. "Wait, now. You were not the author of this letter?"

The door slammed open. Instantly fearful, both men turned to see others arriving, all cloaked, all looking about furtively.

"It appears we're not the only ones bound by our intent," said Montcourt as the new arrivals found pews in which to sit then pushed back their hoods. Nobles, all of them.

"Intent?" asked Cassel. "Which is what, exactly?"

"The intent is revolution," came a voice. A familiar voice. A female voice. The men turned to stare at the front of the church. Beside the altar stood Madame de Clermont. Beatrice. Dressed in a new gown that had been sent to her anonymously the day before. Her face was stony with purpose.

Cassel shouted, "This is a monumental risk! What if these communications were intercepted? Or worse, deciphered?"

"They have been deciphered," said Beatrice.

Montcourt gasped. "Then our location is known?"

"Once a codex is broken," Beatrice answered, "it offers opportunity. I wrote a new message and made sure it was found. It proposes a rendezvous today, on the other side of Paris. We are quite safe where we are."

Chevalier stood in the back of the church and pounded his fist on the pew.

"Cousin!" he shouted. "What on God's Earth are you doing here?"

Beatrice gave Chevalier a cold, challenging look as Chevalier waited for an answer. But then Beatrice turned her attention back to the crowd. "We're from different denominations," she said, "but we pray at the same altar – the church of the living France. Our prayer is for deliverance from the tyrant Louis, and for a new France to rise from the ashes." She paused and looked at each man in turn. "A great moment is upon us. The King has a fever. His sickness grows. We must plan in this moment for our future. But I bring joyous news. We are not alone. We have powerful and wealthy friends, some already at court, and others abroad are watching closely. All stand ready to help." Beatrice reached into the sleeve of her dress and removed a paper that had been sewn into the fabric fold. "A message of support from the Dutch Republic. William of Orange will soon be stadholder, commander of the armies and admiral of the sea. He vows here to support those who would move against King Louis. Not just with words but with money, materials, influence, and arms."

"I've heard enough," said Chevalier. "Thank you for the puppet show."

Beatrice pointed at her cousin. "Chevalier de Lorraine! Don't confuse the woman you have known with the woman you now see. You haven't the faintest idea who you are dealing with. You stand to gain a great deal from our cause. A gathering in Paris awaits you. Canvass your supporters there. I know there are many."

Chevalier glanced at the others then back at Beatrice. "I'm beginning to wonder whether we *are* related."

Beatrice lifted her face to the rafters. "France will be born again, and Versailles will be a forgotten folly. The dream of a sick King. Divided we will fail, united there is nothing we cannot achieve. Long live the noble republic. Long live the true inheritors of France!"

*Fabien galloped his* horse along a winding road south of Paris, followed closely by two musketeers, and then reined the animal up in a weed-choked field. In the center of the field stood an abandoned abbey, its stone walls covered in vines. Fabien slid from his horse and motioned the musketeers to be silent but at the ready. Slowly, quietly, Fabien crept to the entrance and peered inside, ready to confront the traitors whose cipher he'd translated.

The abbey was empty.

Fabien spun about and stormed outside to his horse. "Someone has played tricks on us!"

*Jacques was ushered* into the King's bedchamber by a footman. His eyes were narrowed and his steps uncertain. He looked from Bontemps to Claudine to Louis, sweating, waiting to be told what to do.

"Do not address the King unless he addresses you," advised Bontemps.

Jacques nodded. Then Louis stirred in his bed and opened his eyes.

"Closer," said the King.

"Sire," said Bontemps, "your doctors forbid it."

Louis looked at Jacques. "Are you afraid to approach your King? Are you afraid of death?"

"No, Sire," replied Jacques. "It holds no mystery to me."

"Come, then."

Jacques went to the King's bedside.

Louis' cheeks hitched and he swallowed with effort. "Tell me a story about my father," he said. "Your mother suckled him before you. Which makes you milk brothers, yes?"

Jacques nodded.

"A story, then."

Jacques nodded again. "An emissary from Japan once came to our shores," he began. "He brought your father a text from China, one he said had been read by every samurai in the Imperial Army. The author was a man called Master Sun. The text, *The Art of War*. Your father, to my knowledge, never read the book but one of his ministers did. From it came a most vital maxim. 'Appear weak when you are strong, and strong when you are weak.'"

"My father never told me about this volume."

"Perhaps he planned to but did not have the chance."

"You killed for my father. And one day, I may ask you to do the same for me."

The two exchanged smiles.

"Now you must rest, Sire," said Jacques.

Louis tried to smile but the pain was too much. "You would order your King to bed?"

"If it would protect him."

Louis shifted his face on the pillow. "I trust only four men in this world. Bontemps, my valet. Fabien, my commissaire. Rohan, my oldest friend. "And you." He coughed then said, "My enemies are close."

"They are, Sire."

"They see me. They see my family, my friends, my ministers and associates." He motioned for Jacques to lean in. "But they do not see *you*." Then Louis began to cough, deeply, loudly.

Bontemps ordered the gardener out and frantically motioned the priest forward. The priest made the sign of the cross on Louis' forehead, and murmured the prayer of Extreme

Unction. Louis tried to pull away from the priest, for the man's touch was as hot as the flames of Hell, his words burning coals in his ears. He tried to order the priest gone, but the heat was so great he could not speak.

*Go! Be gone! I am on fire!*

And then a rainbow formed above him, arcing over the bed, painting the air in colors that were brilliant and alive. Louis sat up, reaching for it through the pain, seeking relief in the shimmering hues. Beside his bed a nymph appeared on a pale green horse. She wore a suit of mirrored armor that reflected the King's face, and she held a large sword in her hand. She smiled at Louis and her teeth were those of a wolf – sharp and covered in blood.

Louis moved to the edge of the bed. The nymph raised her sword and Louis bowed his head in surrender. *Let it be done! Let it be done!* He heard the *whoosh* of the blade as it cut the air on its way down.

The King fell back onto his bed, spitting blood. "Death is here and Hell will follow!" he screamed as Marie-Therese rushed to him and gathered him in her arms. The nymph and rainbow were gone, vanished into the realm of nightmares.

*The room was* chilly, the fire warm. Henriette sat close to the hearth, staring at the crackling, golden flames. Sophie was seated beside her, silently adding lace to a handkerchief. Henriette heard the Montespan enter the room. She glanced around then looked back at the fire.

"I hear more people talking," the Montespan said.

"Rumors," said Henriette.

"What if they're true? They're saying we might go back to Paris."

Sophie stopped stitching and frowned. "Why would we do that?"

"We are not going to do that," said Henriette.

The Montespan went to the fire and held out her hands to warm them. "With the King so ill, what if he cannot oppose them? What if all he's built is taken away?"

"His men are loyal. They would never betray him."

"Wake up. Please."

Henriette stood abruptly. "I am fully awake, Madame! And I more than you know what the future might hold if our worst fears are realized."

The Montespan flinched but kept her eyes fixed on Henriette. "If they are your influences would grow. I would hope you might still look kindly upon your friends."

"We support our men," said Henriette, looking back at the fire, "but men think only of themselves. Who is there to support a woman, but a woman?"

*Alone in her* apartment, Beatrice put the finishing, elaborate touches on several sheets of paper. She fanned them to dry them then scuffed and creased them to age them. She collected them and left her apartment.

She found Colbert in the War Cabinet room, reading at his

desk. Announced, she waited at the door until he beckoned to her. "Ah. Madame de Clermont."

"As promised," she said, approaching him. "Our proof of noble heritage."

Colbert took the papers. "I will review in due course."

Beatrice nodded, curtseyed slightly, and left the room, praying that her skill at forgery would save her and her daughter.

*Philippe entered the* King's bedchamber to find Marie-Therese, Bontemps, and Fabien watching on while Claudine held the King's hair back as he spit vomit into a bucket.

"What is she doing here?" Philippe demanded.

"The King's new doctor," said Marie-Therese.

"His Majesty requested it," said Bontemps.

"Right now he could request you bring him the moon in an egg cup but I doubt you'd attempt it!" yelled Philippe. "We cannot leave the King's health in the hands of a child! My brother should be in Paris. I've readied my own carriage. I will take him there to recuperate."

"He cannot travel," said Claudine, keeping her eye on the King.

"An hour by horse, at the most."

The Queen shook her head. "It could kill him."

Philippe stared at her. "It's this palace that is killing him."

*The palace slept* uneasily, and in the morning the King's Circle gathered once more in the War Cabinet room. Colbert, Louvois, Bontemps, and Rohan stood by the table as Henriette and Marie-Therese sat in chairs by the windows.

"The nobles who seek to discredit the King will slake their thirst on this, I've no doubt," said Rohan.

Marie-Therese frowned. "How can you be so sure?"

"They're nothing if not predictable," said Louvois.

"A rumor can be more harmful than a hard truth," said the Queen.

Fabien opened his satchel and removed a piece of paper. "I've compiled a list. On one side, those I believe are for the King. On the other side, those who move against him."

The door banged open and Philippe entered, late to the gathering, looking both annoyed and anxious.

Rohan snatched the paper from Fabien. "Let me see that."

Fabien took it back. "Careful," he said coolly. "My father was a printer. I'm very fond of paper."

Rohan paced around the table, shaking his head. "The whole of France must offer prayers of health and recovery for the King. Let all those who love him move together. And let those who disagree show themselves and their true colors."

Fabien nodded. "A fine idea."

"I'll speak to Bishop Bossuet myself," offered the Queen.

"But the issue of regent remains," said Rohan.

Philippe stepped forward. "Will no one vouch for me?"

"It's not you who lacks the merit, Your Highness," said Colbert. "Our concerns fall instead on those who would place themselves around you."

"Why don't you say Chevalier's name?"

Marie-Therese stood and walked into the midst of the men. Her voice carried calm and regal authority as she addressed Philippe. "We need someone whose behavior is more becoming of a monarch. Someone who is his own man. I hope I make myself clear."

Philippe blinked, shocked at the criticism. Then he regained his composure as best he could. "Perfectly," he answered.

"Her Majesty and Monsieur Colbert would, to my mind, ensure a resilient transition," offered Bontemps.

"Then it's settled," said Colbert, and the Circle was dismissed.

Philippe went straight to his apartment, his blood cold with the Queen's reproach. He walked in to find a valet packing a bag as Chevalier barked instructions.

"All those shoes," Chevalier said with a wave of his hand, "and those shirts there on the bed, and for God's sake be careful nothing tears."

"What are you doing?" asked Philippe, slamming the door shut.

Chevalier scratched his head and sighed. "All this rumor throughout the palace makes a man giddy. I'm going to Paris for a few days to un-giddy myself."

Philippe stepped between Chevalier and the valet. "You

told me you thought I would make a great king."

"And you would."

"This is not idle chat. What are you up to? You make a vow to me."

"And I kept it," said Chevalier.

"Then be truthful in return."

"That is all for the moment," Chevalier said to the valet, who bowed and left the room.

Chevalier went to the sideboard, began to pour a glass of wine then put the bottle down. "Have you been hiding under a rock these past months, Philippe? We're on the verge of great change. People want that change, one that would not deny the monarchy but rather share in its burden. You can see it in your brother, even now. One man cannot rule the land. He's drowning in it. And you are the man to save him."

"You tread a dangerous path, Chevalier."

"The only danger is smelling smoke and not acknowledging that a fire is burning."

"You side with the nobles."

"I side with you. Just as the soldiers side with you." Chevalier held out a hand. "Would you side with me?"

"You cannot know what you're asking."

"I know exactly what I'm asking."

"Unless death forces my hand, I cannot answer."

"Very well." Chevalier crossed his arms and raised a brow. "But know this. Our future is changed no matter what happens now."

*Rumors were fast* and furious throughout the palace. Nobles had witnessed Bishop Bossuet sweeping through the corridors to the King's apartment, and speculation was rampant. A crowd gathered to whisper in the hallway as portraits and statues looked on, impassive, motionless, silent.

"They've closed his outer doors," said one noblewoman. She crossed herself and cried in the arms of a friend.

Another lady turned to Cassel. "Did you hear?" she asked. "The King?"

Cassel nodded. "I did. Terrible news. Simply…" He paused, turned, and offered a small, dark smile to the Montespan who stood not far away, "…awful."

Chevalier, followed by his valet, worked his way through the gossiping humans and nearly ran into Henriette, who was quietly taking in the chatter.

"Oh, I beg your pardon," he said with a chuckle, "I didn't see you there!" He glanced at her protruding belly. "Which, from the looks of you, is quite an achievement."

Henriette sighed. "I've no desire to engage with you, sir. This is no time for pettiness."

"I agree, my dear. You were once someone to talk to, of course. When you had the affection of the King. But now that it's gone, I don't suppose I know why anyone would speak to you at all." And without waiting for a reply, Chevalier vanished within the sea of troubled nobles.

*There was a* soft scratching sound, a rustling that woke Claudine on her pallet in the corner of the King's bedchamber. She rubbed the sleep from her eyes to find Louis at his desk, his head resting in the palm of one hand and scribbling on paper with the other. Stunned, she scrambled up and shook Bontemps, who was asleep on his cot. He woke immediately.

"Sire!" said Bontemps, pulling himself to his feet. "We rejoice at your recovery!"

Claudine felt Louis' forehead and she gasped. "The fever has broken."

Louis put down the pen and looked up at her. "Where is your father?"

Claudine took a shuddering breath.

"She gave up her father for you, Sire," said Bontemps. "He was killed by a poison we believe was meant for you."

Louis' eyes narrowed. "Was this poison responsible for my fever?"

"I do not think so," said Claudine.

"The court must know nothing of my condition."

"But surely," said Bontemps. "Your brother must be informed."

"Send for Rohan. I wish to see him. And my tailors. I want some new clothes." Louis wrote a few more words then handed the paper to Bontemps. "As for the rest of the court, this is the only message I wish you to convey."

Quickly and obediently, Bontemps left the King's apartment and summoned the King's Cabinet and Circle to the War Cabinet room to share the message. Fabien and Rohan were the only ones not in attendance.

"I am saddened to report that His Majesty's health has not improved," Bontemps reported. "He has passed on instructions for government to continue under his word."

"How can he make decisions in such a condition?" asked Colbert.

"The King wishes that France be informed immediately of his condition so that they might offer their prayers."

The Queen and Henriette covered their faces and wept. The men struggled against their own tears.

Bontemps watched them all then added, "His Majesty would also have the court learn a new dance."

Philippe gaped. "A dance?"

"It is one he has composed himself in his moments of peace. To raise our spirits in anticipation of his recovery." Bontemps held up the paper on which Louis had written the dance and the others gathered close to have a look. "Monsieur Lully is to create a melody."

*Claudine stood in* her father's clinic, sobbing over his body as it lay on the examination table. Once so vital and busy in life, Masson was now as many of his patients had been. Cold. Dead. Decaying flesh on a slab.

Fabien waited and watched as patiently as he could, considering this young woman who had abilities that should have been reserved for men. After he'd had enough of her crying, he spoke. "If I'd not seen your work first-hand I might have thought you were a witch."

Claudine wiped her eyes. "And have me burned."

Fabien considered this. "I don't know many unburned witches."

"We're all condemned in one way or another. I must examine him. Under the knife. He died by a poison I believe was destined for the King. If I can trace the cause I may find its remedy."

"And," added Fabien, "the poisoner."

*Louis stood beneath* the portrait of Philippe and himself as children as Rohan entered the bedchamber. The drapes were drawn and the room was dark. Rohan moved cautiously and slowly to the bed, his head forward, straining to see the King.

"You look like death, old friend."

Rohan spun toward the voice to find Louis against the wall, smiling.

"Praise God!" said Rohan. "It cannot be!"

Louis stepped out and clasped Rohan's hand. "When a man is ill he retreats to his past, to the perfect summers of youth. You were always there by my side. You are my oldest friend and I am grateful for it. Because of this, I'm giving you this gift – the gift of truth. But in return you will give me the gift of silence on this matter."

"I await your command."

"I've told my council to inform the entire country of my imminent demise. In this way, I hope to root out all those opposed to me, since they would be the first to make plans for my absence."

Rohan laughed. "What a mind you have, my friend."

"You approve?"

"I applaud it. We did the same with our foxhounds in Fontainebleau. Send the bad news down the holes and see what scampers up."

Louis nodded, satisfied, trusting. "You are my eyes and ears. Ensure the word goes out."

"I will not fail you."

Louis pulled back the drapes and the two men sat in a pool of sunlight and talked. Recalling. Reliving.

And while the friends visited, there came a pounding on the King's outer chamber door. Bontemps ordered the guard to open the door and found Philippe with a crowd of brawny men bearing swords. Their expressions were hard and determined.

"I'm here to fetch my brother," Philippe said. "It is plain to see his life depends on it."

Bontemps put his hand on the door. "The answer was no and it remains so, Your Highness." He turned to one of the guards and snapped his fingers. "Fetch Fabien Marchal at once."

Philippe snarled. "Your little dog won't help you now, Bontemps. You forget who you are addressing."

"Good day," said Bontemps, and he shut the door.

"Do not shut me out!" shouted Philippe. He gestured toward his men to force their way in but at that moment Fabien and eight of the King's largest, best-armed Swiss guards arrived. Their hands were on their weapons and they were more than ready.

"I would choose your next decision carefully, Your Highness," said Fabien.

Philippe bared his teeth and turned on his heel.

*Having spied Beatrice* quietly conversing with Cassel in chapel during morning prayers, and anxious to find something more to offer Fabien and please him, Laurene dressed herself as a chambermaid and made her way into Beatrice's apartment. She hid in the shadows until she was certain she was alone, and then searched the shelves, armoire, and desk, checking each paper and feeling each drawer in case there might be a false bottom.

And there was.

The base of the lowest desk drawer slid open to reveal more papers, papers that were covered in ornate writing and appeared quite old. One in particular caught her attention. It was the same as the others yet half-finished. She suspected it was quite important, and folded it to put into her skirt.

"Hello," came a voice from behind. "I'm looking for my mother."

Laurene stood and spun around to find Sophie standing there.

"I…I found this," Laurene managed, holding out the paper. "It was on the floor. Where does it go?"

Sophie shrugged. "I don't know. I don't live here anymore. I sleep close to my lady. I can take it if you like."

"I'll put it away," said Laurene. Sophie nodded and went

to the armoire to draw out a scarf. Laurene pocketed the paper, made a ruse of dusting, and then hurried from the room.

*Resting on his* pillows, his strength not fully returned, Louis beckoned Claudine over to his bed. He saw the sadness in her eyes from the loss of her father yet also saw the wisdom and courage.

"Your sacrifice will not be forgotten," he said. "My deepest sympathy for your loss. I know now my replacement for your father."

Claudine nodded. "What is his name?"

"I only know he stands before me now. You will find many who oppose you, who would rather I chose someone from my circle of physicians. But you must be deaf to their judgments. Will you accept the position? If the answer is yes, there is no going back. Your life will be changed forever."

Claudine nodded slowly. "I accept."

"Then it is yours. Medicine is a fine career."

Claudine curtseyed, stunned at this news.

Louis called to Bontemps, who came to stand beside Claudine. "Send for Madame de la Vallière," the King ordered.

Louise came quickly and uncertainly, entering the King's bedchamber with her rosary fumbling in her hands. She approached the King and curtseyed.

"The child's name is Louis?"

"Our son? Yes, Sire."

"His governess is in Paris. The same as his brother?"

"Yes."

Louis was silent for a moment. Then he said, "I hoped you might stay here. That you might think of this as home."

"I cannot."

"Not even for your children."

"For their sakes and my own, I must show contrition for my life."

"I know. You may go."

Louise let go of her rosary. She stared at the King. He had not meant leave the room, but leave Versailles. "Majesty, thank you with all my heart."

"Arrangements will be made."

"I pray God for a healing angel to be with you." She smiled at Louis, then at Bontemps, and left the chamber with a new lightness to her step, one that seemed much like a dance.

"*I must sadly* report the demise of the King's doctor, Masson," Fabien said as Colbert sat hunched over his desk in the War Cabinet room, processing a stack of nobles' paperwork. "Died of a condition of the stomach, I'm told."

"We must appoint another royal physician at once."

"The King has a preferred candidate already in place."

"Oh?" Colbert looked up. "Is the King recovered?"

"He is not."

Colbert considered Fabien, waiting for more information,

but not receiving it he looked back at the stack on the desk.

"Are your noble papers complete?" asked Fabien.

"Mine?" Colbert scratched his ear. "Oh, well, I've yet to submit, in fact."

Fabien tapped the stack. "And these people here. Are they in order?"

"Yes. Beauvilliers. Poitou. De Clermont. That makes twenty this evening."

"Madame de Clermont? May I see?"

Colbert handed him the paper. "Yes. I forgot you're known to each other. Her lineage extends several generations. This document proves it. I must say I'm quite relieved."

Fabien held the paper, studied it, and put it down. "Thank you." He turned to leave but then his heart tightened and he looked back. "Might I see that paper again?"

Colbert nodded and Fabien picked it up. "You're likewise relieved, no doubt," said Colbert.

"It's a fine piece of paper. The grain is very smooth." And as he studied it closely his eyes narrowed and his heart tightened.

Fabien hurried back to his office, clutching Beatrice's paper. He shut the door and went to the table on which a large scroll lay. On one side was a long list of names. On the other, a map of France marked with red spots, many of which were located in Paris.

Hearing him enter, Laurene came out from a side room and approached him, breathless. "I saw Cassel in conversation with several new nobles," she said. "Including Madame de Clermont."

Fabien glanced at her. "Who else?"

"Poitiers. Anjou."

"Since the court became aware of the King's condition, the number of conversations between these individuals has increased markedly. Anjou, you say, and Poitier, both to Cassel –"

"And Madame de Clermont."

Fabien nodded vaguely, trying to dismiss her comment, wanting to dismiss his suspicion and focus on the traitors of which he was quite sure. He drew long lines connecting the red spots on the map.

"I checked with the stables," said Laurene. "Both Anjou and Poitier are riding to Paris."

"They aren't the only ones." Fabien spread Beatrice's paper out and studied it again. "Laurene, I dispatched a messenger to Pau a week ago. If he returns in my absence, secure his findings in a lock box."

"Your absence? Where are you going?"

Fabien grabbed his cloak. "To Paris."

*The chapel was* quiet and somber; even the shadows on the floor seem softer out of respect for the nobles who had come to pray for the health of the King. Henriette and Sophie entered, crossed themselves, and moved up the aisle. Henriette selected a pew near the altar while Sophie found her mother and slid in beside her.

"Mother," she whispered. "I've missed you."

Beatrice looked up from her folded hands. "Your duty to me is to do well for your lady."

"Yes. Yet my first thought is always to talk to you. Like when I found the chambermaid in your drawer today."

Beatrice's hands abruptly unfolded. "Chambermaid?"

"She found papers of yours on the floor. I think she was putting them back."

Beatrice slowly put her hands back together. "Of course. How kind of her. You must point her out to me so I can thank her."

"I will." Sophie looked around, then said, "So few here this morning. Where is everyone?"

Beatrice stared straight ahead.

"Mother?"

"Don't you remember?" replied Beatrice. "They are practicing. The King has us learning a new dance. Shh, now!"

Sophie folded her hands then looked down at her feet to see if she could remember the dance steps. She tapped them back and forth as quietly as she could.

*Chevalier was hurled* to the floor of Fabien's office where he skidded and slammed against the base of the desk. He struggled to right himself, getting up onto his knees, his cheeks and forehead bruised and bleeding, his face contorted into a mask of rage and utter disbelief.

"I captured you, Chevalier, in Paris!" said Fabien as two guards stood beside him, hands on their swords. "Paris, where the traitors have been gathering! And I've brought you back to Versailles."

"The Duc of Orléans will have your head for this!"

sputtered Chevalier. "And when your head is on the block, do you know what he will say to you? He will tell you –"

Fabien kicked Chevalier in the chest, knocking him down again. "I'll tell you this. You are to be executed in the morning, along with the others."

Chevalier pulled himself to his feet where he stood, heaving, glaring. "The King would never permit it!"

"That seems to be the problem being a traitor," said Fabien. "It never seems to end well. In any case, I hope you're fond of horses."

*In the early* evening Beatrice found Laurene alone in the palace laundry room, a place filled with vats of lye and bubbling cauldrons and crisscrossed with clotheslines upon which socks, trousers, shawls, and gowns were hung to dry. Laurene was placing wet garments into baskets as Beatrice came up behind her.

"Might I trouble you a moment?"

Laurene flinched and looked around. "Ah, yes, certainly, Madame."

"Laurene, correct?"

Laurene nodded.

"Do you know Fabien Marchal?"

"I do."

"I've a problem to discuss with him." Beatrice ran her hand along a clothesline, tugging on it slightly, watching it bounce. "I'm embarrassed to even mention it. I believe a gown of mine has gone missing and I'm worried sick that it is lost."

Laurene wiped her face with her sleeve. "That cannot be true."

"I fear it might be," said Beatrice. "Last time I looked, it was over there." She pointed across the room, and as Laurene turned to look, Beatrice yanked a clothesline down and looped it around Laurene's neck. Laurene spun around as Beatrice twisted the line. Laurene lashed out with her hands then clawed at her neck. Tighter. Tighter. Laurene's face grew purple and her throat began to bleed. Her eyes bulged as she kicked and fought the noose. After what seemed like an eternity, she fell in a heap, tipping over a basket and spilling gowns on the floor.

"Burn in Hell, Catholic cunt," said Beatrice.

As the quarter moon resumed its place in the night sky, a hooded man hauled a heavy sack down the path from the palace to the stable and around that to the pigsty. He put the sack down, made sure no one was nearby in the darkness, then removed Laurene's dismembered hand from the sack and threw it in to the pigs. The pigs snorted and scrambled over each other to get at the tasty morsel. One by one the man tossed the freshly butchered chunks of Fabien's former assistant to the pigs, upending the sack to shake loose the last bit, her foot, and the pigs chewed their evening snack with selfish snorts.

Back in the laundry room, Beatrice felt her hair and ran her hands along her face to make sure all was in order then pulled on her best palace smile. She walked out, taking the servants' stairs to the main corridor where she encountered a clutch of noble ladies, with the Montespan in the middle, posing their feet in various positions.

"Beatrice! My dear!" called the Montespan. "We're all practicing the King's new dance. Will you join us?"

"Isn't it wrong to apply ourselves to joy while he suffers so?" replied Beatrice.

"Ah, but it is the King's wish."

"Of course."

Beatrice excused herself and hurried on to her apartment, where she removed a box from a drawer and took from it a piece of charcoal and a small bottle of tincture. She swallowed the charcoal and forced it down with a glass of wine. It scraped painfully all the way to her stomach, but the discomfort was a small price for the protection it offered. When it was time, the charcoal would prevent the solution from taking effect. She slipped the bottle into her bodice and headed for Fabien's office.

He was not there. Slipping out of her clothes, Beatrice lit two candles and stretched out on Fabien's bed. It was not long before the door rattled and he entered. He looked around in the dim light as if seeking Laurene, and then his gaze fell on Beatrice.

"I've something to aid us," she said, licking her lips and running her hand seductively along her breasts.

Fabien came close. "Aid us with what?"

"Endurance." She opened the bottle, took out the dropper, and squeezed a drip into her mouth. "A love potion."

"When I look at you," said Fabien, "I need nothing else."

"I'm the same," said Beatrice, licking her lips. "But I think this might be fun."

Fabien's expression was a mixture of lust and doubt, and lust won out. He knelt by the bed, opened his mouth, and

Beatrice put several drops on his tongue. Then he climbed into the bed, onto Beatrice, and he was on fire.

*Philippe looked up* from his evening prayers to see all other nobles had left the chapel. Standing in the doorway was Louis and several guards. He leapt to his feet and raced down the aisle, his arms open to embrace his brother.

"My God!"

Louis stepped back and away from the embrace.

"I…I was told you were dying," said Philippe.

"I was," said Louis. "Then I recovered."

"And did not think to tell me?"

"I told no one."

"Why?"

"So I could see who it is upon whom I can truly depend."

"You did not trust your own brother?"

"I do not trust the company he keeps. You're blind to Chevalier's failings and dumb to his faults."

"Do not say such things!"

"A conspiracy in Paris was uncovered. The nobles plotting against me even as I lay in my fever bed. I arrested them all. Chevalier was a ringleader."

"Impossible!"

"He is a traitor. He is now in jail awaiting execution."

Philippe's knees went weak. Blood ran cold in his arms. "Brother, please!"

"He shall be hanged, drawn, and quartered in the morning."

"NO!" Philippe dropped to his knees, his hands tearing at his hair.

"And your presence is expected at the dance this evening. I hope you've learned the steps."

*The largest palace* salon was decorated for the party. Candles blazed from the chandeliers and golden and ivory stands, music played in every corner by trios and quartets, servants carried platters of the most aromatic and sumptuous foods. In the center of the room, nobles danced the King's new dance wearing gowns and coats of such an array of hues that it was as if a rainbow had descended from the heavens. Around, back, bowing and dipping, spinning and circling, all smiling at the King's dying command.

Suddenly the music stopped. The dancers came to a standstill and looked at each other curiously. The doors opened and a most peculiar warrior entered. He was dressed entirely in armor made of mirrors from helmet to plackart to greave. The armor flashed in the light of the candles and reflected the faces of the nobles, who moved back, a bit frightened. The warrior stopped, turned slowly, and then lifted the visor. It was Louis.

"Your Highness!"

Nobles gasped and fell into bows and curtseys. The King was recovered. The King was among them once more.

In the midst of the celebratory commotion, Philippe threw back his chair and fled the room, and Fabien, his stomach cramping, stumbled out not long after.

*Oh, God!*

Chevalier stood in the palace prison yard with his arms lashed behind his back, watching as one of the nobles accused of treason was laid out upon the ground between four nervous horses. The man's arms and legs were each bound with rope, and the ropes' ends were secured to the harnesses that extended from the horses' hindquarters. Each horse faced a different direction and was held in place by a guard with a whip. The executioner stood beside Chevalier, watching with eyes bright with purpose.

*God, no!*

The executioner shouted, "Now!"

The guards whipped the horses. They reared, whinnied then bolted, jerking the man's limbs and tearing them from his body with a loud snapping of bone and ripping of flesh. Blood sprayed and the man, now a wretched, red-soaked torso, screamed, gurgled, and died.

Chevalier whimpered and vomited on his shoes, a man broken in spirit, broken of hope.

*The day was* crisp and bright, laced with spicy scents of wet wood and decaying humus, filled with the rustle of creatures in the undergrowth gathering food for the winter ahead. Louis and Philippe rode side by side through the forest beneath trees shedding golden foliage. For a long time, Philippe said nothing, enraged that his brother had commanded he take this ride.

At last Louis spoke. "There will be others."

Philippe stared at the ground as his horse stepped over a log. "Not like him."

"Chevalier's a traitor. I had no choice. My advice is to take the matter less to heart."

Philippe drew up his mount. "You have put my dearest friend behind bars! Yesterday he witnessed a most grisly execution. He may be next! How else, then, would I take it?"

"Your dearest friend was plotting against me."

"He was trapped. He's gullible. He meant no harm."

"I took the decision as your King, not as your brother." Suddenly, Louis spurred his horse into a gallop, off through the trees, and with a huff, Philippe set off in pursuit.

The two men knew the forest well, the risings and fallings of the land, the densest thickets and outcroppings of great boulders. The horses knew the land, as well; they snorted with the sudden adventure of speed and competition, leaping ditches and fallen trees with what seemed like true abandon.

Ahead was an ancient black poplar tree where Philippe and Louis had, many times before, ended their races. Philippe slowed his horse and let Louis pass the tree ahead of him.

Louis spun his horse back around. "You could have won, brother!"

"But then the King would have lost. And we can't have that."

They turned back in the direction of the palace, their mounts breathing heavily.

"If I were of a suspicious nature," said Louis, "I would have you arrested, too."

"You believe I would plot against you?"

Louis shook his head sadly. "I believe you are capable of anything," he answered, and then urged his horse into a gallop in the direction of the palace.

*Claudine hurried with* Bontemps through the main palace corridors, trying to keep her composure, hoping no one would see through the ruse. Bontemps had said she looked presentable dressed as a man, complete with the black clothing and hat of a physician and wearing a small mustache she had affixed to her lip with a sticky concoction, and it seemed true; courtiers she passed gave her no more than mildly curious glances. She feared her voice might give her away so Bontemps had recommended she speak as little as possible. It had been the King's decision that she serve as his physician and that she no longer sneak in and out. The disguise was the only solution.

Yet greater than her fear at discovery was her fear for Henriette. Claudine entered the room and found her in her bed, muttering incoherently, her lady Sophie mopping her brow with a damp cloth, the King holding her hand and watching her intently. The bed sheets were soaked in blood.

"Doctor Pascal, Sire," said Bontemps.

The King looked over and Claudine curtseyed.

"It's customary for men to bow to the King," said Louis.

Claudine bowed awkwardly.

"Your services are required, doctor."

Claudine whispered a quick prayer, opened her medicine box, and went to work. Yet for all her efforts, within the hour Henriette delivered a tiny, miscarried fetus. Sophie wept, the King was silent, and Henriette, at last, fell asleep, worn out from pain and her fruitless efforts.

As Claudine removed the soiled sheets, Philippe entered the bedchamber. He stared at his wife. "Will she recover?"

Claudine lowered her voice. "Yes, Your Highness. I shall prepare an herbal infusion to fortify the blood."

Philippe sat beside his wife and touched her face. Henriette stirred in sleep then went still again.

Louis joined Bontemps at the door. "I'm expecting our visitor from England today," he said. "Bring him to me without announcement. In private."

Bontemps nodded. "Yes, Sire."

"And where is Fabien? I've not seen him since the party and dance last night."

"I've been looking for him, but with no success."

"I want him to interrogate Chevalier," Louis said, trading cold glances with Philippe across the room. "He has a loose tongue and I'm certain he has much to tell us."

*He could barely* swallow, and his eyes felt fat and hot. His muscles shook uncontrollably and there was a burning in his stomach. *She said it was a potion. A love potion…*

"There's nothing to fear." Beatrice's voice pierced the fog of his mind. "Don't fight it."

Fabien struggled to open his eyes and caught a wavering glimpse of his lover standing by the bed. Her bed. They were in her private chamber, alone but for a fire dancing on the hearth.

"Rest, love," she said. Her smile was so familiar, but now, even through the haze of his misery, he spied what looked to be a hardness lurking there.

He reached up for her wrist. "What…did you give me?"

Beatrice stroked his forehead. "Shh. It was a potion. I told you. The same as I had. Close your eyes now."

"I'm thirsty."

"Of course. I believe it was something you ate. Don't worry. I won't leave you until you're recovered. I'll fetch some water." She smiled again, more widely this time, and then got up and went into the anteroom where she kept the pitcher. In that moment Fabien forced himself off the bed and staggered from the room.

*What have you done to me, Beatrice? What have you done?*

Nauseous, barefoot, and in his nightshirt, Fabien found his way through a rear palace door, down through the gardens, and onto the road leading to the village of Versailles. He knew where he needed to go and hoped he could find it. Rocks bit into the soles of his feet, bruising and cutting them, but he moved on. There were few travelers and those who passed him turned up their noses, seeing him as a beggar.

In the glare of late afternoon he reached the village center and pounded weakly on a familiar door. When it was opened he fell inside and passed out on the kitchen floor.

"Wake up!"

Someone was jostling him, shaking him, causing his head to rattle. His eyes snapped open. Claudine knelt beside him, her face drawn up in worry. She probed his face with her thumbs and felt his hands.

Fabien coughed then heaved vomit onto the floor. He wiped his mouth with his sleeve. "Have I been poisoned?"

"I believe so."

"By what?"

"The symptoms I see indicate the main ingredient was arsenic."

Beatrice helped Fabien to a chair at the table, where

he leaned over and vomited again into a bucket Claudine hastened into place. He groaned. "Will I live?"

"If I can find an antidote. But first I must apply an herbal salve to your eyes. It is the only way to save your sight."

Fabien nodded with effort. "No one must know I came here."

"Very well."

Claudine ground dried herbs from a rack over the stove then brought the paste and a cup of brown liquid to the table. She handed the cup to Fabien.

"What is it?" he asked.

"Cognac."

"I don't drink."

"This will be beyond any pain you've ever known."

He put the cup down. "Pain holds neither fear nor mystery for me."

"Prepare yourself, then. Close your eyes."

With a flat wooden stick, Claudine spread the paste around the rims and then dabbed it directly onto Fabien's eyes. He sucked air and grit his teeth, and his eyes watered mightily.

"Changed your mind about the cognac?" asked Claudine.

"I told you, I don't drink."

Claudine shrugged. She applied the bandages to his eyes and then kneeled down to treat the cuts on his feet.

*Certain now that* Henriette would recover, Louis gathered with Louvois and Rohan in his outer chamber.

Louvois explained that the prisoners involved in the plot against the King were now in the Bastille, ready for Fabien to question them.

"They will say whatever they think will save their skins," said Louis, standing by the window with his arms crossed. "The question is, are they acting on their own or is someone behind them pulling the strings?"

"Don't worry too much about the nobles, Sire," replied Rohan. "For all the bluster, they are a lazy, cowardly bunch."

Louis smiled slyly. "Are you not a noble, Rohan?"

"My point exactly. I'm lazy and a notorious coward."

"If I may suggest, Sire," said Louvois. "They are traitors and should be executed."

"What are they saying in the palace salons?"

"They are frightened. Most have a friend or relative imprisoned."

"Good," said Louis. "I want them to be frightened."

Bontemps entered and Louis motioned him over. He whispered into the King's ear. "Your visitor has arrived, Sire."

"Take him to the War Cabinet room."

Surprised, Bontemps said, "But, Sire –"

"I want him to see the plans for the palace. Our visitor is a lover of architecture."

Bontemps bowed and withdrew. Louis turned back to Rohan and Louvois.

"I believe you should release the prisoners, Sire," said Rohan.

Louis' brow raised. "Why should I do that?"

"Because their gratitude will translate into obedience and fidelity."

Louis stared out the window, considering the suggestion. "Perhaps," he said at last. "But I should like them to taste the cold floor of a prison cell for a little longer."

The men agreed, toasting the decision with goblets of wine.

Louis found Sir William Throckmorton in the War Cabinet room, studying the palace diagrams with great interest. Throckmorton was an English diplomat, an aging man of serious face and modest stature. He bowed at the King's entrance. "I note and admire your ambition," he said, nodding at the drawings.

Louis closed the door. "I thank you for coming."

"An honor, Your Majesty."

Louis took a cushioned seat and directed Throckmorton to take the chair beside him. "I've asked you here because I have a proposition for your King."

Throckmorton leaned forward, his hands clasped. "Which I'll hear with great interest."

"The substance of our discussions is to be divulged to no one but your King and those in whom he has complete trust. No one else."

"Of course."

"I want to invade Holland."

Throckmorton's mouth opened and it took a moment before sound followed. "I…see."

"The only thing that could stop me is her principal ally, England. How could I persuade England to join me in this venture? Money? Perhaps. A share of the Dutch trade routes? Almost certainly. But that's not enough. What does one give a King who has almost everything? You give him what his family so carelessly tossed away. His Catholicism."

Throckmorton drew back. "Your Majesty, I don't know –"

Louis held up his hand. "Your King claims he is Protestant but in his heart he is Catholic. He seeks to renew relations with Rome but cannot because in their eyes he is a heretic. I, on the other hand –"

"Your Majesty, I fear you are pushing ahead too fast."

"The agreement I propose is simple. We invade Holland. England provides a third of the troops and ships, with all costs borne by France. And I effect a reconciliation between the English crown and Rome."

Throckmorton's feet shifted on the floor. It looked as though he wanted to get up and turn away, to give himself time to think. Yet he knew he could not insult the King in that fashion.

"What better way to seal an alliance between friends?" asked Louis.

Throckmorton's gaze went from Louis to the far wall and back as he considered the offer.

"I suggest a meeting ten days hence. At Dover Castle."

"And Your Majesty will come in person?"

"I've not yet decided."

*Through a window* in his outer chamber Louis watched Throckmorton leave the palace, taking the wide front stairs and climbing into his carriage.

"May I congratulate His Majesty on his plan," said Colbert, his voice filled with admiration. "Brilliant."

"Its brilliance remains to be seen,"Louis said as the carriage pulled away, the horses bobbing their heads and moving into a trot."What counts is that Charles become an ally, not a foe."

"Who will go to carry out the discussions?"asked Louvois. "You, Sire?"

Louis walked over to his ministers."No. I don't want them to think I am desperate for their support."

"If I might be so bold, Sire," said Colbert,"I would send Feuquières. He is an experienced diplomat and cares only for the good of France."

Louvois shook his head."I suggest Chanut. His trip to Sweden was a great success."

"A loose cannon,"said Colbert."Croissy, perhaps. He is a committed Anglophile, and –"

"Henriette will go," said Louis as he walked back to the window.

Louvois and Colbert blinked at one another, stunned at the pronouncement."What is the meaning of this?"whispered Louvois."Perhaps His Majesty has not recovered from his illness!"

"I am perfectly recovered, thank you,"said the King.

Colbert stepped forward."Sire, with due respect, she has no experience with such matters, and the stakes couldn't be higher."

"And she's a woman,"said Louis."But she has the wit of any man here, and courage beyond. Furthermore, she is Charles' sister and knows his weaknesses. She has one thing no French diplomat has. His ear."

"But can she be trusted?"asked Louvois."Is there not risk she will lean in favor of the interest of her country of birth?"

Louis looked at Bontemps, who waited by the door with the guards."What are your thoughts?"

"We might consider her health," offered the valet."That her mind is willing but following her miscarriage, her body might not be."

"She is willing, mind and body."

"Could we wait a few months?"

"No. William of Orange has been given a place in the Dutch government. The republicans are retreating and the House of Orange is ascending. He will be King within two years. If we don't negotiate with England, he will. Louvois, you organize the transportation. Colbert, you ensure that the *Gazette* carries a story that Her Majesty, Henriette, is traveling to Vichy to recover from a minor illness. Bontemps, make sure my doctor prepares her for the journey. As for security," Louis' voice tightened, "I notice that Fabien is still missing."

"I'm still looking for him, Sire," said Bontemps.

"If you fail, you will assume his responsibilities."

The King strode toward the door. Bontemps paced him, speaking softly, earnestly. "Sire, please reconsider. You risk losing the support of the entire council!"

Louis stared at his valet, but did not reply, and then he was gone.

Colbert and Louvois left the King's apartments for their respective duties. They paused in the corridor, close to the wall, voices low, as the Montespan and several noble ladies passed by.

"Her Highness, Henriette, is an admirable woman," said Colbert, "but she is in no fit state."

"Sending a woman!" said Louvois. "And if she stays in England, what then?"

The Montespan dropped her handkerchief then picked it up, moving slowly as if trying to hear the conversation. Colbert hitched his head, indicating Louvois to continue on, away from the lady's ears.

"At any rate," he said as they turned a corner, "we can be sure that His Majesty is motivated by the soundest of reasons."

*Every sound outside* his prison cell caused Chevalier to flinch and stare in dread at the door. The day before, a man whose face was cloaked by a large hood and whose voice was deep and raspy had spoken through the bars of the door, threatening slow death by evisceration should Chevalier give up any information due to fear or torture. And now, each thumping or clattering beyond his cell brought to mind images of the man and his gutting knife or Fabien and his torture tools. In either case, he would suffer greatly. This morning, as the key rattled and the door swung open, Chevalier, chained to the wall by his ankle, tucked his head and prepared for the worst.

"Tell me," came the voice. "Are you faithful to my brother?"

Chevalier looked up. Louis stood there on the filthy straw, wrinkling his nose at the stink and at the mice who scampered two and fro.

"Sire," gasped Chevalier. "He is always in my thoughts."

"Give me one reason I should spare you the axe."

Chevalier swallowed hard. "I cannot, Sire. I've betrayed

you. I allowed myself to be led astray. I beg forgiveness."

Louis kicked at the bent pan that held Chevalier's moldy dinner. "Give me the name of the man who led you astray, then."

"I cannot, Sire, on my honor."

"Your honor? What a novel concept."

Chevalier rose on his knees. "I swear, Sire, I never set eyes on him. I don't know who he is or what he wants."

"Did you think you were helping my brother in plotting against me?"

"No, Sire. I acted without thought, through fear alone."

Louis sniffed. "I've killed mice with more courage than you. My brother deserves better. Now the question is, what to do with you?"

Chevalier bowed his head, waiting for the answer, but it did not come. And he was left alone with the stench and the vermin and the dread.

*Claudine heard Fabien* stir on the pallet on the kitchen floor. He grunted and reached for his eyes, only to find the bandages securely in place. Then she looked back through the magnifying glass at the foul-smelling sample in a petri dish.

"I hear you there. What are you doing?" Fabien asked.

"Examining your vomit."

"Is it the same poison that killed your father?"

"I'm not certain. It's very similar. Whoever created it knew what he was doing."

"He?"

"What about your antidote?"

"I administered it while you were unconscious."

Fabien forced himself to sit up. "What do you know of love potions? Stimulants to the act of intercourse?"

"Why do you ask?"

"Imagine two people took a love potion that contained poison. How is it possible for one to suffer the effects of the poison while the other did not?"

Claudine put the magnifying glass down. "Either that person succeeded in vomiting the poison before it took effect or they took an antidote prior to taking the potion."

Fabien rubbed his neck and bent over, clearly still feeling the aftereffects. "I want you to send a message to Bontemps, the King's valet. "Tell him I need to see him."

Claudine nodded, then knowing he couldn't see her, answered that she would.

*The dilapidated farmhouse* sat beside a low-flowing stream, and countless snakes and turtles had come up from the water to make it their home. Montcourt was the first to arrive and spent his free time stomping reptiles and kicking them out of the house. Cassel came next. He watched Montcourt boot a particularly long snake through the doorway. Then he studied Montcourt's torn, faded clothing with a look of disgust.

"I must give you the name of my tailor in Paris," he said.

Montcourt wiped his face. "Fine clothes serve little purpose when one lives in a hut in the forest. I've nothing and no one to help me. Indeed, I wanted to ask if we could start our little business enterprise again?"

"Noble residents at the palace are barred from all forms of commerce."

"I thought you hated Versailles."

"I do, but it's not without attraction."

A moment later the door opened and Beatrice entered with several other noble conspirators. Cassel turned to her. "Why are we here?"

She frowned. "I don't know."

"Didn't you summon –?"

"It was me," came a deep, raspy voice from the shadows on the far side of the room. The nobles looked at one another then turned to listen. "I've good news for our cause. The King is sending his sister-in-law to England to see her brother, King Charles. For whatever reason, she will not survive the journey."

"You will kill her?" said Cassel. "And then what?"

"You will learn soon enough," said the unseen man.

Beatrice shook her head. "I say we kill the King."

"Come now," said Cassel. "I hate the King as much as you."

"I doubt that. He destroyed your castle. His father destroyed my entire family and thousands of Huguenots."

"Madame de Clermont," said the shadowed man, his arm rising like a dark, accusatory wing, "you tried to poison the King, without our say-so and without success. No, we will first seek to force him from power. Our ally William of Orange grows stronger by the day. He will give us the money and men we need to strengthen our position, to buy friends and influence. Go now. When the time is ripe, each of you will be given a list of people at court susceptible to persuasion."

"Where is Chevalier?" asked Beatrice.

"He was caught and is in prison, charged with treason."

Cassel grimaced. "What is to stop him from talking?"

"Fear."

The nobles exchanged glances then turned back toward the door. As they filed out, stepping over several snakes making their way back in, Montcourt crouched against the wall and waited. As the unseen man moved off into a side room, Montcourt sneaked along the splintering floorboards and held low beside the door, listening in.

"I don't trust that woman," said the unseen man to another in the room.

"Concentrate on your own duties," said the other.

Montcourt peered cautiously around the door. There was faint daylight filtering through the broken walls. He saw the face of the one who'd addressed the nobles and he stifled a gasp. It was Mike, the thug with whom Montcourt had robbed and killed under Cassel's direction. Montcourt could not see the face of the other man who was seated at a table with his back to the door.

"At what time does the convoy leave?" Mike asked.

"Shortly after dawn. She'll be accompanied by six armed guards on horseback and two bodyguards inside the carriage. They'll be joined by a second convoy at Marly."

Mike chuckled darkly. "I'll kill her in the forest, then. I know the perfect spot."

"I've told William of Orange that once she's dead, we must strike swiftly. We'll need men and weapons."

"You trust him?"

The man put his left hand on the table and his little finger began tapping an arrhythmic staccato. Then he said, "Yes. Our enemies may differ, but our means are the same."

Montcourt eased back to the front door and hurried across the field to his horse.

*Dressed in her* finest silk gown, Henriette was escorted from her apartment to the King's private chambers by Bontemps. Philippe followed them up the corridor, anxious as to the summons, pressing for answers.

"I'm her husband," he demanded as they reached the King's door and a guard opened it. "I have the right to know!"

Bontemps ignored him.

"He'll be plotting something, of that we can be sure," said Philippe. "So let me do the talking."

Bontemps stood back, allowing Henriette to enter first. "The King will talk to Her Highness alone." Then Bontemps followed Henriette inside and shut the door.

Philippe stood alone, trying to stem his anger and regain his composure, and then, as the King's brother, ordered the guard to let him enter. As he crossed through the outer chamber he could hear Louis in an anteroom, speaking to Henriette.

"…he'll endeavor to include the treaty in his favor. You must remain firm. Unless he agrees to join us as an ally, the agreement is worthless. If you return without his signature, your mission will have been a failure."

Philippe stormed into the anteroom. Louis turned to stare at his brother. Colbert and Louvois, standing beside the King, gave Philippe a hard stare.

"What do you want of my wife?" asked Philippe.

"I'm sending her to negotiate a treaty."

"I don't understand."

"It is so often that way with you. I'm sending her abroad as my ambassador."

"Where?"

"I won't tell you," said Louis. He motioned to Colbert and Louvois and they quickly left the room.

"Henriette," said Philippe, "is this true? How can you let him do this to you?"

Henriette calmly replied, "Do what?"

"Use you!"

"Is that what irks you, dear brother?" asked Louis. "Or is it that she has been given a role which you, yourself, might have coveted?"

Philippe raised his fist. "What irks me is that you would take away all that is or should be mine!"

The royal brothers locked gazes, eye to eye, royal wolves circling each other mentally, knowing each other all too well. Then Louis said, "Before I forget, your friend Chevalier has just been released from prison. You will find him in your rooms."

Philippe's fist lowered and he drew a sharp breath.

"But if he betrays me again, he will be hanged in public. I'm counting on you to ensure he does not."

Philippe returned to his apartments, his heart pounding. He found Chevalier seated at a mirror, dressed in frilly blue and white, his hair cleaned, combed, and in place, dabbing powder over a fading bruise beneath his eye.

"Darling!" Chevalier hopped up, smiling broadly, his arms outstretched for an embrace.

Philippe stepped back and shook his head.

Chevalier stopped. "I…I thought my return would please you!"

"You betrayed your King. And me."

"May I explain myself?"

"No."

Chevalier's lips pursed. "In that case, I shall go find myself something to eat. Preferably devoid of maggots."

Philippe sighed. "No, wait. Stay."

"Ah," said Chevalier. He leaned in for a kiss but Philippe turned his head away.

"If you betray him again," Philippe said, "the King will have you hanged in public."

"Rest assured I've learned my lesson." Chevalier folded his hands and offered a small, teasing grin. "And the thought of being hanged…in public!"

Philippe went to the sideboard and lifted the wine decanter. "I would not let that happen."

"Thank you, my love!"

"Because I would kill you myself." Philippe poured a full glass, raised it to his lips, and downed it in two angry gulps.

*Beatrice enjoyed card* games for they required strategy, skill, and sometimes trickery. And so she found herself at a table in a palace salon, playing a lively game of whist with the noble Cassel and the lady Montespan. The Montespan studied her hand then played an ace, the winning card.

"Luck is with me today!" she said. "Another game?"

Beatrice chuckled. Cassel smiled through gritted teeth and said, "All right. But I believe you wish to play cards simply to humiliate me."

The Montespan shuffled the cards. "Why would I want to humiliate you?"

"The suffering of others gives you pleasure."

The Montespan winked and dealt.

A messenger, disheveled from what must have been a long and tiring trip, entered the salon with a guard. Bontemps beckoned the messenger over and they stood not far from the card table.

"I've a message for Monsieur Marchal," said the messenger. Beatrice looked at her new hand of cards but turned her ear in the direction of the messenger.

"He's away on business. Deliver it to me," said Bontemps.

"I'm sorry," replied the messenger. "I'm to deliver only to Monsieur Marchal."

"In his absence, his duties defer to me. Give me the message."

Reluctantly, the messenger handed Bontemps the paper.

"From where have you traveled?" asked Bontemps.

"From Pau."

Beatrice's mouth went dry. Without thinking she took her turn, laying down a heart. The Montespan sighed. "Dear Beatrice, you've played a heart. The rest of us are playing in spades." Beatrice snatched up the heart and put down a spade. She glanced over her shoulder to see Bontemps reading the note.

He looked at her for the briefest moment and left the salon.

"Hm. Aren't you from Pau, Beatrice?" asked the Montespan. "That messenger said he'd come from Pau with information for Monsieur Marchal. For some reason, I thought of you."

"I am not the only person to come from Pau."

"Oh, of course," said the Montespan. "I'm sure it's just a coincidence." She touched her cards to her chin, wrinkled her nose, and smiled.

*With guards keeping* a safe yet attentive distance, Louis and Henriette walked a path in the outer gardens, past stately evergreens and holly bushes. Winter was settling in, washing the sky in the color of iron and chilling the air.

"Are you not cold?" he asked Henriette, whose shawl was of a thin, rose-colored fabric.

"No," she answered.

"Of course," said Louis with a smile. "Your English blood!"

They walked a few more moments. Henriette's silence was troubling.

"Do you know why I'm sending you to England?" he asked, leaning close.

"To test me?"

"There's no need for that. I want you to go, not to please me but because it is your wish."

"Is there a difference?"

"I don't know. Is there?"

Henriette stopped and stared at the path in front of her.

Then she turned to Louis. "Did I do something wrong? We used to be close."

"Are we not close now?"

"I don't know. Are we?"

Louis took several steps away and then back. He would not discuss their relationship now. He did not have the time or desire. "When you're with your brother," he said, "you must betray no emotion. Silence is more important than speech. Hold his gaze when you do speak. Play on his weaknesses. Flatter him. Be strong when you need to and give in to his demands when there is nothing at stake. On this mission, you are not his sister nor wife to my brother. You are France. You are me."

Henriette lowered her face and curtseyed.

*Two courtiers stood* at the base of the front palace steps, watching an unkempt man stroll up and into the palace. "Who is that?" one asked.

"It looks like Montcourt," the courtier's companion, his nose wrinkling with disgust.

"But he was banished!"

"I heard he was dead!"

Montcourt ignored the comments. Taking a main corridor he headed for Louis' apartment, bringing with him delicious news that had the power to open those doors.

Louvois was chatting with several ladies in a salon doorway. When he saw Montcourt stroll by he hurried after him and grabbed his arm.

"What are you doing here?" he demanded. "The King will have you hanged if he learns of your presence!"

Montcourt pulled free and continued walking. "Not when I give him information that has fallen into my hands."

"Of what nature?"

"I'll only talk to His Majesty."

"And why would you give him this information?"

"In exchange for my return to Versailles."

"Why would you want to come back?"

Montcourt looked at Louvois, his eyes hardened. "Do you know what it's like to be cold and alone?"

The King was eating his lunch when Louvois and Montcourt were announced at his door. Bontemps and Colbert, who were in attendance, stared in stunned silence as Montcourt entered, bowed, and declared he had news of utmost importance.

Louis motioned Montcourt forward but did not give him permission to sit. He took another bite of bread.

"I was in a tavern," said Montcourt, "and overheard a conversation at an adjoining table."

"And?"

"Only one of them spoke, Sire. He boasted that he was going to kill Your Majesty's sister-in-law on her way to England."

Louis put down the bread and leaned forward, no longer merely tolerating the intrusion but clearly riveted by Montcourt's claim. "Do you know this man?"

"Yes, Sire. From a former life. He's a thief and a killer."

"Did he see you?"

"No, Sire."

"Where is he to be found?"

"He's now a member of your police force."

Louvois stepped forward. "He must be arrested!"

"He will simply deny all knowledge of the matter," said Montcourt. "To catch him red-handed is the only choice. I know his methods, where he will station himself."

Louis considered this. "If what you say is true, France will be in your debt. But until then, you will be placed in custody. Do you understand?"

"Yes, Sire."

Louis hitched his head and Louvois took Montcourt to the door where he turned him over to the guards.

"And Louvois," said the King, "find him new clothes. He looks like a skeleton."

As Montcourt was led away, Louis stood and stared at Louvois. "This means there is a traitor in our midst."

"Sire?" asked Bontemps. "Might it be good to postpone Her Highness' departure?"

"And lose the chance to discover the identity of my enemies? No. In Monsieur Marchal's absence, security for the journey is in your hands. Find out what Montcourt knows. I need not remind you of the consequences if the King of England learned his sister was murdered on her way to see him."

As Bontemps left the King's apartment, he found Claudine in the corridor, dressed as Doctor Pascal, waiting for him.

"*What happened to* you?" asked Bontemps.

"I've a cold," grumbled Fabien. He sat on the cot in Claudine's kitchen, his eyes still bandaged, his shoulders hunched. Claudine stood at the table, peeling away her mustache.

"Who gave you this cold?"

Fabien ignored the question. "My absence from court has been noted?"

"His Majesty is less than pleased. And I went to your office to find your assistant, Laurene, missing."

Fabien touched the bandages then let his hands drop. "I fear we will not see her again. And I would be grateful if you could tell the King I've gone to Paris on a matter of urgency."

Bontemps nodded hesitantly. "Very well. And before I forget, I've a message for you from Pau."

"Did you read it?"

"I did."

"She is a liar?"

"She is. The real Madame de Clermont died in a fire ten years ago. What made you suspect her?"

"Her documents of proof were dated thirty years before the paper on which they were written was made. The weave was modern, made with a windmill known as a Hollander beater. Older paper has more fiber."

"How can you know that?"

"My father was a printer."

"Why did you not have her arrested?"

"I doubted my own convictions," said Fabien. He turned his head in the direction of the door as if seeing it. "I will not doubt them again."

*Chevalier lay on* Philippe's bed, wrapped in a blanket and twirling a feather in his hand, watching as two valets put the final touches on Philippe's hair and helped him on with his coat. "Where are you going?"

Philippe buttoned his coat. "To see my wife."

"Oh. Her."

Philippe waved his hands, dismissing the valets. Then he turned to Chevalier. "I'd prefer you not to speak about my wife in such an insulting tone."

"I've often heard you use the same tone."

Philippe passed the bed on his way to the door, and Chevalier grabbed his arm. "What exactly do you want of me?"

Philippe pushed Chevalier's hand away. "I want you to give without taking. Would you do anything that benefits me but not yourself?"

Hopping from the bed, Chevalier dropped the feather and blanket and stood naked and aroused. "Of course."

"Not that," said Philippe. "And you will sleep in your own rooms tonight."

Chevalier drew back. "But I don't have my own rooms!"

"I'm sure you can find some slut ready to offer you his pillow or buttocks. Or both."

Philippe left Chevalier standing by the bed and went to Henriette's rooms. He found Sophie dressing her for the trip in new jeweled shoes, pearls, and fur-trimmed coat. He watched for a moment.

"It's not too late to say no," he said.

Henriette looked up. "I want to go."

"But why?"

"He asked me to."

"No, he didn't." Philippe came close and fingered the pearls at her neck. "He ordered you."

"I'm pleased to be of service to the King and to France."

"You won't win him back. You know that, don't you?"

Henriette smoothed her coat. "That's not my intention."

"Then," Philippe said slowly, "I wish you a comfortable voyage."

*The morning broke* with a sheet of frost over the lawns and gardens and a cold scent of impending snow in the air. Louis stirred from his sleep and was drawn to the window by the sounds of horses nickering and stamping about. He pressed his forehead to the glass and looked down to watch servants scurrying back and forth, loading trunks and boxes into carriages and Henriette, flanked by guards and surrounded by her ladies, preparing to leave.

The Montespan, naked but for a sheet around her shoulders, moved up beside Louis and kissed his bare shoulder.

"I do admire her," she said, watching Henriette step into her carriage.

"Why?"

"For going away when she is unwell."

"She is going away to get better. Don't you read the *Gazette*?"

"Of course. She's going to Vichy. Silly of me." The Montespan nuzzled Louis' ear. "I'm honored that His Majesty visited me last night. I feared I'd lost your favor."

Louis drew the Montespan close and caressed her cheek. "You will have to try harder if you wish to lose my favor." The Montespan kissed him again and shuffled back to bed. Louis looked back out at the carriage, at Henriette's pale face at the carriage window, and his breath fogged then obliterated the scene.

*Beatrice caught Sophie* by the arm as the girl moved toward the carriage steps. "I want to remind you to take care," she whispered to her daughter. "There are dangers everywhere. You understand?"

Sophie frowned. "But Mother, we're heavily guarded and in complete security."

"If something happens, be sure to place your own safety before that of your mistress."

"I…"

"Enjoy your time in England."

"England? But we're going to Vichy…"

Beatrice stepped back and Sophie, watching over her shoulder, followed Henriette into the carriage.

They traveled away from the palace, past the outer gardens and into the forest along a twisting, turning path heading east. Henriette watched silently out the window, deep in thought, as Sophie struggled with her mother's words. Then she could no longer hold her thoughts to herself.

"Your Highness, we are not going to Vichy, are we?"

Henriette looked at the girl. "How did you know?"

"I…I overheard one of the chambermaids."

Henriette nodded vaguely. "His Majesty is sending me to England to meet my brother, King Charles."

"Why?"

"Stop asking questions, Sophie. Your duty is to comport yourself with discretion and tact."

Sophie nodded meekly. "Of course."

Henriette looked back out the window. "We're entering the world of men. That does not mean we have to behave like men."

The carriage slowed at a sharp bend in the road, and Sophie looked out her own window to a flock of white doves perched on the low branches of a roadside tree.

What she could not see was the large, hulking man staring at the carriage from a knoll above that tree, his face locked in a defiant, blood-thirsty sneer, his crossbow trained on the driver of the carriage. Mike waved a fly from his eyes and hunched his body, preparing to pull the trigger, when the muzzle of a pistol was pressed against his temple. Mike turned to see six musketeers and the King's valet, Bontemps, staring with a sneer as defiant as Mike had ever seen.

*A portly wine* merchant spread out his wares in a palace salon, decanters on the tables, barrels resting on stands. His eyes were wide and his hopeful smile even wider as Rohan, Cassel, and other nobles sampled the wine and discussed it with each other. The King stepped up for a glass and the merchant watched anxiously as Louis took a sip and rolled the wine around in his mouth.

Bontemps entered the salon and eased up beside the King. "The assassin has been apprehended, Sire," he whispered. Louis nodded and swallowed the wine. Then he looked straight at the merchant.

"Monsieur Gruand! You are a magician!"

The merchant let out a loud breath and smiled as the King turned to the nobles. "Try it, try it. It is the perfect blend of sturdiness and refreshment." The nobles came forward as the merchant poured more glasses and handed them out. Rohan lifted his toward the King in a silent salute, and Louis returned the toast.

Montcourt entered the salon, dressed in his new clothes. "My good friend Montcourt!" said the King.

Nobles turned with their wine glasses, surprised to see the outcast back in the fold.

"A few years ago," Louis announced, "I banished this man from court. It is with open arms that I welcome him back. He is a shining example that fidelity has its reward." Louis hugged Montcourt and Rohan led the nobles in applause.

As Montcourt approached the table for a taste of wine, Cassel sidled up to him. "How the hell did you acquire the King's forgiveness?"

"I begged for it," said Montcourt, lifting the glass as if toasting himself. "I told him that life away from Versailles is not worth living."

Cassel's lip twitched furiously. "And what of our other activities?"

"We shall have this discussion in private." Montcourt turned from the table and moved toward a cluster of smiling nobles. "Now, if you will excuse me, I must say hello to some old friends."

*Fabien sat without* flinching on the cot as Claudine carefully unwound the long bandage from around his eyes. She was careful, though certain the man was still in pain. His forehead was covered in sweat and his lips were red and blistered.

"Is it possible," he asked, "that the same person who tried to poison me killed your father?"

Claudine nodded. "Whoever is the poisoner is an expert. Do you believe you know who killed my father?"

"Not yet, but I'm close."

With the bandages gone, Claudine plucked the patches of cloth from each eye. She studied each one as he stared back. "Your right eye seems well recovered. The left still shows signs of the poison. Now, what do you see?"

Fabien blinked hard, then looked at her. "The truth," he said. He swung off the cot and grabbed a coat off a kitchen chair.

"You're in no fit state to move!" said Claudine.

Fabien buttoned the coat. "You've saved my life. I thank you." He marched past her to the door and grabbed a pair of boots from the door-side mat.

"The coat is my father's. And those boots are, as well."

Fabien stepped into the boots and pulled them up. "They say one shouldn't wear a dead man's shoes. I will make an exception."

*Mike stood in* the torture room with his arms tied behind him, his leg chained to the wall. He grinned a blackened-toothed grin as Bontemps tried to question him. He refused to give his name and only chuckled as Bontemps grew angrier with his feeble efforts.

"On whose orders did you try to kill Her Majesty?" demanded Bontemps.

"You won't believe it," snorted Mike, "but I can't remember."

Bontemps grabbed Mike by the throat. "Who?"

Mike laughed aloud. "You're too old for this, and far too much a gentleman."

Bontemps drew back in rage and frustration. There were torture tools all around him, yet he'd never once been required to hurt another man to gain information.

The door opened and Fabien strolled in. He stared at Mike and Mike stared back.

"What is a member of my police force doing here?"

Bontemps wiped his brow. "He tried to kill Her Highness, the Duchess of Orléans."

Fabien nodded. "I see. Tell me, where is the King?"

Bontemps and Fabien left the torture room for the King's apartment. The guards admitted them, and Bontemps found Louis asleep in a chair in his bedchamber. His face was at peace, as if reliving loving, peaceful times.

"Sire?"

Louis' eyes snapped open.

"It's Bontemps. Monsieur Marchal is with me, Sire."

Louis sat straight and turned to Fabien. The peace of his face bled away and anger took its place. "I am the King of France. We have recently uncovered a plot to destroy me and everything I have built. My brother's wife was almost assassinated by a member of your police force. William of Orange is seeking ways to destroy me. And you…!" Louis took a breath and roared, "*You! My head of security! You were in Paris!*"

Fabien lifted his chin. "I was not in Paris, Sire."

Louis looked hard at Bontemps. "That is what I was told."

"Sire, the fault is mine," said Fabien. "An attempt was made on my life. I did not wish the person responsible to know my whereabouts or condition."

"An attempt by whom?"

"A woman."

"Madame de Clermont."

"Yes. May I ask how you knew?"

"The whole court knows. You thought you could keep your relationship secret? I've given orders for her to be ejected from court. I believe she has a daughter, who will also be —"

"The daughter is lady-in-waiting to Her Highness," interrupted Fabien. "Where is she now?"

"She will be almost arrived in Calais, Sire," said Bontemps.

Louis face darkened. "I pray the daughter has no part in the mother's plotting."

"Sire," said Fabien, "it's imperative that Madame de Clermont remains at court and ignorant of the case against her. I have reason to believe she has committed forgery and was behind the disappearance of my assistant. That she attempted to poison Your Majesty, killed your doctor, and made the attempt on my life. I have no concrete proof, but please allow me to find it."

Louis nodded. Then he angled his head. "What happened to your eye?"

"It wandered, Sire."

*Seated at her* mirror, removing her make-up, Beatrice flinched at the knock on her chamber door. "Yes?" she called.

Fabien stepped in, smiling coolly. It took the barest of moments for Beatrice to gather her composure even as her mind raced. "Monsieur Marchal, I…I was so worried about you."

"So was I," said Fabien, closing the door behind him.

Beatrice stood to face Fabien. His arms were by his side and there was a shape that looked like a pistol beneath his buttoned coat. One eye was cool and clear, the other reddened like that of a devil. "You ran out while I was pouring water for you. I've been looking for you for two days."

"I didn't know where I was or what I was doing. As luck would have it, someone found me and took me to a doctor. I thought I'd been poisoned. But you were right. It was something I ate."

"I'm gratified to hear that." Beatrice felt her courage wavering, and it seemed that Fabien was well aware of her discomfort and pleased with it.

"After my recovery I had to go to Paris on behalf of His

Majesty, and now I'm back and have come for my boots."

"Of course." Beatrice slipped behind the screen that divided the room, gathered Fabien's boots, and snatched up a knife from the table. She tucked it into her belt behind her back and came back around the screen.

"I had them cleaned," she said.

Fabien reached for the boots and for the briefest second she saw raw passion in his good eye, passion that could mean either sex or death.

"I'm glad you're recovered," she said.

"I bid you good day." Fabien bowed and left Beatrice in her room, her legs trembling, her arms shaking.

*The bathwater was* warm and Philippe nearly at peace when the King entered his brother's private chamber and ordered the chambermaid, who was washing Philippe's shoulders, to put down the cloth and leave the room.

Philippe did not turn around but stared at Louis' shadow on the wall. "She may not come back," he said.

"She will, I know it. I trust her."

"How simpler things would be for her if she waved farewell to life in a madhouse where two brothers were always at each other's throats. Do you have any idea what sort of place you are creating?"

"I know you're going to tell me."

"Your palace of dreams is a haven for plotting, treachery, infidelity, and depravity. Did I miss anything?"

Louis stepped around the tub to face his brother. "It is on that subject that I came to see you. You're angry that I sent your wife to England. She now has a purpose in life. You do not. I'm here to give you one."

"Truly? What have you in mind?"

"Etiquette."

Philippe scoffed. "Etiquette?"

"The nobles behave as if this were their home. They do not know how to address members of the royal family or each other, how to eat at dinner, how to *be* at Versailles. I want everyone to know their place and status. I want every minute of every day structured. From now on, everyone must abide by the same set of rules."

"Including the King?"

"Especially the King. And who better to control the King than his brother?"

Philippe stood and shook bathwater from his arms. "Could you not give me a task which would add to the glory and reputation of France?"

"I just did."

*The noise in* the salon was deafening, with nobles gambling, laughing, drinking, and grabbing one another as unabashedly as would the lowest of commoners. Louis passed through the room, seeking Rohan. The Montespan came up to him but Louis brushed her aside. Those nobles who were sober enough bowed as the King passed. The others sat about in bleary-eyed stupors.

"Where is Rohan?" Louis asked.

No one answered.

"Where is Rohan?" the King shouted.

"Behind you, Sire."

Louis turned. "Come, I need a friend tonight." He grabbed a bottle of wine and two glasses from a passing servant and led Rohan out from the noise and bright light.

They went outside and sat on a marble bench behind the palace, looking out through the frosted moonlight at the gardens. Guards stood at a distance.

"Everything use to be so free of fog and thicket," said Louis. "We knew who we were, what we wanted, where we were going, and who our enemies and friends were. But now…"

"There is no turning back?"

Louis shook his head. "The path is too narrow for turning. Every decision taken is a stride forward and cannot be revoked."

Rohan unstopped the wine bottle and filled the glasses. "What is your greatest fear?"

"To be alone."

"You will never be alone."

Louis looked at Rohan fondly, and lifted his glass for a toast. "Spoken like a true friend. To the things and people we left behind."

"And to a brighter future," said Rohan. Both drank deeply under the canopy of night. Then Rohan put his left arm around Louis' shoulder, and his little finger began tapping a soft, arrhythmic staccato.

# 9

*The scene was* serenity itself – the King strolling a garden pathway, past towering statues and elegant fountains gone silent with the season, white winter clouds streaking the ice-blue sky – and Bontemps watched on with awe and love. Yet responsibilities trumped the beauty of the moment, and he hurried to Louis and bowed.

"Good morning, Sire. It is time."

Louis sighed and gave the garden a look of longing. "Of course."

"Any news?" he asked as they strolled back to the palace through evergreen hedges and rows of winter roses.

"A messenger arrived during the night, Sire. The ship carrying Her Highness left Calais the day before yesterday. All being well, she will have arrived in Dover by now."

Louis rubbed his chin pensively. "Was I wrong to send her?"

"His Majesty always does what he considers best for France."

"If she does not return?"

"She will, Sire. I am certain."

"What makes you certain?"

"She is loyal. And because her place is here."

"But what is her place? To be a dutiful wife?"

"That is not for me to say."

"Would you want to be a woman, Bontemps?"

"Oh, no, Sire."

Louis smiled vaguely. "Neither would I."

In the King's bedchamber, the dressers quickly and expertly changed the King from his morning clothes into newly polished shoes, white ruffled shirt, and black velvet vest, while Bontemps read the list of the day's scheduled meetings. When Bontemps mentioned the mid-morning meeting with Bishop Bossuet regarding the Protestant question, Louis shook his head. "Cancel it. I've neither the time nor humor for one of his endless speeches."

"Very well, Sire," said Bontemps. "At eleven the royal astronomer Cassini will deliver an address, and between eleven o'clock and noon you are due to sit for a portrait. After lunch –"

Louis held up his hand. "Yes, yes, it's all fine." He stood still as the dressers added the final touch, an embroidered, gold coat. The King considered his reflection and duly satisfied swept from the room for his busy day.

The State Room was bustling with royal business. Beneath the vaulted, painted ceiling and seated at his desk, Louis signed the countless documents handed him by Bontemps. Colbert and Louvois stood apart, waiting their turn to speak to the King. Rohan lounged nearby in a window seat, the morning sun warming his shoulders.

As Louis handed Bontemps a signed paper, he noted Louvois and called him over. "You've a letter for me?"

"From the King of Sweden, Sire."

Louis put down the quill. "Open it. Tell me what it says."

Louvois broke the seal and read the letter aloud. "The King has agreed to break his alliance with the Dutch and support us."

"Good. All we need now is England at our side." Louis retrieved the quill, dipped it in the inkwell, and signed yet another of the papers given him by Bontemps.

"What word of the prisoner?" asked Rohan from the window. "The one who tried to kill Her Highness?"

"Monsieur Marchal is questioning him," said Bontemps.

Louis signed the last paper. "Tell Marchal I want to see him." Bontemps bowed and left the room. Then the King motioned to Colbert. "What news of the Trianon?"

"They're experiencing problems with the tiles, Sire," Colbert said. "They keep falling off. Le Vau wonders whether Your Majesty would consider changing the façade?"

"No. Without the façade, the building holds no interest. And the canal?"

"Le Notre believes it will be filled with water by summer, Sire."

"Then we shall need some vessels."

"Vessels?"

"Yes. Rowing boats. Miniature ships. Gondolas. Water is not merely there to be looked at."

$\mathcal{T}$*he voyage across* the English Channel had been surprisingly calm, with a cold wind countered by a kind sun. Henriette hoped the pleasant trip predicted a likewise successful task ahead, though as she entered Dover Castle's courtyard with Sophie and her servants, the grave importance of her assignment caught her heart and it took effort to retain her smile and appearance of confidence.

Dover Castle sat upon the cliffs overlooking the channel, a large, somber fortress of gray stone covered with vines and brine. Sir William and his guards met the party in the courtyard, and he bowed respectfully. "Welcome home, Your Highness! How was your journey?"

Henriette nodded daintily. "Pleasant enough, thank you."

"I apologize in advance," Throckmorton said as he led the entourage through the courtyard toward a door at the far side. "The castle is a little chilly this time of year."

"Is it just His Majesty I shall be seeing?"

"No. The Count of Arlington and Lord Arundell will also be in attendance."

"Would it be possible for me to see His Majesty before the official discussions begin? In private?"

"I fear not, Your Highness. That would be most irregular."

Henriette stopped and turned to Sophie. "A handkerchief, please. I've something in my eye." Sophie removed a handkerchief from a pocket in her cloak and held it up to Henriette's eye. As she leaned close, Henriette whispered, "I was not made for this. I do not have the courage."

Sophie pretended to wipe the eye. "You will find the courage in the doing of it, Your Highness."

Throckmorton, ahead several paces, looked back. "Is something amiss?"

Henriette pushed the handkerchief away, squared her shoulders, and lifted her head. "Not at all," she replied.

When they reached the door, armed guards allowed Throckmorton and Henriette to enter and the others were told to remain outside.

The corridors of the castle were much darker than those of Versailles, yet Henriette remembered them well. The stairs and gray walls, the echoes that traveled the unadorned stone floors. Throckmorton escorted her into a large room furnished only with a single, regal chair and a table on which an inkwell and bowl of quills had been placed.

"His Majesty is in conference and will be with you shortly," said Throckmorton.

Henriette shivered and hoped Throckmorton had not noticed. "Thank you," she said.

*The back of* his head slammed against the pillar behind him, sending stars across his field of vision and causing him to bite his cheek, but he made himself smile at Fabien, who had delivered the blow.

"Now then," said Fabien, as he checked the ropes that held Mike in place against the pillar. He held up a leather strap. Two guards stood back, watching. "Who gave you orders to kill her?"

"I don't know."

Fabien slapped the leather strap across Mike's forehead

and secured it around the pillar, making it impossible for Mike to turn his head. "How did he contact you?"

"I don't know."

Mike watched as Fabien selected a hammer and metal spike from the torture table. Mike's nerves jumped.

Fabien placed the tip of the spike against Mike's skull behind his right ear. "Did you know," he said, "that if you drive a spike through a precise spot in the skull, the victim will retain the capacity for speech and thought but will be otherwise paralyzed for the rest of his life?"

Mike began to struggle against the bindings. "I…I never saw him. He left me a note, always in a different place."

"What did you do before entering my police force?"

"I worked in a tavern."

Fabien put the spike down. "Do you know who William of Orange is?"

"No."

"Are you scared?"

Mike snarled. "Of what?"

"Do you visit him or does he come to France?"

Mike fought the restraints. "Who? What do you mean?"

"William of Orange."

"I don't know him!"

"Where is the tavern?"

"In the south, near –"

Fabien leaned close, his lip curled. "Does he give you money?"

"Who? *Who?!*"

"William of Orange?"

"I tell you!" shouted Mike, spittle flying from his bloodied mouth. "I don't know who he is! I've never even been to Holland!"

Fabien stood straight and smiled a cold, thin smile. "I never said he is from Holland. You did, however."

The door to the torture room banged open and Bontemps entered. Fabien turned on the valet, furious at the interruption, but Bontemps did not flinch. "The King would like to see you."

Fabien looked back at Mike.

"Immediately."

Fabien wiped his hands and turned to the guards. "Don't take your eyes off him, don't talk to him, don't give him anything." Then he followed Bontemps out of the torture room.

Mike glared at the guards, who just stared through him as if he were a chair. Minutes later the torture room door opened. Mike braced himself, ready to face Fabien again. But it was Rohan. The guard immediately blocked him.

"Where is Monsieur Marchal?" demanded Rohan. "The King wants to see him."

"Already gone, sir," said the guard.

"So, that's the traitor?" Rohan brushed past the guards, who frowned yet eyed each other, uncertain as to confronting the King's friend.

Mike and Rohan locked stony gazes. "If I had my way," said Rohan, "I'd have you hanged, drawn, and quartered." Rohan scooped up the spike and turned it over in his hands. "Gruesome. What is this for?"

"For killing people," said Mike.

One of the guards approached Rohan. "Sir…"

"Killing?" said Rohan. "Like this?" He spun around with the spike and shoved it deep into the eye of the guard, who fell with a hideous wail. Rohan snatched the guard's dagger as the second rushed forward, and he hurled it, catching the guard in the throat. The guard gurgled and grappled for the knife for only a second then he collapsed to the floor. As both writhed, whimpered, and died, Rohan cut Mike free. Then he drew a monk's cloak from beneath his coat.

"Here," said Rohan as Mike took the cloak and slipped it on."A guard is expecting you by the laundry room. He'll show you how to get out. Visit our friend in Paris. Tell him I want the best men he has at his disposal. You will take them to the usual place and wait my instructions. Hurry!"

*A cozy fire* popped and danced in the fireplace in Philippe's outer chamber, warming the room but not the tension. Seated side by side, Philippe and Chevalier stared at the fire, watching the logs heave and crack.

"Do you remember the first night we spent together?" Chevalier asked.

"No."

"And do you remember what I said to you in the morning?"

"No."

"I said,'Henceforth every day I do not touch you, taste you, feel you, breathe you, will be a day of death and mourning.'"

Philippe shrugged slightly.

Chevalier leaned over in his chair, trying to meet Philippe's gaze."I meant it then and I mean it now. I've made a mistake. I offended the King and I offended you. But my love remains as strong as the day we met."He held out his hand.

Slowly, his focus still on the fire, Philippe likewise reached out, and their fingers touched.

*After a wait* that dragged on mercilessly within the chilly, barren room, King Charles II of England entered, dressed in an ermine-trimmed robe. He was followed by Henry Bennet, the Earl of Arlington, Lord Henry Arundell, Sir William, and four blank-faced guards. Henriette curtseyed. In return, the men bowed, their lips smiling yet their eyes showing hints of condescension.

"My dear younger sister," said King Charles, stretching out his arm. "The last time I saw you, you were scared there was a ghost under your bed. I hope you got rid of it."

Henriette kissed Charles' hand. "I come not as your sister but as an emissary of France."

"Indeed," said Charles. The advisors looked at one another and then at Henriette as if she were merely a child to be tolerated. "And more besides, I understand."

"I…I represent His Majesty King Louis XIV," she said. *I cannot even speak calmly! I cannot do this!* She glanced down and away from her brother and the moment she did, she knew she'd made a mistake.

"I'm pleased to see you," Charles said in the arrogant, regal tone she knew so well. "Now to business. Sir William has outlined your King's proposals and I fear I cannot accept them in their entirety. He seems to see England as a small, insignificant neighbor with no ambitions of its own…."

*I should not be here,* she thought. *This was a mistake!*

And then Louis' words to her flooded back. *"Your every move and gesture must indicate self-control. Betray no emotion."*

"…he wishes us to stand by while he invades Holland and steals their trade. This is unacceptable. He proposes to aid us in our relations with the Pope…"

*"Hold his gaze. Play on his weaknesses."*

Henriette's eyes scanned the room. It was then she truly saw what was before her. The crumbling walls. A rat sniffing in the corner. The shoes of the guards badly worn and splitting at the seams. A broken window and water on the floor from a leak in the ceiling.

"But with what guarantee?" said Charles. "In short, his proposals lean too heavily in France's favor."

Henriette turned her face back to her brother. *"Hold his gaze. Play on his weaknesses."* She took a deep, silent breath of rediscovered self-confidence and looked the King in the eye. "How much do you want?"

Charles frowned slightly. "I beg your pardon."

"You may seek to impress me with your castles and defiant speeches, but you do not fool me, brother."

The frown increased. "Fool you?"

"You are bankrupt."

Charles forced a chuckle. "What a charming thought!"

Henriette felt the tables turn. She now held the winning cards. "Six years ago, the city of London was struck by a plague. Two years after, it was destroyed by fire. You are bankrupt but don't care to admit it. I repeat, how much?"

The King's advisors watched the brother and sister, yet said nothing.

"This is not how we conduct such matters," said Charles.

"It is how I conduct them."

"My dear sister —"

"I prefer you address me as Your Highness."

Charles' jaw tightened. It was a moment before he spoke. "We had in mind something in the region of half a million per month for a year. In return —"

"Three hundred per month for six months."

"But one can do so little with that."

"Two million crowns spread over a six month period. Furthermore, we will provide you with a personal armed guard of five thousand men."

"Whatever for?"

Henriette folded her hands primly and tipped her head. "If the people of England choose to rise in rebellion again and demand the King's head as they did our father's you will need a trusted body of men to protect you."

Charles looked at his advisors, and after a moment Sir William gave a slight yet certain nod.

*The King insisted* on seeing the prisoner, and so Fabien escorted Louis and his ministers and guards down the winding stairs to his office.

"You are certain William of Orange is behind the conspiracy?" Louis asked as they approached the door.

"Without doubt, Sire."

"And you believe you can extract the truth from him?"

"I will extract all that he knows, but it is unlikely he knows everything. His masters will ensure he knows only what is necessary."

The men entered the office and crossed to the open door of the torture room. Inside they discovered the bloodied bodies of the guards and the prisoner gone.

Fabien turned to the guards. "A guard on every exit! Now! Organize a search party! Send to every whorehouse and tavern in the town and inform our agents in Paris and Orléans!"

Louis stood in the midst of the carnage, the guards' blood on his shoes. His voice was low and hard as stone. "This is unfortunate. For me because I am no longer safe in my own home. For France because William of Orange will soon be wearing her crown. And for my head of security, because it is not the first time he has failed in his duties. He no longer has the trust of his employer." Then he swung about to face Bontemps. "Tell my former head of security that I wish him luck in his future career." Then he stalked away, leaving Fabien staring silently at the leather strap on the floor.

Bontemps caught up with Louis on the stairs.

"Sire, while it's true that I consider Monsieur Marchal to be driven more by violence than reason, nonetheless I believe him to be a man of trust and duty."

Louis stopped and stared at Bontemps. "He has failed me!"

"Yes, Sire. But believe me, without him Your Majesty would not be alive today."

Louis stood, breathing heavily, and then continued up the stairs.

*King Charles discussed* the offer with his advisors, their voices low. Then he turned back to his sister. "I am willing to accept His Majesty's offer. You will return to France with the treaty signed."

Henriette nodded. "I'm grateful to hear it."

As Throckmorton sat at the table to prepare for the signing, Charles led Henriette aside. "You are sure I can trust him?"

"Yes," Henriette replied. "You share the same ambitions."

"No, he wishes to place himself at the center of the universe. I do not."

"He wants to be known by posterity as a great king. Not you?"

"My ambitions are more modest. I wish to be known as a king who did no harm to anyone. But how thoughtless of me. I forgot to ask how you were."

Henriette smiled. "Well, thank you."

"Do you miss England?"

"I miss my brother. When he's not trying to humble his sister."

Charles took Henriette's hand gently. "But you will not return here. Your life is there, with him."

"Him?"

"Your husband, of course. They say he has unconventional tastes. They also say you and the King are intimate."

Henriette shook her head. "Do not forget that he and I spent our childhood together. It's natural that we should be close friends."

"So it is merely malicious gossip?"

"Exactly. Besides, His Majesty's attentions are elsewhere."

Charles squeezed Henriette's hand then took his place at the table and dipped the quill into the inkwell.

*Fabien studied the* door, the streaks of blood, and the placement of the guards' bodies on the floor. There were clues here to be found, to discover who had the opportunity and wits to not only gain entrance but also the skill to accomplish it cleanly and quickly. He picked up the spike, weighed it, then swung around, imagining he was the traitor. He came face to face with Bontemps, who had entered unheard.

"The King has been kind enough to allow you to continue in your duties," said Bontemps, stepping back from the sharp point. "This is in spite of your repeated failures. This is your last chance."

Fabien ignored the valet and turned back to his investigation. Bontemps shrugged and left the room alone.

*Giovanni Cassini was* a most eloquent and dramatic astronomer, silver-haired and energetic, and he stood before the gathering of nobles in the State Room, discussing space and distances and the solar system. Louis, however, seemed to be elsewhere in thought. The Montespan, seated beside the King, whispered, "His Majesty seems preoccupied."

Louis shook his head. "On the contrary."

"And," Cassini said with a grand bow, "on behalf of all science, I should like to thank his wonderful Majesty for the generosity and patronage in helping us in our quest for the truth."

Louis stood and led the nobles in generous applause. Then he called out, "Monsieur Cassini, do you adhere to the theories of Copernicus and Newton regarding the relation between the sun and Earth?"

Cassini smiled. "Yes, Your Majesty. The sun is the center, the heart, the mother of the universe. Without its warmth and light, all life is gone. Man will cease to exist."

"Perhaps you could apply the same technique of measurement for France?"

"The topography of France is already begun, Sire."

Louis nodded thoughtfully. "Splendid. Let's hope we have not exaggerated the extent of our possessions."

Cassini's smile faded. The nobles shifted in their seats. "I regret, Sire, the preliminary results indicate that France is not so big as we thought."

"You mean to take away with your calculations the lands I gained in war with the Spanish Netherlands?"

"Ah," said Cassini, his face reddening, "no one can argue with the truth, Sire. Not even a king."

"Then I bow before the power of scientific truth." Louis left the room, followed by an entourage of noisy nobles, and fell in beside Philippe.

"I confess to my disappointment in you, my dear brother. I asked you to take charge of court etiquette and you promised to think about it. Your thinking has led nowhere."

Philippe did not slow. "You know perfectly well that your proposition does not interest me."

Louis pressed close, causing Philippe to stop. "It was not a proposition. Think about it again, in the hope that this time your thinking bears fruit."

*There was a* knock on the door and Cassel looked up from the ledger on his desk. "Who is it?"

"Your old friend." The door opened and Montcourt entered. He glanced around at the size of the room and made a face.

Cassel pushed a decanter across the desk. "Help yourself to some wine."

"No, thank you."

"You'll have heard that our plot to kill the King's sister-in-law failed," Cassel said, closing the ledger, " and the would-be assassin was captured and imprisoned."

Montcourt sat on Cassel's cot. "I did. I knew it was a risky venture."

"I have to wonder," said Cassel. "Who could have revealed the plot to the King? Not many of us knew it."

"Rest assured, it wasn't me."

"No, though it seems curious that you secured a royal pardon with such ease."

"Even if it had been me, what would you do? Tell the King? Knowing full well I have the means to take you to the gallows with me? You'd do nothing, that's what. And if you see our mysterious friends again, tell them I'll take no further part in their plotting. I've suffered at the hands of the King, but I've also been blessed by his generosity."

"And I do not wish to be rid of the King," said Cassel, "but only to put him in his place and return affairs to their former state."

Montcourt stood and brushed his trousers as if Cassel's room had dirtied them. "Things will never return to their former state. We'll both spend the rest of our days at Versailles. Let us ensure they are happy ones." Striding to the door, he paused and looked back. "Please pass on my regards to my former allies. I look forward to never hearing from them again."

*The foods brought* in by the servant were fresh, plentiful, and tastefully arranged, but Philippe had no appetite. He picked up a grape, studied it, and threw it into the fire. Then he lifted a pastry, sniffed it, and put it back. "I can't remember the last time I was actually hungry."

Chevalier selected a grape. "What did the King mean about etiquette?"

"Some hare-brained idea to make me look the fool. He wishes me to create a list of rules telling people how to behave at court. He wants us all to be puppets."

"Is that such a bad idea? I think you underestimate your brother and allow envy to blind you to his talents."

"I merely see him as he is."

Chevalier rolled the grape in his fingers. "What better way to keep everyone under control than by dictating their every word and movement? Brilliant. Besides," Chevalier put the grape to his lips, drew it in, chewed and swallowed it. "He gave me back to you."

"So I'm indebted to him."

"Yes."

Chevalier hopped up and went over to Philippe's desk. He lifted the quill and tapped it on his chin. "We're going to turn the nobles of Versailles into obedient servants. From now on, everyone will know how to be from dawn to dusk. How to walk, to talk, to address a man or woman, to sit and behave in front of the King. And you, my darling, will be master of ceremonies."

Philippe leaned back in his chair. "You're mad."

"Let's be mad together." Chevalier took paper from the desk drawer and smiled.

"*For some reason,* I feel lucky tonight," said Louis as he scooped up the cards Colbert had dealt, held them close, and studied them. He was deep in a late-night game of piquet with Rohan and Colbert in a cozy palace salon while the Montespan, Philippe, Chevalier, and hand-selected courtiers looked on. The Montespan stood close to the table, and he could smell her perfume.

Rohan peered at his cards, discarded two, and picked up two more. Louis replaced four of his own.

"I seem to remember, Rohan," Louis said over his hand, "you were rather good at cards when we were children."

"I cheated. But you never noticed."

"Ah! Now he tells me. Of course, you wouldn't dare cheat now."

"I fear I don't need to."

The players each laid out his cards; Colbert studied them and grimaced. "His Majesty scores forty-seven points. Lord Rohan fifty-six. His Majesty owes Lord Rohan 2,500 francs."

The room went silent and everyone watched the King. He smiled and waved his hand. "Another? But let's up the stakes."

Rohan raised a brow. "Very well."

*I will make this next wager a true wager.* "What is the name of the horse your rode to hounds yesterday?"

"Tarquin."

"If I win, you give me Tarquin. If you win, I give you two million francs."

"Very well!"

The nobles applauded the challenge. The Montespan stepped even closer.

As Colbert scooped up the cards and began to shuffle them, Fabien moved through the nobles and leaned down to the King's ear. "My men have searched the palace and surrounding area without success, Sire. The prisoner is without doubt long departed. I've sent my best men to Calais to accompany Her Highness on her return."

*This will not sour my night.* Louis nodded then jerked his head, sending Fabien on his way.

Colbert dealt the cards again. The men leaned over their hands, elbows on the table, watching carefully, playing strategically, sipping wine. At last Rohan grunted triumphantly and slapped down a line of aces. Louis raised his glass in admiration.

"I owe you two million francs, my friend," he said. "You will receive them in the morning. Now if you will excuse me, I'm a trifle weary."

The King stood and moved to the door. Colbert joined him, his face tight. "Sire, it is not certain that we have two million francs here at the palace."

Louis gave Colbert the briefest glance. "If we don't, my reign will have been shorter than I would have liked."

*Fabien had seen* Beatrice among the nobles watching the King's card game and so, with her well occupied, he slipped away to her apartment and let himself in with his passkey. Lighting a candle, he began a methodical search of her room. He rummaged beneath her bed, in every drawer of the desk and table, and in her purses and satchels and trunks. At last he opened her wardrobe. He felt each dress carefully, running his hands along the satiny sleeves, the soft bodices, the full skirts, the smell – Beatrice's scent – drifting from the fabric and stirring a rush of passion in his mind and his body. *Beatrice.* He paused, remembering her touch, her taste, and the beat of his heart quickened.

*No. Enough of that. Keep looking.*

Drawing his fingers along the base of one gown he stopped. Felt again. There was something small yet heavy sewn into the hem. He picked out enough threads to feel inside and withdrew a small ornate box. Opening it, he discovered a brown power inside. He sniffed it and could not identify the substance.

*I know who will know.*

Fabien left Beatrice's apartment, and went out into the snow-scented night, heading for the town of Versailles.

He found the young physician at home, dissecting a pan of human body tissue in the clinic. She invited him in, wiped blood from her fingers and hair from her eyes, and opened the box Fabien handed her. She stared at the powder then at Fabien.

"Where did you get it?"

"In a lady's dress."

"A lady?"

Fabien nodded.

*W*ith the *King* retired and all the other nobles departed, the Montespan and Rohan were left alone in the salon. The Montespan slid into the chair where Louis had sat and challenged Rohan to a game. She shuffled and dealt the cards.

"Why is it you've never been chosen to play with me before?" she asked as Rohan picked up his hand.

Rohan arced a brow. "We're talking cards, are we not?"

"I am." She discarded two and drew two more from the deck. "Are you scared of losing to a woman?"

"Not at all. At least, not to a woman like you."

"And what sort is that?"

"A woman who will do anything to win."

They played in silence for several minutes. When the Montespan placed her cards down, she leaned over to give

Rohan a clear view of her cleavage. He stared yet he did not make a move.

"You are an enigma," she said at last.

Rohan fanned his cards. "How so?"

"I've always wondered what lies beneath that boyish smile and jovial demeanor."

"You're wasting your time," said Rohan. "Behind the smile and demeanor there is nothing. I like the simple things in life. Wine, hunting, women. What need for anything else for a happy life? I'm not one for politics or intrigue."

"That is why the King is so fond of you."

Rohan smiled. "We all have trump cards. The key is when to play them."

"Never a truer word spoken." Montespan placed aces down, winning the game. She winked and left Rohan at the table, alone with the portraits on the wall and his shadow on the floor.

Montespan entered the King's outer chamber and found Bontemps reading in a corner. "I need to speak to the King," she insisted. The valet gave her the disapproving look she'd seen all too often, so she repeated her demand. Bontemps put the book down and knocked on the bedchamber door. "Lady Montespan wishes to see you."

"Let her in."

Louis sat up in his bed as the Montespan stepped in and closed the door. He looked her up and down. "Am I still King?"

The Montespan nodded coyly. "Still King and still my master."

"And how did you subdue your enemy?"

"By playing the silly little girl, by using my feminine wiles. And by being better than him."

Louis smiled, amused. "Feminine wiles. I'm jealous. Perhaps you would like to try them on me."

The Montespan removed her gown and unpinned her hair. Naked, she joined Louis in the bed. "I feel lucky tonight," he said into her hair, then rolled on top of her.

*The powder was* a puzzle. Claudine sat at her desk in the clinic, placing drops of various liquids onto samples of the powder but the results proved nothing. Her frustration grew with each worthless test. As Fabien paced the room, Claudine took down the case that held her collection of herbal extracts. She selected one, sat down again, and put two drops into the powder. It immediately bubbled and fizzed.

"Yes," she said. "Without a doubt the powder is poison, and quite possibly the one that killed my father and almost killed you."

Fabien leaned over the dish. "You found the missing ingredient?"

"Oleander. Do you know the person who made this?"

Fabien took a measured breath and grabbed his coat to return to the palace. "All too well."

He waited until morning to talk to the King, though the news tormented his thoughts and he was unable to sleep. He found Louis in a lower garden, cloaked against the cold, practicing with his musket by shooting a straw deer set up at a distance. Between shots the King listened as Fabien explained his newest discoveries.

"With your permission, Sire, I will deal with Madame de Clermont as I see fit."

A valet took Louis' spent musket and handed him one that was freshly loaded. Louis aimed it at the deer, his right eye squinting down the barrel. "You would have her tortured?"

"No, Sire. I fear that would give her more pleasure than pain."

Louis fired. The ball hit the chest of the deer and straw sprayed. "And the daughter?"

"If she were involved in the plot, Her Highness would be dead."

Louis lowered the musket. "Everywhere I look, I see the hand of William of Orange. He seeks to undermine our alliance with England and weaken our position."

"Perhaps this failure will put an end to his efforts, Sire."

Louis accepted another musket, aimed. "On the contrary. It will only encourage him to go further." He pulled the trigger and with a *BAM*, blew the deer's head off.

*William of Orange*, dressed in the stiff, royal frills of the Dutch, sat with King Charles in the State Room of Dover Castle, dining on mutton, eggs, and potatoes. Throckmorton stood obediently and attentively by the window. They were well into the meal before the dark-haired Dutch prince spoke his mind.

"I understand a ship sporting French colors left port a few days ago," he said, lifting his wine goblet.

Charles nodded. "I believe a cargo of wine and cheese has recently arrived on our shores."

"From what I'm told, the cargo was not destined for a banquet."

Charles rubbed his chin, maintaining his air of detachment. "I shall inquire if it bothers you so."

"No need. I should merely like to know what the King of France's sister-in-law was doing here."

"Visiting her brother. Do brothers and sisters in Holland not visit each other?"

"If I were in Louis' shoes and wanted to attack Holland, I would first approach her allies. I would tell Sweden to turn a blind eye and convince England to join me. I'd offer money in return. And I'd send a diplomat or someone close to the King of England to discuss it."

"Your argument would carry much weight but for one weakness."

"Which is?"

"Would I join forces with Louis and attack Holland if I was about to propose a marital alliance to the man who will soon be King of Holland?"

Charles nodded to Throckmorton, who went to the door and opened it. He led in a young girl not yet ten years old, with pale hair and green eyes. She stared at the floor as she curtseyed.

"You've not met your first cousin, my niece Mary," said Charles.

"It is an honor."

Charles put his arm across the back of his chair. "Mary is looking for a husband and you, I believe, a wife."

*Henriette was due* to arrive in the afternoon. Louis waited impatiently, walking back and forth from one State Room window to another, looking out at the gardens and the road that wound through them. As he watched and paced, Louvois studied a map of Holland and France that had been rolled out on the center table.

"We now have a base for supplies and munitions in Dunkirk, Courtra, Lille, Brisach and Pignerol, Metz and Thionville."

"Enough for how long?" asked Louis.

"A six month campaign, Sire."

"Good. Start preparing the troops."

Louvois looked up. "Already?"

"I want them in uniform, ready for battle by spring."

As Louvois began to speak again, Louis spotted the carriage in the distance and hurried from the room.

*Henriette watched the* trees flash past, barren trees shed of their foliage and standing stark against the cold, with only an occasional evergreen and red-berried holly breaking the gray monotony. Soon she would be home at Versailles. Yet her heart was torn. Being in England had awakened memories and feelings deeper than she would have imagined, had stirred a longing for what had once been.

Now, with her carriage traveling along King Louis' royal road through the forest, she wasn't sure where she belonged. She tucked the blanket more tightly across her lap and fought back tears.

As the carriage reached the front of the place she saw Louis hurrying through a line of servants, his face radiating joy. He reached out and Henriette took his arm as the carriage door opened. It was all she could do to keep from stumbling into his arms.

"Thank you, Sire," she said. "It's not customary for a monarch to perform the tasks of a servant."

"We are all servants of France, are we not?" replied the King.

As the carriage was unloaded, Louis led Henriette up the steps. He nuzzled her shoulder. "How was England?"

"Cold."

"I've never been to England, but I'm told it rains perpetually and its inhabitants are forever apologizing."

"I'm sorry for contradicting His Majesty, but that is a myth."

Louis smiled and led her out of the winter sunlight and into the palace.

She took her time changing, having a small meal, and trying to regain her strength. Louis had already called for the ministers to meet with Henriette for a debriefing. She preferred to sleep, to un-shoulder the mantle of political responsibilities for a while, but the King would not be denied. She donned a fresh dress, let Sophie comb and style her hair, then joined the men in the State Room.

Louis sat at the center table and read the document Henriette had brought from England.

"The two Kings will declare war against the United Provinces of Holland. The King of France will attack by land and will receive the help of six thousand men from England. The King of England will send fifty men-of-war to sea, and the King of France thirty. His Britannic Majesty will be content to receive Walcheren, the mouth of the Scheldt, and the Isle of Cadzand, as his share of the conquered provinces. The King of England will make a public profession of the Catholic faith and will receive the sum of two millions of crowns in the course of the next six months."

Louis looked up from the paper. "We were ready to go up to three million."

Henriette, seated across from the King, said, "I wasn't."

All the men smiled and nodded.

Louis put the paper down and stood. "This calls for a celebration!"

Henriette nodded weakly, and as she stood her legs gave out and she braced herself against the table to keep from falling. Louis' smile vanished. "Bontemps," he said, "see that my doctor attends to her immediately."

*"Mother!" Sophie hurried* into Beatrice's apartment, filled with energy and enthusiasm. "Mother, Her Highness has promised to present me to the Duc de Quercy. She says he may be a good match! Can you imagine? Me, a duchess!"

Beatrice stood at the wardrobe, rummaging through her dresses. She glanced over her shoulder and Sophie saw the tension in her face. "I thought you were in love with a builder," she snapped, turning her attention back to the dresses.

"You told me to forget him."

Beatrice continued to paw through her gowns, feeling the hems as if something were missing.

"What are you doing?"

"I lost a brooch."

Sophie put her hand on her mother's shoulder. "What is wrong, Mother?"

"Nothing."

"What news of our situation?"

Beatrice pushed Sophie aside and hurried over to the trunks by the wall. She opened the first and searched inside. "I believe our situation may soon be resolved."

"If I marry a duke, we will be safe, will we not?"

"Yes."

Sophie watched as her mother flung garments here and there. "The day we left, you wished me a happy trip to England. How did you know I was going to England?"

"Court gossip."

"Mother, you're hiding something from me, I know it."

Beatrice stared up at Sophie. Her eyes were hard and frightening. "If I'm hiding anything from you, it is for a good reason."

*Philippe and Chevalier* gave their list of new etiquette rules to Bontemps, and ordered the valet, by word of the King, to transmit the information to all nobles living in court, regardless of how they might balk. It was clear Bontemps wanted nothing to do with it, but Chevalier also knew that Bontemps was Louis' lap dog and while he might question, he would never disobey.

Retired again in Philippe's apartment, Chevalier sat at the desk and held up a napkin. "Napkin," he said.

Philippe, whose mind was clearly elsewhere, paced back and forth. "What of them?'

Chevalier unfolded the napkin and placed it on his lap. "At dinner last night I saw the Count of Evremonde using his napkin to polish his teeth. We must construct rules for napkin use."

Philippe went to the window and crossed his arms. Chevalier knew that look all too well. "She may be your wife," he said, "and she may be a good woman. But she's not a good wife."

"And am I a good husband?"

Chevalier tossed the napkin onto the desk. "You allow her to eat away at your mind. Yes, she is returned from England. But don't go see her, I beg you. If you do, the whole nightmare will begin again."

Philippe slammed his fist against the sill and stormed out of the room.

*Henriette sat at* the table in her outer chamber, her head bowed with exhaustion. Claudine, dressed as Doctor

Pascal in dark clothing and mustache, instructed Sophie. "Your mistress must be given only bouillon with sorrel and rosemary for a week."

"Of course," said Sophie.

Claudine turned to Henriette. "You need sleep and repose."

Henriette nodded.

Suddenly the door slammed open. Henriette gasped as Philippe stalked in, his face tight and red. "Both of you! Get out!" he shouted.

Sophie scampered into an anteroom and Claudine quickly packed her case and exited. Then Philippe turned on Henriette. "You! You chose to see him before you saw me!"

Henriette wiped her hair back from her face. "He came to greet me. My husband did not."

Philippe stood, breathing hard, looking at his wife. At last his face softened. "You are right. I'm sorry."

"I understand."

For long moments they considered one another, their unspoken thoughts a silent song of regret and uncertainty. Then Philippe walked up to Henriette and put his hand on her cheek. "Do you forgive me?"

Henriette closed her eyes. "Always. Though sometimes I truly believe you would be happier if I were suddenly not here anymore."

"I cannot live without you."

"Nor can you live with me."

*He was descending* the winding staircase to his office when he heard the voice behind him. "Monsieur Marchal?"

Fabien turned to find Beatrice following. "I'd hoped I might see you. I wonder whether I might have a word with you?"

"Of course."

Beatrice's smile looked as if it had been nailed on. She was nervous. That was fine. That was good. "I had conceived the notion you were upset with me."

"Why should I be upset with you?"

"Because I lied about who I am."

Fabien started down the stairs again and Beatrice kept up. "You used the wrong sort of paper," he said. "The paper you used was of Swiss origin. Such paper was not available in France at the time you claimed to have been born."

Beatrice chuckled lightly. "I underestimated you."

"Why did you lie to me?"

Beatrice grabbed Fabien's arm and gazed at him intently, pouting her lips in an attempt to seduce. "Because I care for you. I first came to court to find a match for Sophie. Then I discovered another reason to stay."

"Have you found a husband for your daughter?"

"No. May I ask what you intend for us? Will you have us banished?"

Fabien put his hand on her shoulder. "I'm sure the matter will be resolved favorably." He felt her tremble but couldn't tell if it was from relief or fear. It didn't matter. Then he left her on the steps and continued to his office.

When mid-day arrived, Fabien went out in search of the King's favorite gardener. Builders were at work, moving wooden beams and stones, busy on the palace's roof and expansions as well as new foundations, pools, and statuary. He found Jacques on a bench eating a piece of chicken.

"Do you know who I am?" Fabien asked.

Jacques rubbed grease from his mouth with his sleeve. "I know who you are and what you do."

"I've noticed you in discussion with His Majesty."

"Spying on him?"

"I keep close watch on those whom he takes into his confidence."

"I served his father."

"And now you must serve the son."

"I already do."

"This is not a case of digging flowerbeds."

Jacques looked away, then back. "What is it you would have me do?"

"*What is the* news from court?" Henriette asked Sophie as the girl smoothed her lady's gowns out on the bed.

"Everyone's talking about the masked ball tomorrow."

A short, round-faced chambermaid entered the room with a tray on which sat a bowl of soup and plate of bread. She put the tray on the table and turned quickly away.

"What is your name, again, miss?" Henriette asked.

The maid glanced back. "Marie, Your Highness."

"Thank you, Marie," said Henriette, and Marie skittered out.

*Morning sunlight and* shadows flickered across the floor of the King's bedchamber. Louis stirred, turned, and stretched his arms out from beneath the blankets. Then he opened his eyes to find Philippe standing over him. Bontemps stood behind, his expression hard to decipher.

Louis pushed himself up and blinked. "Good morning, brother. What are you doing here?"

"I'm here to watch a piece of theater."

"In my bedroom?"

"Yes. It's called the Grand Levee. A comedy of manners with tragic undertones."

Louis, intrigued, got out of bed. His barber sat him down for his morning shave. As the barber applied the lather and drew the razor along the King's face, Philippe explained.

"From now on, your life does not belong to you. All you do is designed to be seen and admired. Dressing, shaving, eating, drinking. They are no longer actions but a performance. All noblemen at court are required to present themselves at the appointed hour. Only a few, however, will be given the privilege of entering, observing, and in some cases, participating."

The barber made the last stroke with the razor and a valet held a mirror up for Louis to check the work. Louis tilted the mirror slightly, and saw reflected in the doorway a queue of nobles waiting to enter the room. They shifted impatiently from one foot to the other. Rohan and Louvois were first in line.

Philippe nodded at the footman by the door, who in turn held out his hand, indicating it was time to enter. The nobles moved into the room. An anxious noble stepped forward but was pushed aside by Cassel, who looked down his nose. "Dukes before marquises, I believe," he said. The noble frowned and then stepped forward again, only to be pushed back by Montcourt. "I'm with the duke," Montcourt muttered.

Rohan, Louvois, Cassel, and Montcourt were escorted to a corner where they stood to watch the King's morning rituals. The other nobles filed in and out in a quiet, orderly fashion, each bowing in turn.

"All entrances and exits will be supervised," Philippe told Louis. "Self-control and order are paramount." Then he added, "Basically, it's the opposite of fucking."

Louis grinned. It was the dressers' turn to do their job. They removed the King's nightshirt and attired him in a new shirt, trousers, vest, scarf, and jacket. Nobles continued to walk past quietly, bowing and watching the royal show. When his outfit was completed, Louis reached up to straighten his collar, but Philippe shook his head. He waved a noble forward.

"Not him," the King said. He nodded at Montcourt. "I want all here to know that Versailles rewards those who show loyalty and humility." Montcourt approached the King, tugged gently on the collar to smooth it out, then stepped back and bowed.

Bontemps announced the Queen and she entered, escorting a young boy dressed in velvet and silk. Then Bontemps ushered the remaining nobles from the room but put his hand on Rohan's arm. "His Majesty wishes you to stay."

Louis approached his son, the young Dauphin. The child was much like his father in face, with dark eyes and hair and a piercing, confident stare. Louis led the Dauphin around the room, showing him the swords, the shields, and the portraits of the royals of France's past. "The time has come to teach you how to rule," Louis said. "To be King is to have power beyond imagining. All you ask for will be given. You will have power but with power comes duty. Duty to your subjects and friends, to justice, to truth."

The Dauphin nodded.

"But with power comes danger. When I was young like you, there were those who sought to destroy us." Louis took the child to the window. As they looked out his voice grew tight. "People we thought were friends. They came hammering on our doors with blood on their hands and murder in their hearts. I will never allow this to happen to you. Do you understand?"

Again, the boy nodded.

Louis turned to Rohan. "My son will be spending a few days with us. I will teach him how to rule a country, you will teach him how to hunt a wild boar."

Rohan smiled and bowed as the boy eyed him shyly. "It would be an honor."

*Clutching the note* that had been slipped under her door, Beatrice hurried out to the west gardens. Fabien had agreed to meet her. He was her chance. If need be she would strip naked and make love to him there in the frigid waters of the Neptune pool. He would forgive her ruse and she and Sophie would be safe at court, as she'd always planned.

She reached the appointed spot on the path and waited. The wind whipped up leaves that danced around her ankles. Still she waited.

Then she saw the crusty old gardener approaching.

"Madame de Clermont?"

Beatrice frowned. "Yes?"

"Monsieur Marchal is waiting for you. Follow me."

"Where is he?"

"It's to be a surprise." Jacques turned and took the curving pathway to the end of the gardens, then across the tall wild grasses to the forest's edge. Beatrice followed, holding her skirt so she would not trip, her heart sensing what her mind didn't want to accept. "You are sure he is here?"

"Yes."

They walked several more minutes on the flat land then climbed a knoll along which a line of pine trees swayed back and forth. Jacques stopped. "This is the place."

Beatrice also stopped. Her mouth was dry, her stomach hollow. She nodded, more to herself than Jacques. "He remembered," she said.

"Remembered what?"

"I told him I would like it to end in a forest, looking down a line of green trees swaying in the wind."

The two stood listening to the rustling trees. Then Jacques said, "Kneel down."

"I would have hoped he had the courage to do this himself."

"If you are prone to prayer, now would be a good time."

She looked at the ground. "It's too late for that." With all her courage she forced her knees to fold and she went down. From the corner of her eye she saw the glint of a long, sharp blade as Jacques removed it from his sleeve. She lowered her head, baring her neck, and clenched her jaw so she would hold her dignity until the end. *Sophie, my daughter, I'm sorry my sweet one. If only I —*

There was the whisper of metal slicing the winter air, a moment of bright agony. And then there was nothing at all.

*There were several* gowns tossed over the screen, and Sophie, in her undergarments, studied each one, trying to decide which to wear to the masked ball that evening. The ball was to celebrate her lady Henriette, and the success she'd had in England. Henriette, as weak as she was, had decided to join the festivities. Sophie had helped her dress and was then given leave to prepare herself for the ball.

The door banged open and the screen was knocked over. Fabien stood there, giving Sophie a stare that drove ice water through her veins.

"What are you doing here?" she managed. "Are you looking for my mother?"

Fabien stepped over the fallen screen, kicking gowns out of the way, and picked up a trunk. He dropped it at Sophie's feet. "I was looking for you. To tell you to leave."

Sophie stared. "I don't understand!"

"I think you do. Pack your affairs and get out. You have no place here."

Sophie's hands went to her throat. *This is impossible!* "What…what about my mother? What have you done to her?"

The pitiless expression on Fabien's face told her the truth. *Oh, God! Please no!*

"You will be making the journey back to wherever you come from alone. I shall return tomorrow morning. If I find you still here, I shall have you tossed into the gutter."

Sophie's legs gave way and she grasped a chair to keep from falling. Fabien spit on the floor and turned, slamming the door on his way out.

*Rohan strolled through* the night shadows of the garden, listening to the muffled gaiety of the ball inside the palace. In his hand was a mask of Apollo which he would don when back inside.

A guard appeared from behind a tall holly bush.

"Have my orders been carried out?" asked Rohan.

"Yes, sir. The men are ready."

Rohan nodded. "I will leave a message in the usual place."

"When?"

"When the time has come."

"What is our plan? We shall capture the King?"

"No," said Rohan, turning back toward the palace and pulling on the mask. "The King is not our prey."

✦ ✦ ✦

*The masked ball* was festively noisy and perfectly elegant. A newly commissioned fresco of radiant angels ascending to the sun covered the arched ceiling, and dozens of faceted, crystal candelabra sent rainbows of light dancing across the floor. Courtiers chatted, laughed, and savored the King's best wines, while wearing a menagerie of masks – foxes and horses, sprites and elves, feathered birds and sharp-toothed demons.

Fabien entered the salon without a mask, earning glances from those nearby. Yet this did not bother him. He was not a man for parties but a man for business. As he watched the crowd, someone touched his elbow. He turned to see Sophie, dressed in her mother's most seductive gown, revealing her full, rounded cleavage and the ivory smoothness of her arms and neck. Her eyes peered out from a jeweled nymph mask.

"This is an unwelcome surprise," said Fabien.

Sophie lifted her chin. "I've come to make you an offer."

"Of what?"

"Of me."

"Life as a builder's wife was unpalatable to you?"

"He would not take me."

Fabien smirked. "So I'm your only hope. You've come to me for deliverance."

"Yes."

"At least you have courage."

"And value. I'm unmarried and pure."

"Or you are seen to be. Which is all that matters here." Fabien studied her bosom, her hair, her neck. "Very well. If you wish to stay here, you will work for me. Everyone apart from the King and I believe you are of noble birth. That will remain the case. You will attend court, dance, flirt, seduce, gossip, just as you do now. But you will do it in my service. You will tell me what people are doing and saying, who is sharing their bed with whom, who is cheating on his wife or at cards. Disobey and you will suffer the same fate as your mother. I will own you. That is my offer."

Sophie's eyes winced behind the mask, but she nodded.

*Louis chuckled to* see his brother wearing the same feathered owl mask as he wore, but assured him it was charming and appropriate. He took Philippe's arm and they wandered the crowd together. Masked nobles bowed and curtseyed in their wake.

"I want to thank you for sharing my vision," Louis said. "All too often, I've had the impression that the petty differences between us have proved too great an obstacle."

"I'm sure the fault is all mine."

"Not entirely."

Philippe glanced around the salon, at the nobles, the candelabra, the musicians, the fresco. "It is magnificent."

"There are still those who would destroy it."

"My dear brother, I've spoken to him and –"

"I'm not talking of your friend, but of forces far stronger and more determined."

"Who?"

"I'm not yet sure."

Louis turned to see Henriette entering the room in a white gown and Pierrot mask. She moved slowly yet directly to the King. He took her hand and found it clammy.

"Ah," said Louis. "The princess we've been waiting for. You will dance with me?"

Philippe feigned a pout. "Why not with me?"

"She shall dance with us both," said Louis.

A minuet began. Louis led Henriette onto the floor and Philippe followed. The masked nobles moved into position and the dance began.

*She was swept* along with Louis guiding her, surrounded by the other couples pacing graceful patterns on the floor. It was all she could do to keep her feet moving, to keep from stumbling. Her legs were weak and the music was too loud.

"None of this would have been possible without you," said the King.

"I'm honored you think so," Henriette managed.

The men traded partners, with Louis stepping away and Philippe sweeping in to take his place. "His Majesty is in a flattering mood this evening," her husband said.

Henriette licked her lips. "Why do you say that?"

"Because I know him. And he knows you."

Another change of partners and Louis was back again. He

turned Henriette around, the motion making her head spin. She struggled to stay focused.

"It strengthens me to know I have you at my side," said the King.

Henriette fought a rising nausea as sweat beaded on her forehead. "You…you have many advisors better qualified than I."

"But you are so much more than an advisor."

Partners changed again, a discomfiting swirl of fabrics and candlelight, masks blending into a frightening collage of fangs and hollowed eyes. Philippe took Henriette's hand and turned her about. His smile was twisted and his voice distorted.

"He no longer loves you. Yet you dream of hearing his footsteps on the floor and the midnight knock at the door." Henriette could not reply.

Then Louis was spinning her. "You were and are my first love. Whoever I'm with, a part of me will always be with you."

Then Philippe. "He will promise and beckon and you will continue to hope."

And Louis. "You would have made a wonderful queen."

And Philippe. "But you are just a puppet now."

Back and forth between the two, the music becoming more discordant, the room swaying violently, Louis and Philippe's words bleeding together. Henriette rocked with the room, feeling it rising up around her like a sea determined to drown her. She tried to speak, to cry out, but there was no voice in her throat, and she crashed to the floor.

# 10

*Rohan's chamber was* modest in size yet furnished with the best Louis had to offer. A bed with the best feather mattress, an elegantly designed writing desk, table, cushioned chairs, a fireplace always stocked with wood. Clocks and statuary on shelves, portraits of royals on the walls.

The masked ball was long over and the palace slept, but not Rohan. He sat at his desk, staring at the portrait of young Louis on the wall. His eyes were narrowed and his hand tight around his half-filled goblet. Beneath his bed was a duffle bag, packed for a trip. Rohan lifted the glass, held it up to the portrait in a mock toast, and then drank the last of the wine. He pulled a small dagger from beneath the chair cushion and hid it in the stocking of his right foot. With a deep breath he got up, nodded at the portrait once more, and left the room.

*Louis lay awake* in his bed next to Marie-Therese, who was sleeping soundly with her face against the pillow. She had come to his chamber through the secret door, reminding him that he had promised to visit her yet had not, refusing to be ignored. Their lovemaking had been warm and affectionate but now, with Marie-Therese slumbering beside him and Bontemps asleep on his cot, Louis' thoughts were of Henriette. She had fainted at the masked ball and was now in bed with her husband. Philippe's concern was touching and genuine but Louis envied his brother this night of intimate care. Yes, Henriette needed rest. Several weeks, maybe, or a month. Whatever it would take, Louis would insist on it, yet that she was with Philippe stung his heart. Louis closed his eyes, thinking of her fragile beauty, her soft voice, and her courage as Marie-Therese sighed quietly in her dreams.

Moments later, or hours – through the haze of night it was impossible to know – there was a creaking upon the floorboards. Startled awake, Louis saw Henriette standing near his bed in a pool of pale moonlight. Her eyes were as wide and white as alabaster stones, her body thin and trembling beneath her sweat-soaked nightgown. Blood trickled from her nose and the corners of her mouth.

"Help me," she gasped.

"My God!" shouted Louis.

The King's cry wakened both Bontemps and Marie-Therese. Bontemps leapt from his cot and the Queen flew from the bed to throw her arms around Henriette. Louis stared, horrified. *Henriette! My dearest! What is wrong?*

Henriette slipped through Marie-Therese's arms to the floor. "My King!" the Queen cried.

Louis regained his wits. "Fetch my doctor, Bontemps! Now!"

Bontemps nodded at the footman, who raced from the room. As the door slammed shut on one end of the room, the secret door opened on the other. Philippe appeared, panting, his face streaked with blood. "Henriette!" He knelt and gathered his wife from the Queen's arms. "I...I followed a trail of blood. Of her blood on my pillow, in our room, across the floor...!"

Louis moved to his brother and his love, both crumpled on the floor, one barely alive, the other weeping with fear. He reached out his hands to touch them both.

The door opened and Fabien entered with the several guards.

"Sire," said Bontemps.

"Do not speak it," said Louis.

"Sire," Bontemps repeated carefully, "protocol demands. If the air is impure you are at risk. You must leave immediately."

"Close the doors," Fabien ordered the guards.

"Move Her Highness to my bed!" ordered Louis as Henriette threw back her head and screamed in pain. Bontemps and Philippe obeyed, moving her slowly, carefully.

Then Fabien turned to the guards, "Take His Highness out to safety! Now!"

Guards moved in around the King, grasping his arms and forcing him toward the door. Louis struggled against them, enraged, recalling a time years past when guards had forced him from his room at the threat of assassination. He'd been so vulnerable then, so at the mercy of others. But no more. *No! Never again!*

"Take your hands off me!" he ordered. The guards reached the door.

*NO!*

Fueled by anger and the utter conviction of his power, Louis bellowed, "*I command you!*" He wrested himself out of the guards' grasp and barked military orders. "Full halt! Column right twice left! Column left twice right!"

The guards were instantly, mindlessly obedient, falling into compliance, moving aside into two straight lines. Louis stared at them, his men, his subjects, who would never defy him again. Then he went back to the bed where Henriette lay, her pained eyes staring at him, her hair wild and damp. It seemed as if she were silently pleading with him to stay with her. But in spite of his desire to, he knew he could not.

Louis turned to Bontemps. "Let me know when the doctor arrives." Then he walked out the door alone, passing through the line of guards. "Please God," he said to himself, "let it be soon."

*The pink light* of dawn poured silently through the windows, touching the walls and tingeing the floor. Candles on the tables had burned low and the fire in the hearth glowed red in need of more fuel. Claudine, dressed as Pascal, stood by the King's bed and listened as Bontemps, Philippe, and Marie-Therese explained the events of the past few hours. Henriette lay abed, breathing heavily and groaning. Several servants stood, wringing their hands as

Fabien waited by the door with two guards.

"She collapsed," said Bontemps.

"She whispered to me something about a poison," said Marie-Therese.

Claudine looked from the Queen to Henriette, her brows furrowed. "Poison? How could she know?"

"She bled from the mouth then doubled over with pain in her side," said Bontemps.

"Which side?"

Bontemps said it was the right and Marie-Therese said it was the left.

"Both then?" asked Claudine.

"It was the right," said Philippe. "She has always complained of it."

Claudine called to a servant. "If it's poison she must purge. If sickness, the remedy may make her worse. I will need emetics and charcoal, iced water and cloth. Go." The servant hurried off.

"Where should we take her?" asked Bontemps. "She cannot stay in the King's bed."

"She stays," said Claudine. "There is no choice."

Philippe touched his wife's face. His voice shook. "And so will I stay."

Claudine squared her shoulders under her jacket. "How did she come to be here in the first place?"

"She walked," said Philippe. "I followed her...her trail of blood."

"Blood?" asked Fabien. "From where?"

"Leading from my chamber. I took her there to rest after she collapsed at the ball."

Fabien's mouth twitched slightly and his face darkened. He left the room without another word.

"All right, then," said Claudine. "If she was strong enough to walk she is strong enough to survive."

"She's strong, all right," said Philippe. "Like a Breton mare."

Marie-Therese walked to a corner of the room where she knelt on the bare floor. "God help her in her hour of need," she said, and then began to pray.

*Louis stood at* the window of the War Cabinet room, gazing out at the light cover of snow upon the gardens. Bontemps, Colbert, and Louvois stood nearby, giving the King this moment. A tray of breads, apples, and cheeses had been brought in, and Colbert selected a slice of cheese and raised it to his lips. At that moment Fabien entered the room, followed by several guards.

"No food or drink shall be consumed until its safety has been confirmed," ordered Fabien. He snapped his fingers and a guard collected the tray and took it away.

Colbert frowned. "You believe Her Highness is poisoned?"

"This palace is a symbol of our King, his power, and his country. Our enemies have stopped at nothing to destroy it. From the moment the first stone was laid in this expansion, His Majesty knew this day would come. Do I believe our enemies would dare poison the sister of King Charles of England? Yes. But I also know their greatest plan is yet to show itself."

"And if she is merely ill?" asked Louvois.

"Then your appetite will be merely inconvenienced."

A middle-aged man with sparse hair and pudgy cheeks appeared at the door. He twisted the edge of his coat in his fingers. "You sent for me, Monsieur Marchal?"

Fabien waved the man in. "Congratulations, Nicolas La Roux. You've been promoted. You are now chief taster to His Majesty's kitchen."

"But..." La Roux blanched. "But Monsieur de Vernon is the King's First Taster."

"Not any more."

La Roux forced himself to smile and bow, and then took his leave.

Louis began to pace the room, his fists clenched and his face turned upward. His grief and anger seemed to rise from him in waves. Back and forth and back, and then he stopped and turned to Bontemps. "How is Madame de Montespan? Is my lady risen?"

"I will send a footman to check," said Bontemps.

"No. I will do it myself." With that Louis strode for the door. He paused before exiting and turned back to Fabien. "Secure the palace," he said. "No one enters. And no one leaves!"

Within minutes the command reached throughout the palace and every door, window, apartment, and gate was shut and locked.

*The shutters covering* the Montespan's bed-chamber windows were opened and the flash of bright light caused the lady to stir on her pillow and angrily cover her eyes. "Too bright!" she complained. "Who compels me to wake?"

"The Sun," said Louis, moving in front of the window and blocking out the strongest of the light.

The Montespan sat up, squinting, and brushed back her hair. "Where did you go? I had to kiss my pillow in the night." Then she sensed Louis' dark mood. "What's the matter?"

The King sat down beside her. His eyes were red-rimmed. "Our dear Henriette," he said.

*Ah, Henriette. I must be careful what I say. I must not offend him.* "I'm not surprised she fainted. She hardly eats a thing."

"She is gravely ill."

The Montespan angled her head. "I must go to her, then! She's in her chamber?"

"No, she is in mine. She came to find me."

Jealousy turned in the Montespan's heart. "I know I would do the same," she managed. She rose and beckoned her lady to help her dress.

Louis watched as she was changed from nightgown to day gown. "I've sequestered the palace," he said at last. "All movements are restricted. If you wish to go, you best go now."

The Montespan nodded, hoping the King would escort her or at least kiss her before she left, but he only sat and looked at the wall, and so she went out alone and unsatisfied.

*A servant had* added more wood to the fire in the fireplace and stoked it to warm the room, but a chill no fire could touch hung in the air. Marie-Therese prayed anxiously in the corner, her appeal to God muttered over and over. Bontemps waited beside his cot, ever attentive should he be needed at a moment's call. Philippe stood by Claudine, watching Henriette's every move.

Claudine placed her hand on Henriette's belly and pressed gently. Henriette screamed and thrashed, kicking Claudine in an attempt to push her away.

"Restrain her!" Claudine shouted, and several footmen rushed over, snatching up scarves and belts to tie Henriette's legs and arms to the bedposts.

"You're killing her!" shouted Philippe. "This is madness!"

"I know it's painful," said Claudine, "but I have to find the source. I have to do this." Then to Henriette she said, "Will you help me? Your Highness, please?"

Henriette stared, her breathing fast and shallow, her face streaked with tears and blood, but she nodded. She closed her eyes. She readied herself for the fresh agony ahead.

*Bontemps entered the* Montespan's chamber to find the King sitting on the lady's bed. "Is there any change?" the King asked.

"No, Sire."

"Is she worse?"

"Yes."

Louis got up and went to the window. He wished to see the gardens, to see new wisps of snow falling and covering his world in a blanket of white, but all he could see was his reflection and the dread in his eyes. "I don't regret sending her to England," he said. "Not for an instant. She brought honor to herself and glory to our court."

"We are all proud of her, Sire," said Bontemps.

Tears pressed Louis' eyes but he knew he had to fight them. *Kings do not cry,* his mother had said. *No matter what they face. I am the Sun. I am King!* With that he felt his whole being harden, and he turned abruptly from the window. "Someone is trying to destroy me. By destroying her."

"But they will not succeed," said Rohan from the door.

Louis looked over. "Madame de Montespan is not here, Rohan."

Rohan nodded grimly. "Yes. When I heard the news I came as soon as I could. I was seeking her out and saw your guard outside her door, Sire. I wish to offer myself to you as your subject and friend."

"Is my son still at court?"

"Yes," said Bontemps. "With the sequester, the Dauphin was confined with his governess."

"I want him far away from my chamber. He is not to hear her pain."

"If I may, Sire?" said Rohan. "If I were to school him in riding today, with your blessing, of course, the fresh air and distance might do him a world of good –"

"And it would keep him occupied in body and mind," said Louis. "Yes. Thank you."

Bontemps nodded and Rohan smiled a small smile. "We'll ride to the woods. You have my word. Although, with the sequester –"

"Allow them full passage in court," Louis ordered Bontemps. "At once."

" *Madame?* "

The Montespan wiped a tear from her eye and looked up at Bontemps.

"Madame, the King is waiting for you."

The Montespan rose from her chair in the King's bed-chamber.

"I need a moment to compose myself," the Montespan said.

"Of course, Madame," said Bontemps.

The Montespan walked to the fireplace, put her hand on the mantle, and bowed her head. Close enough to continue listening to the discussion on Henriette's condition.

"Her Highness is resting now," the doctor told Philippe. "But I fear we're not through the worst."

Philippe rubbed his arms. "My brother always trusted you."

"I'm honored."

"I don't believe I know what that feels like."

"This must be frightening for your wife. And for those who love her."

"We're all of us in sickness here. Just waiting for it to take root."

"Maladies affect different people in different ways. Some

fall easily. Others are born to fight."

Philippe's face fell and so did the tears. He put his hand over his eyes and turned away.

The Montespan stepped from the fireplace, ready to leave. The Queen rose from her knees to accompany her. "Allow me to join you in prayer," she said.

"I'm not praying," said the Montespan.

"You should be." Marie-Therese leaned uncomfortably close. "Believe me."

"I'm confused by your tone, Your Majesty."

"Be careful what you wish for, my dear. Those closest to the Sun have a tendency to be burned."

*Rohan, in his* riding attire, checked himself in his mirror. His new jacket was finely tailored and his boots freshly polished. His feathered cap sat at the right angle on his head and his scarf was properly tied. As he reached for his gloves on the table, there came a scratching at the door.

"Come," said Rohan.

The chambermaid Marie entered with a broom but she did not make a move to sweep.

"The room is dirtier than when I left it," said Rohan.

"Where is my money?"

"You will receive payment in due course."

Marie gripped the broom. "I want the money now."

Rohan smiled then grabbed Marie by the throat. He slammed her into the wall and leaned so close he might have bitten her face off. His lip curled and his eyes flashed. "It is not yet clear to me what you did to earn it."

Marie gasped and whimpered. Rohan licked her cheek, chuckled coldly, and then let go. As he strode out the door he called back, "Make sure you leave my rooms spotless."

*As valets and* servants hurried in and out of the King's bedchamber with bloody sheets, medical tools, and supplies, Colbert and Louvois cornered Fabien in the War Cabinet room, glancing around, on edge.

"She cannot possibly be treated in the King's chamber," said Colbert. "She must be moved immediately. What if the poison were to spread?"

"Poison?" The three men turned at the King's voice as he entered the room. "Did you say poison?"

"Ah, it is not certain, Sire," said Louvois.

"Colbert thinks otherwise?" said Louis.

"Conjecture, Sire," said Colbert. "But the facts remain stark. There was an attempt on Her Highness' life during her journey to England, it could be so again. Even if we do discover a poison how do we find the poisoner?"

"Eliminate the suspects," said Fabien.

Colbert pursed his lips. "Eliminating suspects doesn't mean the same to me as it does to you."

"Either way," said Fabien with a shrug, "it will have the desired results."

"By which logic," said the King, "we must also question

all of whom were with her on the journey to England, either departing, in transit, or arriving."

"Indeed, Sire," said Fabien.

Louis spied Bontemps and left to speak to with him. The ministers' conversation continued, more quietly.

"Are you seriously suggesting we interrogate all those people?" asked Colbert.

Louvois nodded. "I agree with Fabien. There are many in court and in France whose only wish is that His Majesty was also sickening in that bed."

"Whatever method expedites the truth," said Fabien. "I will talk to anyone who had access to Her Highness, or access to the food or drink provided to her."

Colbert frowned. "King Charles himself, perhaps?"

Fabien looked at each man in turn. "No one is above suspicion."

Philippe stormed into the War Cabinet room, his face twisted in exhaustion and desperation. The ministers moved away to give him room to speak to his brother, though even apart they kept their eyes and ears turned to the interaction.

"You," Philippe said, his voice thick with accusation. "*You* did this!"

Louis shook his head. "Brother –"

"You did this to *her*! We warned you. We begged you, yet you heard nothing but your own voice, your own desire for glory. How much pain are you willing to endure to get what you want?"

"Why are you casting this rage at me?"

"Because you deserve it. The whole world gave you counsel but the advice you took came from only one source." At that moment Philippe saw the Montespan at the door, her hands folded, her face stoic. "Or two, perhaps," he added.

*Montcourt fastened his* trousers, buttoned his hunting jacket, and drew his belt around his waist, a favorite with two silver inlay angels set into the leather. He left his room for the hallways, footfalls echoing as he passed door after door, all shut under the King's order of sequester. He reached the end of the hallway, turned into the next, and came face to face with Chevalier.

Chevalier stared with suspicion. "The court is under lock and key, Montcourt. What are you doing?"

"My apartment has a piss pot. The hallway is sadly lacking. And I do hate to urinate in the stairwells."

"That's never stopped you before."

Montcourt lifted his chin. "To live as a gentleman I find I must try to act like one."

"Challenging days, gentlemen." Cassel strode up the corridor to join them. "I hear Fabien and his security lurchers are making inquiries."

"Henriette's lady was taken this morning," said Montcourt. "Sophie de Clermont."

"I don't understand what they hope to get from her," said Cassel.

"I know what I would ask," said Montcourt.

Cassel shook his head. "If she was told anything by her mother, it was how best to hold a fork."

"If any case," said Chevalier, "her lady is ill. What more is there to say?"

"Very little, I should hope," said Cassel. "For her sake."

Chevalier looked up and down the hall. "We cannot be seen together any more. Is that understood?"

"Or what, exactly?" asked Cassel.

"I believe you might be able to guess."

"In times like these," said Montcourt, "it is good to know who one's friends truly are."

"I didn't know I had any left," said Chevalier.

"I've always found my closest allies have been those with whom I can share the silence," said Montcourt.

Chevalier made a tisking sound. "I couldn't have put it better myself."

The men parted, each taking different directions. Montcourt walked on, glad to be free of his room if only for a short while. When he reached a south corner of the palace he saw Rohan at the end of the hallway. The King's friend, dressed in hunting gear, was talking to a guard. The Dauphin, the King's young son, was also dressed for a hunt, and he stomped about impatiently, pretending to shoot arrows at the ceiling.

Then Montcourt noticed Rohan's left hand. The little finger was tapping an irregular rhythm, a nervous gesture. Something Montcourt had seen before.

*Yes. Ah, yes.* As he watched from his distance the guards, Rohan, and the little boy went out into the sunlight.

"*I have interviewed* all Her Majesty's ladies," said Fabien. "And now, you."

Sophie stood before the Chief of Police in his torture room, tears streaking her face yet her head high and defiant.

"You accompanied Her Highness on her mission to Dover," said Fabien, circling Sophie, leaning close. "You had close and intimate access to her person."

"It was my duty."

"What contact did you have with her, in particular?"

"I served her."

"Tea?"

"Tea? Yes. Chicory tea. It gave her great comfort."

"Do you know who prepared it?"

Sophie swallowed hard. "Yes."

Fabien leaned even closer. "Then tell me."

"What happened to my mother?"

"I'm not here to answer you."

"Then neither am I."

Fabien snorted. "I would recommend very strongly that you reconsider."

"I've nothing. So what would I have to lose, except that?"

"Your life, for one."

"I don't have a life. My mother told me who I was. But that was a lie, and so I have no idea who I truly am."

"You're the daughter of a Huguenot conspirator against the King. Funded and supported by William of Orange."

"My mother has paid the price for her treachery. I'm merely trying to survive. I had thought your protection would ensure it."

"Unless you are more like your mother than you care to admit."

Sophie's eyes flashed through her tears. "Make no mistake, Monsieur Marchal. My mother fooled many people with her treason, but the biggest fool was you."

Fabien dug his fingers into Sophie's arm. "Who prepared the tea?"

She took a deep breath. "I did."

"*You look very* pale, my dear," Cassel said to the Montespan as the lady, caught up in her own thoughts, passed him unaware in the corridor. "Like a guilty child with an éclair in her petticoat."

The Montespan spun toward him and glared. "My dear friend is ill. That is enough to worry about without you lurking in the shadows."

Cassel pushed away from the wall. "My rooms are cold. I hear one of the salons is more convivial. Awash with rumors, of course."

"What rumors?"

"That Henriette was poisoned by a jealous rival at court."

The Montespan blinked and then found her voice. "In terms of beauty, she has no rival. In any case, I've not heard such talk."

"That's surprising. Who would have the most to gain, they say, should her rival Henriette be bedridden? What did this rival know, that the rest of us did not?"

There was a spark of fear in the Montespan's eyes. But then

she tossed her hair and the spark vanished. "I'm sure I cannot imagine. But considering how many nobles sought his demise in the past, I'd imagine the only thought in the King's head is which of you is seeking to harm him now?"

*H*enriette's cries had grown worse over the past hours, piercing the walls of the War Cabinet room and slashing Louis' heart like a dagger. Guards stood at the doors, eyeing one another, eyeing the King with each new scream. Louis walked the room, sat and tried to read, and then got up to walk again. He gazed out the window, seeing nothing, then turned away. He didn't realize for several moments that Philippe had entered and was staring at him.

"She knew what she had to do, and did it willingly," said Louis.

"Because you told her to."

"Because she was born to it."

Philippe took a shuddering breath. "Because she loves you."

Louis flinched at this truth but quickly regained himself. "If we do not have the English then we cannot attack the Dutch. You do not understand politics. Or survival."

"You don't hear me."

"The state is a person," continued the King. "And a person either asserts himself or is subjugated to the will of others. We stake our claim or are ploughed into the field. It is one or the other."

"You acted out of pride. I risked my life for our vanity, to rescue your wife's dowry."

"And I acted for France because I am France. Without me the country will consume itself in noble squabbles. Music, dance, art, fashion, beauty…" Louis gestured out the window at the gardens, "…*all* these things have the power to change a nation from within, to affect the hearts and minds of a people, to bring them over to us. We could never invade the entire world but the world can imagine us to be their center. And one day, my brother, it will. The cost is justified a hundredfold."

"The *cost*?"

"If I taught you a piece of music, if it were to strike you in the heart, and then the sheets were burned, you might still play it from memory to a salon of a hundred. And they might take it on and play it. And on and on. The song we sing here, I mean it to be played forever."

Philippe lunged for Louis but the King shoved him back. As Philippe lunged again, Henriette screamed. Philippe jerked his head toward the sound. "There is your music, brother!"

Bontemps hurried across the room toward the brothers. "She was calling –"

"I will come," said Philippe.

Bontemps shook his head and looked at Louis. "For you, Sire. Alone."

Philippe spun away to the window, stunned and angry. Bontemps leaned in to the King and whispered, "Poison."

"So it is confirmed," said Louis. He crossed the room to join Colbert and Louvois who waited at the door.

"Are there English diplomats at court?" he demanded.

"Sir Thomas Armstrong in Paris, Sire," said Colbert.

"Throckmorton remained in England."

Louis' jaw clenched. "We must assume word will reach Paris by tonight, reaching Sir Thomas by morning and with him to London the next day. When King Charles hears his beloved sister has been poisoned in France it is only a matter of hours before a declaration of war."

"A war they cannot afford to win," said Louvois.

"Sire," said Colbert, "in addition to war, should Philippe lose his wife a power shift might emerge from her death."

"How?"

"Henriette's very existence strengthens your position, keeps your brother's power in check and offers a direct connection to England. It unfortunately follows that her absence would weaken you in every possible way."

The King stood silent at the truth of the words. Then he gave Philippe another glance and left for his bedchamber where he found Henriette breathing irregularly but, for the moment, peacefully.

*Fabien threw a* clot of mud across the torture room and it slammed into the wall where most stuck and the rest slid to the floor. *Throw it against the wall and see what sticks,* Fabien thought. *An old saying. Dramatic, to the point.* He turned to Montcourt, who sat in the center of the room on a small chair. It was mildly curious – the room had stunk of fear when the chambermaids had been interrogated. Montcourt, on the other hand, seemed utterly undaunted.

"Madame de Clermont conspired against the King," said Fabien, his voice deep and threatening. "And she told me the names of all who shared her alliance."

"I only knew her in passing."

"You knew she had malevolent intent."

"It might have escaped your notice, but everyone in this building has malevolent intent. Though only a few act on it."

"Why did you return to court?"

"Why does a sunflower turn to the sun?" Montcourt grinned slyly then shrugged. "I became aware of a threat to Her Highness. It was my duty as a noble and steadfast friend of the King to inform him."

Fabien snorted. "I find that hard to believe."

"Living away from court can be cold and dark indeed. Although I'd imagine should Her Highness pass away, and you were found wanting, such as your lack of judgment concerning the late Madame de Clermont –"

"What judgment would that be?"

Montcourt leaned back and cocked his head. He hooked his thumbs into the belt, his fingers drumming the silver angels. "I believe you were seen together a few times, walking in the gardens and such. But then, the card tables always were so full of idle gossip."

Fabien stared. "Who would seek to harm Henriette?"

"Whoever harms her, harms the King. And so you are wondering who, despite his grace and glory, might yet plot against His Majesty?"

Fabien nodded slightly.

"I've an idea, if you are interested."

"Go on."

"It's been my experience that it is only those closest to a man who can inflict the greatest pain. Military strategists tell us when we are near we must make the enemy believe we are far away. When far away, we must make him believe we are near. When we are the King's enemy, we must make him believe we are his friend."

Fabien sent Montcourt away and immediately called for Louvois. The King's friend. The King's confidant.

Louvois arrived and Fabien gave him a chair in the office. Then Fabien stood before his desk, arms crossed. Without an offer of wine, Louvois seemed uncertain as to the summons. *Exactly as he should be*, Fabien thought. *Uncertain. Worried, perhaps*.

"I've been watching you for a very long time," Fabien said. "And I must say, your behavior concerns me."

"Yes? And have you spoken to the King?"

"Your behavior is consistent. It is also highly critical of His Majesty."

The uncertainty in Louvois' face faded. Now he looked annoyed. "Before you speak to me, Monsieur Marchal, I suggest you speak to the King."

"I'm His Majesty's ears and eyes. I speak to whomever I like."

"True. I'm merely suggesting you might save some time."

"Did you have any interactions with Her Highness on her mission to Dover?"

"I did not."

"But you were not convinced of the merits in the plan."

"No, and I made my opinions clear to His Majesty."

"Do you ever agree with His Majesty's ideas?"

"I agree with most."

Fabien took a step toward Louvois, glaring down at him. "Why, then, are the utterances that emanate from your mouth so loudly critical of the King?"

"Because I asked him to."

Fabien's head snapped up. The King and Bontemps stood at the door. Louvois began to rise from his seat but Louis put his hand on his shoulder, allowing him to stay seated.

"Sire…" began Fabien.

"You are diligent, Fabien," said the King. "But in this case, quite mistaken."

"His Majesty asked me to assume the role of critic and conspirator, Fabien," said Louvois. "One I do not relish."

The King smiled. "But one you perform admirably."

"Ah, I see," said Fabien. "Attracting flies to the paper."

"Almost everyone has some complaint over time," said Louvois. "But those who truly move against His Majesty are becoming known to me."

"This is a task you yourself excel in, Fabien," said the King. "But I prefer to maintain two springs from which to draw my water. What is more, as an honest critic, Louvois often speaks the truth."

Louvois nodded. "I did not believe in Versailles at first. But I have always believed in my King."

"I trust that," said Louis. "You and Fabien are the angels at my shoulder."

Fabien smiled even as the word snagged in his mind. *Angels. Why do I remember something about angels?* "Louvois," Fabien said, "you have my apology and my admiration."

Louvois clasped Fabien's hand. "And you have mine, sir. Now, let us find this poison toad and skin him."

"Or her," said Fabien.

The three left Fabien's office, followed by Bontemps and the guards, and climbed the winding stairs. Fabien turned the word over in his mind. *Angel. Angel. Angel.*

Then he stopped on a stair and his eyes opened wide. "Sire!"

The King looked back.

"You once made a request of me, Sire," Fabien said.

Bontemps scowled. "His Majesty did not bid you to speak."

But Fabien spoke, regardless. "You requested to see the faces of those who killed the Parthenays. I believe I might deliver him to you now."

"*Clear the room!*"

The King's voice boomed through the salon. The nobles stopped in their card playing, gambling, and gossiping and turned in unison to watch the King and his guards enter.

"And seal the door behind them!"

Immediately, the men and women put their cards and wine glasses down and skittered out, glancing at each other anxiously. Montcourt put distance between himself and Cassel and headed for the door, a confident smile on his face.

But Louis held up his hand. "Not you, Montcourt."

Montcourt stopped as the other courtiers exited and the doors were shut. Louis stared, his gaze hard as stone, daring the man to move another step.

"Sire," said Montcourt, with a bow, "my prayers have been with Her Highness all day."

"Do you think God will hear you?"

"I don't know, Sire. I would think –"

Louis stepped closer to Montcourt, his voice steady, threatening. "What about the angels?"

"Angels?"

"Do you see them now?"

Montcourt looked at Fabien as if for an explanation. "I… do not."

"I've heard many say they see angels before they die," said Louis, nodding at Montcourt's belt.

Montcourt's mouth opened silently.

"Guards, out!"

The guards left quickly, quietly, shutting the door behind them.

Alone with Fabien and Montcourt, Louis stepped even closer to his prey. He tipped his head back and forth like a viper. "Charlotte de Parthenay saw angels. And then there were others. The many killed on my road. Members of my court. Even attempts on my own life. And now Her Highness, my beloved Henriette, lies dying."

"I don't know what you mean, Sire."

"That makes you a liar, Montcourt."

"No, Sire. I'm a true friend of the King."

"And 'when we are the King's enemy, we must make him believe we are his friend,'" said Fabien.

Louis walked around Montcourt to the fireplace. Montcourt spun to Fabien and pointed an accusing finger at the Chief of Police. "You… you are a fool! You are accusing me? You are –"

"And you are a murderer!" The King grabbed a poker and swung it against the side of Montcourt's head. The noble grunted and dropped to the floor, blood pouring down his face. "Fight me!"

Montcourt coughed, snarled. "You have the wrong man, Sire."

"I let a wolf back into my barn!"

Montcourt pushed himself to his knees. "I saved Her Highness from certain death!"

Louis' heart pounded and rage burned in his soul. "You used her to find my favor! Then had her poisoned!"

Montcourt stood, panting, coughing blood. His hand slipped into his jacket. "I did not seek to harm –"

"Lies."

Louis swung the poker around again, slamming it into Montcourt's hand and sending the blade he'd taken from his jacket across the room. Montcourt drew his shattered hand to his chest, growled, grabbed a chair with his good hand and slammed it against the King. Louis stumbled and fell, his head striking the corner of a table. He bit through his lip with the impact. Montcourt darted for the door.

Fabien snatched up Montcourt's dagger and jumped into the noble's path, lashing out, and cutting deeply into Montcourt's shoulder. Montcourt grabbed Fabien's wrist and twisted it, jerked the dagger free, and flipped it around to point it at Fabien.

Bellowing, Fabien drew his own dagger and the men circled each other, the light from the hearth glinting off their weapons, hatred glinting in their eyes. Montcourt dove forward, and Fabien parried. Montcourt snarled and leapt sideways before jabbing at Fabien again.

Louis clutched the table's edge and spit red onto the floor.

His head spun with the pain, but his thoughts were clear and sharp as any dagger. With every ounce of effort he pushed himself to his knees.

Montcourt and Fabien fought furiously, spinning and slashing, expertise meeting expertise, rage meeting rage. Montcourt did his best to work the fight closer to the King as they slammed into tables, splintering wood, breaking glass.

"Guards!" shouted Fabien.

But from the floor Louis said, "No! The room stays sealed!"

In the brief moment Fabien glanced at the King, Montcourt lashed out and stabbed the police chief in the gut. Fabien stumbled, grasped the back of chair, and held himself in place as blood soaked his shirt.

"Good idea, Montcourt," said Louis. Montcourt turned as the King made it back onto his feet, his fist clenched around the poker, his face a mask of murderous resolve. "Kill them, then me. Blame it on him. If I were you, that's what I'd be thinking right now. But your first strike would have to be true. And that is the problem, Montcourt. You've never been a man who was true. Today is your lucky day. Today you have the chance to kill a king."

Montcourt's lip curled. "But what kind of king will I dispatch? To me you seem like all others, talking of change, of course. But in the end, it is the same. Your own glory at the expense of everything. You talk of light and dream of gods. But your soul is stuck in darkness."

The viper was ready for the kill. "You forget, Montcourt. It is always darkest before the dawn." Then Louis swings the poker. It cracked Montcourt in the ribs. As he staggered the King jumped forward and drove him back against a table.

Montcourt rolled free, shoved the table over, and slashed out with dagger, nearly catching the King in the throat, then ducking out of the way.

Louis and Montcourt crashed around the salon, locked on one another like animals in the forest, their anger thick and hard and deadly, keen in their abilities to skip back from the worst blows and in their strength to fight on. King and enemy. Betrayed and betrayer. And as Montcourt ducked to escape a sideways blow, the King arced the poker up and drove it down onto Montcourt's head, striking a solid, powerful blow, cracking his skull. Blood gushed from the wound and from the noble's ears and nose. He doubled over.

"Bow to your King," snarled Louis.

Montcourt fell in a heap, his legs drawn up, howling.

"Majesty," gasped Fabien.

Louis stood over his foe, the bloodied poker in his hand. "Let him bleed." He threw the poker down and turned to the door.

"I fear…" began Fabien. And then his eyes rolled up and he crashed to the floor.

Louis hoisted Fabien up and over his shoulder then hurried from the salon. "Guards!" he shouted. "Don't just stand there!"

*Rohan and the* Dauphin's horses stood tethered to an oak near the forest path, nibbling at the dried leaves as Rohan and the young boy played at war with sticks. Two guards stood nearby, silently watching.

"You must learn to fight," said Rohan with a grin. "For someday you shall be King!"

The Dauphin giggled and waved his stick sword at Rohan. "I am King! Obey me!"

"You must defeat me first," teased Rohan. "Oh, you are a strong boy!"

Their laughter echoed through the trees. And the guards smiled, watching.

*Jacques pulled a* large cart out past the stables and barns, past the pigs' pen and down a slope to a long, sleet-muddied trench. There he upended it, dumping the body of Montcourt into the mass grave where the bodies of countless degenerates lay, decomposing, glassy eyes and empty sockets staring out at one another as if in eternal surprise.

*The door to* the War Cabinet room opened, and Louis walked in, streaked with blood but victorious in posture.

Philippe stared at his brother. "You look different."

Louis poured a goblet of wine and took several long drinks. "I ordered Monsieur Marchal to interrogate you."

"So you dared to think it."

Louis put the goblet down. "I only thought this – if exonerated, the cloud of doubt will dissipate."

"Then bring him here. Dissipate me further."

"He's currently indisposed. So answer me. Did you seek to injure her?"

"I did. And took every chance I could."

"To what end?"

"By hurting her, I hurt you. As she hurt me on your behalf."

"You wished her pain."

"Never. I wished you pain. Always."

"For sending her to England."

"For not sending *me*!" Philippe shook his head and sighed. "Do you remember our fort?"

"Which one?"

"The first. I don't expect you to remember but I do. Years and years ago. We came here on a visit. You, Henriette, me. We were taking air with our governess and made a break for freedom. We ran away, laughing, through the trees, down to the millstream. We found an old shack made of stone and moss. You wanted it to be your castle and I said let's make it our fort. For once you played along. We defended our position from the Spanish all morning. Do you recall?"

Louis said nothing.

"Henriette found a piece of yellow topaz, shaped like a teardrop, in the mud. In honor of your distinguished service we presented it to you. I was so proud of you. So was she. I felt that if the world came running for us, we might fend off all who would do us ill. Hold on to the moment, I told you. Never forget." Philippe shook his head sadly. "Not that you remember."

Louis held Philippe's gaze, then slowly reached into his jacket, into a small pocket, then pulled his hand out again.

There lay the yellow teardrop. He placed it on the table in front of Philippe and walked out.

And Philippe stared at it, tears stinging his eyes.

*The Dauphin grinned* as he sneaked through the brush with his stick musket. He was hiding from Rohan, ready to capture the man at first chance. He held low, peering through the trees.

There was a crunching of leaves behind him. He whirled about, his stick at the ready. "I see you –" he began, but a man in a black hooded cloak threw his arm around the boy and put his gloved hand over his mouth. The Dauphin kicked and twisted, but the man easily lifted him off the ground. In that instant the boy could see over the brush where another cloaked man pressed his musket against the face of a guard and pulled the trigger, blowing his head apart. Then he watched as Rohan yanked the other guard's head back and slit his throat.

The Dauphin struggled as he was carried to a small clearing, bound, gagged, and thrown into a sack. Then all but one man removed their cloaks, revealing the uniforms of palace guards. The other was Mike, former employee of Cassel and of the King's police. He wore the clothes of an ordinary man. "To the road," Mike ordered. "Now!" He hoisted the squirming sack over his shoulder and followed his men down through the trees.

*Another morning dawned.* Henriette lay in Louis' bed, breathing with effort, her face sallow, her moans faint and hoarse. A servant laid a fresh coverlet over Her Highness then carried the soiled one away. Louis and Philippe stood next to Claudine as she felt Henriette's forehead.

"How long does she have?" asked Philippe.

"I don't know. But it is her wish to see you both," said the doctor. "I'm so deeply sorry, Your Majesty. Your Highness."

Louis nodded.

"She asked to be carried outside to be surrounded by her favorite flowers."

"Then do so," said the King.

"It would cause her too much pain. It would be torture."

Louis turned to Bontemps. "Bring the garden here."

Within the hour the room was converted into a lush garden filled with white winter roses, blue snapdragons, and hardy pink pansies covering the windowsills, the mantle, the tables and desktops, and in vases on the floor. Henriette stirred, and her eyes opened slowly.

"Is…is there a breeze today?" she asked.

Louis nodded at Bontemps, who unlatched a window and opened it. Henriette sighed into her pillow, so frail she seemed almost a part of it. "Is there anything more beautiful than the scent of blossoms in the air?"

"There is. And I'm looking at her now," said Louis.

Henriette tried to smile but was caught in a wave of agony.

She drew her head down to her chest and moaned. When the pain at last subsided, she whispered, "I'm scared."

"There is nothing to fear," said Philippe.

"How do you know?"

"Do you remember before you were born?"

Henriette shook her head.

"Then how can you feel scared?"

"I do not remember a heaven before I lived." Another wave hit and Henriette's legs thrashed beneath the coverlet. Her face folded into a mask of anguish.

Louis grabbed Claudine's arm. "Do something!"

"There…is nothing to be done," Henriette managed. "I feel so cold now." Her breaths came even more rapidly, more shallowly, and her arms were splotched and blue in color. "Philippe, I'm so sorry. I…I could never love you well."

"You did the best you could," whispered Philippe.

"How handsome you both are. How…different things might have been."

"Please," said Louis. "Rest."

"Oh God!" she screamed. "It hurts so much to breathe!"

Louis took her hand. "The pain will go if you lift your head."

"I can't!"

"Let me do it for you," said Philippe.

"I don't want to!"

"Henriette."

"Make it go away! Make it go away!"

"Put her on another pillow!" cried Louis.

"She doesn't want to move," said Philippe.

"But the pain will go away!" said Louis. But then he saw in his brother's eyes the truth of it all. The cold and brutal fact. It would not go away. She would suffer. She would die.

Henriette screamed. Spittle flew from her lips and her eyes blinked madly. Louis reached out for her hand and she caught it. Her nails dug deep into his flesh. "Don't look at me, please!" she begged. "I want to look beautiful for you. Not like this!"

Louis forced down a sob. "You are beautiful. I fell in love with you the first time I laid eyes on you."

Philippe watched, tears streaming down his face. He did his best to smile at his wife, with nothing left to offer her.

The priest Bossuet entered the room. "Get him out!" cried Henriette.

"Henriette," said Philippe.

"I will not hear it yet!" Then she screamed again, a deep, hellish wail.

"Something for the pain!" shouted Louis. Claudine poured liquid into a cup and brought it bedside. She held it to Henriette's lips and the lady managed a few sips before vomiting it back up. Her breaths were reduced to desperate gurgles.

"Her throat is closing," said Claudine.

"Open it up!" said Louis.

Philippe touched Louis' shoulder. "Brother."

"What must be done?" cried Louis. "Something must be done!"

Henriette's eyes darted back and forth in terror as the fluid in her lungs began to drown her.

"Now the pillow!" said Philippe.

The brothers lifted Henriette and drew a second pillow under her head. The gurgling grew less intense.

Bossuet stepped to the other side of the bed, made the sign of the cross, and began to intone the last rites. Louis clenched his fists, wanting to drive them into something, to kill whatever it was that was killing his love.

"Let…me live," whispered Henriette.

"My love," said Louis.

"Let go now, my sweet," said Philippe.

Henriette tried to lick her cracked lips. "Let me bathe in the lake and feel the sun." Her gaze met Louis'. "Let me feel the sun upon me."

"You will," he said.

"Oh Lord, receive me!" Henriette gasped, choked, and went silent.

Louis and Philippe looked at one another, weeping. They leaned over the bed.

Henriette's eyes opened, glazed, unfocused. "Listen. Can you hear that? The flowers. They are singing." And then she gasped once more, shuddered, and her final breath eased from between her lips. The priest continued the rite, his voice quieting in respect.

Philippe dug the tears from his eyes, glared at his brother with anguish and loathing, and left without looking back.

*Fabien awoke on* the cot in his office. His gut ached and his arms throbbed. There were bandages around his stomach and chest, and several on his arms. He tried to sit up but the pain kept him prone.

Then he realized he was not alone. He turned his head to find Sophie standing by his desk.

"Are you in pain?"

"What are you doing here?"

"Helping."

"You were under arrest."

"And now I'm not. Where is my mother? Her body?"

"This is not appropriate."

"I agree. You should be standing in the presence of a lady."

Fabien grit his teeth, rolled over, and forced himself to his feet. "I need your help," he said as he dropped into the chair behind the desk. "I must write something."

Sophie held out the quill pen. As he reached for it, she pulled it away. "Why did you kill my mother?"

"I didn't. Damn it, the quill!"

Sophie shook her head.

Fabien pushed himself up and struggled to the door, every nerve in his body shrieking. If he could not write it, then damn it to Hell, he would deliver the message in person.

He sought the King in the War Cabinet room, but found only Bontemps.

"You are injured," said Bontemps, noting the bloody bandages. "Let me —"

"Listen!" Fabien said, brushing the valet's concerns aside. "There are only two men in court who move freely between the King's Circle and the world outside. But only one has never raised a single voice against him."

"The King's brother…" began Bontemps.

"Is a critic. But we ignore another who has lain hidden before us. Rohan."

415

"The King's oldest friend."

"He means to destroy him as he has destroyed Her Highness."

"You said Montcourt was to blame."

"He killed many, but not her."

"How can you be sure?"

"The King warned me once that his enemies would seek to kill those closest to him. Montcourt was trying to tell me the same. We must move the King, Queen, and yourself to safety."

Bontemps' face went pale and his mouth opened in horror. "Oh, my."

"What is it?"

"The King's son. The Dauphin! Rohan took him hunting."

"On whose word?"

But Bontemps could not answer. "Call the guard!" he cried, flinging open the door.

Flanked by two guards, Fabien took the corridor to Rohan's room. He kicked in the door to find it empty but for a chambermaid named Marie, who lay on the bed, her throat cut from ear to ear.

*In their orderly*, prescribed line the nobles passed through the King's bedchamber to pay their respects to Henriette, who lay in state upon the bed with roses and pansies adorning her hair. Ladies wept softly; men bowed their heads. Louis and Marie-Therese kept vigil at the foot of the bed, acknowledging the visitors, maintaining a regal stoicism. Cassel hesitated in the line, his hands trembling, his forehead slick with sweat. He looked at Chevalier, who gave him an iron-hard stare.

Philippe entered, pushed through the line, and grabbed Chevalier by the arm. "We're leaving," he said, "and never coming back." As nobles watched apprehensively, the two headed for the door. Louis quickly moved over with three guards to block their exit.

"Excuse me," said Philippe.

"I cannot permit it," said Louis.

"I'm not asking permission. I'm leaving."

"You would defy me, even in this moment?"

"I know what this moment is."

"We are grieving."

"And I grieve alone."

Louis looked from his brother to Chevalier and back. He saw noble faces turned in their direction. He lowered his voice. "You will marry again, brother."

"I simply want to live."

"It is your duty."

"I've had my fill of duty."

"Then you set yourself against me."

Philippe's lip drew up in disgust. "Gladly."

"And sacrifice your future to see me suffer?"

"Sacrifice?" said Philippe. "What does a king know of sacrifice?" He moved around Louis, taking Chevalier with him. Louis nodded and the guards parted to let the men pass.

"What does a king know of sacrifice?" Louis whispered to himself. "Too much."

He left the vigil, ordering his footmen to prepare his horse for a ride. Wrapped warmly against the frigid day, he rode through the gardens to a path that led to the edge of the royal forest. There he stopped and looked back at the palace, so much larger and grander than years before, still a work in progress, still much to do. Such anguish was life for a king. Such burdens to be borne, and such loss. A cold drizzle began to fall. He blinked back tears, for he would not cry.

There was a sound of hoof beats. Louis turned in his saddle. Perhaps Philippe had realized his error and was returning to make amends. But no, it was Fabien and Bontemps coming his way.

Louis held up his hand. "I am not to be disturbed."

"Sire," said Bontemps, reining in his mount, his face grim. "You must come at once. The Dauphin –"

"He is with Rohan," said Louis. "A riding lesson."

"Sire," said Bontemps. "Your son's boots were found in the woods near Marly. All his guards were killed. We fear –"

"He's been taken," said Fabien.

Louis drove his heels into his mare and the three men galloped out together.

*D*istraught, the *M*ontespan wandered the palace corridors, looking for the King, seeking solace in his arms. She opened several doors in her search, and on the third one, an anteroom to the royal kitchen, she found Nicolas La Roux, the new chief taster, splayed out at a table, his face turned to the side. His eyes were red and popped, his face bloated. Black vomit was pooled around his mouth, along the table, and onto the floor where countless flies probed the foul mess hungrily.

*The night brought* more sleet upon the land, driving wolves and squirrels to their dens and nests and peasants home to their wives and hearths. In a muddied trench at the far reaches of the palace grounds, bodies lay rotting and stiff. And deep within the human carnage a hand spasmed and fingers scrabbled. A leg twitched. Then Montcourt, very much alive, pushed himself up and free, gasping for air.